124

By Heather Fawcett

Emily Wilde's Encyclopaedia of Faeries
Emily Wilde's Map of the Otherlands

Emily Wilde's
Map of the Otherlands

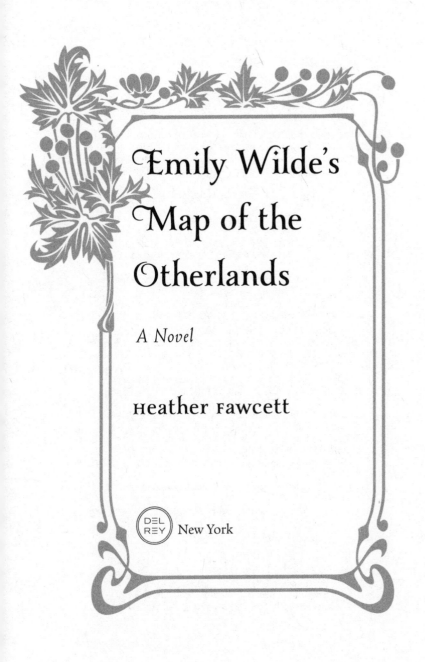

Emily Wilde's Map of the Otherlands

A Novel

HEATHER FAWCETT

DEL REY · New York

Published in the United States by Del Rey, an imprint of Random House, a division of Penguin Random House LLC, New York.

DEL REY and the CIRCLE colophon are registered trademarks of Penguin Random House LLC.

LIBRARY OF CONGRESS CATALOGING-IN-PUBLICATION DATA
Names: Fawcett, Heather (Heather M.), author.
Title: Emily Wilde's map of the Otherlands: a novel / Heather Fawcett.
Description: New York: Del Rey, 2024. | Series: Emily Wilde; 2
Identifiers: LCCN 2023036750 (print) | LCCN 2023036751 (ebook) |
ISBN 9780593500194 (hardcover; acid-free paper) |
ISBN 9780593500200 (ebook) | ISBN 9780593724682
(international edition)
Subjects: LCGFT: Magic realist fiction. | Novels.
Classification: LCC PR9199.4.F39 E46 2024 (print) |
LCC PR9199.4.F39 (ebook) | DDC 813/.6—dc23/eng/20230816
LC record available at https://lccn.loc.gov/2023036750
LC ebook record available at https://lccn.loc.gov/2023036751

Printed in the United States of America on acid-free paper

randomhousebooks.com

2 4 6 8 9 7 5 3 1

First Edition

Book design by Virginia Norey
Floral art by Alexandr Sidorov/stock.adobe.com
Ornamental frame by 100ker/stock.adobe.com

Emily Wilde's Map of the Otherlands

14th September 1910

The foot would not fit in my briefcase, so I wrapped it in cloth and wrestled it into an old knapsack I sometimes carry with me on expeditions. Surprisingly—or perhaps unsurprisingly, as it is a faerie foot—it is neither dirty nor foul-smelling. It is, of course, long mummified and would probably be mistaken for a goat's foot by a casual observer, perhaps an unlikely offering excavated from the tomb of some ancient pharaoh. While it does not smell *bad*, since bringing the foot into my office I have at odd moments caught the scent of wildflowers and crushed grass carried on a little breeze whose source I cannot trace.

I gazed at my now-bulging knapsack, feeling entirely ridiculous. Trust me when I say that I would rather not cart a *foot* around campus with me. But faerie remains, mummified or not, have been known to slip away as the fancy takes them, and I can only assume that feet are particularly inclined to such wanderlust. I shall have to keep it with me until its usefulness has been exhausted. Good grief.

The soft chiming of the grandfather clock alerted me that I was late for breakfast with Wendell. I know from experience that if I miss our breakfast appointments he will bring the meal to me himself, in such a quantity that the entire department will smell of eggs, and then for the rest of the day I shall have to suffer Professor Thornthwaite sniping at me about his delicate stomach.

I paused to pin my hair back up—it's grown far too long, as I've spent the past several weeks descending into one of my obsessive periods, when I can think of little else beyond the subject of my research. And the question of Wendell's door has consumed me more than any other academic mystery I can remember. My hair is not the only area of my appearance I have neglected of late—my brown dress is rumpled, and I am not altogether certain it is clean; I found it in a heap of other questionably laundered items on the floor of my closet.

"Come, dear," I said to Shadow. The dog roused himself from his bed by the oil heater with a yawn, stretching his massive paws. I stopped for a moment to glance around my office with satisfaction—when I was recently granted tenure, I also inherited a much more spacious office, now three doors away from Wendell's (naturally he has found a way to complain about this additional twenty feet of distance). The grandfather clock came with the room, as did the enormous damasked curtains lining the sash window that overlooks Knight College's pond—presently dotted with swans—and the magnificent oak desk with its drawers lined with black velvet. I added bookshelves, of course, and a ladder to reach the uppermost volumes, whilst Wendell insisted on cluttering the place up with two photographs from Hrafnsvik that I did not even know he took, one of me standing in the snowy garden with Lilja and Margret, the other of a village scene; a vase of dried flowers that somehow never lose their scent; and the newly reframed painting of Shadow he commissioned for my twenty-eighth birthday—all right, I cannot complain about that. My beast looks very fetching.

I passed several students sunk deep into the armchairs of

the dryadology department common room, an open space beyond the faculty offices that boasts a cosy fireplace—unlit on
this warm September day—as well as an impressive row of windows taller than several men, with little half-moons of stained
glass at the top, which face the Gothic grandeur of the Library
of Medicine, its proximity the subject of innumerable wry remarks concerning a dryadologist's susceptibility to strange
injuries. In one corner is a bronze urn filled with salt—campus
legend has it this began as a joke, but many a whey-faced undergraduate has visited this vessel to stuff their pockets after
sitting through their first lecture on wights. Not that there is
much to worry about, as we do not ordinarily have Folk wandering into the department to hear what we mortals are saying about them (Wendell excepted). The thick rugs scattered
on the floor must be trodden on with care, for they are lumpy
from the coins stuffed beneath them. Like the salt, this tradi-
tion most likely originated as a humourous diversion rather
than any serious design to ward the Folk away from our halls,
and has now largely devolved into a sort of good-luck ritual,
with students pressing a ha'penny into the floor before an
exam or dissertation. (Less superstitious young scholars have
also been known to raid this lowly hoard for pub money.)

Shadow gave a happy grunt when we stepped outside—he is
ordinarily a quiet dog—and plunged into the sunlit grass,
snuffling about for snails and other edibles.

I followed at a more sedate walk, enjoying the sun on my
face, as well as the cool edge to the wind that heralded the
coming autumn. Just past the main dryadology building was
the ivy-clad magnificence of the Library of Dryadology, which
overlooks a lawn dotted with trees known in this part of Britain as faerie favourites, yew and willow. Several students were
napping beneath the largest of these, a great hoary willow believed (erroneously, I'm afraid) to be the home of a sleeping

leprechaun, who will one day awaken and stuff the pockets of the nearest slumberer he encounters with gold.

I felt a pleasant sense of kinship as I passed into the shadow of that library. I can hear Wendell mocking me for having familial feelings for a library, but I don't care; it's not as if he reads my personal journals, though he is not above teasing me for continuing the journalling habit after we left Ljosland. I seem unable to quit it; I find it greatly helps me organize my thoughts.

I continued to gaze at the library as the path rounded a corner—unwisely, as it happened, for I collided with a man walking in the opposite direction, so forcefully I nearly lost my footing.

"I'm so sorry," I began, but the man only rudely waved my apology away. He was holding a great quantity of ribbons in his hands, which he seemed to be in the process of tying together.

"Have you any more?" he demanded. "These won't be enough."

"I'm afraid not," I replied cautiously. The man was dressed oddly for the weather, in a long, fur-lined cloak and tremendous boots extending to his knees. In addition to the ribbons in his hands, he had a long chain of them looped multiple times round his neck, and more spilling from his pockets. They were a highly eclectic assemblage, varied in both colour and size. Between the ribbons and his considerable height, the man had the look of a maypole given human form. He was perhaps in the latter stages of middle age, with mostly brown hair a shade or two lighter than his skin, as if bleached by the elements, and a scraggly white beard.

"They won't be enough for what?" I enquired.

The man gave me the most inexplicable glare. There was something familiar about that look that I could not put my finger on, though I was certain I had never met this strange person before. I felt a shiver glide along my neck like the brush of a cold fingertip.

"The path is eternal," he said. "But you mustn't sleep—I made that mistake. Turn left at the ghosts with ash in their hair, then left at the evergreen wood, and straight through the vale where my brother will die. If you lose your way, you will lose only yourself, but if you lose the path, you will lose everything you never knew you had."

I stared at him. The man only looked down at his ribbons with an air of dismissing me and continued on his way. Of course I turned to see which direction he went, and was only mildly surprised to find that he had disappeared.

"Hm!" I grunted. "What do you think of that, my love?"

Shadow, though, had taken little interest in the man; he was presently eyeing a magpie that had descended to the lawn to yank at a worm. I filed the encounter away and continued across the leafy campus grounds.

Wendell's favourite café perches on the bank of the River Cam adjacent to Pendleigh Bridge. It is a fifteen-minute walk from our offices, and if it were up to me, we would eat somewhere more conveniently situated, but he is very particular about breakfast and claims that the Archimedes Café—it adjoins the mathematics department—is the only place that knows the proper way to poach eggs.

As usual, Wendell was easy to locate; his golden hair drew the eye like a beacon, glinting intermittently as the wind tossed the branches to and fro. He was seated at our usual table beneath the cherry tree, his elegant frame folded into a slump with his elbow on the table and his forehead pressed against his hand. I suppressed a smile.

"Good morning," I chirped, not bothering to keep the smugness out of my voice. I had timed it well, for the table had recently been filled; the bacon and eggs were steaming, as was the coffee in Wendell's cup.

"Dear Emily," he said as I sat down, not troubling to lift his head from his hand but smiling at me slantwise. "You look as if you've come from a wrestling match with one of your books. May I ask who won?"

I ignored this. "Something peculiar happened on the way here," I said, and described my encounter with the mysterious ribbons man.

"Perhaps my stepmother has finally decided to send her assassins after me," he said in a voice that was more disdainful than anything, as if there were something unfashionable about the business of assassins.

Of course I didn't bother pointing out that the stranger had not mentioned Wendell nor seemed in any way connected to him or his problems, knowing this would fall on deaf ears, and merely said, "He didn't seem very threatening."

"Perhaps he was a poisoner. Most poisoners are strange, irritable things, with a great fondness for talking in riddles. It must be all that hunching over measurements, breathing in fumes." He eyed his coffee morosely, then dumped another scoop of sugar in and tossed the whole thing back.

I filled a plate for Shadow with eggs and sausages and set it under the table, where the dog happily settled himself, then slung the knapsack casually over the back of my chair. Wendell continued to take no notice of the powerful faerie artefact I had brought with me to breakfast, which I found entertaining. "Do you notice that smell?" I said innocently as I again caught the scent of wildflowers emanating from no particular direction.

"Smell?" He was scratching Shadow's ears. "Are you trying

out a perfume? If so, I'm afraid it's been overwhelmed by your usual aroma of inkwells and libraries."

"I didn't mean *me*," I said a little too loudly.

"What then? My senses are utterly incapacitated by this damned headache."

"I don't think that's how it works," I said, amused. Only a little, though; he really did look like death. His ordinarily rosy skin had a greyish pallor, his dark eyes underscored with shadows. He mumbled something unintelligible as he rubbed his forehead, tangling the golden locks that had fallen into his eyes. I suppressed the familiar urge to reach out and brush them back into place.

"I have to say I've never understood this annual ritual of poisoning oneself," I said. "Where's the appeal? Shouldn't a birthday be an enjoyable affair?"

"I believe mortals wish to blot out the reminder of their inexorably approaching demise. I just got a bit carried away—bloody Byers and his drinking games. And then they brought out a *cake*—or was it two cakes? Anyway, never again."

I smiled. Despite Wendell's habit of complaining of fatigue, sore feet, and a myriad of other ailments—generally when confronted by the necessity of hard work—it's rare to see him in any actual distress, and on some level I found it gratifying. "I managed to mark my thirtieth—as well as my thirty-first last month—without drinking myself into stupefaction. It *is* possible."

"You also retired at nine o'clock. Reid, Thornthwaite, and the rest of us celebrated your birthday longer than you did. Yours is only a different category of excess, Em." Something—perhaps a twitch in one of the faerie foot's toes—must have finally alerted him to my knapsack, for his bleary gaze snagged upon it suspiciously. "What have you got in there? And what is all this smirking about? You're up to something."

"I don't know what you mean," I said, pressing my lips together to contain said smirk.

"Have you gotten yourself enchanted again? Must I begin plotting another rescue?"

I glared. I'm afraid I have not gotten over my resentment of him for saving me from the snow king's court in Ljosland earlier this year, and have made a solemn vow to myself that I shall be the one to rescue *him* from whatever faerie trouble we next find ourselves in. Yes, I realize this is illogical, given that it requires Wendell to end up in some dire circumstance, which would ideally best be avoided, but there it is. I'm quite determined.

"I'll explain everything tomorrow," I said. "For now, let us say that I have had a breakthrough in my research. I am planning to make a presentation out of it."

"A presentation?" He looked amused. "To an audience of one. Can you not do anything without waving around a pointer and a stack of diagrams?"

"An audience of *two,*" I said. "I suppose I must invite Ariadne, mustn't I?"

"She would be put out if you didn't."

I stabbed my knife into the butter and applied it to my toast in unnecessarily sharp strokes. Ariadne is my brother's eldest daughter. She arrived at Cambridge for the summer term with a deep-rooted love for dryadology, which my brother, unsurprisingly, has added to the extensive list of items he holds against me. Only nineteen, she is easily the brightest student I have ever taught, with an impressive alacrity for getting what she wants, whether it be a research assistantship, after-hours tutoring, or access to the faculty-only section of the Library of Dryadology, where we keep our rarest texts, half of which are enchanted. I'm afraid that her habit of reminding me how frequently she writes to Thomas has more to do with this than her powers of persuasion; much as I tell myself I could hardly care less about my brother's opinion of me—he is a full twelve years my senior, and my opposite in every way—I cannot help picturing his frowning face whenever she mentions their correspondence, and would, on the whole, prefer not to provide him with additional points for his list.

"Is this about my door?" A youthful hope enlivened Wendell's drawn face.

"Of course," I said. "I only regret it's taken this long to develop a workable theory. But I'll reveal all tomorrow. I have a few more details to pin down—and anyway you have two lectures this afternoon."

"Don't remind me." He buried his forehead in his hand again. "After I get through them—*if* I get through them—I am going home and burying myself in pillows until this bloody pounding ceases."

I nudged the bowl of oranges in his direction. He seemed to have eaten little, which is unlike him. He took one, peeled it, then gazed at it a moment before setting it aside.

"Here," I said, handing him my buttered toast. He was able to force this down, at least, and it seemed to settle his stomach somewhat, enough to tackle the eggs I spooned onto his plate.

"Where would I be without you, Em?" he said.

"Probably still flailing about in Germany, looking for your door," I said. "Meanwhile, I would be sleeping more soundly without a marriage proposal from a faerie king dangling over my head."

"It would cease to dangle if you accepted." He rested his hand over mine and teasingly ran his thumb over my knuckles. "Shall I write you an essay on the subject? I can provide an extensive list of reasons to acquiesce."

"I can imagine," I said drily. A slow shiver travelled up my arm. "And what would be the first? That I shall enjoy an eternity of clean floors and dust-free bookshelves, as well as a constant refrain of nagging to pick up after myself?"

"Ah, no. It would be that our marriage would stop you from charging off into the wilderness in search of *other* faerie kings to marry, without first checking if they are made of ice."

I made a grab for his coffee cup—I did not *actually* intend to empty it into his lap, though I could not be blamed if my hand had happened to slip—but he had already snatched it away, a motion too quick for my mortal reflexes to counter.

"That is unfair," I complained, but he only laughed at me.

We have fallen into this pattern of jesting over his marriage proposal, though it is clear he is no less serious about it, as he has informed me more times than I care to count. For my part, I wish I could see the whole thing in a humourous light—I have indeed lost sleep over it. My stomach is in knots even as I write these words, and in general I prefer to avoid thinking about the whole business so as not to be sent into a minor panic. It is in part, I suppose, that the thought of marrying anyone makes me wish to retreat to the nearest library and hide myself among the stacks; marriage has always struck me as a pointless business, at best a distraction from my work and at worst a very *large* distraction from my work coupled with a lifetime of tedious social obligations.

But I am also keenly aware that I should have refused Wendell long ago, and that allowing him to hope like this is cruel. I do not wish to be cruel to Wendell; the thought gives rise to a strange and unpleasant sensation, as if the air is being squeezed from my body. But the reality is that one would have to be an utter idiot to marry one of the Folk. There are perhaps a handful of stories in which such a union ends well and a mountain of them in which it ends in madness or an untimely and unpleasant death.

I am also, of course, constantly aware of the ridiculousness of my being the object of a marriage offering by a faerie monarch.

"Give me a hint at least," he said after we had spent several minutes attending to our food.

"Not until you've made a start on that essay."

"Much as I appreciate that you cannot stop thinking of marrying me," he said, "I was referring to this breakthrough of yours. Have you narrowed down the possible locations of my door?"

"Ah." I put my crêpe down. "Yes. Although, as my research points to many possible locations, it would be more accurate to say that I have landed upon one that seems particularly promising. How familiar are you with the work of Danielle de Grey?"

"De Grey? Not very. Bit of a rebel; disappeared decades ago after wandering into some faerie realm. Her research has been rather discredited, hasn't it?"

"*She* has been discredited. She was arrested in four different countries, most notably for stealing a faerie sword from the estate of a French duke. Undid a curse upon his family in the process, not that he ever thanked her for it. I have always found her research to be exemplary. It's a pity it's no longer cited. I tried once, in graduate school, and my supervisor informed me that it would not be politic."

"That's hardly a surprise. Scholars are a conservative lot. De Grey sounds like she was far too much fun."

"Her ideas are innovative. She believed ardently that the Folk of different regions are in closer communication than scholars assume—back then they called this the Trade Routes

Theory. She also came up with a classification system that would still be useful today if it had ever gained traction. When she disappeared, she was investigating a species of faun."*

Wendell made a face. "I hate fauns—we have them in my kingdom. They're vicious little beasts—and not in an interesting way. I don't know why dryadologists make such a fuss over them. What on earth do they have to do with my door?"

I leaned forward. "In fact, you have several species of faun within your kingdom, don't you?"

He sighed. "Don't ask me to name them, I beg of you. I have as little to do with the creatures as possible."

I pulled out a book from my pocket—naturally I hadn't stored anything else in the knapsack, in case the foot decided to hop out as soon as I unclipped the flap. I opened it to the marked page and handed it to him. "Does he look familiar?"

"She," Wendell said absently, looking at the drawing. It showed a blurred, hairy creature with a goat's legs and hooves—many fauns alternate between bipedalism and a sort of crouched, apelike lope. Rising from the faun's head were two majestic horns, sharp as knifepoints. "Yes. They live in the mountains to the east of my court."

"De Grey called them tree fauns—not because they dwell in forests, but because their horns resemble tree rings, the intricacy of them. It's a feature unique to their species."

I took the book from him before he could read the caption below the illustration—I wanted to surprise him tomorrow. He seemed to guess this and smiled.

"That's all I'll get for now, is it? A story about a disreputa-

---

* Despite objections by Evans (1901), Blanchet (1904), and others, "faun" remains the accepted nomenclature for all species of hoofed common fae regardless of size or origin, one of several terms whose lineage can be traced to dryadology's roots in early-seventeenth-century Greece.

ble scholar and a lecture on the common fae? And you are always after me for being mysterious."

"I'm sure that the person who spent ten years failing to locate a simple faerie door can wait another day without grumbling about it," I said, only half suppressing my smugness. "Pass the tea."

He picked up the pot and filled my cup. I froze, staring.

"What?" he said, setting the pot down. Wordlessly, I gestured. The tea in my mug was blue-black, and floating across the surface were tiny lily pads, each cradling a perfect white flower. Shadows flitted across the surface of the water, as if above it was a canopy of dark trees admitting only the thinnest of sunbeams.

Wendell swore. He reached for the cup, but I was already cradling it. "Are they *blooming*?" I said. Indeed, as I watched, another flower opened, petals waving in a wind that did not belong to the calm Cambridge weather. I couldn't look away.

The bizarre concoction smelled divine—both like and unlike tea, bitter and floral. I tilted the cup to take a sip, but suddenly Wendell's hand was covering the rim—that unnerving trick of his of moving more quickly than my mortal eyes could follow. "Don't," he said, pressing the cup towards the table.

"Poison?"

"Of course not. It's just tea. Commonly served at breakfast in my court."

"Ah." The general rule is that mortals should avoid consuming anything in Faerie—particularly faerie wine, which erases human inhibitions. Most commonly the drinker, who has been lured into some faerie revel, dances until they die, or until the faeries tire of them, which is often the same thing.

"I'm not in the mood to dance at present," I said. "Thank you for ruining my tea."

"Obviously I didn't *mean* to. I don't—" He frowned and shook his head.

I emptied the tea onto the grass—the pot, anyhow; he was still holding the cup. "I've never seen you lose control of your magic before. Were you thinking of home just now?"

"No more than usual." He sipped the tea, closed his eyes briefly, then shrugged. "Some effect of the hangover, I suppose."

I eyed him thoughtfully. He flagged down a waiter and requested a fresh pot of tea. Our conversation turned then to a familiar debate concerning department politics; Wendell ordinarily takes little interest in the subject, but given his skill for charming his way into others' confidences, he is nevertheless an excellent source for gossip. Currently we are all placing bets on the outcome of an ongoing feud between Professors Clive Errington and Sarah Alami, which began over a misplaced tea tray in the faculty lounge and devolved into accusations of professional sabotage. Alami is convinced Errington broke her glass mirror containing a captive faerie light, while Errington believes Alami followed him to the Wiltshire downs in order to leave out mouldy scones for the brownies he was investigating, about which they purportedly took great offence.

"Excuse me?"

I turned and found a young scholar hovering at my shoulder, a hesitant smile on her ruddy face. "I'm sorry to trouble you, Professor. I'm in one of your classes—Dryadology in the Early Modern Period?"

"Oh, yes," I said, though I could not place her. Well, there are more than a hundred students in that class, after all.

"You'll think this is silly," she said, clutching her book more tightly to her chest—which I realized was my encyclopaedia of the Folk, published earlier this summer. "But I wanted to tell you what an inspiration you are. I came here to study architecture, you know—well, that's what my parents wished me to study. But now, because of you, my mind is made up. I'm going to major in dryadology like I always wanted."

"I'm happy to have been an inspiration for you. But it's neither an easy profession nor a safe one."

"Oh, I know," the young girl said, her eyes alight. "But I—"

Her gaze fell then on Wendell, who was tilting his chair back and smiling at me, and she seemed to forget what she had been saying. At first I thought it was merely his appearance that had distracted her—not an unusual occurrence even among those who know him well. I think if it was just a matter of good looks, one could get used to him, but Wendell has—I can think of no better way to put it—a *vividness* that is difficult to ignore. It is largely indefinable, and perhaps all faerie monarchs have it; I don't know. There is a sharpness to his presence that snags one's attention.

It was only when her eyes darted back to me that I realized. There was in her expression something I had seen before in the villagers of Hrafnsvik, and I felt my mouth tighten.

The girl thanked me again and departed with some haste. I turned to Wendell with a frown.

"What now?" he said.

"I believe the rumours about you have reached Cambridge," I said.

"Oh, good grief."

In Hrafnsvik, the villagers had known Wendell's true identity—there had been no avoiding it. Wendell and I had not worried overmuch about this—it is such a small, out-of-the-way place, and we'd assumed his secret would be easily kept.

He was rubbing the bridge of his nose, his eyes closed. "How did it happen?"

"I don't know. But this is the modern world, Wendell. The Department Head has a telephone in his office now. Not that he knows how to use it, of course . . ."

He reached for the coffeepot, and I realized I had misjudged his reaction—he was not anxious at all, merely preoccupied with his hangover. "Oh well."

"Oh well?" I repeated. "We don't know how many people have heard this rumour, nor how many believe it. We'd best take it seriously. At the very least, you will have to be more careful from now on. You don't always guard yourself—I am not the only observant person on the planet, you know. And I hope that is the last pot of tea you accidentally enchant."

"The faculty won't believe it," he said. "Can you imagine? They'd feel like common dupes. You know they'd go to any lengths to avoid *that.*"

"I don't know," I said. "You have plenty of enemies. Some would jump at the chance to villainize you, and I think a rumour that you are here playing some cruel faerie game aimed at making us all look ridiculous would suit that purpose nicely. We cannot lose our funding, Wendell. We need that if we are going to find your door."

"All this is not helping my headache." He took my hand. "It's all right, Em. It's only a rumour. One would think you cared more about finding my door than I do!"

"I doubt that's possible." For he is constantly complaining of homesickness.

"I hadn't thought so."

I withdrew my hand, which was feeling overheated. "Of course I care about your door. It is one of the most interesting mysteries I have encountered in my career, and I intend to solve it. You know how I am."

He smiled. "Yes. I do."

+ + +

He left me shortly thereafter, saying that he would nap for an hour or so before his first lecture in the hopes of ameliorating his headache. I remained at the table to finish off the tea and toast as I worked on my latest letter to Lilja and Margret. I have a regular correspondence with them, as I do with Aud and—more sporadically—with Thora. I pictured Lilja opening the letter by the fireside in the little cottage she shared with Margret—no doubt they would be already thinking ahead to the winter in Hrafnsvik.

Lilja and Margret continue to demonstrate a great deal of interest in Wendell's marriage proposal, and they ask if I have come to a decision each time they write. I began by scribbling vague things about the ill-advisedness of marrying one of the Folk, but as their questions persisted I have simply been ignoring them. I miss them both and very much wish I could see them again—I always found Lilja in particular an uncommonly easy person to converse with.

My worries receded as I made my way back to my office with Shadow at my side. I have resided in a sort of contented haze since being granted tenure—a highlight of any academic career, but even more so for me, as Cambridge is the only true home I have ever known. The ancient stonework has an aura of friendliness now, the paths more comfortable beneath my feet.

It was as I strolled along, thinking of the stack of papers on my desk that still needed grading, that I realized what had been so familiar about the glare the man with the ribbons had given me. It was the same look I have seen numerous times from older professors, often when I have challenged them on a point of scholarship. There had been a quality of disappointment in it that is particular to scholars, which would explain my reaction—I had felt, for a brief moment, like an undergraduate who had forgotten to do the assigned reading.

"Hm," I said again as I turned the encounter over in my head, examining it from new angles. But I could make no further sense of the mystery, and thus I set it aside.

14th September, evening

Well.

I am not quite sure where to begin.

The ghastly scene in the lecture hall seems the most obvious place, but my thoughts dart away from it like fish from a shadow falling over the water. How Wendell could sleep after something like that is beyond me, and yet I hear him in the next room, snoring peacefully. I suppose it's like him to put more energy into fretting about a hangover than a murderous attack.

When I returned to my office after breakfast, Ariadne was already waiting for me. I had made a detour to the Museum of Dryadology and Ethnofolklore in the hope of borrowing a few exhibit pins to stick into the ruddy foot, which had begun twitching every few seconds. The pins are made of iron with heads shaped from old pennies—both metal and human currency are despised by many Folk, and thus the pins help to subdue any lingering enchantments imbued in their artefacts. But the curator—one Dr. Hensley—merely gave me a baleful glare and informed me that pins were in short supply. We are not friends, Dr. Hensley and I. She took great offence when recently I asked to borrow a particular artefact for Shadow, declaring that the museum was not "a library designed for the idle amusement of scholars." This grated on my patience as only an insult to libraries could, and after a terse argument we parted on bad terms. I suppose I should consider myself lucky that I wasn't chased out of the museum under a hail of dusting cloths.

"Are you all right?" my niece enquired when I stormed in, my good humour in tatters. I replied in the affirmative, but she nevertheless ran to fetch me some tea from the lounge, despite my calling after her that I had no need of it.

Ariadne looks a great deal like my brother, round-faced with a long nose covered in a smattering of freckles, with her mother's hazel eyes and light brown complexion. Unlike my brother, though, whose disposition is decidedly taciturn, Ariadne is possessed of a wearying amount of energy. This would not be an issue were she not so often underfoot, having appointed herself my assistant, something I have never sought nor desired.

"Don't *all* scholars of your standing have assistants?" she asked me once, fixing me with a look of guileless admiration. I could only splutter in reply and wish that my ego were not so easily stroked. The truth is that I do not *always* mind her presence.

"Did you locate the Spengler maps?" I demanded when she returned, ignoring the tea, which she had paired with a plate of my favourite biscuits. My brusque demeanour did not penetrate her high spirits, which seem indefatigable, and she hurried to fetch her briefcase, from which she drew a folder containing two carefully folded sheets of parchment.

"Thank you," I said grudgingly. I had not expected her to locate the maps so quickly. "Then they *were* hidden away in one of the basement stacks?"

She shook her head. "They'd been moved to the Library of History—the Germanic cultures floor. I had to speak with half a dozen librarians, but once I worked that out, they weren't difficult to locate."

"Ah," I said, quietly impressed. Ariadne is perhaps the most competent student I've ever taught. This, though, is irritating in its own way—were she demonstrably inept, I would have an excuse to get rid of her.

"Would you like to see?" she said. She was actually bouncing slightly up and down with excitement, like a child half her age, and I had to suppress the urge to step on her foot to restrain her.

"Put them here."

She spread them over the desk, weighting the edges with a few of my faerie stones. I ran my hands over the old parchment—they were not the originals, but rather copies drawn by Klaus Spengler in the 1880s. Those originals, which have since disappeared or been misplaced in the depths of some university archive, were created by Danielle de Grey more than fifty years ago, and were found amongst her belongings after she vanished in 1861.

As I touched the maps, my gaze snagged, as it did all too often, on the missing finger on my left hand. Wendell offered to create a glamour so lifelike I would scarcely notice a difference from before, but I said no. I am not entirely sure why. I suppose I appreciate the reminder—and warning—the empty space gives me. Wendell claims it is because I see it as a ghoulish souvenir of my sojourn in a Faerie court, an experience to which few scholars can lay claim. This I vociferously deny, even while a small part of me wonders if he might be right.

The first map showed a bird's-eye view of a mountainous landscape. The only settlement was a small village labelled *St. Liesl,* perched upon an elevated plateau amongst the peaks. The second map was a closer view of the area around the village, with many more details labelled, including footpaths, streams, lakes, and what seemed to be geographic features—my German is rusty.

"I still can't believe it," Ariadne said, which made me jump—I hadn't realized she was leaning so close to me. "Danielle de Grey drew these maps. Danielle de Grey!"

My mouth quirked. De Grey may not have the respect of dryadology's *corps d'elite,* but her irreverent character coupled with the mystery of her disappearance have made her something of a folk hero among the younger generation of scholars.[*]

"Will we find out what happened to her?" Ariadne continued in a hushed voice.

"It's certainly a possibility," I said evasively, refolding the maps.

"When do we leave?"

"As soon as Wendell and I can make arrangements. Before the month is out, I hope."

Shadow gave a low huff. He was sat in the doorway, his gaze fixed upon a point down the hall—Wendell's office door. I recalled how he had leaned against Wendell's legs all through breakfast, never stirring even to beg for scraps. At that, several moments and half-thoughts connected in my mind like points in a constellation, forming a troubling pattern.

"Ariadne," I said, "when did you leave the pub last night?"

---

[*] This is partly due to the rumour that de Grey, whose genius was notable from a young age, ran an illicit essay market during her undergraduate years, which was so profitable that it funded her entire education. In an interview following his retirement, Dr. Marlon Jacobs of Durham admitted to having paid de Grey a handsome sum for an essay that was featured in *Modern Dryadology* in 1839, which runs only one undergraduate submission per quarter, an achievement that launched his long career. De Grey is seen by many as a sort of Robin Hood figure, given her impoverished background and habit of charging her wealthy peers exorbitant rates for her assistance. As no one besides Jacobs ever admitted to taking part in such a scheme, however, it remains in the realm of legend. The phrase "pulling a de Grey," which has come to refer to many forms of academic plagiarism, originates from this source.

She grimaced. "Late, I'm afraid. I woke with quite a headache, but fortunately, I have my morning exertions. That always sets me right no matter what sort of night I had. I begin with a quick run around Tenant's Green. After that, I do my breathing exercises, which—"

"Were you with Wendell throughout the evening? Dr. Bambleby, I mean."

"For the most part." She thought. "Though our table was rather crowded. I ended up sat with his graduate students, to make room for the professors."

"And did you know everyone at the gathering? Was it all faculty and students, or were there also well-wishers from off campus?"

"Well—I'm not sure," she said. "Mostly it was members of the dryadology department, and a few of the librarians and art history professors Dr. Bambleby is friendly with. But as the evening wore on, there were a few that turned up whom I didn't recognize."

"Did Dr. Bambleby recognize them?"

She laughed. "I'm not sure he recognized *me* towards the end of the night. Most of us were in that sort of state. It was an excellent birthday party."

I drummed my fingers on the table. I considered visiting Wendell at his apartments—but why would that be necessary? To *check* on him? A king of Faerie?

Before I could make my mind up one way or another, there came the sound of footsteps from the hall. Very emphatic footsteps, paired with equally emphatic breathing, an almost snorting noise. Shadow growled, and I half expected some dreadful faerie beast to come rearing into my office, but Ariadne muttered quickly, "That'll be the Head—he was looking for you earlier—bee in his bonnet about something—" And seconds later, the Head himself burst into my office.

Dr. Farris Rose has served as Department Head for over a decade, taking over from Letitia Barrister, who was abducted by a bogle in the Hebrides and returned several weeks later aged to approximately ninety (she'd been forty-eight when she vanished). Rose is portly with a manelike fringe of white hair framing a bald pate, and of indeterminate age—a common trait among dryadologists—this falling anywhere between fifty- and seventy-something. He is a known eccentric even among the scholarly community, insisting as he does on wearing his clothing inside out at all times—which, while a useful way to evade the notice of the Folk and confound their enchantments, is seen as a bit gauche when adopted as a general practice—and sewing so many coins into the fabric that any sudden movement makes him jingle. He has a network of tattoos extending from his wrists to Lord knows where—I have never seen them exposed, and their terminus is a subject of lively speculation among students and some faculty—that are said to be warding symbols of some sort. His body of scholarship is vast and respected—he is the author of the Sandstone Theory,* after all—but he has few friends and, rumour has it, was only grudgingly appointed to the position of Head, nobody else of equal standing desiring the job. Again, though, there is nothing particularly remarkable about this; a clear majority of dryadologists live like cats, keeping a watchful and antagonistic eye on one another.

It was immediately clear that Rose indeed had a bee in his bonnet, and that this was somehow my doing. He seemed upon sight of me to be rendered temporarily incapable of speech and merely thumped a large book down upon my desk,

---

* The theory that Faerie is shaped culturally and physically by layers of stories, which Rose breaks into two categories: foreign, into which fall all tales told by mortals and Folk in unrelated realms, and domestic, the stories the Folk tell of themselves.

knocking the tea tray onto the floor. Ariadne gave a small yelp and scurried over to gather up the shards.

"What on earth—!" I began.

"Where is he?" Rose demanded. His pale skin was flushed. "You two are thick as thieves."

"I have no idea," I said icily, for naturally there was only one person he could be referring to. Remembering myself, as well as Rose's position, I added more calmly, "He has a lecture in an hour or so; you might catch him before—"

"Never mind," he cut in. I realized that what I had at first taken for anger was in fact a sort of righteous triumph. "Perhaps it's better this way. We'll have to fire you separately, after all."

I stilled. For a moment, the only sound came from Ariadne scooping the teacup shards onto the tray—*plink, plink, plink.* "What?"

"Not as yet," he added grudgingly. "I have to compile my evidence and present it to the senior faculty. But I will be requesting that we convene for an emergency meeting tomorrow. I have no doubt that they will agree with my conclusions."

I felt as if I were trapped in a powerful current drawing me farther and farther from shore. The worst part of it was that my mind had gone blank—all my carefully ordered thoughts and theories deserting me. "I'm *tenured*—you can't—"

"Are you that much a fool?" he said in a voice of such scorn that it froze me to my seat. "We certainly *can* fire you if there is evidence of malpractice. And as I said—I have evidence."

He tilted his chin at the book, which I had completely forgotten about. I thumbed it open with shaking hands. It was a bound collection of journals—*The Theory and Practice of Dryadology*, volume seventeen, which covered the year 1908. I noticed he had marked two articles that had been written by Wendell.

I groaned inwardly. "This is about the Schwartzwald expedition."

"No," he said. "I've been unable to conclusively prove his observations in that case were falsified. Like most successful charlatans, he's good at covering his trail. But he slips up now and then." He poked his finger at the table of contents and read: "'What's Good for the Goose: Evidence of Animal Husbandry among the Hearth Brownies of the Welsh Marches.' In which he argues that simple household faeries are responsible for chasing wolves away from the sheep—with their brooms and dusters, I presume? I spoke with the farmers he supposedly interviewed—they have no trouble with wolves because said wolves were all shot decades ago. And this article on a huge cluster of faerie stones he unearthed in the Dolomites, which he called evidence of a courtly fae battleground—he paid several of the local masons to plant the stones there, following a particular pattern. Most were evasive about the whole thing, but the rumour's out among the villagers, and I eventually managed to convince one to talk."

I thumped the book shut. I have always found Rose an intimidating figure even in small doses, and I struggled to find my voice as he stood there glowering at me. When I spoke, it sounded small contrasted with Rose's sonorous baritone, which has always seemed to me designed for podiums and lecture halls. "What does this have to do with me? My name is not associated with either of these articles. I make no claims as to their authenticity, and *you* are the fool if you think you can jeopardize my career on the basis of who I am friends with."

He smiled thinly. "I've reviewed your paper on the Ljosland Folk, which the two of you presented in Paris this year to all that fanfare," he said. "It's hogwash."

My mouth dropped open in outrage. The anger was a relief—far better than the cold terror that had engulfed me before. "*Hogwash?* How dare you—"

"How dare I? Your claims are so ludicrous I'm astounded you thought you could get away with them. A changeling that behaves like a wight? A Folk so powerful they can draw down the aurora? Utter nonsense."

"If you speak with the villagers of Hrafnsvik, they will inform you—"

"I don't need to speak with anyone. It fits the overall pattern we see from Bambleby—wild, irrational claims unsupported by previous scholarship."

"You will attempt to have me removed because you find the behaviour of the Folk irrational?" I looked him up and down, wondering how I had ever respected this man. "This is about my encyclopaedia, isn't it?"

His face hardened. "I don't like what you're implying, Emily."

I gave a disbelieving laugh. "I don't like being accused of professional misconduct."

His reaction had bolstered my suspicions. I'd heard rumours that Rose was working on his own encyclopaedia of the Folk—a project that had reportedly occupied much of his career. He'd said nothing to me about it before or after my book came out, but there had been a distinct cooling of our already cool relations.

"I don't wish to imply anything untoward," I said. "So I will simply say it: you resent me. You spent years on your own encyclopaedia, obsessing over minor details as you always do, and you were too blinded by your own arrogance to think that someone else might beat you to the punch. Ruining my reputation will be to your benefit, won't it? I've often noticed, sir, that for all we scholars shake our heads at the amorality of the Folk, on many occasions we demonstrate that we lack the high ground."

"That is enough." The words were so cold that I couldn't help flinching. "You haven't the slightest idea what you're saying. Instead of putting in the work it takes to distinguish yourself, you have used deception to advance your career, and you will suffer the consequences." He turned to leave—rather dramatically, I thought, though I wasn't in any mood to smirk about it. I felt ill.

He paused at the threshold. "He's lecturing today, is he? Perhaps I'll observe."

My nausea intensified. Senior faculty periodically evaluate our lectures; this information forms part of our annual performance reviews. But it was clear that Rose had something else in mind. I pictured Wendell entertaining his students with ridiculous claims, or confusing basic facts because he could not be bothered to crack open any of the textbooks he himself had assigned; Wendell skiving off his lectures entirely in favour of an extended nap. Anything seemed possible.

Smiling a little at my reaction, Rose strode off, his ridiculous inside-out cloak jangling as the hem connected with my doorframe. Ariadne was still crouched on the floor beside the broken china and scatter of biscuits, her face pale, and we gazed at each other for a long moment in perfect silence.

🌿 **Wendell was not** at his apartments, which meant he must have retired to one of his other preferred napping spots, either the shade of a willow on the quiet side of Brightwell Green or a bench hidden away in a poplar grove beside the river. Ariadne and I split up to check both locales, but either he had changed his mind about the nap or he had found himself a new hideaway, for we could find no trace of him. After some indecisive fretting, I made my way to the lecture hall.

Wendell had already begun his lecture, which meant he must have started on time—that at least brought me some relief, though I knew this alone wouldn't be enough to save him. As I slid into a seat at the back, I noticed Rose below me near the front of the classroom, which took the shape of an amphitheatre, a notebook and pen at the ready, leaning back with a kind of malicious indolence. Everything about him communicated his ill intentions—were Wendell's tie askew, I suspected this would have been recorded and used as evidence in Rose's case against us.

And as for Wendell? He took no notice whatsoever of the danger he was in. He paced back and forth, largely ignoring the notes in his hand as he delivered what seemed to be a lecture on the faerie mounds of the Channel Islands—I say *seemed* because it was punctuated by numerous tangents, not unrelated but giving the whole thing a confusing structure. I have watched Wendell teach before, and of course present at numerous conferences, and I know that he generally relies a great deal on style over substance, but this struck me as haphazard even for him. Occasionally he would pause to write something on the board, after which he would toss the chalk over his shoulder.

"Excuse me, Professor," one of the young women in the first row called, raising her hand. Those in the first row had the appearance of a group, frequently nudging one another and dissolving into quiet giggles. Mostly young women and a smattering of young men, they had a habit of placing their chins on their hands and fixing Wendell with lingering looks, then whispering into their seatmates' ears.

"Yes?" Wendell said. He seemed relieved by the interruption

and took the opportunity to lean his weight against the lectern and massage the bridge of his nose.

"How long have you been studying the Folk?" the girl enquired. She looked barely a year or two older than Ariadne. "It's just that you seem so terribly *young*, Professor."

Her unambiguous tone gave rise to a great deal of tittering from the first-row cohort and a number of others in the classroom. Wendell either ignored both the tone and the tittering or—as I thought more likely—was too preoccupied with his own suffering to notice. He went back to rubbing his nose, his elbow propped on the lectern. "At times it feels like an eternity," he intoned, which set off a round of laughter. Rose leaned back in his seat, looking disappointed.

He went back to his lecture, skipping over the greenteeth of Guernsey, an odd omission. I could easily guess the reason, as Wendell's knowledge of Channel Islands folklore is patchy—as is his knowledge of the folklore of most regions beyond his home country. Unfortunately, Rose noticed the omission too, and he pounced.

"Professor Bambleby," he said in the carrying voice he uses in his own lectures. "Who was it that first documented the Guernsey greenteeth?"

"Ah." Wendell tilted his head slightly, his gaze sweeping idly over the classroom as if the answer were on the tip of his tongue. He hadn't shown any sign of noticing my presence before, but his gaze went to me unerringly, and I mouthed, *Walter de Montaigne.*

"Walter de Montaigne, if memory serves," Wendell said.

Rose pursed his mouth and scribbled something in his notebook. I held Wendell's gaze, jerking my head in Rose's direction and trying to communicate the danger of the situation, which worked about as well as you might expect. Wendell gave me a blank look.

He began to speak again, but at that moment, the lights flickered off.

"Bloody electricity," Wendell muttered. "Why they wasted the funds converting to a system as reliable as the musket is beyond me. Well, that's all right—we still have the windows. We shall soldier on like the book goblins of Somerset, who work only in the dark of night. I apologize for the lack of honey-milk."

More laughter. I was beginning to wonder if Wendell might actually succeed in not making his situation any worse. Naturally it was then that I noticed the lights.

Not the electric lights that had gone dark above us, but the glittering motes drifting out from under the back door. Wendell hadn't noticed them, but several of his students had and were muttering amongst themselves. The motes were so bright that looking at them scattered blotches of darkness across my vision.

I shoved my chair back, and everything seemed to slow, as if time were caught in a sticky sap. Rose stood a heartbeat after I did, the disdain gone from his face. He met my gaze, and we shared a moment of wordless understanding. He opened his mouth to shout something.

The door burst apart.

The faeries swarmed into the room, silent as a breath of wind. There were four—no, five of them, flowing together like water. They wore oversize cloaks of shadow that rendered their exact movements nearly impossible to track; at times they seemed mere ripples of darkness, and other times they dropped to all fours and moved as wolves, their long muzzles bright with teeth.

I knew—had already guessed—that they were the grey shee-rie, a species of trooping faerie found in Ireland. The grey sheerie, unlike their bog-dwelling brethren, are deadly creatures commonly hired as assassins by the courtly fae. They use their lights, which bob in the air above them, to blind their victims before they strike.

I began shouting something to this effect as the classroom erupted into chaos, ordering the students to shield their eyes, but Rose stood upon his chair and thundered in his most stentorian tones, "Run for your lives!" which had a much more useful effect. Students screamed; half ran for the door and the other half for the tall casement windows, which overlooked a ground-level garden. This is likely what saved them from trampling one another, as it provided two additional points of egress for the fleeing multitudes. Nevertheless, I saw several students knocked off their feet and slammed into desks, and others launched themselves through the windows so energetically that they stumbled into the duck pond.

"Wendell!" I cried, because of course the grey sheerie were here for him. I think the only reason they weren't immediately upon him was that two of his students had bowled him over as they fled, landing in a heap with Wendell beneath them. The grey sheerie are blind and track their victims as wolves do, by scent.

Because the aisle was blocked, I descended to the floor of the lecture hall by clambering over desks, chanting one of the Words of Power over and over. I had no idea if it would bestow upon me an invisibility of scent in addition to the regular kind, but it seemed to, for the sheerie took no notice of me whatsoever. One let out a ghastly howl, half human and half wolf, and they fanned out through the classroom, nipping at the students as they scattered. They sniffed the floor, the air, the corners. Hunting.

Wendell shoved the students off him and stood. The closest of the sheerie whipped around, and suddenly Wendell was engulfed in a cloud of tiny lights like midges.

But I had already wrenched Rose's cloak off him—the man sputtered and shrieked like a child, too shocked to stop me—and threw it over Wendell's head. It was like snuffing a candle: the faerie lights went out as soon as the weight of the coin-stuffed cloak fell upon them.

"Thank you, Em," Wendell said, tossing the cloak aside. Then suddenly I was dizzy and confused, for he had grabbed me and spun me away from the sheerie who had lunged at us; only he had done it so quickly I hadn't seen.

"The Word!" his voice said in my ear, and I remembered myself and opened my mouth to begin chanting it again. Half a breath later my back collided with the blackboard—he had shoved me out of range of the fight, and was already gone. My skin tingled—it was like feeling the brush of a ghost.

"A pencil!" he shouted at me as he leapt over a desk—the sheerie who had lunged at him collided with it and rolled towards Rose, who let out another shriek. "Toss me one of your pencils!"

"Have you gone mad?" I cried even as I removed the pencil from my cloak pocket and threw it at his head.

It began to transform before it even reached him, elongating and flashing through the shadows—a sword. I regretted aiming for his head then, but Wendell caught it with the grace of a trained swordsman, which of course he was.

Watching Wendell with a sword is like watching a bird leap from a branch—there is something thoughtless about it, innate. One has the sense that he is less himself without a sword, that wielding it returns him to the element most natural to him.

He drove the sword into the nearest sheerie, and before it had fallen he had spun round to slash at the one behind him, slicing it open like overripe fruit. The other three fell just as easily.

Most of the students had fled by now, but a few remained, hovering in the doorway at the back of the lecture hall. "Run!" I shouted at them. Then, because they simply stood there, looking worried and afraid, and also like they might attempt to offer help, "More are coming!"

That got them moving. Of course I couldn't undo what they'd seen, but at least what they'd seen had occurred in a darkened room, at a distance.

I looked at Wendell. He was supporting his weight with one hand on a desk, rubbing his eyes. The blood-darkened sword was tucked casually under his arm like an umbrella. "Did you enchant my pencil?" I demanded.

"I enchanted all of your pencils," he said without opening his eyes. "You always have at least one upon your person. I knew they would come in handy." He added, as I continued to stare at him, "Well, I can't carry a bloody sword around with me everywhere," misunderstanding entirely.

"Why didn't you enchant your own pencils?" I groused.

"I would have, but I can never remember where I put them."

Shaking my head, I approached one of the sheerie. They were uncanny in the extreme: though I had initially thought them wolfish, I couldn't say, upon closer inspection, what animal they resembled. In overall form they were closest to human, I suppose, but with overlarge, velvet ears, a twisted snout glittering with teeth, and wispy fur like an ethereal mane. I have seen plenty of strange Folk, but I cannot begin to convey how disturbing these sheerie were, how my mind shuddered away from my inability to connect them to the worlds I knew. What sort of place, I wondered, is Wendell's kingdom?

"You're exhausted," I murmured. "That was the intention, of course. If not complete incapacitation."

He groaned. "Em, you know I find it nerve-racking when

you talk to yourself. What have you figured out, and how will it make this day worse?"

"Someone poisoned you last night," I said bluntly. "Likely a poison brewed in your own kingdom, to ensure its efficacy."

He looked thunderstruck, then hurt. "It was my *birthday party*."

"The fact that you are still standing means, I suppose, that poison can weaken but not kill you. Your stepmother would not have sent the sheerie otherwise, but simply upped the dosage."

"I wouldn't be so certain on that point. You underestimate her sense of fun." He lifted his hands and glared at them. "That explains this feeling—using my magic is like walking into a gale. Well, in any event, how shall I dispose of them?"

This last seemed addressed to himself. I looked at the ghastly corpses scattered about us. "You seem to have disposed of them adequately."

"That was just to give myself space to think," he said. "They'll rouse themselves soon, and be after me again."

"But in the stories—"

"The stories are wrong. Drowning's the only way to kill the bloody things. Stab them, cut them in half even, they'll only regenerate like worms."

As I pondered this deeply unpleasant image, he became very still. I could feel the magic surround him—it set the air humming. I kept quiet so as not to disturb his concentration. Naturally, that was the moment Rose chose to remind us of his presence.

"I have *never*," he sputtered, "in all my years of scholarship, I have *never*—"

"Shut up," I said succinctly. I have not spoken to him in such a way before—I suspect it's been a long time since anyone has—and we had a few blessed seconds of silence as he stared at me in astonished indignation before he recovered himself again.

"What is your purpose here?" This was addressed to Wendell. "You—is this all part of some elaborate trick? Some faerie sport that has gotten away from you, putting the school in danger? Either way, I cannot—will not—allow this to continue. The chancellor must be notified of your true identity. And *you.*" He rounded on me. "You knew what he was, didn't you? Are you *assisting* this creature in some way? Has he enchanted you, or are you so childishly foolhardy that you have allied yourself with—"

"Emily," Wendell said. The sheerie were beginning to rouse; one had propped itself up on its elbow. I marched over to Rose as he grew steadily louder and more indignant and slapped him across the face.

The silence that followed was thunderous, broken by incoherent sputtering, but it was enough. Wendell made an odd gesture with his hands, like tightening a knot or tearing a sheet of paper in two. The floor of the lecture hall split open.

Somehow, none of us lost our balance. Wendell stood for a moment on the sandy floor of a dry riverbed. He made a *come here* sort of motion and then clambered up the side as a wall of water roared towards him. The river swept four of the sheerie away. Wendell moved towards the fifth, but Rose, to my astonishment, seized it by the leg and tossed it into the water.

"Good man," Wendell said, patting the Department Head on the shoulder. The expression on Rose's face was beyond description; I would have laughed if I hadn't been so distracted.

The river crashed merrily along before exploding through the windows. I could not make out the source of the river; it seemed to emerge from a spot in the far wall below one of the blackboards, where there was now a small, dark cavern of rock.

Wendell collapsed upon the riverbank, grey with exhaustion. "I may have overdone it."

"Just a tad," I said. "You realize we could have drowned them in the duck pond. It's just there."

"Well, the river was the first thing that came to mind." Weeds were beginning to bloom in the sandy soil beneath him, their leaves draping in the shallows at the water's edge.

"Can you stand?" I said. "We need to get you back to your apartments so you can rest." I put his arm around my shoulder and helped him to his feet. Then I froze.

More lights were drifting through the broken doors. Upon noticing Wendell, they made for him immediately, and I had to flap Rose's cloak at them like a matador. Startled shrieks sounded in the distance, which I took to mean that the river had reached the lawn outside the dryadology library.

"I'm afraid rest will have to wait," Wendell rasped. "The grey sheerie always travel in two separate packs—an advance party, and a group of reinforcements."

I swore. "And I don't suppose these reinforcements will helpfully leap into the river, will they? Are you up for another swordfight?"

"I'm not wholly certain I'd be up for a stroll in Tenant's Green."

"I have an idea," I said, and pulled him up the stairs. When we spilled into the hall, we found a group of students still there, clearly in the middle of a debate about whether to help us or flee as instructed. One approached, offering to take Wendell's other arm in a display of useless bravery. "They're coming!" I hollered at them, and then, without pausing to see if this took effect, I broke into a run, dragging Wendell behind me.

"Your sword?" I huffed.

"Dropped it, I'm afraid," he replied. He staggered a bit but managed to keep his feet. "Give me another pencil."

"I only had the one on me!"

"One? Who are you?" His teasing didn't allay my worry, though; I had never seen him so spent. Was he truly immune to faerie poison, or was it merely a slow-acting draught? "A pen, then."

"Goddamn you." I found one of my pens in another pocket and tossed it at him. "If you've magicked any of my books, I will shove you into that river with the sheerie."

I became aware of a huffing sound at our backs, and for a moment I thought one of the students had followed us. But it was Farris Rose, a glazed look of panic upon his reddened face, tie flapping behind him.

"What the hell are you doing?" I shouted at him.

"I am not remaining back there with *them*!" he shrieked.

I would have shouted some more, but I hadn't the time to worry about Rose—we had reached the museum.

We burst through the doors—fortunately the museum was closed, so the only occupant was the curator, bending over a display case. She screamed at the sight of us—Wendell and I spattered in river mud; Wendell with his shirt bloodied, brandishing a sword; Rose looking like he'd seen his own ghost.

"Hide," Wendell said, putting enchantment into the command, though I don't think the curator needed the encouragement. She fled towards the back rooms.

Wendell stepped over a rope and sank into one of the museum's two elven thrones. The museum was spread over three galleries; we were in the largest, which housed faerie artefacts from the British Isles. Beyond the display cases was an impossible ship salvaged from the Norfolk salt marshes—

shaped like an enormous coracle, it grew larger with the waxing moon. Its wood frame was half rotted away, but its sail was as bright as if newly made: a blue-and-yellow pattern framing a creature that looked vaguely like a narwhal.

"What is the plan?" Wendell said.

I grabbed his sword and used the hilt to smash one of the display cases. I seized several faerie stones and tossed two his way. "Here—you can break these, yes?"

He stared at them—they were unremarkable, as are all faerie stones, yet if measured you will find they are perfectly spherical. "Yes, but—"

That was when the second party of sheerie made their entrance, smashing through the museum doors in a hail of splintered wood. I wondered if they were unaware of how human doors operated, or if they simply enjoyed a dramatic entrance. I say *second party,* though I can only assume they were different sheerie; the creatures did not look alike, but they were so peculiar to my mortal eyes that I struggled to compare them.

Wendell looked at the faerie stone in his hand, shrugged, and smashed it against the floor.

Out burst a flock of parrots. The birds shrieked and squawked, and the sheerie were momentarily distracted—not afraid, they lunged at them like cats. Each parrot seemed to be carrying a tropical flower in its beak.

Wendell hurled another stone. When it smashed, glittering banners unfurled upon the museum walls, covered in the faerie script.* The ceiling was suddenly painted in frescoes of

---

* Visually, written Faie is like a strange melding of the mortal script of a particular region and something similar to Ogham. It is far more difficult than spoken Faie; Alistair Holywood argues in *A Lexicon of Folklore* that it may remain impossible for mortals to comprehend to any useful degree. Firstly, it is

Folk lounging in forest pools, surrounded by green foliage. Vases of unfamiliar flowers appeared on every surface next to bottles of wine in ice buckets, and the air filled with the muffled sound of violins, as if drifting in from the next room.

"Wendell!" I shouted. "None of this is useful!"

"Well, what did you expect?" The third faerie stone contained only a song, a loud and energetic faerie band of some sort, which merged with the violins to form a cacophony. The fourth was the most ridiculous of all; an entire *hot air balloon* burst forth, made from gaudy silks in a dozen different colours. It drifted a few feet off the floor, bouncing gently off the display cases.

"Can't you sense what enchantments are stored in the stones?" I demanded.

"No!"

I threw my hands up in frustration. "Then why do you keep on breaking them?"

"Because you told me to, you lunatic!"

I grabbed his hand and yanked him deeper into the museum, searching the glass cases for something else, anything

---

far less consistent than spoken Faie; fifteen variations have been documented in southern England alone. Some look almost like the Roman alphabet, only with additional flourishes, while others do not even resemble writing, but some random pattern formed by natural processes. Second, written Faie appears to possess semasiographic elements; i.e., certain words that exist in the written language have no spoken equivalent, making it richer, busier, and less knowable than its oral counterpart. And, as if all this weren't enough, their writing is not static, and one may translate an entire page of text only to find, moments later, that it has rearranged itself into some unrelated subject. Whether this is enchantment wrought by the Folk to make their writings less comprehensible to mortals or a quality intrinsic to the language itself is unknown. The study of written Faie can be dangerous; several scholars were confined to asylums in the 1800s after suffering psychological breakdowns. The most famous of these was Harriet Fairfax-Walton, who claimed to have discovered and decoded a peace treaty between two warring faerie kingdoms in Scotland, only to have it rearrange itself into a recipe for fruit bannock. This document is on display at London's Museum of British Folklore, where it is currently the lyrics for an extremely lewd sea shanty.

else, that might prove useful. The sheerie surged after us, snapping their teeth. Rose was hollering something from the corner he'd backed into—either shouting useless instructions or pleading for his life; I didn't bother to listen.

"There!" Wendell shouted, and lunged towards the faerie coracle. We clambered into the ruin, which felt as ridiculous as it sounds, rather like a child leaping behind a fort made of blankets and cushions.

"Have you strength enough to summon another river?" I said hopefully as one of the parrots dive-bombed a sheerie. The birds seemed to have taken great offence to the creatures' presence.

"No—but the ship has its own enchantment. It is simply a matter of releasing it—ah!"

A rope appeared, tied to the mast. I was certain there hadn't been a rope there before. Wendell sliced through it with the sword, and the ship surged forward.

Surged—yes. Somehow it *surged*. I could hear water rushing beneath us, feel the salt spray upon my face, but there was nothing there—nothing but a silvery ripple of movement. Wendell wrenched the sail around, and the coracle shot towards the sheerie, who were, at that moment, distracted by the unintentionally helpful parrots. The closest sheerie began to howl a warning, but the sound was abruptly cut off as the coracle struck the faerie and sent it headfirst into the—water? For there *was* water beneath the coracle; it was what carried us through the museum, even if I couldn't see it. Wendell wrenched the sail again, and we slammed into the remaining knot of sheerie, who met the same fate as the first. Their screams made a burbling sound before they were silenced.

Wendell tried to adjust the sail again—I think he was trying to slow us down—but his hold slipped, and we only picked up speed. "Emily!" he shouted, and threw himself on top of me, just before we slammed into one of the display cases. He was showered in broken glass, and we were both soaked by a wave that washed, invisibly, over the coracle.

"Are you all right?" he demanded, cupping my face. I was so relieved that we had stopped moving that I could only nod, though my stomach was dreadfully queasy. He shook the glass from his hair and helped me out of the boat.

The sheerie were sprawled upon the floor—or what was left of the sheerie. They had melted into little lights, which hovered where their bodies had been, fitfully sputtering. One by one, they went out. One remained alight, but Wendell clapped his hands around it, as if crushing an insect.

"What a mess!" he said, surveying what remained of the museum, which now had the appearance of a fever-induced hallucination, or perhaps several. The hot air balloon had drifted off into a corner, where it bounced gently between the wall and a display of a faerie village in miniature.

Wendell collapsed into the elven throne again, which had drifted a little, and rested his head in his hands. I was at his side in an instant, splashing through the shallow remnants of the tide that had carried us in the boat. The coracle rocked, creaking, behind me.

"Let's get you home," I said. "Please tell me you have a working knowledge of antidotes to the poisons brewed in your realm."

He lifted his head, flashing me a smile. "I'm going to be all right, Em."

I brushed the hair back from his dark eyes, examining them. "Perhaps there is something in the literature," I muttered, thinking out loud.

There was a noise behind us. I whipped round, but it was only Rose. I expected him to say something to us, but he merely stood motionless, his gaze drifting here and there without appearing to take anything in. His hair was plastered to his head; clearly he had been hit by an errant wave. At least he had stopped shrieking.

I turned back to Wendell. "What should we do about him?"

Wendell made a face. "Why must we do anything about him? *He* wasn't poisoned on his birthday."

It seemed wrong, but as I could not think of an alternative—the man would not even respond to his own name—we left Rose there in the nonsensical wreckage of the dryadology museum, unmoving as a statue. A parrot landed on his shoulder and began cleaning his hair, which he did not seem to notice. It was abundantly clear that he was no longer a threat to either Wendell or myself—not in the immediate future, at any rate.

On the way out, I paused by one of the broken display cases. "Ha," I muttered. I reached in and snatched up the artefact I had been interested in borrowing for Shadow, which the curator had denied me—a seemingly simple leather collar. I felt a little guilty, but not much; I was jittery with adrenaline and the aftershocks of terror, and anyway I reasoned that I would bring it back.

I became aware then that the main gallery of the museum, particularly where the battle had taken place, was alive with tiny lights. They weren't lights like the sheerie had used, but something closer to embers, which drifted through the air as if caught by an errant breeze.

"Whatever is that?" I said, reaching a hand out to trap one of them. It felt cool against my palm, but as soon as I opened my fingers, it fluttered away again.

"Hmm? Oh. Spilled magic," Wendell murmured. He was nearly asleep on his feet, leaning heavily against me. "Some of it's mine—the rest from the artefacts."

"Spilled?" I repeated incredulously. I had never heard magic referred to in such a way, as if someone had overturned a milk bottle.

Wendell muttered something else that sounded like "lint," which I must have misheard. I reached into my pocket and withdrew one of the pouches I use to collect faerie artefacts, velvet with a sort of netting of iron rings encasing it. I scooped several of the tiny embers of magic into the pouch, wondering if they would simply go out as the sheeries' lights had. Then I tucked the pouch into my pocket beside the borrowed collar and helped Wendell through the door.

15th September

I roused Wendell early this morning—he had slept on my couch, at my insistence. Yes, I realize how ridiculous that sounds. As if I could hope to stand in the way of another round of faerie assassins should they come crashing through my door. But given his condition, I felt it best to keep him where Shadow and I could watch over him. Also, his staying at my apartments offered some protection, as many Folk obey ancient laws of hospitality and cannot simply come charging into one's home to murder guests. He slept straight through the remainder of the day and into the early hours of the morning, and awoke still complaining of a headache, but I could tell from his voice and his colouring that he was greatly recovered.

"I refuse to go anywhere at this hour," he replied when I informed him that I had purchased train tickets to Dover the previous day. He was buried so deeply in his blankets and pillows that I could make out only a splash of golden hair and a quarter of his face. "I had a dreadful day and will be remaining here until at least noon."

"Wendell," I said, keeping my voice even through sheer force of will. "Your family has begun sending *assassins* after you. We must make every effort to locate your door without delay. At the very least, we must get as far away from Cambridge as possible, given that *they know you are here.*"

"How on earth will a few hours alter our situation? I must be allowed time to recover if I'm to be of any use in defending myself."

This tedious argument continued until I threatened to make ribbons of his favourite cloak, which he has spent a ludicrous number of hours tailoring to perfection, and he finally roused himself with many muttered complaints about tyrannical scholars.

The campus was still and slumbering at that early hour, the trees blanketing the paths in shadow, and the predawn air had the chill of autumn in it. I had hoped that the dryadology department would be deserted so that we could strategize without fear of eavesdroppers, but there were two students asleep on opposite ends of the common room, and Professor Walters was muttering to herself and slamming books about in her office—she keeps the hours of an owl. Well, it would have to do.

"Let me clean up this mess," Wendell said, waving his hand as we entered his office.

I raised my eyebrows. I've never seen Wendell's office messy—there was no dust, no unwashed cups, and for some reason it always smells faintly of nutmeg—though he often likes to organize it into the kind of disarray that clean people employ for aesthetics. Stacks of heavy books were piled up on the desk, along with a box of immaculate stationery and a row of inkwells, and there were expensive scarves and a spare cloak tossed over chairs—that was about it. Shadow immediately made himself at home in the bed Wendell keeps for him by the window—he ordinarily remains in my office when I'm at work, but has been known to slink over to Wendell's to have some variety in his bedding.

Wendell hung the cloak and folded the scarves away, then

got a fire going, though it was not cold; naturally he was only doing it for the atmosphere. Wendell's office is one of only two in the department with a fireplace—the other being Rose's—which is a source of perpetual resentment among the other faculty. As he was doing that, a light and rapid step sounded from down the hallway.

"That will be Ariadne," I said with a sigh. As predicted, my niece burst into the room, looking far too chipper for six in the morning.

"Oh, I hope I haven't forgotten anything," she said, dropping her suitcase upon a chair. I had informed her that we planned to leave immediately after our morning meeting for the ferry to Calais, thence to board a train east. From the neatness of her attire and the bright gleam in her eyes, she had been up for some time.

"I simply cannot believe it," she continued in a breathless voice, clasping her hands together as she often did when caught up in one of her fits of enthusiasm. "An expedition with two of the greatest dryadologists of the twentieth century! I can hardly contain my excitement."

"We wouldn't have known," I said. "Please keep your voice down—I'd rather the entire department didn't hear our discussion. What have you got there?"

She glanced down at the paper bag she was carrying. "Well, one can't do anything this early without refreshments, so I stopped in at the baker's for croissants."

Wendell perked up. "What kind?"

I left them to divide the spoils. At the end of the hall was a seminar room with a blackboard mounted on wheels, which I dragged to Wendell's office. When he saw it, he groaned.

"You have an addiction to blackboards," he protested. "You haven't even told us where we're going. You are not going to make us sit through charts and diagrams first, surely."

"The Alps," I said shortly. "Specifically, the village of St. Liesl in western Austria. I am particularly interested in the Grumanhorn, a nearby peak where Danielle de Grey is said to have vanished."

He looked blank. "What does de Grey have to do with my—"

"We have a few items to discuss before we turn to that," I said. I wrote *St. Liesl* on the board—not for any particular reason, but because, in truth, he was right about me: I enjoyed writing things on blackboards.

I turned to Ariadne. "I expect you have questions about what happened yesterday."

Her eyes widened. "Yes—well, so does the entire school, really."

I nodded. Naturally, a great many rumours were floating about concerning the sudden appearance of a river in one of the lecture halls, not to mention the mess we had made of the poor museum. I had given the vice chancellor what I felt was a plausible half-truth: that Wendell and I were being targeted by assassins as the result of our unwittingly angering one of the faerie monarchs of Wales—Wendell and I have both spent time there in recent years, and the Welsh faerie courts are notoriously sensitive to slights. The river I blamed on the assassins, of course, rather than Wendell, and on the whole my story was fairly nonsensical, but then scholars are used to this where the Folk are concerned.

Both Wendell and I had been given permission to depart on our expedition, which I had described as a mission to seek out a powerful faerie artefact to deliver to the Welsh court as a gift, in an attempt to petition their king for forgiveness. The vice chancellor was unenthusiastic about the prospect of finding someone to take over our classes at a moment's notice until I informed her that I believed the destructive assassins would keep coming until their court was satisfied or Wendell

and I were dead, at which point she expressed a clear preference for us to be as far from Cambridge and its remaining
lecture halls as possible.

"Sit down," I told Ariadne. She sat, looking apprehensive.

I drew in my breath. "Wendell is Folk. He is the monarch of
a court in the south of Ireland which we scholars call Silva
Lupi. He was overthrown by his stepmother, who has named
herself queen and is now attempting to have him assassi-
nated."

Ariadne stared at me. She seemed to be waiting for me to
add something, but when I did not, she looked dubiously at
Wendell, who was brushing flakes of croissant from his lapel.
"I see," she said.

Well, I suppose I should have expected as much. While
many scholars have had interactions with the common fae—
household brownies and the like—few have encountered
courtly fae and lived to tell of it. It was asking quite a lot of
Ariadne to simply accept that one of them was sat beside her
in a slump, his hair all over the place, clutching his cup of coffee as a drowning man would a life raft.

I looked at Wendell. He raised his eyebrows and said, "What
do I care if she believes you or not? Let's get back to your interest in de Grey. She was investigating faerie doors when she
vanished, is that it? You think she found mine?"

I raised a finger. Though I knew it was silly, I was a little
discouraged by Ariadne's anticlimactic response to my revelation. When I give a presentation, I like it to be appreciated.

"Before we turn to that," I said, "we must answer a more
immediate question: why now?"

"Why now?" Wendell repeated. "What do you mean?"

There was something a little too guileless about the way he
said it, and the way he was gazing at the notes I had scrawled
upon the blackboard as if suddenly fascinated. I narrowed my

eyes. "Why is your stepmother only now sending assassins after you? Surely she could have tracked you down sooner than this. She's had ten years."

"Perhaps she spent the decade yearning for my company. My stepmother is extremely contrary."

"Before you said that she *couldn't* kill you, according to faerie custom. That this would make her too powerful, too secure upon the throne."

He flicked his fingers dismissively and emptied his cup of coffee. "I'm not always right about these things. Ariadne, dear, could you brew up another pot in the lounge?"

The girl jumped to her feet, seeming relieved to have something practical to do. After she left, I folded my arms.

"You are keeping something from me," I said. "I dislike it when you do that. Please do not treat me like some faerie supplicant to whom you must talk in mysterious riddles."

He laughed. "Emily, Emily. How long have we been friends?"

"Seven years this December," I replied promptly. "That is, if you assume we became friends at the moment of our acquaintance, as most people tend to. Myself, I find it a more dubious transition to pinpoint."

"I'm sure you do. Well, I hope that by now you've come to trust me a little. The truth is, I could answer your question, but I'm not sure you'd like it. And in any event, it has no bearing on our situation whatsoever."

I examined him for a long moment as he looked back at me with an expression I couldn't read. Before I could decide upon another line of attack, Ariadne was back with the coffee.

"Thank you," Wendell said, clearing a place on the desk. But Ariadne had been too busy staring at him to notice; she bumped the tray against a chair, and the whole thing overturned, the cups smashing against the floor.

"I'm so sorry," she sputtered. "Professor Bambleby, I—"

"Hold your hands out, please," Wendell said with a sigh.

Ariadne looked at me, then held out her hands in baffled silence. Wendell made a gesture like the shape of a comma. The tea tray darted back into Ariadne's hands in a horribly uncanny motion, the teacups following immediately after, whole again and brimming with coffee.

I leaned against the desk, wincing. I hate when Wendell plays with time. I saw him do it once before, in Ljosland. There is something about it that makes me nauseated—perhaps it is the inability of my mortal mind to comprehend the rewinding of a moment of time, but contained within a single pocket of space. It is—well, impossible. Ariadne's reaction was more dramatic—she lurched backwards into the bookcase, sending several books crashing to the floor, and would surely have dropped the tray all over again if Wendell had not immediately snatched it from her.

"That's out of the way," he said to me.

"I thought you could only do that in Faerie," I said.

"I've been practicing," he replied, to my dismay.

"We could have made more coffee," I muttered, taking a sip. "This tastes like the floor now."

"It does *not,*" he said, as offended as if he'd made it himself.

"Well, I can't stop picturing it, so that's what mine tastes of." I was rattled and trying to hide it. I suppose I'm used to seeing him use magic, but every now and again he does something that unsettles me on a fundamental level, enough to make me almost regret the series of events that brought me to dryadology. Fortunately, these moments are short in duration.

"It seems a trivial use of magic," I said. "I am now certain that you're feeling better."

Wendell took a deep sip and closed his eyes. "There is nothing trivial about good coffee. Ariadne, did you make this?"

"It—it was already brewed. One of the other professors, I expect," she said. She was gazing at Wendell with her whole face alight, as if he'd brought to life her every childhood fantasy. "Then you're really—"

"Yes, he really is; let's move on," I said brusquely, because once again he had stolen my thunder. I opened my knapsack and deposited the faerie foot onto Wendell's desk.

Ariadne screamed. Wendell yelped, "My God!" and snatched the bag of croissants away.

"Good grief," I said. "It's only a foot."

"Only a foot!" Ariadne cried as Wendell said, "*Emily,*" in a scandalized tone. Professor Walters thumped several times on the other side of the wall.

"All right, all right," I said, putting the foot back into the knapsack. "This is the foot of a faun—a tree faun, in fact. We discussed them yesterday at breakfast. Danielle de Grey was investigating the species when she vanished."

"I can't believe you put a *foot* on my desk," Wendell said.

"Is that the only one?" Ariadne said, staring at my bag worriedly.

"Can you please pay attention?" I said. "This is important. That foot is from one of de Grey's traps. Perhaps the creature gnawed it off to escape, in the manner of beasts."

"These creatures you scholars call tree fauns are Irish. De Grey went missing in Austria," Wendell said. Then he froze. "Ah."

I smiled. While he chewed it over, I wrote a list on the blackboard: *St. Liesl, Austria. Corbann, Ireland. Nalchik, Russia. Kolyma, Russia.*

"A nexus," Wendell murmured. "That's what this is all about, isn't it? You think de Grey was chasing a nexus."

"No," I said. "I think she found one."

I pointed at the board. "This species of faun—which is

clearly its own species given the morphology of the horns; these are always distinct—has been documented in these four locations, each separated by hundreds, if not thousands of miles. They may not be native to Ireland at all, despite their long habitation there. As you know, only a small percentage of Russian scholarship has been translated into English, which perhaps is why few scholars have noticed the pattern. Tree fauns have been extensively documented in Ireland, but evidence of their existence in Austria and Russia has been largely ignored. I could find only two references in the Irish scholarship, both to the St. Liesl sightings, which the authors dismissed as erroneous."

"De Grey was studying them."

"Yes—but you know de Grey's reputation. Few scholars were inclined to take her seriously in her era, and fewer still today. She published a preliminary analysis on the subject of tree fauns before she vanished, arguing for the existence of a nexus. It was retracted five years after her disappearance, as were many of her other papers—I had to dig through mountains of archives at the University of Edinburgh, where de Grey was a visiting lecturer, to locate it. That is, by the way, where I also found the foot—squirreled away in the basement of their dryadology museum, with a number of de Grey's other finds."

Ariadne had been watching us with barely contained excitement—she was once again bobbing up and down on the balls of her feet. "What is a nexus?" she blurted. "I've not heard the term in any of my classes."

"There's a reason for that," Wendell said. He got up and took a cloth and a glass bottle of some sort of cleaning solution from one of the cupboards, with which he began to scrub at his desk. "According to scholars, they don't exist."

"They are a theory," I said. "A highly probable one, I've always thought. Where does that door lead?" I pointed at the office door.

Ariadne frowned. "To the hallway, of course. Or to Dr. Bambleby's office, if you are on the other side."

"Quite. Doors in the mortal realm generally connect two places. Most scholars assume that faerie doors are no different—but why must this be the case? The Folk are not bound by mortal laws in other respects. A nexus is a door that connects more than two places. In that sense, they are less like this office door and more like the door of a ship, which moves about and can open onto any number of locations."

"Oh," Ariadne breathed. "Then that would explain the presence of these fauns in so many countries—they are using a nexus, which connects their realms."

"And then, of course, they make forays into the human world, as the Folk always do." I drew a door on the blackboard with lines connecting it to St. Liesl and Corbann. "Ireland has seven known faerie kingdoms. Wendell's is located in the southwest of the country, where lies the mortal village of Corbann and those sightings of tree fauns. Now, Wendell's stepmother has all the doors to his realm closely guarded to keep him out, either by magic or other means—but this?" I circled St. Liesl. "A back door used by the common fae? Perhaps built by the fauns for their own particular use? She likely has no idea it exists."

"I can assure you she doesn't," he said. "Because my father didn't. The only back doors he knew about led to various faerie kingdoms in Britain, and they collapsed long ago. Faerie doors do that if they aren't used regularly. Incidentally, I believe that is how my stepmother sent the sheerie after me—she must have managed to repair one of the English doors."

"Ah," I said, nodding.

He smiled. "This is all going into your book, isn't it?"

"I was not even thinking about my book," I said defensively—I was only half lying. With my encyclopaedia complete, I have, as Wendell knows, turned my attention to another large project—creating a mapbook of all the known faerie realms, as well as their doors. Such a book will be a patchwork thing, unavoidably so—faerie realms are often attached to specific geographical locations in the mortal world, though only a few have been explored in a meaningful way—but I wish to use it to argue Danielle de Grey's point: that the realms are more interconnected than previous scholarship has suggested. Finding evidence of the nexus would be the linchpin of the entire project.

"Are you all right, dear?" Wendell asked Ariadne.

I tore myself away from my reflections and noticed that the girl was looking rather flushed and glassy-eyed. "Why don't you sit down?" I said.

Wendell offered his chair, and the girl sat. "I'm sorry," she said. "It's just—well, it's beyond imagining, isn't it?"

"Are you certain you wish to go with us?" Wendell said.

She stared at him in disbelief. "Of course I'm certain! I've been reading stories of the Folk since I was a little girl. This is everything I've ever hoped for."

"Everything you ever hoped," he repeated thoughtfully. "But if you come with us, you will also find everything you ever feared."

She looked worried—not, I thought, because of the warning, but rather the idea that he might prevent her from going. "I've already decided."

Wendell was still frowning at her. "It makes the most sense for us to attempt to locate the door in Austria," I said, "as opposed to the Russian sites—Austria is where de Grey was working, and thus we have her research to guide us."

"Research that apparently takes the form of a bloody *foot*,"

Wendell muttered. He had finished his scrubbing and began dabbing some sort of wood polish into the desk. The room smelled so strongly of lavender and citrus that it made my head ache.

"Yes." Ariadne cast a queasy look at the knapsack. "Is the foot, er—necessary?"

"You both seem to think I am carrying this around for my amusement," I said, exasperated. "Have neither of you heard the story of the cluricaun's ear?"*

"Oh," Ariadne said. "*Oh.* Then the foot will lead us to the nexus!"

"The foot will lead us to the fauns, which will lead us to the nexus," I said. "That's the idea, anyhow. I hope I don't need to point out that I have never taken directions from a faerie foot before. Fortunately, if it proves uncooperative, we have de Grey's maps to fall back on—and the villagers may know something too."

"You are overlooking one small detail, Em," Wendell said. "The creatures which you scholars have charmingly termed 'tree fauns' are a nasty lot. Even for my kingdom. And we are to go chasing after them, are we? You do realize this is likely how de Grey met her end."

---

* "The Wine Merchant and the Cluricaun's Ear," documented in its most famous iteration in *The O'Donnell Brothers' Midnight Tales of the Good Folk* (1840), is a sinister story in which a merchant is robbed of his stores by highwaymen on a remote forest track. A passing cluricaun offers aid, cluricauns being friendly with pub operators, distillers, and the like, but the ungrateful merchant kills the creature and removes one of its ears, out of the mistaken belief that cluricauns can "hear" gold singing from hidden caches and river deposits (cluricauns, who are often found in taverns, usually have their pockets stuffed full of gold, with which they pay for endless rounds of drink). The merchant lifts the ear to his own and follows the sound of singing on a long, winding path through the woods, where he is soon lost. To his astonishment, after hours of wandering, he ends up back where he began, staring down at the cluricaun's corpse. By this time, the cluricaun's family has gathered to observe their funerary rites. They fall upon the merchant, and he dies a messy death.

I leaned against the bookcase, tapping my fingers on a shelf. "There are no stories of them harming mortals."

"And the conclusion you draw is that they never have? There is another explanation."

Ariadne's eyes filled with a mixture of terror and delight that was concerning to behold. And that was the moment I began to doubt myself. It was one thing to throw myself into these dangers—I made my decision on that front long ago—quite another to bring my nineteen-year-old niece along.

"Ariadne," I began, "perhaps you should—"

"Perhaps she should stay behind?" interrupted a voice behind me. To my astonishment, Farris Rose was looming in the door, a grim look on his face. "You're bloody right she should stay behind."

"I— Dr. Rose," I sputtered. "Have you been listening to our conversation?"

Rose gestured in Wendell's direction. "That creature shows more concern for the child than you do."

I was so outraged that I couldn't immediately reply. Wendell put his hand on Shadow's head—the dog was beginning to growl. "You've overheard everything," I finally said.

"I have, in fact." His face was grey, his eyes reddened, but he was not, on the whole, as dishevelled as I would have expected, given the state we'd left him in yesterday. "Surprising as it may be, I found it impossible to sleep after that business with the sheerie, and spent the night here. That's my coffee you're drinking, by the way."

"I trust my aunt," Ariadne declared. "She knows the Folk better than anyone. I *wish* to go with her."

"How brave," Rose said. "Brave and stupid, which are usually one and the same where youth is concerned. I will go in the child's stead, Emily. You need help with this, that is clear."

"You will *what*?" My head spun, and I had the sense that

the conversation had suddenly bounded several miles ahead of me.

"Farris, my friend," Wendell said, "thank you for the offer, but we do not require your company." His voice was amiable, but with an undertone that made Rose go still.

Dozens of questions flitted through my mind, but the first to emerge was, "Less than twenty-four hours ago you were threatening to have us both turned out of Cambridge."

"I've spent years studying the Folk of the Alps," he said. "You need my expertise if you are to locate the nexus."

I gave a disbelieving laugh. But I couldn't help turning it over in my mind—it was true that Rose had extensive experience in the Swiss Alps, experience that I lacked; many of the same Folk can be found there, as faeries care little for human-made borders. Yes, it would be helpful having someone like him along. And yet—

"That doesn't explain *why*," I said.

He looked at me as if I'd sprouted another head. "You have a reasonable plan to locate a nexus, which current scholarship deems barely theoretical. In the process you will likely unravel the mystery of Danielle de Grey's disappearance, one of the enduring legends of dryadology. Emily, you might as well ask yourself why *you* are going."

"Ah," I said. "I see."

Ariadne was smiling hesitantly at Rose. "I say the more, the merrier."

"Good grief, Ari."

"What?" Her face fell. "Oh, yes. He threatened to have you sacked."

"And I may yet," Rose said. "But should you agree to my accompanying you on this trip, I could decide to overlook the matter of those falsified papers."

I gaped at him. Wendell, however, didn't appear surprised.

He was drumming his fingers on his desk, looking increasingly bored with the conversation. "This isn't really my area, but that strikes me as rather unethical, Farris."

Rose shrugged. "I can live with a lapse in ethics. I can live with a great deal if, in exchange, I find answers to the great scientific mysteries of our time."

Wendell sighed. "You scholars are all mad. No wonder you're always getting yourselves gobbled up by the common fae or trapped in some miserable realm. Emily, there's no point in arguing. He's obviously coming."

"I don't see how that's obvious," I said, glaring at him. Then I paused. "This is because of the coffee, isn't it? *That's* why you are being so amenable."

Wendell raised his eyebrows in an unconvincing display of innocence. "Hm?"

"You are allowing Rose to come because he makes a good cup of coffee."

"Well, you cannot expect me to endure the kind of deprivations we faced in Hrafnsvik," Wendell said.

Rose reddened. "I am the head of the department, with decades of field experience. My role in this expedition will be to provide expertise, not make *coffee*."

"Your role may be more varied than you think," Wendell said irritably, and I could tell that he would have no qualms about enchanting Rose if it suited his whims. Rose seemed to guess this too, and he flinched; I'm nearly positive I saw the first nigglings of doubt appear in his eyes. But before he could get a word out, Wendell's expression changed in that disconcertingly swift way it does sometimes, and he clapped Rose on the back. "Suddenly I'm feeling much more positive about this whole thing. Shall we get going?"

+ + +

Twenty minutes later, I stood outside the ivied pile that housed Wendell's apartments. Ariadne had gone inside to help him with his luggage while I waited below with Shadow. I was already packed, of course. Rose would meet us at the train station.

"Well, my love," I said. "Here we go again."

Shadow gazed up at me with the perfect contentment known only by dogs, and I massaged his enormous forehead. I hoped that the journey would not prove onerous for him. Though he is a faerie beast, they are no more immortal than those of the human realm, and when I found him eight years ago, he was already old—I do not like thinking about this. Of late he has shown more interest in lengthy naps by the fire than romping about the countryside. And yet, the idea of leaving him behind was simply not one I would countenance; nor, I suspect, would he.

Ariadne emerged from the door, panting under the weight of two suitcases.

"Good grief!" I said. "I told him he should bring only *one.*"

She set them down upon the cobblestones. "I reminded him of that, and he put his hands over his face and ordered me out. He is trying to combine the remaining two cases."

I shook my head. "If he is not down in five minutes I will go up there and drag him out. We will miss the train."

Ariadne nodded assent. I noticed she seemed distracted and kept putting her hand to the scarf she was wearing.

"What?" I said, and she jumped a little.

"Nothing," she said, tucking her scarf beneath her coat.

"None of that," I said. "We are about to involve ourselves in a great deal of danger, much of it strange and unsettling. There will be no putting on a brave face or ignoring things that concern you. I appreciate you saying back there that you trusted me. But you must trust me with your thoughts, Ariadne, as well as your safety, if we are to come out of this in one piece."

I knew I was being blunt, and also that there was no help for it. Partly because I struggle to be anything but, and also because we hadn't the time to tiptoe around things. I knew that I had not shown Ariadne much warmth in the few short months we had worked together, and I did not know how to compensate for it; but at least I could offer her this.

She gazed at me nervously. "He doesn't want me to come," she said.

I hadn't expected this. "He said that?"

She nodded. "He said that he had been pondering whether to enchant me into staying behind, but that you would only 'breathe fire' at him."

"I certainly would," I said irritably.

She gazed up at the brightening sky. "I told him that it wasn't any of his business what I did—it's my career. After that, he disappeared into one of the other rooms and came out with this."

She pulled out her scarf, which I realized she hadn't been wearing before—small wonder, for it was too warm for scarves.

I leaned forward. It was a silk scarf, though finer, I think, than ordinary silk—I have no expertise in the area of clothes—in a warm periwinkle shade that suited Ariadne well. Silver thread woven through the fabric made a sort of checkered pattern. I turned it this way and that, wondering if the pattern would change, or if it would suddenly sparkle with enchantment, but it seemed an ordinary scarf, albeit a prettily made one.

"He said it would help to protect me," she said. "That he would not allow any flesh and blood of yours to be harmed by the Folk."

"That was—good of him," I said after a pause. My mind was

busy wondering what the scarf did. It certainly didn't look like much, but looks mean little when it comes to faerie-made objects. "Though I hope you never have need of it."

She tucked it back under her coat, smiling a little. "Me too—I would like to keep it. My own faerie artefact! I will never take it off."

Her voice was wondering, and she went back to gazing up at the sky, which was turning a pretty shade of pink. Something nagged at me, and it took a moment to work out what it was.

"Ariadne," I said abruptly. "I'm sorry—I should have warned you away from this business myself some time ago. This is indeed a research expedition, but it's far from an ordinary one. Wendell is correct in saying that it would be best for you to stay here."

She gave me a startled look, as if astonished that I should express concern for her safety, which naturally made me feel monstrous. "It's all right, Aunt. As I said, I want to come along. I want it more than anything. After all the weeks I've spent helping you with the de Grey research, I simply couldn't bear to be left behind."

"Yes," I said quietly. "You've been very helpful."

She looked pleased at this, and we lapsed into silence. I felt certain that I should say something more, but had no idea what, so after another moment elapsed I escaped inside to find Wendell.

Instead of discovering him in a tizzy of trying to cram every last one of his garments into a suitcase, as I had expected, he was sat on the edge of his bed staring at the cases with an expression of utter woe.

"Please tell me you booked us one of the first-class cars," he said plaintively. "Train travel makes me ill."

"All of our tickets are first-class," I said, amused in spite of myself. "Naturally. We have ample funding for this expedition. I think you will find our accommodations an improvement over Hrafnsvik."

"We'll see. It's been my experience that villages in the middle of nowhere have a way of underwhelming you." He threw a shirt into one of the cases with a sigh and locked it.

"We'll miss our train if you don't get a move on." I went to his wardrobe and removed two jumpers, tossing them in his direction. He rolled his eyes at my selections.

"What?" I said. "I bought you one of those—the green. What was it, four Christmases ago? I have seen you in it before. You cannot always wear black."

"Yes, but it's rather dressy for—oh, never mind." He sighed again and folded them both neatly into the second case. "The problem is not the packing, I admit; I simply dislike travelling. Why people wish to wander to and fro when they could simply remain at home is something I will never understand. Everything is the way I like it here."

"That's no surprise," I said, gazing about me. Naturally, Wendell's apartments are absurdly comfortable, and somehow there is the atmosphere of a forest about them, though I know this makes little sense. The ceilings are very high, rather like the canopy of an ancient grove—I suspect he has enchanted them somehow—and always there is the sound of rustling leaves, though this abruptly ceases if you listen too closely. I would have expected a lot of luxurious frippery from faerie royalty, but his furnishings are simple—a scattering of sofas, impossibly soft; a huge oak table; three magnificent inglenook fireplaces; and a great deal of empty floor through which an impossible little breeze is always stirring, smelling of moss. For decoration there is the mirror from Hrafnsvik with the forest reflected inside it and a few silver baubles, sculptures and vases and the like, which catch the light in unexpected ways, but that's it. And, of course, the place is so clean one feels one may sully it by breathing too hard.

"Thank you," I said.

"What for?"

"For thinking of Ariadne. For being kind to her. I wasn't expecting it."

"No?" He sat on his suitcase to close it. "I'm hurt, Em. I'm really quite kindhearted, you know."

I certainly knew him to be kind when it suited his whims, which I'm not convinced is the same thing, but I didn't argue the point. "You've never made me a magic scarf."

He looked at me in amazement. "Would you wear it? I could make you more than that. Dresses would be the first order of business, to replace those dreadful brown things you always have on. And your *raincoat*."

I rolled my eyes. "Thank you, but I don't require wardrobe assistance from one of the *oíche sidhe*. Any raincoat you made for me would probably have an otter in the hood or something equally mad."

"No otters, I promise." He picked the cases up and looked about glumly. "I suppose that's that."

"Wait," I said.

He tilted his head in exasperation, clearly anticipating some sort of lecture. He went completely still when I strode up to him and kissed him.

For one strange moment, I felt like laughing, because it was so clear that I had shocked him. I soon forgot about that, though, as well as everything else. I had not kissed him since Ljosland, and that barely counted; the first time, I had been so nervous that I barely touched him, while the second he had been in his other, *oíche sidhe* form. Perhaps it was the leaves rustling invisibly or the breeze that plucked at my hair, but I had the sense that I had left the mortal realm somehow, and that when I opened my eyes, I would find myself in some enchanted grove surrounded by faerie lights. This impression was so strong that I pulled away, dizzy.

Wendell's eyes were dark. He took a half step towards me. "Emily—"

"No," I said inanely, without knowing exactly what I meant. I felt flustered and as surprised as he was. Also, a little ashamed of myself—hadn't I just resolved that it was unfair of me to give him false hope, that the only wise course would be to answer his proposal in the negative?

I seized one of his suitcases and added, "We must make our train," before hurrying away as fast as my legs would carry me.

17th September

We made the train from Cambridge—barely—as well as the ferry, and are currently crossing the French countryside in a first-class sleeper carriage en route to the town of Leoburg, Austria, whence we will need to hire a coach to reach St. Liesl. Wendell and Ariadne have retired early, while I sit here in the lounge, enjoying the scenery, or trying to. I tried to take notes for my mapbook, but found it too difficult to concentrate. My mind is overactive these days, sifting through our plans and contingencies for what we might find in Austria. The journey is four days by train.

The ferry to Calais was uneventful. I had expected to find Farris Rose's presence burdensome, but the man kept mostly apart from us, hiding away in his cabin and scribbling in his own journal. It is Ariadne's first trip abroad, and I believe she has spent half her waking moments exclaiming over something, from the view of the Channel to the rumble of the train to the tiny squares of chocolate they serve with tea. More often than not it is her company, not Rose's, which I find myself avoiding. Fortunately, Wendell seems amused by her, and after the awkwardness of the first day of our trip, which she spent staring at him as one might an exotic zoo exhibit, and jumping a foot in the air if he addressed her, they seem remarkably at ease with each other, and have bonded over their mutual love of good food and good clothes—Ariadne was briefly apprenticed to a dressmaker in London before convincing my brother to send her to Cambridge.

My compartment is next to Wendell's. It is adequately spacious, with a bed large enough for myself and Shadow, and a washbasin. I locked the door last night and drew a line of salt across the threshold, in the event that more assassins pay us a visit. I am not too worried, however, as Wendell says that all Folk despise trains and railroads. I stowed the faerie foot under my bed, surrounded by a circle of salt, which I hoped would dissuade it from wandering.

I awoke in the night at the sound of an odd sort of rustling from Wendell's compartment, which was followed by a few intermittent thumps. There was nothing violent about the sounds, and so I assumed that he was finding it difficult to sleep in the train, and was up fixing himself a midnight snack, as he had been wont to do sometimes in Ljosland. I considered rising to check on him, but I have always found trains lulling and almost immediately fell back to sleep.

Shadow's low, rumbling growl woke me this morning. He was crouched beside me, his body one long line of tension, facing the door. I looked, and found there was a man standing at the foot of my bed.

I am pleased to say that I did not scream—my work has involved a great many supernatural frights, and I have learned to tamp down my reactions. And it was clear that the man was supernatural, for he was the ribbons man I had met on campus, and he had come through my locked door.

"*Left*," he told me, as if we had been in the middle of an argument. He seemed to have even more ribbons than before, some of them looped round his neck like a tatty scarf. But besides that—and this is where I feel my mind folding in on itself in a futile effort to make sense of it all—he was *younger* than when I'd last seen him. By twenty, if not thirty years. His hair hadn't any grey in it now, and his dark face was unlined save for the fold between his eyes.

I felt myself grow still.

"Left," he repeated, "and then left again. Do you remember nothing, girl?"

This I found irritating, as my memory is faultless, and though I knew it was ridiculous to argue with a spectre, I said, "If you are referring to the mysterious directions you gave me at our previous encounter, you told me to turn left when I met with an indeterminate number of ghosts with ash in their hair; left at an evergreen wood; and then to carry on through the valley where your brother will die."

He narrowed his eyes. "And then?"

Well, I thought, *this conversation makes the last one seem sane.* "I haven't the foggiest idea. I don't know what you are, nor what place you are directing me to."

He laughed, revealing very white teeth. "Directions? You think me capable of giving directions, you silly girl? I am lost, long lost, though I may yet find my way out again." He held up his ribbons. "But you—you are so deep in wilderness you do not even know it surrounds you."

"That's a bit rude," I said.

"*Lost* is a kingdom with many paths, but they all end at the same place. Do you know where?"

I bit back a sigh, because now that the novelty was wearing off, the stranger was beginning to grate on me. "I imagine you mean Faerie. *The kingdom of the lost,* it is called in some of the oldest tales. Rather poetic, isn't it? But most likely it simply refers to the habit the Folk have of leading careless mortals astray."

He blinked at me, this strange apparition of a man, and for a moment he looked almost sane.

"You just might do it," he murmured after a pause. "A silly child with her hair all in tangles."

I lifted my hand to my head, annoyed by this unnecessary slight, and he looked back at his ribbons. He frowned as if reading something in the varied colour and texture of them, and then he unlocked the door and stepped out.

I shot to my feet and followed him into the corridor, where I collided with Rose.

The man was holding a cup of tea, which overturned all over him. "Emily, what in God's—"

"Did you see him?" I demanded. "That man—the ribbons—"

"I see only *you*," he said, glaring magnificently through the tea on his glasses. "What faerie nonsense have you mixed yourself up in now—"

I banged on Wendell's door. From within came a sleepy murmur of protest, but no footsteps approaching the door. I tried the handle—locked.

"Damn you," I muttered. "Utterly useless in a crisis. Your beauty sleep is more important, is it?"

The door seemed to glare back at me. With a curse, I darted back into my room, threw on my clothes, and charged off with Shadow at my heels, leaving a sodden Rose staring after me.

Ariadne was in the dining car, a half-eaten breakfast in front of her. At that early hour, there were few other passengers about, and she was having an animated conversation with one of the waiters. A wall of grey-green mountains, rocky and shadow-shrouded, took up the entirety of the view beside her.

"Aunt Emily!" she exclaimed, waving me over. "Did you hear that this train runs all the way to Istanbul? Isn't it amazing how much of the world one can see these days? You know, my mother spent her entire life in a village not five miles across—what she knew of other countries she had to read in books. Modern technology is a wondrous thing, isn't it? And I'm sure that the Folk of Turkey are fascinating—oh, dear." She looked me up and down. "Your dress is on backwards."

"Never mind that."

After ordering myself a pot of tea, I told her of my encounter, and she listened in rapt silence, her eyes growing wider and wider.

"How wonderful," she breathed when I had finished. "How terribly mysterious! This is just like the tale of the blacksmith and the boggart.* It must be faerie magic at work."

"With that attitude, I hope our friend visits you next. Myself, I prefer not to be stalked by strange men who can walk through walls."

"Do you have any idea who he is?"

"Several. And I think it would be best if we assume the worst is true: that he is another assassin sent by Wendell's stepmother."

Ariadne worried her lip between her teeth. "If so, he doesn't seem very good at his job, does he? He's more interested in you than Professor Bambleby. And are the ribbons supposed to be a weapon?"

"I believe he's human," I said. "He could be a captive of Wendell's stepmother, someone she sent back into the mortal realm under an enchantment. Perhaps it drove him mad, or perhaps his behaviour is part of some faerie ritual not yet documented by scholars."

---

* There are several tales involving blacksmiths and boggarts, but I assume Ariadne is referring to the one from Skye, which tells of a blacksmith unlucky enough to live in the vicinity of a faerie inn. The man is interrupted by strange Folk at all hours making various demands of him, under the mistaken impression that he is the innkeeper. Only when the blacksmith invites a local boggart into his home do these visitations finally cease.

"I don't think we should jump to that conclusion," came a voice from behind me. To my dismay, Rose pulled a chair up to our table.

"You were eavesdropping again, I take it," I said, tossing a glare at Ariadne, for surely she had seen him standing there.

She looked at Rose guiltily. "Well, as he's part of the expedition—"

"Quite right," I said, waving my hand with a sigh. "I am being petty, aren't I? Dr. Rose, I apologize. Perhaps you can offer your perspective."

He looked surprised, but only very briefly—Rose is the sort of man accustomed to giving opinions; whether others are interested is a question he rarely takes into consideration. He tucked his hands into his vest pockets and leaned back in his chair in what I have come to see as his Department Head posture. "You are assuming that this *ribbons man*—who must be trapped in some sort of faerie realm, given his palavering about paths, only one that is not fixed to any spatial plane—is connected to Bambleby's stepmother. This is not necessarily the case."

"He appeared on the same day the assassins did," I pointed out. "Watkins's First."*

Rose gave me one of his sage looks. "Surely you're familiar with Smith-Patel's critique of Watkins. It runs along the same line as criticisms of Occam's razor; namely, an overzealous application of the Principles can result in oversimplification. In this case, faerie magic may be involved in both circumstances without it springing from the same source."

"Yes, well," I said, annoyed at my own annoyance. I still

---

* Watkins's First Principle of Dryadology: The more coincidences, and the more improbable those coincidences, the greater the likelihood of faerie involvement in any given situation.

cared about Rose's opinion of me; that was the ridiculous thing. "It is only one possibility."

"We must gather more evidence," he said. "Sadly, I am without my personal library here, but I will place a call to the university when we arrive in Leoburg and have my research assistants scour the literature for stories involving ribbons, cross-referenced with the theme of reverse aging—those seem to me the two key details of these encounters. Emily, the next time this man appears to you—as it seems likely he will—you should try to obtain one of these ribbons. It may give us a valuable clue as to his identity." He said to Ariadne, "I'd like you to go round the other passengers and ask if they've seen this man lurking about—particularly those in adjacent compartments."

It was all eminently sensible, which only increased my resentment. "I'll wake Wendell. He may have his own suggestions."

"I don't see how they would be relevant."

I blinked, wondering if I'd misheard. "Surely you're not suggesting we leave Wendell out of this. He is a rather important part of our research."

"He is a subject of our research," Rose said. "And we will sound him out for information when necessary—with the utmost caution—but he is not part of this expedition any more than your ribbons man is part of it."

I gave a snort of disbelief. "You can't be serious."

"No?" Rose leaned forward, his expression darkening. He looked at me in a way he rarely had before, without condescension, only a piercing gravity, and part of me wished to shrink back. "Emily, I may have doubts about your methods, but I have always thought you an intelligent person. Yet you are behaving like an utter fool."

I gaped at him. Ariadne looked as offended as if he'd directed the insult at her. "Professor," she began, "you aren't—"

"I cannot believe I need to explain this to you," he continued. "You have apparently come to trust one of the courtly fae—but not only that, an exiled royal embroiled in a war with his family. Are you blind to the danger this places you in? It is so obvious that I find myself wondering sometimes if you are bewitched. The man you see as Wendell Bambleby—which is not, of course, his true name—is a fiction. He is the natural-born ruler of the Silva Lupi, for God's sake! The most vicious faerie kingdom in Ireland, one responsible for the disappearances or deaths of dozens of scholars, as well as Lord knows how many mortal inhabitants of the region. 'The realm of villains and monsters,' Brakspear called it in his *Histories. That is the home he wants back.* And you see him as an ally? A *friend*? What is the matter with you?"

Each sentence landed like a blow, and I could do nothing but stare as he went on. "The wisest approach—nay, the *only* wise approach—is to focus on the nexus. We will find and document evidence of its existence, which will represent an enormous step forward for science. Should we unravel the mystery of de Grey's disappearance in the process, so much the better. That is *all* we will concern ourselves with. Bambleby's quest is his own business, and if his presence places us in danger, we will ask him to leave. You must act like a scholar, Emily, not some silly mortal in a story whose head was turned by one of the Folk."

"Have you quite finished?" I said levelly, even as I fought the urge to shrink from him as a snail shrinks into its shell. Rose waved his hand, and I shoved my chair back.

Shadow followed, of course, but not before he nipped at Rose's shoe, making him yelp. I walked blindly for several moments and only realized I had walked past my compartment when I reached the door to the next car.

I was not thinking about either Wendell or Rose, but the sheerie: how they were like nothing I'd seen before, and perfectly terrifying. And such monsters were commonplace in Wendell's world.

It struck me for the first time—or, I suppose I should say, the *reality* of it struck me, for I had until then been viewing the whole thing as an abstract issue of scholarship, or at least trying to—that we were searching for a door to that world. Rose was not incorrect in pointing out that it was a kingdom into which a disproportionate number of scholars had disappeared, never to be heard from again.[*]

I leaned against the wall for a moment to catch my breath. One of the porters passed by, giving me an odd look, and so I collected myself and went to Wendell's door.

It was still shut—only it wasn't locked. I had been wrong before. The handle turned, but the door didn't open. This was because there were leaves jammed into every inch of the frame, which acted like a doorstop.

"What the bloody hell," I muttered. I shoved at the door, putting my shoulder into it. With a rustling and a creak, it burst open.

Once I saw what was inside, I hastily yanked Shadow in by the scruff and slammed the door shut behind us. The walls of the compartment were covered in flowering ivy. The floor had

---

[*]   Probably the most well-known of these is Dr. Niamh Proudfit of the University of Connacht, a contemporary of Rose's who disappeared in the 1880s. Dr. Proudfit was investigating a species of imp—the smallest of the brownie-type faeries—believed to be native to the Silva Lupi. Her cane was discovered just beyond a circle of nine dead oak trees, and within the grove was exactly half her cloak. It was such a neat half that scholars theorized it had been caught in a faerie door as she slipped through, and severed by the liminal magic itself.

turned into some sort of stone, damp and mossy, and one of the walls seemed to have vanished entirely, offering a view of a lantern-lit path that bent towards several shadowy dwellings, turreted and roofed in green turf. Wendell lay asleep in his bed like a forest king in his leafy bower, oblivious, covered in blankets apart from a foot that stuck out.

"How does one sleep through a spectacle like this?" I exclaimed, moving towards the bed. Then I shrieked, because a flock of sparrows flew at my head.

At least I think they were sparrows—when one is abruptly pummeled by dozens of wings, it's difficult to focus on particulars. Shadow erupted into barks and caught one of the birds in his mouth, whereupon it exploded in a burst of feathers. Fortunately, Wendell awoke then, and grabbed my hand, at which point the sparrows flitted off.

"What on earth have you done?" I demanded. Then I coughed, because there was a feather in my throat. "It *was* you that did this, wasn't it?"

"I think so," he said, gazing about him with a frown. He was dressed in his bedclothes, a loose silk shirt and pants, and his hair was almost comically askew. The sparrows alighted on the edge of a pond, which seemed to have replaced his washbasin, and began a noisy bath.

"You *think* so." I paused. "Then this was an accident? Like the tea?"

"No, I have simply grown fond of pointless exertions of magic," he said. "Of course it was an accident. I recall that I was dreaming of home, as usual. I suppose part of the dream drifted out of my head."

I touched the ivy—it was quite real, as were the sparrows, as evidenced by the talon marks on my arm. "Will you be able to clean this up? We can't very well leave it for the poor janitors when we disembark."

"Yes, just—give me a moment." He sat heavily on the edge of the bed, rubbing his face. His shirt was haphazardly buttoned and hanging off one shoulder, revealing the graceful line of his collarbone and the lean muscle of his sword arm.

I settled myself gingerly beside him. "Has this ever happened before? This—dream-magic?"

"I'm afraid not." He looked uneasy, as if some other faerie had waltzed into his compartment and made it go to seed. And perhaps one had, but I was beginning to feel an unpleasant prickle of suspicion at my neck.

"What else?" I asked.

"What else what?"

I picked up his hands and examined them, then gripped his chin in a carefully businesslike way and looked into his eyes. I saw nothing peculiar—no *additional* peculiarity, that is; his eyes have always been too green, a blackened green like leaves layered until no light can get through. I don't like to hold his gaze for long; not because I find it intimidating, but because a part of me worries that if I do, I will never wish to look away.

I released his chin. "What other symptoms do you have?"

"None." He stopped and thought. "I am a little tired much of the time."

"And you didn't think to tell me you were still suffering from the poison," I scolded. Wasn't it just like him, to make a to-do about getting enough sugar in his coffee, but not a thing like this.

"I didn't want to worry you," he said.

"You failed miserably."

"Miserably?" He looked so delighted that I pushed him over.

"What is that?" I said, catching a strange flicker of movement through the half-open buttons of his nightshirt. At first

I assumed he was wearing a necklace, which had slid to one side. But when I pulled open the top button, I saw—

Wings.

They were the faintest of shadows, flickering over his skin. But they were unquestionably the outlines of birds, perhaps a half dozen of them; they were so ethereal and swift that I couldn't separate them enough to count.

"Em?"

I realized that he had gone still, and then that I was crouched over him, having nearly torn the buttons open on his shirt.

I withdrew, pulling him upright so that he could more easily look down at his chest. "*Look.*"

He followed my gaze. "What?"

"You don't see it?" Even as I stared, the flicker of wings faded and died. Had I imagined it? I looked around the compartment. Leaves swayed with the movement of the train. Could it have been merely the play of shadow against his skin? I clung to the possibility, even as I felt the ghostly tug of a memory that evaded my grasp. What I had seen called to mind a story—but which one?

"I thought I saw something," was all I could say, because something about that fragment of memory made me wish to recoil from it.

"Oh, dear. Some dark omen?" he said, uncomfortably close to the mark. He pressed my hand between his and drew it against his chest. "Ignore it, Em. I've always refused to be governed by omens; I find them far too dull."

"You can't expire before I decide whether or not to marry you." I had meant it as a continuation of our jests, but it came out sounding wrong, flat. I felt as if I might faint.

"I won't," he assured me earnestly. "It's not too bad."

"Not too bad!" I cried.

He winced. "Yes, this is an inconvenience—but I feel much better than I did. It's clearly the sort of poison meant to confuse my magic, but these"—he glanced about the compartment—"effects should fade soon enough."

"That's remarkably unspecific."

"I'm sorry. I have never been poisoned before, so I find the symptoms difficult to predict. I—" He gazed at me for a long moment, and I felt my dread rise.

"What?" I demanded.

"Em," he said, "you've put your dress on backwards again."

"Good grief." I wrenched my hand away. Still, his nonchalance had reassured me a little. Though I was still trying not to look at the impossible place where the wall had been.

There came a gentle snoring sound from behind me. I turned and found that Shadow had fallen asleep on Wendell's bed.

"I assume that if I avoid using my magic, it should reduce the chances of anything unexpected occurring," he said.

"Ah," I said. "Wonderful."

He blinked at me for a moment. Then he groaned.

"I'll see if the steward has any gardening tools," I said with a grimace, though in fact I was relieved by the distraction. "Let's get this cleared up by noon, if we can."

20th September

Fortunately, with Ariadne's assistance—I did not bother asking Rose, thus sparing myself another lecture on my foolishness—we were able to dispose of the ivy Wendell had inflicted upon the compartment without too much difficulty, tossing handfuls out the window as the train chugged along, which left an odd trail of green upon the deep mountain pass. The sparrows were shooed outside, and we also found, hiding amongst the greenery, one cantankerous vole, which I let Wendell take care of. He was able to magic away the rest without incident, which was a relief.

The rest of the journey was unremarkable—disappointingly, for I had been hoping for another conversation with my beribboned mystery man. Sadly, no coaches were to be had in Leoburg, and so we were forced to hire a wagon drawn by two small, sturdy farm horses to reach St. Liesl, which took more than three hours.

I have been to the Alpine countries of Austria and Ardamia before, but never to this corner of the range, and while the journey to St. Liesl, which perches high above sea level, was not a comfortable one, it took my breath away. The path wound up a mountainside still dotted with the last of the summer flowers, snowbells and cheery buttercups. Mountains cluttered every horizon, many crowned in an eternal snow. Below us was the town of Leoburg with its railroad, its neat stone-and-timber buildings, its sharp and commanding steeple, but the higher we went, the more all this was dwarfed by the wildness surrounding it, the railroad a thin line of stitches connecting us to the world we knew. And then we rounded a bend in the path, and we could no longer see the town at all.

I understand now why the folklore of the Alps is so rich— the many folds and crevices in the mountainsides could hide any number of faerie doors opening onto dozens of stories. Even Rose seemed impressed, and Ariadne kept up a steady commentary that consisted mostly of exclamations. Our elderly driver, introduced mononymously as Peter, seemed to enjoy her appreciation of his native land, and eventually she occupied herself in cobbling together a conversation with him consisting of gestures and her rudimentary German, which came as a great relief to my patience.

Eventually we left the wilderness behind and began to pass a few farms, which seemed largely dedicated to sheep and cattle, some occupying precarious slopes. Peter turned his horses down a rutted lane, below which was a little alpine lake, blue as the sky, that sent Ariadne into ecstasies all over again.

"Here we are," our conductor said in German, stopping outside a two-storey cottage at the end of the lane. It was built of solid, dark wood with ivy clambering up the side, reddening in the autumn air, for autumn and winter come early to high places like this. I saw only farmers' fields around us, but in the distance, around a little treed rise in the landscape, a few columns of woodsmoke rose, which I took as evidence that St. Liesl did, in fact, exist. The place reminded me of a faerie village, hidden away between mountains, which amused me. There was even a scatter of mushrooms by the side of the road.

"This is Julia Haas's guesthouse?" I enquired, naming the woman with whom I had corresponded, and he smiled.

"Only guesthouse in town," he said. "Go in, go in—it will be dark soon."

"Not bad, this," I said after the man had departed, for to my eye the cottage was quite pleasing.

"It's marvellous!" Ariadne enthused, while Wendell maintained a dubious silence.

Within, we found a kitchen and sitting room, humble but clean and smelling of its oak floorboards. Large windows at the back overlooked the fall of the mountainside and the valley below, with another tremendous mountain looming out of the cloud cover opposite. A little grove of beech beside the cottage was putting on a spectacular show of leaves in yellows and oranges, which the wind plucked loose and sent skittering past the window. I have scarcely seen a more prepossessing guesthouse.

"I will take the room farthest to the back," Rose announced. "I sleep very lightly."

With that, he picked up his trunk and stomped up the creaky stairs. Ariadne clapped her hands together in delight and hurried after him.

"Oh," I murmured in sudden dismay.

"What?" Wendell said. He had been gazing about the place with an expression of resignation.

"I forgot—our accommodation has only three bedrooms," I said awkwardly. "Rose being here rather complicates things."

He glanced at the ceiling. "Are you certain about that?"

My face heated. "Well, I—"

"I meant, are you certain there are only three?" He opened a cupboard and shook his head. "Good Lord!"

"It doesn't look dirty to me," I said, to which he responded with a long-suffering sigh. I added, "And if you are going to be an old hen about it and waste your time clucking over every scrap of clutter, you should know in advance that I won't be assisting."

"Old hen!" he exclaimed. "Well, of course you won't help. You'll spend the evening in your preferred manner, hunched over in some dark corner like a troll."

I was spared from replying by the arrival of our host, a woman of fifty or so who might have been the human embodiment of welcome and good cheer, round and red-cheeked with her eyes permanently creased into a smile, her pale skin still showing signs of a healthy summer tan. She was practically attired in sturdy leather boots and a dress of simple blue wool ending below the knee, but she wore no cloak despite the cool breeze.

"We saw you coming up the rise," she said in English, heavily accented but fluent. "It's a relief that you got in before dark—it comes quick around here. We brought you some refreshments after your journey."

"That's very kind of you," Wendell said with a semblance of his usual charm—I could see that our host's warmth had improved his spirits. That and the basket tucked under her arm, which held some manner of buns covered in powdered sugar.

The woman bustled in, followed seconds later by what looked like a younger version of herself bearing a small pot of bacon dumplings in broth, and then by a still younger version with a basket stuffed with cheeses, fruit, cured meat, butter, and freshly baked bread.

"My daughters," Julia said unnecessarily. "Astrid and Elsa. Tell me, how was your journey?"

I happily allowed Wendell to take over the conversation, and within seconds the four of them were laughing at his description of the bumpy cart ride, which he managed to turn into a mockery of his scholarly softness rather than an indictment of our driver's abilities. Ariadne returned moments later, having selected her own bedroom, and soon the cottage was as noisy a place as a country pub at the weekend.

"Where is Rose?" I asked Ariadne.

She covered her smile with her hand. "Out like a light! I don't think he enjoyed the journey up the mountain any more than Professor Bambleby."

"Ah." So much for my hope that I might induce Rose to take one of the couches. The man had essentially blackmailed his way onto our expedition—it was highly unfair that he should have claimed first choice of the sleeping quarters.

As we sat down to our meal—which was very good, particularly the buns, which were soft as clouds and contained a lovely apricot jam—I managed to turn the conversation to our research, which earned me an eye roll from Wendell. Well, he knows I am useless at small talk.

"Oh, we'd be happy to help however we can—we've had scholars stay here before," Julia said. "None for some years, though. They were mostly interested in the story of that Scottish woman, de Grey—and that man as disappeared the next year searching for her, Eichorn. Less him, though." She smiled. "Always felt a bit sorry for the fellow—most folks were all 'de Grey this, de Grey that'—well, he vanished into Faerie just as completely as she did, but then she did have that touch of the glamourous about her, from what I heard." She paused, her gaze drifting to Wendell in an absent sort of way. "That's why you're here, I suppose? To look for her?"

"Well, it's one of the enduring mysteries of dryadology, isn't it?" Wendell said.

"How many scholars has the village hosted?" I asked.

"Ten or so. None found any clue about what happened to her." Julia seemed to notice that this had sunk my spirits somewhat, for she added, "But fresh eyes, you know."

"Do you know the place where she disappeared?" I asked. "Near the Grumanhorn, wasn't it?"

"Her path was a little more to the south," Julia said. "We think. We found one of her ribbons tied round a root. I say *we,* but of course I was just a baby when she came through the village. My husband's father could show you the spot."

Wendell and I stared at each other. Ariadne had gone still with her hand hovering over the cheese.

"Ribbons?" I repeated.

"Yes—it's common custom around here to stuff your pockets with them when you go a-roving. It's very easy to get lost in these mountains, even if you know them like the back of your hand, because there are so many doors to Faerie hidden everywhere, particularly in the mists and clouds that linger here and there. You tie ribbons as you go so that you can find your way home again."

"That seems a bit of a gamble," Wendell said, pouring another cup of tea. "Some bored faerie could simply rearrange them, no?"

He was echoing my own thoughts, but Julia smiled and held up a finger. "We know our faeries well, Dr. Bambleby. We soak the ribbons in a saltwater bath during the full moon. The Folk don't touch them."

"Clever," I murmured. The first half of it, anyway; the second was likely local superstition—the Folk do not generally care if it is a full moon or not, though some do use lunar phases to mark the passage of time. But almost all Folk despise salt.

Julia's elder daughter, Astrid, began pressing Wendell for details about his travels then, and he obliged with a winsome smile and a warning glance in my direction. I understood well enough and set my questions aside—I did not wish to repeat the mistakes I had made in Hrafnsvik. It was in our interest to befriend the people of St. Liesl, and that would be more diffi-cult if I insisted on cross-examining them before we'd even exchanged pleasantries.

I was surprised when, barely half an hour later, Julia glanced out the window and said, "We'd best be on our way. When the shadows climb that high up the Malvenhorn, you know it's near to dark."

I was delighted by the brevity of the visit, but Wendell looked crestfallen. "It's not yet seven," he said. "Won't you stay for coffee?"

"We'd love to," the woman said apologetically, "but we don't leave our houses after dark if we can avoid it."

I was immediately intrigued. "Do the Folk trouble you after dark?"

She gave me a weary look, but there was warmth in it still. "I suppose that's one way to put it."

"And how long has this been happening?"

"How long?" she repeated. "It has never been otherwise, Professor. Now, mind you lock up tight, and don't forget to leave a little food on the doorstep. They've a particular fond-ness for cheese and cooked vegetables. I'll send one of the girls round in the morning with your breakfast. Oh—and I'd advise you to avoid the faerie den down on the lakeshore."

With that, the three of them were rising and wishing us a good night. I held the door open for them, and was surprised to find how quickly the night had come on. The shadow of the peak had fallen over the cottage, and the air had none of the warmth we'd felt on the approach. As Julia and her girls trooped down the lane, waving to us over their shoulders, lit-tle fingers of mist crept in behind them like a door closing.

I looked at Wendell. "What do make of that?"

He shrugged. "Why not take a stroll down to this den?"

"Shall we bring ribbons?" I said, fingering the bunch Julia

had left for us. They were a great deal like those my visitor carried, variable in colour and style.

"Only if you wish to adorn Shadow's fur. Wouldn't he look dashing?"

Ariadne was disappointed when we instructed her to remain behind, though she grew cheery again when I tasked her with the washing-up. I was beginning to understand that she would be happy in any situation so long as she felt useful, a rather dangerous quality in an assistant that I would have to resist the temptation to exploit. Then Wendell and I donned our cloaks and slipped out the door with Shadow.

It was not yet officially sunset, but with the sun gone below the encircling peaks, we had entered that long, cold twilight common to mountainous regions. Wendell and I found a footpath down to the alpine lake we had passed earlier.

"Rather odd, this ribbons business," he said as we navigated the rocky slope. "First that walking cipher appears to you at Cambridge, festooned with them; now here we are, at the other end of Europe, and apparently they're the local pastime. There must be a connection."

"It would be quite the coincidence otherwise," I said.

He looked at me, then laughed. "You've already figured it out."

"What?"

"The identity of your mystery man."

I couldn't quite suppress my smile. I admit, I do enjoy it whenever I can unravel some faerie mystery before he does. "Let's just say that my list of theories has narrowed somewhat. I would like to confirm it with him first."

He waved his hand. "By all means. *I* certainly don't care who he is, unless he wishes to kill me or lead me to my door."

"It's definitely one of the two," I said.

He gave me a narrow-eyed smile. "You would miss me too dearly."

"I would miss the trouble you cause me. It's been a boon to my career. In any case, you can sleep easy; I believe my new friend is more likely to help than harm us."

"Where would I be without you, Em?"

This was another joke between us. I cast about for an answer I had not given before, and said, "No doubt lounging in some sun-splashed Italian villa, bribing the villagers to plant faerie stones in unusual patterns so that you can write a paper about it."

We reached the lake, which had a steep, sandy bank and was half-cloaked in filaments of mist. I tripped over a stone and would surely have gone tumbling end over end had not Wendell caught me in one easy flash of movement. He set me back on my feet, smiling.

"No wonder mortals are always injuring themselves," he said. "You're as clumsy as blind bears and yet still you go charging about as if you aren't the most fragile creatures in the world. Watch your *feet*."

I searched for a clever riposte but couldn't find one. "Thank you."

"No need. It's charming."

"As long as I'm a source of amusement for you," I muttered as he laughed, glad that the darkness concealed my flush. We had been standing chest to chest, close enough to feel his breath on my cheek.

Wendell found a stick and waved it at Shadow, then tossed it into the lake. The old dog lumbered happily into the water, where he swam about in circles for a time before finally catching sight of the stick in the distance and making his plodding way out to retrieve it. Shadow is blind in one eye and not in what could be called peak condition; I'm afraid I have a tendency to spoil him where his meals are concerned.

"This is your idea of searching for a faerie den?" I said.

"There aren't any Folk about," he said, using his arm as a shield as the dog emerged from the water to shake himself.

It was just like him to give up so easily. "What about faerie *doors*?"

He took his time wrestling the stick from Shadow, doling out much disproportionate praise of his athletic prowess before turning to scan the bank.

"There," he said, pointing. "Where that spring emerges from the rock. It's a shallow thing—a cosy little cottage for one of the common fae, I suppose. Don't step in the mist, or it'll sweep you into Faerie."

I hastened over to the spring, squeezing the coin I carry in my pocket to ward off enchantment. But I saw no movement around the spring—which was clearly a faerie door, now that I had a good look at it.[*] The mouth of the spring was hidden by a fine mist that seemed to have no interaction with the breeze stirring the water.

I was startled by a low chittering sound. A fox kit stood in the shadow of the cliffside, its black eyes flashing. It was gone before I could get a good look at it, tucking itself into a narrow crevice. A second followed after the first—I caught only the flicker of its bushy tail.

---

[*]   The term "faerie door" is often a source of confusion for newcomers to dryadology. Only a small percentage of faerie doors are visible to the human eye as *doors* (and even those are wont to disappear at the whim of the Folk). They are, by and large, invisible gateways between our world and theirs. It takes a well-trained eye to spot a faerie door; the best clue is what dryadologists usually call an incongruity. The most common example is an unnaturally round ring of mushrooms, but often the clues are less obvious: a sudden patch of wildflowers; the only bare stone in a creek where all others are covered in moss; a particularly evil-looking grove; and so forth.

"Hm," I said. I took out my notebook and made a few jottings.

"Are you quite done?" Wendell called a few minutes later. "Shadow is getting cold."

Now, Shadow is never cold; he is a grim, and their connection to death renders them immune. "*You* are cold, you mean."

"Well, I forgot my scarf," he complained.

I knew he would only keep it up, so I rolled my eyes and put away my notebook. "Not much to see here, anyhow," he said. "A single door to some humble abode. We'll make a proper survey of the area tomorrow."

"Even a *humble abode* may prove useful."

"Emily, Emily," he said. "As I have reminded you many times, just because they are small does not mean you can make pets out of the common fae; most species are more interested in dining on your entrails than giving directions. And what is the point, anyway? They're foolish creatures, on the whole."

His snobbishness grated on me. "Have you forgotten how Poe helped us?" I said. "Establishing contact with the common fae of this region may lead us to your door."

He looked dubious. "You were lucky with Poe. Your luck will run out if you aren't careful."

"I'd wager it ran out long ago, as I'm presently traipsing round the world on an errand for an indolent monarch," I replied acidly, which only made him laugh again. We threw the stick for Shadow once more, and then we made our way back to the cottage beneath the gathering stars.

The cottage was quiet, Ariadne having retired for the night. Wendell and I set a plate of leftovers outside the door, cheese with a handful of small, sweet tomatoes—I hoped that would satisfy the palate of whatever sinister faeries would soon be creeping about our garden. We added wood to the fire that Ariadne had started and went upstairs.

"Good night, Em," Wendell said, and went with a yawn into the bedroom at the end of the hall, across from Rose's, from which emanated the Department Head's thunderous snores. That left one open door, the one across from Ariadne's—she had left hers ajar, the bright scarf Wendell had gifted her hung on the hook with her cloak.

My own room was small, consisting of a washbasin, a simply carved wardrobe, and a creaky bed, its frame made from woven branches. Shadow immediately made himself at home among the blankets. After placing the foot under the bed and securing it with another circle of salt, I went to the window.

The view was east-facing and painfully lovely, overlooking the lake we had just visited and a rounded sub-peak. The lake matched the indigo of the sky, both scattered with patterns of stars.

I lit the lantern by my bed and spent some time organizing the notes I had brought with me, putting everything in order. I had several sketches drafted for my mapbook—my intention for the first edition was to focus on the best known faerie kingdoms of Western Europe, scouring the literature for references to their doors. Some doors have been documented; more have not, or exist as rumours. While it's true that many faerie kingdoms are tied to specific mortal regions, others are more nebulous, and a tale may place one at the edge of a village a hundred miles from the setting of a later iteration of the same story.

I am aware that mine is no easy task, given that faerie doors can and do move, and what I will accomplish is likely to be a mere snapshot of Faerie during this particular era. Even so, it will be a monumental achievement for scholarship, something for others to build upon—particularly if I can produce evidence of such disputed doors as the nexus.

Eventually, my eyes began to cross, and I was forced to admit I'd accomplished as much as I could that day. I set my books aside, pausing to listen to the gentle groans and murmurs of the cottage settling.

It was only then that I realized: four bedrooms. Not three.

21st September

I slept well our first night, awakening only once for no reason I could discern, perhaps because the wind had sprung up from the valley and was rattling the windows. I thought I heard the foot shuffling around a bit under the bed, but it may have been only my fancy.

I lay there in an uneasy mood, listening to the gale, until Shadow's snores—he was squeezed into a space between my legs and the wall—lulled me back to sleep.

The situation with our nighttime visitors is extremely curious. When I opened the door this morning to let in the crisp air, I found they had taken the food we left on the step, but also left a series of long scratches in the door.

Ariadne went pale when I showed her. "Are they trying to get in?" she demanded.

"If they were, they didn't succeed. We'll take more care with their refreshments tonight—that should please them." I said all this quite calmly, while making plans to lay a line of salt and coins behind the threshold that evening.

I asked Wendell what manner of Folk he thought responsible, but all he said was, "No doubt some charming little creatures with mushroom-cap hats," so clearly he was determined to be quarrelsome.

While we awaited our breakfast—the shadow of the mountain still lay thick over the cottage—I went over the day's plans with Ariadne. I wished to make a full survey of the area using de Grey's maps as a reference, identifying all possible faerie doors. The nexus is a door, after all, and will likely have the same physical markers as the common faerie door. Only after completing our survey would we interview the townsfolk, so that any information they gave us would not bias my observations.

"We will interview the townsfolk first," Rose said. He was occupying the best armchair by the fire, filling the small space with his self-importance. "No doubt they will know the locations of a number of doors, and we must proceed scientifically, from the known to the unknown. It would be foolish to base our research on your intuition, Emily. Ariadne and I will proceed to the local pub, or what passes for it in this place, immediately after breakfast."

My hand clenched briefly around my pen. Even more irritating than Rose's self-assurance was the way a part of me instinctively sought to oblige him—because he was Dr. Farris Rose, Department Head and dryadology doyen.

"*We* certainly will not," I said. "Ariadne will accompany Wendell and I into the mountains. You may do as you please."

Ariadne's gaze darted from me to Rose. Far from being angered, Rose gave me a pitying look. "Emily. While I will always appreciate your ideas, we cannot afford to be divided during this investigation. The nexus is too important." He stood and gave me an absent sort of smile, which managed to imply that my plans had not only been dismissed, but dismissed so surely that he had already half forgotten them. "Well! I'm off for my morning stroll."

"Excellent," I said, hoping darkly that he would stumble across whatever Folk had vandalized our door.

Wendell, who might have backed me up during the argument with Rose, had instead been pacing from one end of the cottage to the other, muttering about the mess in increasingly histrionic tones.

"I don't know why you waste time complaining," I snapped. "You shall never be able to live here until you've cleaned it."

He glared at me, then spent the next five minutes banging around in the cupboards and exclaiming at the lack of this or that or the general disarray. My depleted supply of patience grew increasingly scant until he finally stormed off in high dudgeon, and I had a few blessed moments to myself and my maps. Only a few moments, unfortunately, for he soon stormed back in and, as I had predicted, began straightening things up. Ariadne leapt up to help him, taking a cloth and scrubbing hopefully at random surfaces.

"I don't suppose you'll so much as wipe down a plate," he said to me whilst whacking the dust out of an armchair, achieving nothing that I could see beyond transporting the accumulation from one place to another, except that the chair looked immensely cosy once he'd finished, the cushioning fat enough to swallow one whole, and the dust seemed to have winked out of existence.

"I can't think of a greater waste of my time," I said tersely. I knew I was being unkind, as his need for cleanliness is, I think, more compulsion than preference, but I was too irritated to care. "I don't see any mice—that's all that concerns me. I couldn't care less if the place is dirty."

"Of course you don't, as your type finds its natural habitat under old bridges."

I chose to ignore this and went back to my maps, though I admit I snuck glances at him at regular intervals. It's just that I was frustratingly unable to identify what it was that he was doing—or, rather, why it had the effect that it did. He would adjust a rug an inch or two, and the room would brighten. When he gave the floor a few desultory sweeps, the boards gleamed. Ariadne soon stopped scrubbing and gazed about, marvelling.

Barely a quarter hour had elapsed before he collapsed in the armchair, looking peaky. Grudgingly, I made a pot of tea and brought him a cup along with one of the apricot buns left over from supper, for I couldn't deny that he'd wrought a marvellous change upon the place and felt it only fair to show some appreciation, but also he kept swearing that he would never rise from the chair again if he was not granted some relief from the burden of his exhaustion.

He gave me one of his loveliest smiles as he took the tea, green eyes glinting like dewed leaves when the sun strikes them, all quarrels forgotten. "Thank you, Em. You have saved me."

"Oh, shush," I said, rendered a little breathless in spite of myself.

"Just think," he said, "if we marry, in all your life you will never have to worry about mice again."

I rolled my eyes. "You found mice, did you."

"In the back of the cupboard."

Ariadne let out a yelp and started away from the kitchen. I affected unconcern even as a shudder went through me. I'm embarrassed to admit that there is nothing in the world that disturbs me more than mice. I refilled Wendell's tea, and he looked very smug.

"You missed a few spiders," I said, to offset the indulgence. "Just there."

"Spiders?" He sipped his tea. "I never interfere with spiders. I quite like them, in fact. They are tidy beasts who keep a place clean. Which is more than I can say about some people."

Elsa arrived shortly after with our breakfast—quite a heavy

meal in this part of the world; she had fresh buns with an extensive array of jams, sausages, more cheese, and potatoes fried with onions and bacon and topped with egg.

I asked if she knew what Folk had left the marks upon our door, but she only gave a grimace and replied, "We prefer not to name our Folk here. Give them nothing with salt in it tonight—they may have taken offence."

This confirmed my suspicions. I nodded my thanks, and the girl departed. "Thank God," Wendell said, and he and Ariadne fell upon the food. I ate sparingly, wanting to be nimble for the day's exertions, and as soon as Ariadne and Wendell had finished, I was donning my cloak.

"Good grief," Wendell grumbled as he followed my lead. "She won't even allow for a second cup of coffee."

"Shall we leave some food over the fire for Dr. Rose?" Ariadne enquired. "It'll be cold otherwise."

"I'm sure he'll make do," I replied, surveying the unappetizing remnants of the meal with satisfaction as a field of battle from which I had emerged the victor, and together we trooped outside.

22nd September

We made a good day of it yesterday, or at least I thought so. We used de Grey's maps, of course, which proved highly accurate. The map of St. Liesl and its environs covered a territory of roughly forty square miles, too much to survey in a single day, particularly with such companions as I had, but we were able to cover a lot of it. Of course there are a number of inaccessible crevices and precarious peaks that may hide their own faerie realms, and it's also possible that the nexus may be found just beyond the borders of our map, though I think this unlikely; de Grey's instincts are exemplary, and she would have had good reason to focus her attentions on this area.

Ariadne, while possessed of an abundance of enthusiasm, was also a difficult person to organize. I assigned her the task of making sketches of all the faerie doors we identified, which kept her busy for about five minutes until she became distracted by the view, or by the door itself, peppering me with questions about similar doors I had encountered and what sort of owners they might have, or whether a certain patch of flowers might *also* be a door, and if we had a faerie village on our hands.

"Perhaps the nexus will be larger than the typical door," she said at one point. "Or more strange in appearance."

"Possible, but unlikely," I said. "If so, surely it would have been documented by now. No, I believe it will be little different from the commonest of brownie doors—perhaps even marked by a circle of mushrooms. It is a door, after all. That it leads to multiple faerie lands, rather than only one, makes it strange to our mortal minds, but it is unlikely the Folk are troubled by such an impossibility."

Wendell was uncharacteristically amenable during the first part of the day, clambering over ridges and down steep slopes without his usual protestations. But as the day wore on and his long sought-after door did not suddenly leap out of the landscape in front of us, he grew sullen, stopping often to catch his breath or flop down in some comfortable meadow, and dispensing a great deal of sighs and muttered curses during particularly rough climbs. All in all I was impressed by his fortitude.

"We will find it," I told him during one of our afternoon rests. We were seated in the lee of a rocky outcropping, eating the sandwiches Julia had prepared for us while Ariadne finished up a sketch in the meadow below. The snowy mountain peaks were sharp against the blue sky and close enough to touch.

He let out another sigh. He was lying on his back with his arm over his face, Shadow flopped over at his side.

"We *will*," I repeated.

He sat up and looked at me. His golden hair was woven with small green leaves, and I suppressed a familiar urge to brush my hand through it. "Do you remember that night at that Glasgow pub three winters ago?"

"*That* is what you were thinking about?" I said. "Well, it's not as if you have a kingdom to take back."

"It was after the conference on faerie stones," he said. "You needed a great deal of convincing to come along."

"Bribery would be a more accurate word," I said. "You promised me your copy of Jane Drakos's treatise on Faie."[*]

"And didn't I deliver? Of course I knew you could only tolerate an evening of merrymaking if you had some dull tome to look forward to afterwards. Anyway, not an hour after we arrived you ended up in an argument with Dr. Lemont of the University of Clarywell. Something about vestigial magic."

"The theory of erogation,"[†] I said promptly. "Lemont thinks it's nonsense."

He waved a hand. "Anyway, things turned rather heated. Lemont was drunk again—he is insufferable enough without the assistance of spirits, but with? He was berating you. I actually considered spiriting you away by magic—which likely would have been impossible, given that I was then still barred from revealing myself to mortals. But you simply pulled a faerie stone from your pocket and handed it to Lemont, inviting him to sit down, whereupon he immediately fell asleep. And thus you were left in peace, and I was not required to give myself away."

"I would not have been very surprised, anyhow," I pointed out, for I had suspected him from our very first meeting. "More importantly, I won the argument with Lemont. That faerie stone was broken; the enchantment it held should have been spent. But it retained a remnant of power still, enough to induce weariness when held against the skin. I suspected this

---

[*]   *The Un-Dictionary,* 1905.

[†]   Letitia Barrister's theory, described in an 1890 paper in *Dryadological Fieldnotes,* that all faerie-made artefacts such as faerie stones retain a trace of enchantment long after their magic has been released. Barrister compared magic to wine, which leaves a stain that cannot be got out.

would be enough to send him into slumber, given his state, and I was correct."

He was smiling. "What I enjoyed most was how matter-of-fact you were about it. Here was this dreadful, red-faced boor of a man, looming above you spitting with anger, and you simply slap a little stone into his palm, cold as anything. You might have been dismissing a servant with a coin."

"It didn't convince him, though," I said. "In the morning he claimed to have forgotten the whole thing. Do you have a point to make in all this?"

"Yes," he said. "If there is a door to my kingdom in this godforsaken warren of stones and peaks, I have absolute faith that you, of all people, will find it."

I was mollified. "Of course I will," I said, feeling my anxieties shrink back to a size at which I could almost forget they existed.

"After all," I went on lightly, unable to resist falling back into our familiar banter, "once you work out how to be rid of your stepmother, I understand the office of queen will be mine for the taking, should I want it."

"Yours and no one else's," he said, reaching for my hand. I batted his away.

"I still haven't decided. I'm very particular about faerie kingdoms."

"Oh, I know. You've already discarded one, haven't you? Still, I think you will like mine more than that castle of ice and snow."

"I'm unconvinced," I said. "Given your fondness for decorative frippery, I wouldn't be surprised to find your castle stuffed with useless knickknacks and loud draperies."

"Ah, but what if I give you the final say in draperies?"

I opened my mouth to needle him further, but then I stopped and thought it over.

"I think that is my answer," I said softly.

"What?"

"I would like to see your kingdom first," I said. "Before I decide whether or not to marry you."

He opened his mouth to reply—I believe he assumed I was still jesting. But then he caught sight of my expression.

"Oh?" I had surprised him, and his face broke into a smile. "Em, you will have a map to every province, and a key to every door. I promise you that. You know I would have taken you already, if I could?"

"It's not that I think you're hiding something from me. Not intentionally, at any rate. I simply wish to make sure there aren't monsters lurking in the wardrobes or severed heads adorning the battlements."

"Severed heads!" he said with a shudder. "Can you imagine? What a mess."

Shadow awoke then, and I gave him his customary ear scratches—as much a comfort to me, I think, as it was to him, given the disquiet that had settled over me like a cold fog. Well, you try contemplating taking up a throne in one of the most fearsome faerie kingdoms known to scholarship. I still did not see how I could possibly acquiesce, and yet I found it increasingly difficult to contemplate saying no. In the answer I had given Wendell, I felt I had accomplished something, or come one step closer to it.

"Do you know what I miss the most?" he said.

"Being waited on hand and foot?"

"My cat."

"Ah," I said neutrally. I suppose I should have guessed—Wendell speaks of his dear Orga a great deal, though I am never able to get a sense of what the creature actually looks like.

"She has many talents. Several I'm not allowed to reveal."

"A cat has power over a king?" I said drily, adding a note to the map.

"Faerie cats do not like their powers to be known, and prevent their masters from revealing them, often upon pain of death. Suffice it to say that I would trust her with my life." He gazed wistfully into the distance, clearly lost in memories of his cat. "I hope I will be able to introduce you. You will like each other, I think."

I considered this dubiously. Not only because every time I learn something new about Wendell's cat, it makes me less inclined to make her acquaintance, but because, in my experience, cats in general exist in a state of perpetual resentment and dissatisfaction. Or perhaps that is merely the aspect of their nature distilled by my presence, I don't know. I am not a cat person.

"We should carry on," I said, folding the map and tucking my pencil back in my knapsack. I had the foot with me, of course, though the thing had been nothing more than dead weight all day. Not the slightest twitch had it given that might point us in a useful direction.

Wendell gave me one of his unfathomable looks. It makes me nervous when he does this; it reminds me too much of the snow king of the Ljosland Folk, a creature beyond mortal understanding.

"Is there a moment you would relive more than once?" he said in a musing voice.

"No," I replied, thinking uncomfortably of his power to reshape time, limited though it is. "I'm rather fond of my sanity, thank you."

He brushed a loose strand of hair from my forehead, tucking it behind my ear with one long finger. I felt the ghost of his touch trailing over my brow for some time afterwards.

"That would be mine," he said. "Your hair is always in your eyes."

"You're in a strange mood," I said over my thundering heart.

"Am I?"

I rolled my eyes. "Keep your secrets, then, and your cat's," I said, because I have largely given up trying to decipher him when he is like this. He laughed, and together we rose to our feet.

We located a total of fourteen faerie doors—an impressive number for such a small area. Most, according to Wendell, led to simple households and farms hidden away in the mountain folds, likely belonging to brownies associated with nearby springs and meadows and the like. Two others were abandoned. Four were of particular interest.

"It isn't a household door," he said as we stopped outside the first, visible to myself and Ariadne merely as a hollow tree stump. "It leads somewhere. I don't know how to describe it, other than to say that the difference is like standing beside an ocean as opposed to a tidal pool. But where it leads I can't guess. Likely to a faerie world native to this landscape—it doesn't *feel* like a door to my realm."

I added a note to the map. "We can return here another day and investigate further. Shall we try to find another route to the peak?" The sun was low in the sky, close to dipping behind the mountains, and a chill wind had sprung up, smelling of distant glaciers.

"It will be dark in an hour or two," he said. "We should turn back."

I raised my eyebrows. "Don't tell me you're frightened of these mysterious nocturnal Folk."

"Terrified. You shouldn't take the danger so lightly, Em—there are Folk in this world so vicious the mortal mind cannot fathom it, so ghastly you would spend a lifetime yearning to forget a single glimpse of their countenance."

"You just want to put your feet up by the fire and drink chocolate."

"Well, you try fighting off some nasty beast with ankles this sore. Besides, Shadow is on my side."

Indeed, the old dog had taken advantage of our temporary halt to lie down in a patch of clover, his huge paws stretched out before him. As I watched, he gave a yawn.

"You shouldn't encourage him," I muttered to the dog. Shadow rolled onto his back.

"We still haven't surveyed the woods over there," Ariadne said. She was flushed and merry and did not appear in the least tired. "I could carry on, Aunt."

"No," I said irritably, because the idea of her going off on her own was ridiculous. Her face fell.

Wendell took it upon himself to soothe the girl's feelings. "That scarf is not a fail-safe against *all* danger, my dear."

She touched it. I watched her with narrowed eyes—Ariadne is headstrong, and I fancied I saw disobedience brewing within her. She trusted too much in her magic scarf, that was the trouble—coupled with her overabundance of enthusiasm, I could easily see her sneaking out again when Wendell and I were distracted in order to continue working, requiring us to spend time and resources dragging her out of some faerie den. I opened my mouth to lecture her, but Wendell put his hands on her shoulders and playfully spun her round so that she was facing the direction of the village.

"Come along, come along," he said, nudging her forward as Ariadne began to laugh. "I've had enough of rescuing mad scholars; please don't force me to go climbing hither and thither in search of you tonight. I have never been fond of mountains. Now, hills, on the other hand—green hills, with plenty of shady dales and pleasant streams; hills with paths that slope sympathetically instead of forcing you up a ladder of bloody boulders . . ."

Their voices faded, and I followed at a distance, feeling vaguely chagrined.

On our return to St. Liesl, Wendell suggested we wander through the village and introduce ourselves to the inhabitants. I could tell he was hoping for a hot meal at the local tavern, with plenty of opportunities for talk, but no tavern was to be found. The village was a quaint scatter of timber houses built into a series of terraces, connected by a country lane that rambled through meadow and pastureland. St. Liesl was dominated by a handsome church, which perched upon a higher slope, regaling the village with its bells on the hour. Paired with the mist, I found it an eerie sound, the convoluted topography creating ghostly and unexpected echoes. We passed two goatherds, each busy with their flock—one had a large brown dog who yipped a friendly greeting at Shadow before leaping backwards and cowering behind its master once it got within smelling distance of him.

We ran into Peter on the road, wending his way home with his cart half full of fodder, driven by the same small chestnut horses that had carried us to St. Liesl, a breed which every reasonably prosperous inhabitant appears to favour. He informed us casually that no pub could stay in business in St. Liesl, given the necessity of closing each day before dark to protect its patrons from being torn apart by the Folk.

"Does that happen often?" Ariadne said, her eyes wide with excitement. I elbowed her.

"Well, once is often enough," Peter replied, scratching his head and continuing in his offhand manner. "And it's happened more than once. But they're a lovely people. We're very grateful to have such neighbours."

I waved this aside—it's common in many parts of the world for those who live in close quarters with the Folk to speak of them only in fawning terms, on the off chance they are listening. "Is there a village hall?"

"There's a café," Peter said. "Down the lane, just below the church. Open every morning an hour after sunrise."

We thanked him, and he nodded, then reached absently into his pocket and scattered a handful of seeds among the grass. After he went clattering up the lane, I knelt and scooped a few into my palm.

"It's the fauns he means," Wendell said. "Without a doubt. They've a predilection for that sort of violence. They don't even eat their victims. In my kingdom, they're known for feeding pieces to their dogs while the poor mortal watches."

"Charming." I showed him the seeds. "What do you suppose this means?"

"An offering, I guess." Wendell flicked his hand at the seeds in the grass, and they burst into bloom—a mix of primroses and forget-me-nots. "Wildflowers."

"Of course," I said. "In case he offended the Folk. They have a similar ritual in Provence."

Ariadne lingered by the wildflowers, giving me a quick, astonished look, as if wondering at me for not sharing her amazement. When I turned back, I found that she had plucked one of the flowers and was absently spinning it between her thumb and forefinger as she walked.

"Never remove a faerie offering," I told her. I tried not to sound stern that time, but I must have missed the mark, for she went pale and immediately dashed back to return the bloom. She did not speak to me for the rest of the walk, and kept close to Wendell, the two of them wrapped up in a pointless conversation about the probable contents of our supper. Of course I am aware of how ridiculous it is that my niece should be more comfortable with one of the courtly fae than with me, but then all Wendell has done is make flowers bloom and gift her with a pretty scarf, while I cannot stop myself from snapping at her. Still, I have warned her away from faerie offerings more than once—when will she attend to me?

When we entered the cottage, we found Rose seated at the table, several books open in front of him. Wendell predictably collapsed into the armchair in a display of exhaustion while Ariadne began excitedly regaling Rose with stories of our day, seeming to take no notice of the spectacular scowl on his face. Another characteristic of Ariadne's, I've noticed, is that her good humour is so complete that it often forms a kind of armour, off which the foul moods of others ricochet without leaving so much as a dent.

"Well, Emily," Rose said, interrupting Ariadne midsentence, "what did you find?"

I could not interpret the tone of his voice, besides the fact that it boded ill, but as I had quite definitively wrested away the leadership role that he had assumed to be his, I felt I could afford to be gracious. I showed him the map with the notations I had made, as well as Ariadne's sketches, and provided a brief summary of the most promising of the faerie doors we had located. He said nothing for a moment after I'd finished, just scanned the map, and the only sounds in the cottage were from the crackling fire and Shadow licking his paws. A few leaves drifted past the window like flakes falling from a goldsmith's worktable.

"Well done," Rose said.

He might as well have taken the map and walloped me across the face with it. "What?"

"Your methods are unorthodox," he said. "But effective. You've managed to make some significant discoveries today that will help us narrow our search for the nexus. It seems I should not have doubted your capabilities—I was concerned that your research methods would be slipshod, given how much time you spend with this deceitful creature."

"That's where you're wrong, Farris," Wendell said. He was slouched deep in the chair with his arm draped over his eyes. "Emily is puritanical in matters of professional integrity. It's her only bad quality."

"Wait a moment," I said. "Are you—*apologizing* for your behaviour?"

"Yes," Rose said simply. "I will defer to your judgment from here on out."

"You should have done that from the beginning," Wendell said.

"Perhaps so," Rose said after a little pause, thus conveying that he would have preferred to continue in his habit of ignoring Wendell's existence but was hampered by the sincerity of his apology.

Julia Haas entered then, preventing further quarrelling, accompanied by a third daughter whom she introduced as Mattie. The girl, older than the others, perhaps Ariadne's age, seemed quite interested in getting a look at Wendell—I suspect the other two had been gossiping—but in this she failed, for he remained in his unbecoming, woebegone slump. Julia looked so startled by the state of the cottage that she nearly dropped our supper, a pot of hearty stew that smelled wonderfully of bacon, which she had encased in tea towels.

"Why, it's as if you've had a visit from the hearth kobolds," she said, using a German term I have heard elsewhere to refer to a species of faerie that, like the *oíche sidhe* and other household fae of that ilk, tends to the tidiness of the home in exchange for small tokens of favour.

"I hope not," I said, for I doubted such monomaniacal creatures would appreciate an outsider like Wendell poking his nose into their domestic duties.

Wendell retired early with a mug of chocolate, claiming exhaustion, while Ariadne merrily tucked in to the evening chores with such enthusiasm that I believe she would have taken offense had anyone tried to stop her (I did not). After putting the day's notes in order, I wanted some air to clear my mind before bed, so I called Shadow to me and went outside. I had noticed a little bench behind the cottage that overlooked the valley, but when I reached it, I was surprised to find Rose already in residence, smoking his pipe.

"Apparently it's rather unhealthy to linger outside after dark in this part of the Alps," I said.

He gave a huff of laughter. "You could take your own advice."

I sat beside him. The grass was scattered with orange and gold leaves, which spilled over the edge of the cliff. Shadow nipped at one as it went by. The mountains before us rose into the twilight sky like a series of great waves. "I have Shadow," I said.

Rose folded his arms and assumed a posture I had observed when he settled in to grill doctoral candidates on their dissertations. Naturally he was taking up three quarters of the bench, without seeming at all conscious of the inconvenience to me. "You have *him*, you mean," he said.

I sighed. "You made your point on the train. You needn't repeat yourself."

"It's true he's lived among mortals for ten years," Rose said.

"Unheard of for the courtly fae. And perhaps it's changed him, but how much? Surely not on any fundamental level."

When I said nothing, he went on drily, "I don't offer up tedious warnings for my amusement. I am not quite old enough to relish the role of the gloomy sage. You are, in fact, far from a fool, Emily, and I have some hope that I might penetrate your illusions."

I decided to be blunt. "You lost someone to the Folk, is that it? Your wife? A sibling, perhaps?"

"No," he said. "My wife met a natural end thirty-two years ago—an illness so dreadful and yet so mundane that the Folk could never have devised it." He was quiet for a moment. "It was a very old friend. You are not yet of an age to understand what it's like to lose a companion of nearly half a century. It is an experience that has no comparison."

I looked away as he contemplated his twin losses, and for a moment we both watched the mountains darken. "What happened?"

"We were schoolboys together, he and I. Very alike in our interests, including our fascination with the Folk. We both went our separate ways as adults—me to academia, him to the bar—but still we kept close. He grew quite wealthy, and used that wealth to fund his hobby—that is, visiting sites across Britain that are said to be faerie-haunted. Well, one day—this was perhaps fifteen years ago now—I received an urgent telegram from his wife, saying he'd been taken to hospital in rough shape. Naturally I abandoned the conference I was chairing and went immediately to his bedside, where I found him as I had been warned.

"Eventually I managed to get the story out of him, which I kept from his family," Rose continued after another pause. "He'd fallen in love with a faerie woman somewhere in Exmoor. They'd spent months together, by his reckoning.

Months of impossible revelry and contentment. Then the seasons changed, and she and her kind packed up and left—not unusual, of course; several species of Folk travel with the seasons. He roamed the moors for days and somehow managed to catch up with them as they took their rest. He stumbled into one of their revels, thirsty and half starved, expecting to be welcomed back. But his beloved was irritated by his feat— I suppose she must have been tired of him, or perhaps she simply resented him for following her. She and her family tied him to a tree by his beard, which was quite long by that point. Perhaps they thought it comical, but he was too weak to free himself. By chance, he was found by a hiker the following morning, but the damage wrought by exposure and despair had already been done. He died a few days later."

I grimaced. The story was bleak, as romance tales involving the Folk often are. "I'm sorry."

"I often wish I had warned him," Rose said. "I had studied the Folk more deeply than he—his enthusiasm was that of a hobbyist, and it had blinded him to their darker qualities. I simply didn't think he would do something so foolish."

I let out my breath. "You think I'm making the same mistake. That I have come to trust Wendell too much, and that one day he will leave me dangling from a tree somewhere."

Rose didn't answer immediately, but placed a surprisingly gentle hand upon my knee. "One day, Emily. One day, you will see him for what he is. I only hope it doesn't destroy you, as it did my friend."

I drew my cardigan more tightly about me—it was the chill of the air, I told myself, not Rose's words. "I appreciate your advice, Farris. Genuinely. But I know Wendell."

"Emily." He pointed up at the beech tree boughs, which waved to and fro, scattering more leaves about us. "Do you know the wind?" And with that gloomy koan, he left me.

24th September

The first thing I did this morning, as has become my habit, was check the door for evidence of our nocturnal visitors. We have been careful with our offering every night, leaving only cooked vegetables and cheeses, as instructed, but each morning brings fresh evidence of displeasure in the form of long, jagged scratches.

I examined the lock, and was disturbed to find evidence that the creatures had been at that as well—it was a solid thing, or had been; now it was slightly loose, as if someone, a large and heavy someone, had pounded at the door with such force that the lock had begun to buckle. None of us had heard so much as a creak in the night.

I called Wendell out to take a look, but he continued to demonstrate a complete lack of concern about the whole business.

"It's iron," he said, briefly touching the lock. "What Folk could break in?"

"*You* could," I pointed out. "Surely there are others."

He gave me a bemused look, as if I'd misunderstood something so fundamental that he couldn't fathom how to explain it to me. Well, perhaps he was not worried about being woken in the night by some dreadful faerie mob clawing through our door—Wendell's attitude towards the common fae is one of implacable condescension—but it was not an event I could anticipate with much composure.

"Wendell," I said in a voice of forced calm, "have you not considered that this may be the work of yet another variety of assassin, sent by your stepmother?"

"If so, they are fearsome creatures indeed—just look how, night after night, they occupy themselves with ravaging a plank of wood! Why, the Haases may be forced to apply a plaster," he said in a voice of such amusement that I wanted to throttle him. Fortunately, Julia was coming up the path with our breakfast, and I was able to elicit some sympathy from her, at least.

"This is a muddle," she said, touching the marks with a grimace. "What could have happened to set them off?"

I explained that we had provided only the choicest victuals to our finicky visitors, even hoarding the cheese she served us with breakfast so that we could offer up the lot, and she shook her head.

"I'll make some fried apples," she promised. "Our good neighbours haven't much fondness for sweets, but they make an exception for fried apples. We leave them as offerings on special occasions."

I thanked her, comforted as much by her offer of assistance as her unflappability. But then, forbearance in the face of faerie malice is characteristic of rural folk in all countries. We city-dwellers have trouble comprehending it, for we don't know what it's like to live in such close proximity to the fae any more than we understand the terror of crop failures or predation by wild beasts. Moreau wrote a book on the subject.[*]

---

[*] Mathieu Moreau, *Sketches of Rural Life in Faerie Lands,* 1908.

We finished our initial survey yesterday, and so today we elected to split up: Wendell and Ariadne would probe the series of faerie doors we'd located in the neighbouring valley, while Rose and I would venture to the home of Julia Haas to collect her father-in-law, who had promised to lead us along the final path taken by Danielle de Grey. The locals believe the de Grey mystery to be the reason for our visit, and I saw no reason to disillusion them, given that de Grey's last known location is indeed of great import. It is quite possible—if not likely, given de Grey's skill as an investigator—that she succeeded in her search for the nexus and became lost inside the thing, or was killed in the vicinity by its guardians. Thus, following de Grey's path may also lead us to Wendell's door.

Julia Haas's home is a pretty place, built of dark timbers with well-tended window boxes spilling red and pink flowers—window boxes seem to be as much a requirement in St. Liesl as goats, as most houses have them. But it was tucked into a sharp rise in the earth, and so at that time in the morning it was shadowed and rather gloomy. Her front garden is small, but above the house is a grassy field expansive enough for goats and cows, and beyond that an apple orchard.

One of the Haas daughters greeted us cheerily at the door, bending to give Shadow his preferred greeting of ear rubs— I believe it was Astrid, but in truth they look so much alike that I have taken to avoiding the use of their names in case I am mistaken.

Roland Haas is a small man in his seventies, spry in the manner of many aging country labourers, with a short beard, rosy brown complexion, and an abundance of white hair. I understood that he had once run the Haas farm, the responsibility for which had now passed to his sons, daughters, and various daughters- and sons-in-law (I did not attempt to sort through the Haas family tree and the various names thrown my way, as I have a terrible memory for such things). Now in his retirement, the man primarily performs odd jobs around the village, which today included shepherding two foreigners along the trail of a missing dryadologist, a task he seemed to relish.

"It's been years since any scholars paid us a visit," he said. "There was a flurry of interest after poor Dani vanished, but it passed, as such things must do—been gone near fifty years now, hasn't she? Where do the decades go?"

"Then you knew de Grey personally?" I said.

"Oh, yes. And the other, Eichorn—he was a prickly sort. But Dani was lovely. So vivacious, with a laugh that carried from the foothills to the mountaintops, as we say around here. Good Lord, that can't be what you're wearing."

Rose and I glanced down at our wool cloaks and wellies, the standard uniform of a dryadologist in the field. Before we could reply, Roland had disappeared back inside the house before emerging with two enormously bulky cloaks that I first took to be the newly shorn pelts of sheep.

"It's fearful cold where we're going," he explained. "You'll need these."

"You don't, though," Rose observed wryly, for Roland Haas had only a light coat and scarf over his woolen vest.

The old man smiled. "We're a thick-skinned people, unlike folks who spend their lives attached to desks in heated offices. No offence."

Rose laughed and assured him of our gratitude, and we pulled the ridiculous things on over our cloaks. Not only did I look like a sheep, I smelled like one. I amused myself by imagining Wendell's reaction to being presented with such a garment. Doubtless he would choose frostbite.

We set out into the mountains, following a footpath that petered out beyond the village. Rose steered the conversation to polite pleasantries that I paid little attention to, enquiries about the weather conditions at this time of year and Roland's personal history with the mountains, as we navigated our way down an uneven slope dotted with mossy scree. Roland paused periodically to excavate a ribbon from one of his pockets and tie it to a small rock or root.

"Does the colour signify anything?" I enquired.

"Indeed," Roland said, and informed me that a red ribbon is used to indicate that the rambler's path continued straight on along a mostly level plane; white indicates an ascent; blue, a descent. There are also ribbons that represent a change of course in one of the compass directions, as follows: green, west; yellow, north; orange, east; red, south. These signifiers are primarily of use to search parties, should they be needed, but the rambler who became hopelessly lost could also use the ribbons to gain some form of orientation while retracing their steps. There are also textural signifiers: a lace ribbon tied alongside a blue ribbon indicates that the rambler decided to descend to a lower altitude *and* had met with one of the Folk—again, information that could be of use to rescuers should the rambler fail to return. A coarse muslin ribbon indicates an injury, and so on—I will not record every signifier, as there seem to be as many as there are varieties of ribbons. Families mark their ribbons in a specific way—the Haas family snips a triangle out of each end; other families stitch letters, paint the tips, etc. Ideally, ribbons are placed within sighting distance of each other, but this is not always possible.

I observed Rose scratching all this down in his notebook, his posture a near-identical mirror of mine, and I hastily closed my own notebook around my pencil.

"Fascinating," Rose said. "Did de Grey use this system?"

"Oh, aye—it's how we know whereabouts she fell."

"Fell?" I repeated with some dismay.

He gave me an apologetic look. "Yes—that's how the other scholars reacted. Less interesting, I suppose, than if she'd been stolen by the Folk. Nothing you could write a paper about. But as you'll see, Professors, the particulars are pretty clear, at least as far as I can make out."

It took approximately one hour for us to reach our destination, following the course de Grey had taken. It felt a little eerie, I confess, walking in the footsteps of that doomed woman whose ghost—in the form of her maps and other writings—had so shaped our expedition thus far. This impression was not helped by the changeable weather—clouds kept scudding across the sun like dark portents, and at one point we were pelted by hail. But the terrain was relatively easy, crossing a series of alpine meadows and rounded slopes in the mountainside. Shadow, though not ordinarily fond of the repetitive ups and downs of mountainous terrain, had little trouble keeping up, though I kept him away from the patches of snow we came across, not wishing for Roland to take note of the queer lack of pawprints he would leave.

Then we came up out of a little pass, whereupon the view brought Rose to a comically abrupt halt. I found myself gazing at a precarious spine-shaped saddle between two peaks, the one directly ahead rising to a fearsome point. Over such exposed terrain the wind howled as if determined to tear apart the thin barrier of rock and shrubby vegetation. My hair whipped free of its tie; facing the wind, I found it difficult to breathe. I was immediately grateful for my ridiculous cloak as we followed Roland out onto the spine. It was barely three feet wide in places, which did not make for comfortable hiking, particularly when combined with the battering wind.

"As I said—quite the chill up here." Roland had to shout to make himself heard. "That there's where we found her last ribbon—white."

I looked at the cairn of stones he was pointing to—a memorial, I assumed, built above de Grey's final ribbon—and then I followed de Grey's indicated course with my eye. It was steep terrain, painfully narrow all the way, ascending towards the jagged peak crowned with snow. Yes, I could well imagine it—particularly in bad weather, or later in the season, when the whole ascent would have been coated in a layer of ice and snow. I've had several near misses myself whilst conducting fieldwork in the mountains of Wales and know well the danger posed by the combination of snow, heights, and a lack of familiarity with one's environs.

I could see from the disappointment in Rose's expression that he was coming round to Roland's conclusion, and I might well have done the same, dismissing de Grey's disappearance as a dead end in our search for the nexus.

Had not the bloody foot started twitching in my pack.

I surreptitiously slid the pack from one shoulder, shielding it from Roland's notice with my arm. I scanned the landscape, turning with difficulty from the ferocious view of towering peaks as far as the eye could see. To our left, the land dropped away, dizzyingly sheer—one would have a great deal of time to contemplate the impending landing, if they took a tumble in that direction. But to the right was a gentler slope, traversable without equipment if one was careful, which led to another alpine lake cupped in an elevated valley. Against the leeward slope was a little forest, mostly of hardy pine.

Roland noticed my interest. "We searched the valley," he said. "Found no sign of her. And the white ribbon means she kept on towards the peak."

"She couldn't have changed her mind?" I suggested. "Or chosen the wrong ribbon by mistake? Yellow looks like white in poor lighting. The valley lies to the north, does it not?"

Roland looked dubious. "Why wouldn't she have tied another ribbon?"

"There could be any number of reasons," Rose said thoughtfully. "Perhaps she wandered through a faerie door shortly after she changed course. Perhaps she was disorientated by the weather or altitude."

I kept my own hypothesis to myself. Namely, that this system of ribbons, ingenious as it was, had from the outset struck me as a decidedly capricious method of wayfinding when the Folk were introduced to the equation, salt water or no.

I informed Roland that I wished to conduct a brief survey of the valley, and he showed me an easier route than the one I would have chosen. I encouraged him to return home at this point, as we would likely tarry awhile in the valley, boring him with a lot of standing about, note-taking and the like, and would anyway have no trouble finding our way home again. Roland agreed good-naturedly enough—I think he knew I was up to something, but also did not seem to care much about the designs of scholars. He kindly informed us that he would leave in place his metaphorical trail of breadcrumbs, on the off chance we found the return journey trickier than we anticipated; these we could return to him when we came to dine at the Haas residence.

Naturally, once Rose and I descended, I found the valley larger than it had looked from above, easily a mile across, with innumerable nooks and crannies that might conceal a faerie door. We had not surveyed the valley before, as we had previously approached from the northeast, whence the terrain is too steep to descend, and thus had ruled it out as a possibility. The importance of local knowledge in these investigations cannot be overstated.

I informed Rose about the faerie foot's reaction to the

valley—it maintained its mad twitching in my pack—as well as my suspicions regarding de Grey's ribbons. He nodded peaceably, astonishing me not a little. I had not expected him to give way so easily to my leadership, despite his pretty words earlier.

"We will undertake only a cursory survey so as to be well on our way before the gloaming," he said, "and return in the morning with the others. It will be best to proceed on the assumption that we are near the door used by the fauns, a circumstance requiring the utmost caution. Your cloak, Emily."

Not quite so acquiescent, then. Still, I decided not to be small about it, largely because his thoughts aligned with mine, and reversed my borrowed cloak. I did not bother reversing the one I wore underneath, which Wendell had tailored against my wishes back in Ljosland, as it now has a tendency to bunch and flap about when I do this, as if I have made it uncomfortable and put it in a mood.

The lake was unexceptional, lovely and green-blue, but the forest was a peculiar thing. Among the needles carpeting the floor were clusters of mushrooms and strange white flowers, lantern-shaped, their cupped petals like small orbs. The trees themselves were taller and healthier than such flora had cause to be at high altitudes—indeed, they were quite fat, as if overfed.

"Got you," I murmured. Rose frowned at me, having a scientist's dislike for leaping to conclusions, but it was obvious that there was something faerie-touched about the forest, even if it had nothing to do with the nexus. I removed the foot from my pack and set it among the moss and grasses.

Had I expected it to hop about like a rabbit, I would have been disappointed, for the thing simply sat motionless, not even fidgeting anymore. But Rose and I are professionals, and so we simply waited, keeping an eye on the foot but not focusing all our attention upon it, and slowly it began to move. It did not hop nor stride, but would simply, between one moment and the next, appear to be slightly farther away than I had thought, so slightly that I could have convinced myself I was imagining things. After Rose and I closed the gap, it would gradually drift farther away again. It was impossible to perceive any movement; it was as if the landscape itself moved, stretching itself to place distance between us and the foot.

Initially, the foot seemed to be making for the forest, but then it veered towards the lake, then back to the forest again.

"Perhaps it's lost," I said, intending the remark to be humourous until I realized that a lost faerie foot was neither more nor less ludicrous than one that knew what it was about.

"I don't like this," Rose said. "Put it away, Emily. Better yet, let the thing go."

"It's the reason we found the forest," I pointed out.

"And what *is* the forest? What manner of Folk dwell here? Do not commend yourself until you've answered that."

I heard the echo of an old argument in his disdain and could not stop myself from rising to it. "Is your point that we have placed ourselves in danger by venturing to this place? What safe path is there to a door frequented by a malevolent Folk—a door, let me remind you, which leads to the Silva Lupi?"

"My *point*," Rose said, "as you know, Emily, is that the usefulness of faerie artefacts in resolving faerie mysteries is dubious at best, contrary to the specious claims of the less responsible set of scholars. You disdain the locals' trust in their ribbons, reasoning quite correctly that the Folk may make mischief with them, and yet here you are, placing your faith in a magic foot."

"That is hardly a fair comparison," I replied heatedly. "Would *irresponsible* be a fair characterization of Gabrielle

Goode? Or Marcel Tzara? Both have argued in favour of the cautious use of faerie artefacts in investigations of little-known fae. Goode's faerie lanterns led her to a leprechaun cache, for God's sake—only the third such discovery in history! What our community needs is the kind of innovative thinking we are seeing from the younger generation of scholars, or we shall never advance in our understanding of the Folk."

"Goode's lanterns will lead her over a cliff one day. What we *need* is a return to the tried and tested methods of dryadology, revolving around good, old-fashioned fieldwork and oral accounts. The rest is pseudoscience."

We bickered like this until Shadow began to whine. I ignored him at first, for I admit I was enjoying myself; it was the sort of debate I have sometimes wished to have with Rose, but I had never been able to work up the nerve. Eventually I turned and found it was not the faerie foot that had upset my companion; this I had stuffed back in my pack already. Instead he was snuffling at a bone.

A skull, in fact. Human. It was partly embedded into the sandy soil at the edge of the lake.

"Good God!" I said. "Could it be de Grey?"

"It would be a dramatic appearance on her part." Rose knelt to examine the skull. "She was known for her showmanship, wasn't she? But no. It's male. My graduate thesis included an osteological component, a study of the remains left behind by the Welsh afanc. There's a whole scatter of bones in the sand here—hm! Interesting."

"We should take a look at those caves," I said, motioning to a rise in the land where the rock was riddled with hollows—it was next to a spring, with an odd little mist rising off it. It put me in mind of what Wendell and I had seen at the smaller lake below the cottage. "Many of the Alpine tales of *zwerge* place their abodes in cavernous regions."

"Let me record this first."

I waited impatiently while he paced slowly along the bank, bending to examine the bones. There was indeed a fair number of them, though the distribution grew more concentrated nearer the caves.

"I believe we have bones from two human skeletons," Rose said finally. "Both male. As well as several pigs and at least four goats. Offerings by the mortal residents of St. Liesl? As well as the odd unlucky hiker."

"All right," I said, because this was, in fact, useful information. "Bogles, perhaps? Shall we examine the north bank?"

"I think not." Rose's voice was calm as he tucked his notebook into his pocket. "I've tarried here primarily to avoid the impression of flight. We are being watched, and may be attacked at any moment."

I absorbed this revelation—unwelcome at any time, but particularly when one was stood within some fae creature's extensive bone collection. "Where?"

"Behind us, of course. We should move slowly away from the caves—very slowly. Their power may be tied to the spring."

"How did you detect them?" For I heard nothing, though I'd been paying attention, as I always do.

"My pocket watch. I earned a favour from a household brownie inhabiting a clockmaker's workshop, who enchanted it to cease its ticking in the vicinity of bogles and similar miscreants."

The hypocrisy of it was too galling. "After all that blather about artefacts—"

"Emily. We haven't time."

I looked at Shadow. He was worrying one of the pig bones,

too distracted by his delight to sense anything amiss. But he caught wind of my unease and went rigid, his jaw still clamped round the bone, drool dangling.

Abruptly, he charged—not behind us, but at a small red fox regarding us from one of the caves.

"Leave it," I told Shadow, but he kept barking—the thunderous, unearthly bark he reserves for the most dire situations, rough and rasping like the rattle of death, which brought the chill of the earth below into one's bones. The fox melted back into the shadows of the cave, but not before I sensed something terribly amiss about it, which jarred at my awareness like a toothache.

"Emily," Rose murmured.

I turned. Several more of the little vulpine Folk perched upon a log on the bank—for naturally they were Folk, like the one I'd observed briefly by the cottage; I felt irritated at myself for not realizing it before. Even at close range, they looked a great deal like foxes in all but their faces, which reminded me of a human infant, all overlarge eyes and small rosebud mouths. They might have been small children wearing costumes, but for the unnerving glint of very small, but very sharp teeth, and the wet, all-black of their eyes. They darted in and out of the meadow grass, which was riddled with foxholes, so quick it was difficult to ascertain their number, except that it was great.

Enchantment washed over me, so much that I grew dizzy— that is sometimes what it feels like when a faerie throws a lot of magic at you, a highly disorientating experience. When I was sensible again, I took cautious stock of myself, and found I seemed unaffected.

Rose was not so lucky. He had taken off at an impressive sprint over the terrain, for these were trooping faeries, and like many of their ilk, they love the chase above all else. Rose—

perhaps aided by his inside-out cloak—recovered his senses after a dozen yards or so and trotted to a halt, puffing. "Emily!" he shouted.

"Keep going!" I shrieked at him, because two things had become clear at once: one, these little faeries knew a meal when they saw one; and two, I had some form of protection against them—protection that, I strongly suspected, had something to do with my cloak, which Wendell had perhaps imbued with something more than natty tailoring and an altogether silly swish about the hem.

Rose seemed to have come to the same conclusions, for he abandoned his concern for my well-being and focused his attention on saving his own skin, hurling handfuls of salt about him, which he excavated from a variety of pockets in his cloak that I guessed he'd sewn himself. I wished he'd kept running, as there was a distinct likelihood that the faeries would not harm him beyond the territory they'd claimed as their own; though it was true also that flight would only encourage the appetite of creatures like these—well, we could debate the probabilities later. I hoped.

"Shadow," I said, and the beast took off after the faeries. But they seemed little bothered by him and simply darted into some unseen foxhole when he neared, emerging again in some other location.

Shadow managed to catch one, whipping the faerie back and forth until its neck snapped with a wet gurgle, but several others were already breaking through Rose's salt circle, which he hadn't had time to complete, and dragging him to the ground. The man began to scream.

As I sprinted up the hillside, not knowing what on earth I would do—chant the Word? Hurl more salt?—but needing to do *something*, as Rose's screams were like nothing I had ever heard nor wished to hear again, the faeries scattered, wailing at me. Their dismay sounded for all the world like the tantrums thrown by small children denied a treat.

I was baffled by their reaction and glanced behind myself on pure instinct, as if there could be some far more intimidating personage there who had been the cause of their fright. That was when I noticed that my cloak had expanded—impossibly, nonsensically—and was now trailing behind me like a terrifying shadow. It billowed like silk and seemed to have no fixed end; it simply grew more and more insubstantial as it expanded, the distant hem no more than a blur of grey. Good God! First my pencils, now this.

I hadn't any time to dwell upon the shock of it, though. Since the faeries seemed so afraid of my cloak—I own I could not blame them, as instinct screamed at me to shake the horrifying thing off like a spider—I gathered up the trailing portion, which felt like silken cobwebs, ever so slightly sticky, and hurled it at them. The throw was clumsy, but it had the effect I had hoped for; the faeries fled, sobbing desperately at this frightening disruption of their fun. Several were caught beneath the cloak, and these vanished like snuffed flames. Shadow chased the faeries all the way to the forest, howling self-righteously—I believe he'd convinced himself that they'd at last comprehended his intimidating nature—then came trotting back with his tail held high.

Rose, meanwhile, was bleeding copiously and clearly in a great deal of pain, judging from his clenched jaw and the sweat pouring from his brow. Of the wounds, the most disconcerting was his left ear, which dangled from a narrow flap of skin, the blood running thick down his face and neck. I tore apart my scarf with my pocketknife and did what I could to bandage him up, but he could not stand, and I could not very well carry him.

"Shadow?" I said.

He understood me, of course—he always does. I do not entirely comprehend the bond between us, as Shadow is the only grim I know of to take a human master, but the beast immediately shed his glamour, growing to a size closer to a bear than anything else, his huge paws tipped in jagged claws. I slung Rose over his back, and we made our way home as quickly as we could manage.

27th September

I've not had time for my journal these last few days; Rose's condition has been touch and go, and I've felt disinclined to take up my pen until he was safely on the path to recovery.

Shadow and I made it back to the cottage without incident, and fortunately without crossing paths with any villagers, to whom I would have had to explain the presence of a Black Hound.* Ariadne was beside herself at the sight of Rose, oscillating between tearful expressions of dismay and panicky rambling as to the likelihood of his attackers having followed us. It was several moments before she was able to attend to my queries about Wendell's whereabouts and finally informed me that he had gone to the café.

"Well, fetch him! Go!" I shouted at her, and the poor girl fled through the door without even pulling on her cloak.

I did not immediately notice when Wendell arrived. Rose had regained consciousness—reassuring, but also appalling, given his condition—and was moaning and attempting to

---

* Black Hounds can be found in the folklore of almost all regions of Europe, including the Alps.

push me away as I ineptly dressed his wounds. When finally my attention was free, I found Wendell leaning against the doorframe, arms folded, watching the proceedings with an expression I could not interpret.

"Of all the times to disappear to the alehouse," I snapped, but in truth I was nearly weeping with relief. "Come here. The ear looks the worst, but as you'll see, it's actually the wounds upon his side—look."

Wendell gave me a look of mild puzzlement that could not have been more discordant with the grisly scene before him. "What am I to do about this?"

"I don't know! Why should I know?" I was shouting at him, and could not stop. Rose's blood was all over my hands, my cloak. "Heal him!"

"Emily," he began, his voice growing gentle as he at last seemed to process my distress, "this is not my sort of business—"

"Yes, you told me so!" I cried. "We were careless today, Rose and I. You were right about the common fae, and I was wrong. Do I need to say it three times before you are satisfied?"

I was nearing some sort of breaking point. I don't know if it was on account of Rose—who, distant as we were now, had been my colleague for nearly ten years, and for whom I've always had a grudging respect, despite our disagreements. It feels ridiculous *not* to respect Rose, even while resenting him; you might as well shake your fist at some august old turret. But also, my experience with incidents this gruesome has heretofore been limited to secondhand accounts, dutifully recorded in my notebook. My hand clenched around the bloody bandage I still gripped in my fist.

Wendell covered my fist with his hand and drew me into his arms. The gesture surprised me—not for its own sake, but because of how easy it felt to lean my head against his shoulder. I was oddly unnerved by it, and drew back—well, we can't have things between us becoming less fraught, I suppose.

"What would you have me do?" he said quietly.

"Heal him, for God's sake." Then, realizing what he was asking of me, I repeated it another time, to make three.

Wendell went to stand beside Rose, who had slipped into unconsciousness again. The quantity of blood was so great that it was as if he were not bandaged at all, and I wondered if there was some form of toxin in the teeth of the vulpine faeries.

"You can do it, can't you?" I demanded.

"Oh—naturally I can," he said, but there was a glibness about it that raised the hair on the back of my neck.

"What were you saying before? That this isn't your kind of business?" I pressed, for I was suddenly afraid, my mind full of all sorts of faerie bargains gone horrifically wrong—not a short list, that. Was it possible that Wendell's efforts might harm Rose in some ghastly way?

"Nothing," he assured me. "I misspoke—I only meant I do not *commonly* undertake the business of healing. But why should I not be as adept at that process as I am at any other form of enchantment? I'm very sorry that I upset you, Em. I didn't realize you liked him so much!"

This took me a moment to process. "Then—you have absolutely no idea what you're doing?"

At that moment, Rose stirred, letting out a moan. He opened his eyes to find Wendell at his bedside, gazing down at him in contemplation, and his face seized with horror.

"No," Rose croaked. "Not him—"

"My dear Farris," Wendell said, "would you prefer to bleed to death? All over this clean floor, I might add. I hope you're aware that blood is the most difficult thing in the world to remove from a surface. Anyway, I see no reason why you should prefer certain trauma over an uncertain one."

"Emily, stop him." Rose's gaze fixed on me even as his voice grew fainter. "This creature cannot—malignant realm with malignant Folk—whatever he intends, it could only—"

"You are very lucky Emily considers you a friend," Wendell said darkly. "You don't know the first thing about my realm, and I will thank you to refrain from mentioning it if you have nothing positive to say."

"I will not be beholden to you," Rose cried. "I will not—"

"In fact, Farris, this has nothing to do with you," Wendell said. "Good night."

This last was an enchantment—I felt the air hum, and Rose went as limp as if clubbed over the head.

"Hm," Wendell said, tilting Rose's chin to examine him. "I haven't done that in a while. Still, he needs a good sleep in his condition, doesn't he? You see, I am not wholly unschooled in the field of human health. Ariadne, will you be so good as to fetch the scissors and some clean cloths?"

The girl hurried to do as she was bid. "Thank you," Wendell said when she returned, giving her a warm smile. "Now, why don't you sit down, my dear? How unpleasant it must have been for you to return home to this."

"I'd rather be of assistance, if I can," Ariadne said, standing up a little taller.

"Brave girl." He absently tapped the end of Ariadne's scarf, which she'd draped over her shoulder. "You know, if he'd had this, those little menaces could not have touched him."

Wendell cut Rose's shirt away and washed each of his wounds. Rose's tattoos, I noted distantly, which had always been the subject of much salacious speculation, ended at his elbows, which would no doubt come as a great disappointment to the Cambridge gossips.

"These just need a good cleaning, I'm sure," Wendell muttered, seemingly to himself. "There! The poison washes right out."

Ariadne shadowed him the entire time, fetching cloths and changing water whenever directed. The terror in the girl's eyes had vaporized, replaced by determination, which seemed to strengthen every time Wendell gave her a word of praise, which he did frequently, even for such trifles as ensuring the water was a pleasant temperature.

Wendell at first seemed at a loss. He washed the wounds and then prodded one with a fingertip. Abruptly, it began to spill rose petals.

"Not that," he said hastily, making the same gesture in reverse, which stopped the flow of foliage. "Of course—only checking."

"Wendell," I began, then simply stared in an inane sort of way. I couldn't seem to do anything except stand there. It was partly fascination—my hand itched for my pen and notebook—but mostly shock, I'm afraid.

"Ah! I've got it," Wendell said. For a moment, I thought I saw a flicker of silver over Rose's prone form, like the flash of tiny sewing needles. Rose groaned in his sleep, and some of the tension seemed to leave his body.

Ariadne made a choking sound. "Good God," I murmured. Rose's wounds had closed, yes, but they had left the most uncanny scars, pure silver and somehow geometrical, like crisscrossing rows of stitchery. His ear was the most jarring—not only was it half silver, no doubt due to the extent of the injury, but Wendell had affixed it backwards.

"That was badly done," he said apologetically. "Still, who knows? It could come in handy. And there are always hats."

"Will there be any—side effects?" I said.

"Oh, probably," Wendell said with perfect unconcern. He

looked immensely pleased with himself. "I couldn't predict. I suspect he'll be more susceptible to some fae enchantments, and immune to others. But he's healed. That was what you asked for, wasn't it?"

"Yes," I said. I had a strong desire to sit down. It was a few seconds before I realized I was already sitting. I was having one of those moments, like the one on the train, where I realized, fully and painfully, that I had stepped beyond the world I knew. Before me lay a world of dangers, of sharp edges and deep shadow, and for all my knowledge, I was a mortal woman without an ounce of magic to guide me.

Do you know the wind? Rose had asked. I had been so dismissive at the time! Now the memory of the words sent a shudder through me.

"One thing more, Em," Wendell said. "Your cloak."

I came back to myself and found him regarding the article with a grimace. "My cloak?"

"Yes. Would you mind?"

Silently, I unbuttoned the cloak and passed it to him. He held it by the collar between his thumb and forefinger, his nose wrinkled in a way that prompted me to protest faintly, "It isn't *that* dirty."

Wendell made no reply. He went outside and began shaking the cloak vigorously in the garden. Ariadne and I trailed after him. "Wendell?" I said.

"This won't take long," he replied, utterly unhelpful. He gave the cloak a few sharp *thwack*s against the side of the stair, as if it were a dusty rug. At that point, the cloak began to twitch, and Ariadne leapt backwards with a cry, colliding with me.

"There," Wendell said with satisfaction. He gave the cloak a few more shakes, and out tumbled a faerie. One of the fox faeries, in fact.

"Bloody *snámhaí*," Wendell said, aiming a kick in its direction. The little faerie shrieked and fled sobbing into the mountainside, and Wendell turned his attention back to the cloak, muttering curses in Irish. He gave it another shake, and out tumbled a second faerie.

"They owe us a debt now," he said as the faerie followed its companion, shrieking even more loudly. "Because I let them go, I mean—you may claim it whenever you wish. You see? Contrary to the sentiments you regularly express, I am capable of foresight sometimes. Good Lord, how I hate the smell of injury! This place needs a good airing."

He disappeared within, and seconds later we heard the sound of him flinging open the windows.

I awoke in the early hours of the morning. The fire was down to a few flickering embers, and I had a terrible cramp in my neck. I'd decided to sleep in one of the armchairs so as to keep an eye on Rose—we'd not any of us had the energy to hoist him up the stairs to his bed, so he slept upon the table with a blanket over him.

Unable to drift off, my mind began sifting through the day's events, dwelling upon the vicious trooping fae. Eventually I got up and retrieved the notebook in which I had been compiling my addenda and updates for the second edition of my encyclopaedia, which I hoped to submit to my publisher within the year. I quickly grew engrossed in the task of describing the grim little faeries we had encountered at the lake, and how I might revise my entry on the trooping faeries of the Alps to accommodate them—lupine fae have been documented elsewhere, certainly, but never in this part of the world, and viewed objectively, it had been a momentous and exciting discovery that would make for a very fine paper; I could easily see it earning me an invitation to the annual conference of the Berlin Academy of Folklorists—not as large as ICODEF, but prestigious in a different way, as they are exceptionally choosy.

As I write this entry, I realize that it was cold of me to sit there revelling in daydreams of scholarly triumphs while the victim of one of my emendations lay insensible nearby, covered in strange wounds, but at the time I had no consciousness of this.

After finishing my notes, I turned my attention back to the draft of my mapbook. I had several scholarly articles on faerie realms in Germany that I wished to cross-reference with my book of German faerie stories from the medieval period, which contained its own rudimentary map indicating possible locations of Germany's five faerie kingdoms. I was startled out of my abstraction by the awareness that, at some point, a man had appeared out of nothingness in the chair opposite mine. Though surprised, I was also a little irritated by the interruption, and finished what I had been writing before I looked up.

"The cold goes straight through you," the man informed me. It was, of course, my enigmatic stalker, pockets full of ribbons as always. The firelight played upon his face; he was perhaps a little younger than the first time I had seen him, and a little older than the second. "At these heights, the wind is strong enough to snatch away your soul. Did you see its shadow?"

"I would like us to move past these tedious riddles," I said, closing my notebook.

He gave me an odd look—lost, almost childlike. Then his expression grew dark again, and he intoned, "You must keep to the path even as it unravels."

"Which path?" I enquired. "The one with the ghosts and

the ashes, or is this another route? I'm not sure I see the point of these visits if we cannot understand each other. Can you at least give me your name?"

"My name," he repeated. Some of the abstractedness faded from his eyes, and he seemed to see me clearly. "Did I have one?"

"A poor beginning," I said. "But perhaps I can assist: you are Professor Bran Eichorn of Cambridge, who disappeared in this very region in 1862 while searching the mountains for Danielle de Grey. You were born in Munich in 1817. Your father was a German diplomat of Egyptian descent, your mother a scholar and distant relation of the then queen of Ljosland. Your family relocated to London in 1820, where you were educated at a rather exclusive public school by the name of Collingwood. You received your doctorate in dryadology from Cambridge in 1841—does this aid your memory, sir?"

Eichorn neither confirmed nor denied any of this. But I saw him returning to himself, piece by piece, as I spoke, and I knew my supposition had been correct. By the end of my speech, he appeared almost sane, and had stopped clutching at his ribbons.

"Did she get out?" he said quietly. "Did Dani get out?"

I suspected I should attempt to soften my reply, but I couldn't think how. "Danielle de Grey has never been found."

He gazed into the fire. I wondered if it warmed him. Certainly he *seemed* to be there, and yet I had the odd certainty that if I let my attention drift, he would vanish. I've had the same feeling with the common fae, who are apt to disappear into the landscape whenever it pleases them; this is how I knew he was still somehow trapped in their realm, even as he sat at my fireside.

"I had hoped she escaped the Otherlands at last," he said,

using an antiquated word for Faerie. "It gave me a kind of comfort to think of her growing old somewhere in the mortal world even as I endlessly paced the borderlands of their realms, searching for her. You see, Professor Wilde, I have been chasing after Dani in one way or another for most of my adult life."

"What is the nature of the faerie realm you are imprisoned in?"

"As I said—it is a borderland. I stumbled into a fog one day—it was a door, and after wandering for a time I found a little house in which several brownies were sitting down to tea. They laughed at me, and declined to show me a way out, and while I attempted to retrace my steps, I was never able to free myself. I have been wandering the edges of different, overlapping realms ever since—time lost all meaning long ago. Sometimes I encounter the Folk in the form of common fae, and each time I entreat them for information about Dani, but they laugh and make sport with me, often endeavouring to make me more lost. Most of the time, though, I am alone in a strange, twilight sort of place."

I nodded. I had a similar experience myself last year in Ljosland after departing the faerie market. The borderlands of Faerie can be especially tricky for mortals to navigate; they are like the edges of a turbulent stream, where can be found innumerable eddies and whirlpools to ensnare the hapless wanderer.

He seemed to shake himself. "What year is it?"

I told him, and he nodded grimly. "How do you know my name?" I said.

"Sometimes I am with you without you seeing. I've overheard your conversations."

This was an unwelcome revelation, though it was quickly

dwarfed by scholarly fascination. What a curious faerie realm he was trapped in! How on earth did it connect to myself? "And what is your interest in me?"

"I have none. I would much rather spend my time searching for Dani than being continually drawn into your orbit."

"Hm," I said. Curiouser and curiouser! My mind was humming with excitement as it attempted to puzzle out the mystery. Still, I remained focused. "Where is the nexus?"

He let out a sharp breath. "Damned if I know. Dani did, though."

"She found it," I murmured, and he gave a grim nod.

"The Trade Routes Theory was her obsession. She was determined to prove the faerie realms are all connected, despite the resistance she encountered from her peers." He paused, and warmth lit his face. "You might think this obsession stemmed from resentment over the mockery she endured in scholarly circles, but nothing could be further from the truth. Dani never cared one whit what others thought of her. Her motive was science."

"So she found the nexus. What then?"

"What then, indeed! The last letter I had from her said that she intended to spend several days observing the nexus and its Folk from a safe distance before returning home."

"Is it possible she went through the nexus herself? Or became trapped in its interstitial space?"

"Dani knew better than to walk through such a door. Something else happened to her. These mountains are riddled with faerie doors leading to God knows where, and God knows what manner of Folk."

"Indeed." I regarded him. "Knowing this, it was brave of you to come here in search of her."

"You say *brave*," he said. "But I see your true meaning. Well, I don't care if the entire world thinks me a fool. I will search for her until my dying day, and perhaps beyond—perhaps I am already half a ghost. You say I have been gone half a century—at times it feels longer than that, at others it could be mere days. I have energy and life left to continue searching." He leaned forward abruptly. "You want the nexus. For the same reasons she did, perhaps. Find Dani, Professor Wilde. She will lead you to it."

I frowned. "How am I to do that?"

"You are clever," he said. "And you have the help of one of the Folk—yes, I have seen him. You could set her free."

Well, how was I to respond to this? His voice had taken on a desperate urgency, and as I gazed at him, he reached out and clamped down hard on my hand—his skin was so cold and wind-roughened it was like touching stone, and I could not help crying out. What does one say to this kind of appeal? He spoke not a word for his own sake, but instead begged me to pull de Grey from Faerie, leaving him to wander the mountains, perhaps for an eternity, chasing her shadow.

"Say you will try," he pleaded. "As I have failed her utterly, say that she might not spend the next half century desperate and alone. Give me that small hope."

I opened my mouth to reply, but in that moment Ariadne's door creaked open, and she came clattering down the stairs in her slippers. "I heard you shout," she began, brandishing her scarf as if it were a club, clearly under the impression that I required her inept form of heroism. I wrenched my gaze back to Eichorn, but it was too late: the man was gone, and I was staring at an empty chair.

2nd October

A nasty storm has kept us confined to the village for much of the week. This morning, it finally lifted, and we were able to return to the valley; but we found little of note, apart from a single door to a brownie home in a tree. Happily, we saw no sign of the vulpine fae, which Julia Haas informed us are known locally as *fuchszwerge*. But the valley proved far too vast to search in a day, particularly after the recent deluge, which has rendered it exceptionally boggy.

Naturally I gave Wendell a full account of Eichorn's visit. He was initially uninterested in the idea of focusing on de Grey, reasoning that we could find the nexus without her help. His opinion changed, however, when I related all that Eichorn had said of his decades-long search for his beloved.

"What a tragic tale," he lamented, looking misty-eyed. "He sounds properly heartbroken about the whole thing. Yes, of course we must remove de Grey from Faerie, and Eichorn too. But how? He has never appeared to me, and Lord knows where de Grey is at this moment."

"If she isn't a scatter of bones below that ridge," I said, for the weather had me in a pessimistic mood. "Yet Eichorn's suggestion is a sound one. If we find de Grey, we will find the nexus. We have traced her final path to the valley of the *fuchsz-*

werge, which the foot was also drawn to. It may be that we will find both de Grey and the nexus there."

Our midnight vandals remain unappeased by our offerings, even Julia Haas's fried apples, a local delicacy of battered apple rings dipped in sugar after cooking. Each morning, the food is eaten or spirited away, and each night, our door is scoured as if with enormous claws.

This morning was particularly troubling. I came downstairs to find the door not only scratched, but dented, the lock buckled in the frame.

"Perhaps an animal makes off with the food in the night, before the Folk pay their visit," I suggested to Ariadne. "That would explain their anger; they believe us to be stingy guests."

Ariadne nodded and seemed about to suggest something, but held her tongue and continued with her breakfast.

I suppressed a sigh. It seems clear that my relationship with my niece has taken a turn for the worse. Only moments before, she was wrapped up in a spirited debate with Wendell about the offerings at the village café; she remains full of opinions and happy to voice them, but not with me. I'm afraid that, after she startled Eichorn away, I lost my temper and shouted at her. I apologized the following morning, but I believe it came across as rather frosty. It's just that it was the height of foolishness for her to come barging in like that— why on earth would she assume I needed her assistance? I might have questioned Eichorn further.

My niece's reticence towards me, though, together with the dreary weather, has me feeling in low spirits—trust me to make a muddle of things, and not know how to fix them.

We spent most of our days over the past week in the village café, to Wendell's delight and my resignation. The café occupies a high point in St. Liesl, a little rise that slopes down from the church before cresting up again to form a flat-topped hill crowned with two stunted spruce trees, between which the café is neatly tucked. It is an attractive timber structure with the requisite window boxes filled with flowers of all colours, and is attached to a little shop offering basic necessities as well as tourist trinkets, for St. Liesl does see tourists sometimes, in hiking season. Given its elevated situation, the views in all directions are simply breathtaking, though the wind whips across the hill at all hours, and any scarf or jacket left thoughtlessly draped over a chair will likely be swept off to adorn one of the roofs below, if not carried all the way to a neighbouring peak. The chairs and tables are nailed to the wooden terrace. The locals seem to take little notice of the weather, and many dine al fresco even in the worst of the wind.

I mentioned this to Wendell in the context of some remark about the hardiness of rural folk, and he replied, "Almost all of these villagers have faerie blood," in the offhand way he sometimes dispenses such revelations.

"Good Lord!" I cried. "Are you certain? No, don't answer that—of course you are. How much?"

"Only a little in most cases. Roland Haas likely has a great-grandparent among the common fae." He tightened his scarf, frowning at something—likely the wind. "I've seen it before in villages like this, out-of-the-way places where mortals and Folk live in close quarters. Twice in southern France, once in the forests of Bulgaria."

"I had no idea!" I said, filled with curiosity. "Do such people inherit special abilities?"

"Oh, I don't know," he said dismissively. "Apart from a greater comfort in their environments, no matter how unpleasant, I've never observed anything of note—you'd be astonished how mortal blood muddies faerie power; even halfbloods can barely invoke the most basic glamours. Less than that and it's generally a wash. But one thing that's consistent is that the mortals in such places are more willing to defend their Folk, often in very silly ways. You could have wights storming their barns each night, making off with the livestock, and they would recoil at the thought of driving them off. In any case, we should be careful around these people."

"Were the villagers of Hrafnsvik of a similar lineage?"

"Lord, no. Most hadn't a drop of faerie blood. Why do you suppose we found them so rational and even-tempered?"

"I've never heard such self-awareness from you," I said with some amusement, though I admit I was also genuinely surprised.

"Emily," he said, "I'm quite capable of recognizing faults in other Folk," quashing my surprise entirely.

Naturally we settled ourselves *inside* the café, which was cosy and bright, the ceiling thick with massive oak beams, no doubt a necessary anchor against the hungry winds. Decorating the walls were what one might expect to find in such a place: namely, a collection of hunting trophies, primarily stag antlers, and the enormous skin of a brown bear sprawled across the floor. But there were also a number of musical instruments dangling from hooks—harps, zithers, and some sort of unusually shaped accordion. For the inhabitants of St. Liesl are very fond of music, and almost everyone here can play *something,* or at least carry a tune. Additional evidence of their faerie-touched lineage, perhaps, or simply a pleasurable pastime in such an isolated place, where winter occupies more than half the year?

We received a warm welcome from the owner, one Eberhard Fromm. Peter Wagener, our cart driver, did the introductions, assisted by Astrid Haas, with whom Ariadne has become fast friends, somehow managing this feat within the space of a few days. Wendell happily situated himself at the heart of the place, the massive fireside, for a chat with Eberhard, which established them as the centre of attention among the indoor patrons. I do not have the sense that any of the villagers warmed to me, with my inept small talk and persistent questions, but they were charmed by Wendell and Ariadne and impressed by Rose, and thus they seem willing to accept the small amount of water in their wine that my addition to the party represents.

To my delight, the locals have been eager to share their folklore with us, seeming to regard it as a source of pride. Two revelations were of particular interest:

1. Sightings of both Eichorn and de Grey are commonplace within St. Liesl and its environs.

Scholars have documented numerous sightings of Bran Eichorn in this part of the Alps. He appears as a shadowy figure in most cases, demanding whether the traveller has seen de Grey, or simply as a voice in the distance, calling her name. But what astonished me was that several of the villagers have also seen de Grey.

Over forty years ago, Eberhard was searching for a lost hound in the Adlerwald, a forest that fills one of the nearby valleys. Just off the path he came across a strange Scottish woman with vividly green hair,* dressed for the snowy heights, not a forest walk. She was carrying several ribbons—a strange

---

* Danielle de Grey is not a difficult person to identify by description. Her biographer, Matthew Chauncy, states that her green hair was most likely the result of a faerie curse, probably a hob's, a species de Grey studied extensively early in her career, and which is known for inflicting such disfigurements upon those who displease them. De Grey herself never spoke of how she came by the colour, and even claimed to enjoy "how loudly it clashed with everything under the umbrella of fashion."

thing in the valleys, where locals are generally less cautious about the Folk—as well as some sort of animal horn. When Eberhard asked if she required help, she demanded that he inform Bran Eichorn of Cambridge of her whereabouts. When told by an astonished Eberhard that Bran had disappeared in search of her some years ago, she launched into a volley of curses and stormed back into the woods, ranting, "I must do everything, mustn't I? I put his shoes away, I remind him to brush that hair of his, and now I must fetch him *and* myself out of Faerie."

Julia Haas's mother—now deceased—also came across de Grey more than a decade ago. This time, the woman seemed younger—around forty, de Grey's age when she vanished. This suggests that de Grey, like Eichorn, is lost not only in space but in time. How old she will be when—*if*—we ever extricate her from Faerie is anyone's guess. In this case, de Grey simply asked Frau Haas for directions to the village without mentioning her plight, then vanished along the path indicated.

Three other villagers attest to having seen de Grey over the years, each time from a distance. Oddly, she appeared greatly occupied with the horn she carried, noting the villagers' presence but appearing disinclined to speak with them, holding the horn before her as if it were a lantern that might light her tortured path.

Sightings of Eichorn over the years are far more numerous. Ernst Graf documented more than two hundred of them, which include eighty-five firsthand accounts.[*] Intriguingly, Graf makes no mention of the de Grey sightings, not even as a passing aside; nor does any other scholar that I have come across. I believe I have an explanation for this: the villagers dislike speaking of them. Most believe that de Grey met her

[*]   *When Folklorists Become Folklore,* 3rd ed., 1900.

end by human error, not faerie mischief, and seem disinclined to entertain the possibility that she is trapped in Faerie. Wendell believes this is tied to the villagers' sympathetic feelings for their Folk; de Grey being a more charismatic figure than prickly Eichorn, they have greater difficulty acknowledging wrongdoing towards the former than the latter, and as sightings of her are more rare, they are more easily dismissed. It is only on account of Wendell's ability to charm that we have been able to induce the few individuals with knowledge of her wanderings to confide in us.

Eichorn shows even less inclination to speak to the villagers than de Grey does, and Graf documents only one instance of back-and-forth communication, which involved a shepherdess whom Eichorn seems to have confused with de Grey. Upon realizing his mistake, he unleashed a torrent of invective upon the poor woman for her stupidity in venturing into such a dangerous, faerie-infested landscape alone, then stormed back into the fog in high dudgeon. I spoke to the woman, Julie Wiesenthal, and she still looks back on the incident with fear some thirty years later. That the man is less fondly remembered than de Grey is a mystery indeed.

2. Locating the tree fauns may be more dangerous—and more essential—than we supposed.

Happily, most sightings of the creatures so fundamental to our search have occurred in the vicinity of the fox faeries' valley, a region the locals informally call the Grünesauge, which is also the name of the lake.

The locals take a dimmer view of the tree fauns than other Folk—they cast no aspersions upon them, but encourage us to avoid the creatures at all costs. They are woven into the folklore of these mountains, and while few villagers would consent to name them, those who did referred to them either as *krampuslein* or *krampushunde,* as some tales depict them as helpers to the infamous horned Krampus figure. It is said that they prefer to abduct children, but the *krampushunde* do not confine such attacks to the Yule season.

Few have caught sight of them, and those who have seem superstitious about describing the encounters in detail, despite generous applications of Wendell's charm. "They don't like to be looked at" was the most I could get out of one of Eberhard's sons.

4th October

This is my third attempt at writing—the fire is almost down to the embers. This time, will I succeed in recounting all that has happened, or will I again drift into stunned blankness and drip ink upon the page?

I arose early yesterday morning to go over my notes. I find I enjoy sitting by the window before dawn, Shadow dozing at my feet, to watch the stars fade and colour spill across the valley, the ghostly snowcaps shedding their moonlit radiance. The cottage is particularly comfortable at this hour, with the *tick-tick* of the clock and rustle of the flames a counterpoint to the wilderness beyond the windows.

As I worked, I kept darting glances at the front door, tempted to see if I could catch our vandals in the act. But I was not foolish enough to confront them alone, and also, I was afraid. I could not specifically hear anything moving about out there, but the wind was rattling the doors and windows, and this might have covered many sounds.

I capped my pen and gazed about the little cottage. Naturally, it is now as snug as the winter den of some fanatically hygienic bear. Wendell sent Ariadne to the local shop with her pockets weighted with Lord knows how much money—no doubt a decision factored into the shopkeeper's friendliness towards us—to acquire a variety of useless items: rugs woven from wool dyed a vivid blue, a fashionable commodity in St. Liesl; vases painted with musical notes; wildflower-scented candles; and decorative knickknacks of all descriptions, including a small version of the local accordion, intricately carved. Ariadne seemed to enjoy this unscholarly task, and the two of them exclaimed over everything when she returned home, Wendell rearranging it all to his liking to a chorus of compliments from my niece. I have decided to suffer this in silence; it is no concern of mine what he spends his money on. The effect of the changes is pleasant, I suppose, and somehow he has made the place brighter, so that reading is rarely a strain on my eyes. Julia, when she came round with breakfast the other day, was insistent that the "hearth kobolds" have been hard at work in increasing the cottage's comfort. It is a quality that seems to deepen as time passes, though Wendell has done little that I have observed in recent days. I wonder if the mere presence of one of the *oíche sidhe* in a home is enough to alter its character.

I put my work aside in order to give Shadow his daily salve, which I rub into his toes and the joints in his legs. I've had occasion to worry about him these last few months, as his ordinary lumbering gait has grown stiffer, particularly in cold weather. He rests his head on my knee as I work, his eyes closing.

I'd only been up a half hour or so before Rose came down the stairs, moving carefully. He is looking much better—fortunately, most of his scars can be covered by his clothing. Nevertheless, he will spend the rest of his life explaining to scholars and layfolk alike how his left ear came to be fastened to his head backwards with a curious silver scar. Dryadologists, of course, are known for our strange injuries—my missing finger; Lightoller's stone elbows—yet I can think of nothing that compares to this.

Eventually, I had to rouse Wendell myself—he is sleeping a great deal these days, which is concerning, as I can only assume this is another symptom of poisoning. He is no help whatsoever in easing my concerns, merely repeating his refrain that he has no idea what the symptoms are, and why should he as he has never in his life been poisoned before, and on his birthday too.

With half of the morning gone, we finally set off and came upon the Grünesauge an hour later. The weather was fair for our hike, though the wind remained an encumbrance, howling over any attempt at conversation and sometimes shoving the lighter half of our party—Ariadne and myself—off the path. Shadow takes little notice of the wind, though it tosses his dark fur about, but then an enviable quality of his is that he is comfortable in any weather.

The sight of the picturesque valley with its lovely bright lake reflecting the soaring peaks was a great relief—given the amount of time we've spent there, I almost felt a sense of homecoming. I doubted my thought would have been appreciated by Rose, though, so I did not share it.

"Where to?" Rose enquired. He didn't flinch from the valley, and I reminded myself that his decades of experience with all manner of Folk had no doubt provided him with enough dark memories to put his latest experience in context.

"We shall search the forest again," I said grimly. "I am still convinced it is the likeliest location."

Wendell gave a skeptical murmur. "I would have sensed it by now, Em."

I made no reply to this, nor did he press the point; we'd had this debate before. For my part, I wonder if his senses where the doors are concerned are truly as heightened as he believes. Faerie intuition is one thing, the evidence another, and the evidence points to this part of the valley. I suppose we will see which of us is correct.

We split up before entering the little wood, though we kept within sight of one another. I did not bother removing the foot from my pack—sadly, it has continued to prove itself a useless burden. Well, perhaps *useless* is too harsh; it did point us to the Grünesauge, but it seems unable to narrow its directions in a helpful manner. Like a tour guide only superficially familiar with a locale, it wanders to and fro, starting off confidently in one direction before doubling back to try another.

As a branch slapped me in the face for the dozenth time, I found that I was beginning to lose hope. It's possible that Wendell's faith in me is misplaced, and we shall never find the nexus.

The problem, of course, lies in the nature of faerie doors.

Were they actual doors, made of wood or stone, with a knob and frame and all the rest, the process would be simple: scour the countryside, opening each door we come upon and poking our heads inside until we locate the correct one. But what if a door can lie within any fold in the mountainside, any ripple of fog?

Add to this, then, that faerie doors can move, as well as the mundane issue of the physical landscape: it is next to impossible to search every square foot of terrain as varied as the Grünesauge, with its steep slopes and mist-haunted peaks.

After spending a disheartening hour in the little forest, we made our way up the scree-laced mountainside that formed the western flank of the valley, following a vague little path none of us could remember noting before.

"Ah," Wendell said abruptly. "The trail itself is the door. Wait here."

And so we waited, trying to anchor ourselves to the unpleasant slope as the wind blew dirt and mist in our faces, whilst he wandered up the trail and then, without the faintest warning, disappeared into the landscape. I cannot adequately explain how disorienting it is when he does this. It is like watching someone vanish around a corner, and yet there is no corner; there is nothing at all. Shadow gave a huff of displeasure and started forward as if to follow. Ariadne wobbled, then sat with a heavy thud; not a wise move on an unstable scree slope, and she slid a little way. Rose had to grab her scarf to stop her.

"Nothing," Wendell informed us when he reappeared again, just as unpleasantly as he had vanished. "The door leads to several brownie houses, but they are all abandoned."

We turned off the path then, following a line of red, cup-shaped wildflowers that I had not seen before. And then, abruptly, we came to a door—an *actual* door, because the Folk are maddeningly inconsistent, even when it comes to their inconsistencies—tucked into a little hollow.

It was only about two feet tall and painted to look like the mountainside, a scene of grey-brown scree with a few splashes of green, so realistic that it was like a reflection on still water. The only thing that gave it away was the doorknob, which looked like nothing that I can put into human terms; the best I can do is compare it to a billow of fog trapped in a shard of ice.

"It has the look of a brownie house," Wendell said. "But perhaps I should make sure."

He shoved the door open and vanished into the shadows within—I cannot relate how he accomplished this; it seemed for a moment as if the door grew to fit him, but I was unable to get a handle on the mechanics as not one second later he was racing out again and the door had shrunk to its old proportions. Several porcelain cups and saucers followed in his wake, about the right size for a doll, and one made contact, smashing against his shoulder. Behind the hail of pottery came a little faerie who barely came up to my knee, wrapped so tightly in what looked like a bathrobe made of snow that I could see only its enormous black eyes. Upon its head it wore a white sleeping cap. It was brandishing a frying pan and shouting something—I think—but its voice was so small that I could only pick out the odd word. It was some dialect of Faie that I could not understand, but as the largest difference between High Faie and the faerie dialects lies in the profanities, the sentiment was clear.

"Good Lord!" Rose said, leaping out of range of the onslaught.

"I don't—what on—would you *stop*?" Wendell cried, shielding himself with his arm. "Yes, all right, I should have knocked, but is this really necessary?"

The faerie kept on shrieking, and then it launched the frying pan at Wendell's head—he ducked—and slammed its door.

Rose and I stared at each other. Ariadne looked blankly from Wendell to the door, clutching her scarf with both hands. "Bloody winter Folk," Wendell said, brushing ceramic shards from his cloak.

"*Winter* Folk?" I repeated.

"Guardians of the seasons—or anyway, that is how they see themselves," he said sourly. "Really I think they just want a romantic excuse to go about blasting people with frost and zephyrs and such. It seems I woke him earlier than he desired."

I had never heard of such a categorization, but as I was somewhat numb with surprise, I filed the information away rather than questioning him further. I fear that working with one of the Folk is slowly turning my mind into an attic of half-forgotten scholarly treasures.

A fast-moving cloud bank was rolling over the valley, reaching thin fingers towards our precarious perch on the mountainside. It was difficult to see the trail back down to the forest. Rose looked grey with fatigue during the descent, inching his way down, and Ariadne slipped twice, sliding several feet on her backside.

"Do you see what I mean?" Wendell said, and at first I thought he was lodging some complaint about the terrain; but no, he was only indulging his snobbery in regard to the common fae. "What information could be gleaned from a creature like that? Useless, temperamental little monsters, the lot of them."

"A characterization solely applicable to the common fae, I'm sure," I said, and would have gone on had not one of the rocks given way underfoot, making me stumble.

Wendell took my hand, steadying me, then led me sharply to the left.

"Another door," he explained. "In the fog. I haven't the patience to investigate after enduring that tantrum up there."

"I think you just want to hold hands," I muttered, though I did not mind.

"That wouldn't be very gentlemanly."

"You aren't a gentleman."

"In fact, plenty of Folk are gentlemen. And plenty of mortal men are not."

The forest too was wreathed in cloud, so thick it muffled sounds. I caught a flicker of movement—a faerie crouched behind a tree, watching us. I started back in shock, because there was something nightmarish about it, though I didn't catch more than a flash of its countenance before it faded back into the trees. I was reminded of the grey sheerie, the only other Folk from Wendell's kingdom I had encountered, the singularity of them. And something about its head—was it horns? I would have followed the creature, but Wendell distracted me.

"Emily," he said, gazing intently up at the sky, now covered in rippling cloud, with little tears in it through which the sun shone fitfully, "I believe we should return home."

I blinked. Wendell had used Faie, which we sometimes speak together when we do not wish to be understood by those around us, albeit quietly, for Faie is a strange language, with a musicality absent from any of the tongues of Man. One of its many fascinating characteristics is that it has local dialects; these generally contain words from the mortal tongue most common in the region. Thus Wendell's Faie has some words of Irish sprinkled throughout. I am fluent in Faie, but not Irish, and sometimes must ask him to explain things.

"Please don't tell me you're tired already," I replied. Rose was glaring at us—the older generation of scholars did not believe it possible to become fluent in the language of the Folk, and thus few ever made the effort. Ariadne is studying the language but presently has the knowledge equivalent of an entry-level course—perhaps she could ask for the location of the nearest faerie library or train station, should such things exist in their realms, but her frown indicated she had not understood our exchange.

"I don't like these clouds," Wendell said. "Don't say this to the others. Make something up."

It took me a moment to puzzle this out, and when I did, I drew a slow breath to calm myself.

Some Folk are drawn to mortal fear like sharks to blood. Wendell believed such Folk might be near, and thus wished to avoid creating anxiety in the others. Though what the clouds had to do with anything I could not guess.

"We're going back," I informed Rose and Ariadne. "The

weather's turning. We don't want to be trapped in an early snow squall."

Neither looked inclined to argue after our fraught journey down the mountainside, and we hastened back to the ridge. Unfortunately, by the time we reached it, the sky had darkened and the clouds had grown more strange, like the frayed edges of cloth. I felt one brush my face and shuddered, for it had a clammy roughness to it, nothing like cloud at all. Here and there I caught sight of what looked like the outline of a horse's head, but each time the mouths yawned wide until they broke apart. Shadow, at my side as usual, began to growl.

"How is it possible?" I murmured to myself.

Wendell glanced at me. "You've worked it out, Em? Of course you have."

"If you two don't explain yourselves," Rose blustered.

We came to a stop on the ridge, clouds swirling about us. "It's pointless to flee," I said. "It seems we will soon be paid a visit by the elder huntsmen."[*]

My voice was unnaturally even; I might have been delivering a lecture to my students. I am often like this when confronted with dangerous Folk, only this time I could sense a towering wave of terror on the other side of the calm.

Rose stared at me. "Have you gone mad? The elder huntsmen are Irish Folk. True, they roam the Irish realms freely, but what on earth would they be doing on the continent?"

"Yes," I said, still with that terrible calm. These creatures

---

[*] Recurring characters in Irish folklore, often described as old men astride monstrous horses made from cloud. Their reputation has diminished somewhat, as sightings, for some reason, have grown fewer and farther between in recent generations, but it was once common practice in the southwest of Ireland to shelter at home when the wind grows wild and *beithíoch* clouds mass overhead, a formation that is long and stringy, like a horse's mane. It was said that the elder huntsmen were riding on those days, and while deer were their preferred quarry, they would hunt mortals if the fancy took them.

had come to kill Wendell. "It's extraordinary. But the signs are clear."

"How much time do we have?" Ariadne demanded. She was clutching her scarf so tightly her fingers were white.

"In the stories, it always takes a few moments for the huntsmen to take shape from the clouds," I said.

"A few moments," she repeated faintly.

Wendell was muttering to himself, pacing back and forth. He dug a pencil from his pocket and shook it angrily until it grew into a sword, with which he slashed at the clouds over and over again. Rose and Ariadne took several steps away from him.

I grabbed him by the arm and shook him. "Wendell! How is it possible that the huntsmen are here? Did they use the nexus?"

"What?" he said, as if my voice had crossed a great distance to reach him. "No, they wouldn't need to. The elder huntsmen don't wander much these days, but their hunting grounds once included England, France, and a good portion of Germany. It's not improbable that they would have tracked me here."

I shook my head. "But how did your stepmother enlist them to her service? They are not ordinarily in the business of assassination quests."

"My beloved stepmother excels at soliciting favours. She knows precisely what a person desires and offers it to them on a platter. She is much cleverer at reading people than my father ever was. Perhaps she gave them the run of Wildwood Bog, where we keep our prize boars, or—"

I seized Wendell's arm and dragged him back, for a figure had coalesced from the fog—a wizened old faerie perhaps four feet tall astride a massive warhorse. The size of the beast more than compensated for the diminutive height of its rider, who was dressed with ridiculous foppishness—ruffled collar; tall feathered cap; yards of silken cape—that might have been amusing had it not been attached to a faerie commonly described by scholars as death incarnate. The faerie himself was one of the most hideous Folk I had ever laid eyes upon—and that is saying something—for his face was swollen and divoted with horrific scars, as if he were in the business of wrestling wild dogs.

The warhorse charged—it moved like a gust of wind, its hooves barely scraping the ground. Wendell shoved me aside, and I tripped over a stone and rolled several yards down the slope. When I stopped moving, the horse was half-headless—far worse, I can assure you, than being entirely headless, as Wendell had simply sliced his sword through the creature's neck and then left it stuck there in the gore, and the head was now flopping about horribly like a fish left on a dock. The beast continued past him, its rider screaming in fury until he was thrown from the horse's back—unlucky for him, for he fell right into Wendell's path. In one smooth motion, Wendell slashed the faerie's head off with another sword.

I could hear Rose retching as the horse staggered over the cliff, followed by its rider's tumbling head. My vision was swimming, but I managed to clamber to my feet and reach Ariadne in time to tackle her to the ground; another rider had appeared behind her. I felt the *whoosh* of air as the sword slashed past my scalp, likely claiming a few hairs, as the rider galloped by. I clambered to my feet, searching for Wendell, but suddenly he was at my side.

"There are too many of them," he said, seizing my hand. "I must take you elsewhere—you are too much in their path."

"Shadow," I cried, but the dog was lunging back and forth, nipping and snarling at bits of cloud, and did not hear.

"Leave him," Wendell said. "They won't touch a grim."

"I will *not* leave him," I snapped, but he was not listening to me; there was a terrifying calm about him that I recognized from the Ljosland wilds, when he had slain an entire troop of bogles by tearing them apart with his bare hands. I seized Ariadne's arm, and Rose grabbed my shoulders—thinking on his feet again, though a distant part of me wished he was not gripping me quite so hard.

And then Wendell did something I have only observed from a distance. He stepped into the landscape, and took me with him.

I will endeavour to describe the experience to the best of my abilities, because I am certain I will write a paper about it. Such a paper would no doubt secure me an invitation to any conference I desired, though I will note that, as we fled the assassins surging out of the clouds, I was not worried about conferences, or at least they were not at the forefront of my thoughts.

It was not like stepping into something solid, thank God, but rather some sort of dark tunnel, cold as the heart of the mountain, a cold that left me gasping. Did Wendell actually drag us through the mountain? Or did he create a pathway of sorts, a temporary causeway through Faerie?

Before I could begin to sort anything out, I was staggering forward, slipping on wet stones and sedges. I coughed, trying to clear the sensation of ice in my throat.

"Where are we?" Ariadne demanded.

I had no answer. Mountains surrounded us, which threw cold shadow over the forsaken patch of bogland we had stumbled into. It was an inhuman wilderness, the Alps jagged and sheer, the bog frigid, of uncertain depth; I could see no bank upon which we could rest, no path out. In the shallows clustered the loveliest flowers I had ever seen, purple and white and every shade in between, which filled the air with sweetness. I found myself irrationally annoyed by their presence; it was like being laughed at after tripping over your feet.

"Where were you trying to go?" I shouted at Wendell over the wind as we floundered in the muck.

"The cottage!" This was followed by another stream of curses. He doubled over, one hand pressed to his head.

I stumbled to his side in time to catch him before he went headlong into the frigid bog, guiding him to sit upon one of the mossy stones that jutted out of the water.

"Bloody poisoners," he rasped.

"What is happening?" I demanded. He did not seem entirely *there*—his outline blurred, and I felt as if I were trying to grasp a slippery wind. I gripped him tighter, wrapping my arm around him. I had seen this before—in Ljosland, after I accidentally stabbed him with an axe.

Wendell cast his gaze heavenward—at first I thought he was rolling his eyes at my concern, until I saw the rippling cloud boil through the nearest pass and spill towards the bog.

Wendell drew himself to his feet, grabbing for my hand again. I barely had time to grasp Ariadne's—fortunately, she was still holding on to Rose, who stood as if frozen in place with his mouth hanging open—before he pulled us into the landscape once more.

This experience was worse. After a brief interval of cold, a clammy cold this time, with something slimy underfoot, we emerged into a village square.

We were still in the Alps—but that was the only certainty I had. There were the soaring peaks and saddles, ragged as if hewn by an unskilled apprentice, but St. Liesl it was not. This village was lower in elevation, for one thing; I could feel it in the warmth of the breeze, and beyond the gabled rooftops I caught a glimpse of an expansive blue lake, larger than any in the vicinity of St. Liesl. The square had a restaurant with tables set outside it, and there sat several villagers, staring at us with astonished faces.

"What place is this?" Rose cried. "Stone the crows! Can it be Banns? That's fifty miles away."

"Wrong village," Wendell murmured. He was sitting on the cobblestones with one leg drawn up and his forehead resting on his knee.

"I need—" He thought it over. "I need elevation. The hunts-men hate snow."

"In your state, you're just as likely to take us to the bottom of a lake!" I cried. "We will find lodging here until you are well again."

"Emily," Rose sputtered in a scandalized voice. "We cannot unleash the elder huntsmen on a *village*."

"Unleash?" I repeated. "What on earth are you talking about? If this *is* Banns, we have surely gone far enough that they have lost the trail, at least for now."

"Don't be an idiot," Rose snapped. "The huntsmen are ex-pert trackers—how long do you think it will take them to real-ize where we've gone? We must leave at once, and I don't care where we go—back to that bog, if necessary. At least we will hurt no one but ourselves."

"Wendell isn't well enough to take us anywhere!"

We bickered on like this for a time—we were beginning to attract a crowd, and two villagers began approaching slowly, as if we were injured animals they wished to help, but were uncertain of our temperaments. Wendell paid no heed to any of it—he simply sat with his head upon his knee, breathing deeply, his body shaking despite the warmth of the square.

"Professor Bambleby!" Ariadne cried. Wendell thrust him-self to his feet before the last syllable died on her lips and grabbed my hand, hauling me towards the little oak grove at the centre of the square, which is what we must have emerged from. I realized as he whipped me around what had drawn Ariadne's attention, though I had guessed it already—a strange cloud was approaching from the lake, rippling like a thousand horses' manes.

When we staggered out into the world again, Rose began to shriek. We were at the icy pinnacle of some godforsaken ridge, just below a summit. The mountain was all spine, a jagged, narrow pathway into a realm of sky. The ground looked miles away, and the wind howled and pummeled us with ice crystals. *Well,* some part of me noted distantly, *at least we're above the clouds.*

"Ariadne!" I shouted, grabbing for the girl's hand. She would have fallen if I hadn't, swept away by the wind, for she stood upon the narrowest part of the ridge, which was barely as wide as a shoe length.

Wendell half sat, half crouched in a hollow in the mountainside, one hand over his eyes, showing no interest whatsoever in our impossible surroundings, and I realized what was happening: somehow, the poison had curdled the magic inside him, and any use of enchantment pained him.

I knelt at his side and wrapped my arm around his shoulders. "Is there anything I can do?"

"Yes," he murmured. "Say that you'll marry me."

"God." So he was well enough to tease me, at least—that was some relief. "Perhaps I will refuse you here and now. Disappointment in love may provide a welcome distraction from the poison."

"Only you, Em, would refer to heartbreak as a *distraction*. I think I would receive a more sympathetic response if I asked to marry a bookcase."

He stiffened suddenly, and I saw it out of the corner of my eye—clouds were rising from the valley below. He forced his head up and flung out his arm as if in frustration. The mountainside above us split apart with a booming crack, flinging rock and ice in all directions. I turned and found that, tucked into the side of the summit, where seconds before had been only rock and snow, there was a castle.

It was a small, awkward sort of castle—the two turrets were of different shapes and sizes, and there were a large number of windows but no door in sight. A great quantity of moss and ivy adorned the stonework, which contrasted spectacularly with the violent wasteland of wind and ice and gave off the impression of a flamboyantly dressed guest at a sombre wake.

"You made a castle," I said faintly.

"An abomination of a castle," he said, and I assumed his objections to be aesthetic until he said, "Keep to the main hall and away from the turrets—there's some type of void inside them, and Lord knows you don't want to meet the sort of Folk who take up residence in voids." He staggered to his feet and gave me a shove. "Go!"

Rose needed no encouragement; he was already charging towards the castle with surprising agility, but then I suppose the imminent prospect of falling to one's death has a way of sharpening the reflexes. He grabbed hold of Ariadne, who was windmilling alarmingly, and hauled her along in his wake. Wendell, meanwhile, patted my pockets until he excavated another pencil. I don't know where the other sword went; perhaps he dropped it en route and it's now buried at the centre of a mountain.

"Wendell," I began, because surely I could think of some other means of escape than fighting our way out. He could barely stand upright and kept passing his hand over his eyes as if wiping away a film.

"Farris," he called, and Rose returned, glaring ferociously, and seized my arm. I gave a cry of outrage as he dragged me up to the ridiculous castle, for I was furious with both of them, but particularly with Wendell. But as struggle would only pitch us off the mountain, I was forced to allow myself to be dragged inside whilst Wendell marched off with my pencil—now a curving sword—to confront the nightmarish clouds gathering below.

I expected the castle to be as nonsensical within as it was without, but it was a simple structure: a large room with a fireplace at one end and a flight of stairs at the other, which led to two floors of rooms that were pale and empty, like seashells, every one of which had a fire burning. I suppose it would be more accurately termed a castle gatehouse than a castle, as there was only the central stone structure flanked by its turrets. The strangest thing about it—beyond the disquieting turrets, I suppose, but those we did not investigate—was that it seemed uncertain about which size it wished to be. At times, I had the impression of standing in an immense ballroom; other times it might have been some cosy country tavern.

We had to enter the thing by clambering through one of the windows. These had no glass, yet once we were inside, there was no wind at all.

Wendell marched down a winding path in the mountainside —he must have conjured it himself—to engage the elder horsemen in a square of meadow tucked between two crags. I don't know if it was some inane faerie custom or simply the custom of the horsemen, but the one who appeared to be their leader—judging by the size of his horse and the number of scars he bore—stepped forward as if to challenge Wendell to single combat. Wendell, still with that calm detachment, somehow cut out the beast's heart in two sharp movements and hurled it at the rider in a stomach-churning spray of blood, knocking him from his saddle.

At that point, the remaining horsemen decided to abandon honour and charge him together, but their horses were, wisely, terrified of Wendell by this point, and shied away when he neared, some throwing their riders off, which Wendell dispatched in various appalling ways, sometimes appearing to forget about his sword entirely. Rose stood there the whole time, aghast, but I was familiar with Wendell's murderous moods and turned away after the third or fourth death, drawing Ariadne with me to the fireside. I was still shaking with fury. So he would risk killing himself rather than pausing to think our way out of things, would he?

The castle was very clearly the product of no more than one second's thought on Wendell's part. It contained no food whatsoever—perhaps for the best, as I was uncertain if all food summoned by faerie enchantment would be inherently intoxicating to mortals—but naturally there was a large kettle of drinking chocolate bubbling lightly over the fire. I went outside to gather snow for melting, exiting through one of the back windows. The northern side of the castle was more sheltered, and I took a moment to admire the ridiculous view. St. Liesl was visible in the distance, tucked into an immensity of peaks and waterways. I hoped the villagers would not mind an unexpected architectural addition to their prospect.

"There," Rose called a little later, and I hurried back to the window. Wendell was making his way up the path, very slowly. Ariadne and I ran to assist him—he seemed to have abandoned yet another sword, and the part of me that had thought about conferences as we were fleeing the assassins wondered if I was to be left with any pencils at all, and noted that this was not an item sold in St. Liesl's shop.

Rose had done absolutely nothing to ready the castle for our return, though I supposed that witnessing Wendell in one of his violent rages would be unlikely to inspire an interest in his health, and so Ariadne and I threw blankets down by the fire for a bed and laid him there, where he fell instantly asleep. We could have put him in one of the rooms upstairs, as each housed an eerily identical four-poster, but I did not like the castle—all right, I liked it quite well from an intellectual stand-point, but on no other account, I assure you. With its uncertain proportions and ghostly atmosphere, it struck me as the sort of faerie-made place into which one could disappear like spare change into a sofa.

I stayed at Wendell's side throughout the night. I don't believe I've ever been so worried about him—not because it seemed that at any moment he might disappear before my eyes, but because he hadn't said a word of complaint about the bloodstains on his cloak. I lay beside him, and I can't be certain if I slept at all, but I recall many moments drifting by as I watched him sleep, worried that he might slip away without meaning to, to Faerie or some in-between place where I would not be able to find him.

Increasing my dread was the fact that, when I opened his shirt, I found the same flickering bird shadows I had observed before, only darker. I pressed a hand to his chest. At first I felt nothing, but then, when one of the birds seemed to dart closer, I felt a faint thrumming beneath his skin, as of wings beating against the bars of a cage. I drew back, and the memory tugged at me again—the disturbing sight recalled a story I had read before. But it slipped from my grasp.

We remained there until mid-morning, subsisting on melted snow and the chocolate, which fortunately did not inspire in us a mad urge to dance. Wendell seemed a little better when he finally awoke, but was still weak and shivering all over, as if with fever. He pulled us through the landscape again, aiming for our cottage in St. Liesl. But once again the enchantment warped, and we ended up in a grassy meadow high in the alpine. Fortunately we were close enough now to hike the remaining distance, though it took us all day. Shadow, thank God, had returned to the cottage in search of me and greeted us on the road in a frenzy of relief, licking every inch of my face.

I must set my pen aside now—I am in Wendell's room in a chair beside his bed, writing by candlelight. It is late, and he has slept many hours, and certainly he seems no worse, but nor does he seem better. I know that I will be unable to sleep if I try, and I would rather be near if he awakens in the night and says something that is actually helpful (all he did today was mutter complaints about mountains, with the occasional aside of "on my birthday"). I think I will mend his cloak—no doubt it will turn out a shambles, but the prospect of his indignation when he is well again is distantly amusing. When he is well again.

I have found the story.

I didn't have it with me, but Rose did, in an old edition of *Beidelmann's Collected Tales.* I'm surprised I didn't recall it right away—but perhaps it isn't surprising at all. Perhaps I simply didn't wish to remember.

The story concerns a princess of one of the Irish faerie realms, who elopes with a faerie from a rival court. Her father, enraged by her betrayal, follows them, lures the young man away, then stabs him through the chest with a spear of iron, leaving him for dead on a lonely hillside. Fortunately, his bride finds him before he expires and pulls the spear free. They are married and spend several years in peace and contentment until the princess begins to observe something peculiar about her husband's chest while he lies in sleep: it seems to house six dark and shadowy birds, which beat against his skin as if trying to escape. She sees them more and more frequently, even during the day, and at the same time, he begins to fall ill. The princess eventually realizes that, when she removed the iron spear, it left behind one small sliver, which has been steadily working its way to her husband's heart. One day, he collapses, and a flock of ravens pours from his mouth. The sixth and final bird is carrying her husband's heart in its beak, and the princess wraps him in her arms as he breathes his last. Grief-stricken, she drowns herself, whilst the bird flies off with its prize, back to the court of the vengeful king, who puts the heart on display in his court as a warning to his other daughters. It is an unpleasant tale, told in a way to appease the moral sensibilities of a bygone era.

Beidelmann interprets the symbolism logically, cross-referencing this with several other Irish tales, and I can find no fault with his reasoning. The shadowy birds are, quite clearly, an omen of death.

5th October

After I finished the cloak, I attempted to nap in the chair by Wendell's bed, but could only manage an intermittent doze. I could not shake the sensation that the walls of the cottage were closer than before. I realized how foolish I had been to assume we would be safe here, that in leaving Cambridge we would be going beyond the reach of a queen of Faerie. The deaths of a dozen or more elder huntsmen would not stop her; she would send others. And Wendell would be unable to defend himself. How much time did we have?

An hour or so before dawn, I put sleep aside and focused all of my mental energy, scattered as it was, on the problem at hand. The poison, of course, was the equation that needed solving, more so than the next round of assassins, for even if they did not come, could we locate the nexus with Wendell in such a condition? And if we did, what would be the point? How could he overthrow his stepmother?

Twenty minutes later, I had come up with several ideas, none of which inspired an enormous amount of hope. But one held particular appeal.

I touched Wendell's hand—he murmured something, but whether it was sweet nothings or another complaint, I've no idea—and left him.

Shadow rose when I did and followed me into my bedroom. I changed my clothes, put on my cloak, and stuffed a few items into my pack. I was not bringing the foot this time; it could stay in its circle of salt beneath my bed, and damned if I cared whether the bloody thing escaped or not. I tiptoed downstairs and put my hand on the doorknob.

There I paused. I *thought* I heard something—but what? The brush of the wind? The creaking of boughs? Or was it the shuffling of preternaturally light feet upon the step, the talons of some fell beast upon the wood?

I realized how idiotic I was being. The villagers must have warned us a dozen times against venturing outside after dark. Why risk being gored to death on my own front step with dawn not twenty minutes away?

And so I waited. Shadow, meanwhile, seated himself by the door and fixed his gaze upon the knob, growling low in his throat, not at all unnerving behaviour. I kept expecting the thing to twist and some ghastly troop of bogles to charge into the cottage, but it was still. All was quiet.

As soon as the grey beams washing over the floor gained colour, I rose and opened the door. Birdsong and autumn light greeted me; there was no one there. And yet there upon the door was another long gash, deeper than the others.

When I touched the outer knob to pull the door shut behind me, I had to stifle a cry. The metal was warm. As if another hand had just released it.

My first instinct was to go back inside and slam the door behind me, but when one studies the Folk, one learns to ignore those instincts, wise as they may be, and carry on.

It took only ten minutes to reach the lake below the cottage, and five more to reach the spring with the strange mist hovering about it. There I did what I have never done before, and which would perhaps prove the most unwise venture of my career: I put my trust wholly and entirely in Wendell.

I knocked smartly on one of the stones beside the mouth of the spring. It felt ridiculous, but I affected not to notice, which is one of the key rules for interacting with the Folk.

Nothing happened, and nothing stirred apart from the wind, which made the lake ripple with waves. Shadow sneezed. It was very cold in the shade of the bank, and I drew my cloak tighter around me. I knocked louder, aiming for an irritated rap rather than a desperate pounding.

Finally, one of the fox faeries poked its head out of the hollow. The fur that grew atop its head stuck straight up and one of its huge ears was bent, and it had a blanket wrapped around itself, which seemed to be made of a felted, nestlike material of dried grass and fur scraps. The contrast could not have been more jarring. This was one of the beasts that would have devoured Rose alive.

The creature scowled its little face at me. "What?"

Its voice had a slight rumble in it, like a purr or a growl, but apart from that it reminded me of Poe's, small and boyish. I attempted to set aside my befuddlement and said, "I have come for my favour. My friend spared the lives of your compatriots, and thus you owe a debt—"

"You woke me," the faerie said.

Instinctively, I opened my mouth to apologize, then forced it closed again. "Well," I said eventually, "you ate my companion."

"Only a little," the faerie protested. "We didn't know you were allied with one of the high ones. Why does he bother with a sour-tasting old man and a little frowning woman?"

"The high ones have strange ways," I said.

"Hum!" the faerie said. My answer seemed to please him. "*That's* true. What do you want?"

I reached behind the collar of my dress and drew out the necklace I wore almost every day, tucked securely out of sight: a silver chain from which hung a small coil of bone. A key, Poe had called it.

"I need to visit another friend," I said. "Is there a path from these lands?"

The faerie snatched the pendant from my hand—he had small, human fingers tipped with black claws. Carefully avoiding the silver chain, he sniffed at the bone and said, "The winterlands! I haven't visited my friends in *that* realm in so long. What fun!"

I was too astonished to reply immediately. Of course I had hoped for an affirmative answer, but I had not expected this. "Is it—far?"

"Nothing is far in the winterlands," the faerie replied comfortably. He returned the key to my outstretched palm and sprang across the water—Shadow bristled and stepped in front of me, but the faerie slipped past him.

I hurried to catch up. "Do you mean to say that *your* realm—these mountains—are part of the winterlands?"

The faerie laughed. "How stupid mortals are!" Which I know from experience is often a faerie's way of saying *yes*.

I had a hundred more questions, of course—what a revelation for my mapbook! Were there faerie paths, then, connecting every snowy region? And every temperate one? Or was it that the Alps, uniquely, were rich in such paths, as they are rich in Folk?

I was panting as I tried to keep up with the flash of the faerie's tail, Shadow loping along beside me. The faerie slipped into a cleft in the mountainside—clearly a faerie door, given the sudden carpet of mushrooms at the threshold, like a welcome mat. I took a deep breath and followed.

I stumbled onto my knees. My hands hit snow, my left arm

disappearing up to the elbow. I wrenched it free and looked about me.

We seemed to have emerged upon a snowy curve of mountainside below a glacier—I believe we were in Faerie, for there were two little stone houses tucked in amongst the jagged icicles at the glacier's edge, with smoke curling from their chimneys. One had an apple tree in its yard, the apples coated in a rind of ice. The icicles themselves were like a forest of glittering trees, through which the fox faerie was darting, deeper into the glacier.

"Hurry up!" the faerie called.

I hurried, against my better judgment I might add, but then that is almost always the case when interacting with the Folk; stumbling into an impossible forest of icicles is not the most ill-advised thing I have done in my career. The forest made little plinking sounds and reflected our darting shapes strangely. In the distance, there was music.

I don't know when we went through the second door, if there was a door at all or if it was simply a long path in which time and space narrowed to the depth of a shadow. I was walking hurriedly, chasing the faerie. I held out the "key" before me as if it were a lantern, because why not? I felt a little silly about it, but clearly it was the correct thing to do, for shortly thereafter, one of my steps took me to the Kyrröarskogur and the familiar spring.

I staggered forward a little, dizzy. It was not only the change in the light—for it was not yet dawn in Ljosland—but the change in *everything*. The air was warmer, wetter, and scented with sea salt and the familiar sulphur of the spring. For a moment, the ground felt unsteady beneath my feet, or somehow insubstantial, as if I were not yet entirely *there*. But then the feeling faded, and I stood staring about me in an inane sort of way, heart thundering. Shadow had no such hesitancy; he stretched contentedly, then flopped down at the edge of the spring where warm mist greened the grass, which had always been his preferred spot when we visited Poe.

I spotted Poe immediately. He was raking the leaves around his tree home, a lovely aspen. The whiteness of its bark seemed brighter than the other trees, the knotholes darker; the moss creeping up the south side was luxurious with fat purple flowers, and the leaves were a riot of green in every shade with veins of pure gold. It was, in short, the prettiest tree in the Kyrðarskogur, which was Wendell's doing, but Poe was clearly taking his responsibilities as the owner of such a fine specimen seriously. He had built a trellis against the tree, up which climbed a vine of wild roses, and he had made little furrows in the ground to irrigate the tree's roots. Poe himself was a much more striking figure than the faerie I had first met; in place of the tattered ravenskin, he wore a luxurious cloak made from the bear fur I had given him, which he obviously cared for to a meticulous degree. It had not a speck of dirt and was very shiny.

"Hello!" Poe said when he noticed me there. He seemed happy to see me but not at all surprised, his black eyes aglitter, as if it had been but a day or two since our last meeting. In fact, it had been several months since Wendell and I had visited Ljosland for Lilja and Margret's wedding. "Have you come for bread?"

I hadn't, of course, but I found myself saying, "I would love some. Thank you."

He looked pleased, and darted into his tree home, beckoning the fox faerie to follow, as if his presence too was nothing particularly remarkable. I suppose I should have a name for the fox faerie as well. A variety of unkind appellations spring to mind, each appropriate for a murderous little beast. But then I think of the snowbells that dot the shore of the Grünesauge—Snowbell it is.

I removed my boots and sat at the edge of the spring, dipping my feet into its warmth. The dizziness had faded, but I still felt as if I'd walked headlong into something solid. It was very strange to be back. I could almost believe that I could walk down the path to the cottage with the turf roof and find a fire blazing; Wendell with his feet up pretending to work; Lilja there to give me another lesson on woodcutting. I can't say my associations are all positive; I knew I took a great risk each time I returned to Ljosland. According to Lilja's most recent letter, the snow king and his court have vanished into the northern mountains for the summer, but that means little, given his reach and power. Should he ever realize he was deceived into believing his mortal fiancée was dead, his wrath will shake the mountains. Not because he has been mourning me, but because all faerie lords despise being tricked.

I felt an ache of longing to follow the forest path to the village and Lilja and Margret's cottage, so strong that it surprised me. What a relief it would be to confide in them all that had happened! But it was too dangerous, and not only that, I had no time.

I opened my notebook and scrawled out a quick letter, rather scattered, I'm afraid, recounting all that had happened since last I wrote, and apologizing for not visiting them in person. Then I tucked it beneath a stone in the spring where I knew Lilja left her offerings to Poe—she and several of the other villagers have become regular visitors to the little faerie's spring after hearing of the help he gave me last winter. The simple act of writing to my friends was soothing, and I smiled at the thought of Lilja's astonishment at finding the letter there—well, it *was* my turn to write.

Poe interrupted my reverie. He handed me a perfect loaf of bread sprinkled with sea salt and some form of herb I did not recognize, but which reminded me of rosemary. Snowbell emerged with a sweet bun clenched in his fists and plopped down by the spring to gnaw at it in a rather disgusting manner, slobbery crumbs flying in all directions. Had I not recently watched him and his friends dine on my colleague, perhaps I could have endured it without shuddering. His mouth becomes very large when he eats.

Poe leaned against my leg as I picked at the bread and began to tell me all about the improvements he had been making to his home, dwelling at great length on his gratitude to Wendell as well as the compliments of sundry Folk who, according to Poe, were forever coming round to gawk at his tree's splendor.

"I would not mind," he said. "For my mother always said: 'A guest is a gift, little one,' but I wonder if the same is true of *many* guests, who arrive at all hours, and sometimes make such a noise that my lady cannot sleep through the night? But I do not wish to offend. Last night I baked bread for three kind trolls, who said they could not rest until they watched the light of the rising moon frame the beautiful boughs of my home, and so we sat together and watched the moonrise, and they told me secrets they had learned from the birds about the care of trees. They say they will honour my tree by sending me a flock of tame ravens who will eat any bothersome caterpillars. Isn't it wonderful? I have many friends now. My mother would be so pleased. 'You are too shy, little one,' she always said. 'You must try your best to make friends, for those who are small cannot easily stand alone.'"

It was the first time Poe had paused for breath, so I decided to take advantage of it. His conversation rarely flows in straight lines, and thus he is untroubled by non sequiturs. "How am I here?" I asked.

Poe blinked his enormous black eyes at me. "You have the key."

"Then—then the key created a door? Or did it transform another door, to make it point in a new direction, to Ljosland?"

"Other doors?" I could see I had confused him. He tapped the coil of bone with one needle-finger. "To find me, you need only this."

I turned this over a few times in my mind. And then I had it.

"The key *is* the door," I murmured. "But how?"

"My home needs only one door, which you see there," Poe said, growing enthusiastic now that he was speaking of his tree home again. "There was a second made of bone, around the side, but it was easy enough to take it down and fold it up. In its place I put a lovely window, at the advice of my lady. There she likes to sit and bask in the morning light."

I was gripping the piece of bone too hard and forced my fist to unclench. Poe had *given me his door*. It was both perfectly logical and utterly impossible. Still, I had to pause a moment to rub my eyes. I was acutely aware of how little sleep I'd had in recent days.

"Am I in Faerie now?"

"Yes," Poe said, after an astonished pause. Clearly he had thought I knew all this already. "And no. This is a borderland, where Faerie mixes with *your* world."

I nodded slowly. I thought of the path I had followed with Snowbell, past the faerie homes and into the glacier. "Then in order to use your door, I must be in Faerie myself?"

"In the winterlands," Poe said. "The summerlands are too warm and wet—the door will crack and fall apart there."

"But—" I stopped and shook my head. I was still not convinced I understood, but for the time being, the mechanics of the gift Poe had given me were immaterial. I replaced the key around my neck.

"Your kind knows a great deal about the doors between faerie realms," I said. "More than the high ones. Isn't that right?"

Poe nodded vigorously. "The high ones don't like to visit other realms. They have their courts and their servants. But other realms are good places for hiding, good places for making friends. There are none here in the Kyrrðarskogur—I did not lie to his lordship," he added quickly. "But in the mountains—yes."

I nodded—this confirmed what I had already guessed. It explained why Wendell and his stepmother knew of so few back doors to their realm, but the fauns travelled between multiple realms and countries as they pleased. Likely there were other doors to the Silva Lupi in other countries, also used by the common fae, boltholes too lowly to warrant the attention of any lord or lady of Faerie. An ignorance born of snobbery and privilege, then, of never needing to concern oneself with the world beyond one's backyard.

I was also beginning to realize that, while Poe may not have lied to Wendell when Wendell had questioned him about faerie doors, he had certainly not told him the full truth. "You did not tell Wendell about any doors in the mountains," I noted.

Poe looked terrified. His sharp fingers wrapped around the hem of my cloak, as if in supplication. "There are no doors to the summerlands! Not here. He—he could not have had any use for them. I did not mean—he is great and good, and surely he will forgive—"

"It's all right," I said soothingly. "He isn't angry with you."

Poe shivered and picked absently at my cloak. "'Keep away from the lords and ladies, little one,' my mother always said.

And I tried! When he came here with his questions, I hoped only that he would go away again, and quickly. But then his lordship made me such a lovely tree. They cannot *all* be terrible, can they?"

"Certainly not," I assured him. "And in any event, Wendell will not be visiting here anytime soon. He is very ill."

Poe shook his head. "Wickedness! He has enemies then. The high ones always have enemies. I am glad that I am small."

It was my turn then to be astonished, that Poe had guessed the nature of Wendell's illness—but then, what other reason was there for a faerie king to fall ill?

"I've come to ask a favour," I said. "Once, many months ago, you made us cakes that kept us warm in the snow. Can you make something that might help Wendell? I do not ask for a cure—I know you have no power over poisons used by the high ones. But is there something that might relieve his symptoms? Or give him strength?"

A constellation of emotions filled Poe's face. There was terror again, but also a kind of awe and helpless delight. "He wishes this?" he breathed. "To—to be our *fjolskylda*?"

I had not anticipated this, though upon reflection I can see why Poe would have made such an assumption. It is the nature of many household brownies—which Poe is, after a fashion, despite making his home away from human settlement—to tend to their mortal families when they are ill. But this attentiveness never extends beyond the members of the household. Asking for this degree of assistance for Wendell would be the height of strangeness, unless—

"Of course he does," I lied; I could almost see Wendell rolling his eyes at the prospect.

Poe knitted his fingers together and pressed them to his mouth. "Oh!" he breathed. "If Mother could see me now!"

He vanished into his tree home, from which came a great

clattering and clanking noise. I settled down next to Shadow to wait and took the opportunity to wash his paws in the spring. Snowbell had finished his meal—his little face was now covered in cream, which was an improvement over the alternative, I suppose—and watched me beadily.

"Would you like to wash?" I enquired, more to distract the faerie than anything else.

"I don't like the steam," he complained, but he came closer to me anyway and dipped a hand in the water before leaping back again when the steam drifted his way.

Feeling more than a little ridiculous, I cupped a handful of water and rinsed Snowbell's hands—the two front feet—and paws—the two back ones. Then, using a curved leaf as a sort of bowl, I helped him wash his face. He swiped his hands over his ears a few times, like a cat, and then, to my astonishment and dismay, he hopped into my lap, curled himself into a ball with his tail over his nose, and went to sleep.

I was calculating the odds of receiving a bite on the knee for disturbing Snowbell's slumber versus the odds of him clawing me in his sleep when Poe came hurrying out again, a basket clutched under his arm.

"I hope these will please his lordship," he said, excitedly lifting the cloth for me to see. "My mother made them for me whenever I was sick, for they are good for headache, stomachache, and all other ailments besides."

I examined the contents. They were small, roughly triangular cakes, which put me in mind of a sort of spongey scone, except that they were iced and smelled like—I don't know. Something warm and sweet and leafy—sap, perhaps?

"Thank you," I said, swallowing to clear the obstruction in my throat. For a moment I thought I might cry, but I mastered myself, partly because I did not wish to distress the little creature, who gazed at me with his black eyes luminous with anticipation. "Wendell and I are proud to have such clever *fjol-skylda* as yourself. Would you do one other thing for us?"

Poe swelled. "Anything."

"You say you are visited by other Folk, from other lands," I began.

Poe nodded. "Wanderers. Some Folk wander. I do not understand it, but perhaps their trees are not as comfortable as mine."

"And these Folk may speak with other Folk, who may talk among themselves," I said. "I wonder if you might see if any of your visitors have heard news of Wendell's court?"

"Oh, yes," Poe said, looking relieved. "That's easy. The trolls might have known—trolls love to gossip. But they have gone away again."

"Well," I said, "if you see them again, or any other Folk who have a similar love of gossip, perhaps you will make enquiries?"

Poe promised me that he would. He seemed excited by this new request, though there was an edge of terror there, too, and I soothed him with many assurances of Wendell's gratitude, together with reminders that Wendell was indisposed to visit Poe for the foreseeable future. Poe then returned to his tree and selected three leaves that he hoped I would show Wendell as evidence of the tree's health and how well Poe was tending to it. I tucked these in my pocket and reluctantly shook the fox faerie awake, who did, indeed, snap at my hand, and would likely have made a snack of my thumb had I not anticipated the mongrel's movement. Then, somehow, we returned to St. Liesl. This involved walking around the side of Poe's tree home, at which point we found ourselves back in a glacier, only it seemed a different glacier, for the faerie homes

I saw there had no apple trees in their gardens. Then we went through another door, I think, and then I was standing beside the lake below our cottage, and Snowbell was nowhere to be seen.

I have read that over again. It makes little sense, but how could it be otherwise?

6th October

Wendell slept most of the day yesterday, waking only briefly in the afternoon. I was sitting beside his bed, writing in my journal. I handed him one of Poe's cakes, which he initially turned his nose up at.

"They smell of sulphur," he muttered, and would have pulled the covers back over his head had I not gripped his hand.

"Enchanted scones?" he said, examining them more closely. He was still shivering in spite of the blankets, though he seemed more substantial than before.

"More or less."

He ate one and then lay down again, seeming to fall instantly back to sleep. I sagged back against my chair with a stifled gasp. I hadn't thought I was foolish enough to anticipate some sudden and miraculous cure—but apparently, a part of me had.

Hands trembling, I pushed back the covers and opened his shirt. There was no flutter of wings there, at least, though I could not say I was comforted.

I brushed the hair back from his face. It is very soft—ludicrously so, in fact, more like rabbit down or dandelion seed than human hair—and I found I could not stop stroking it. He murmured something, and the crease between his eyes faded.

I spent the rest of the day in St. Liesl, interviewing the villagers, while Ariadne and Rose went yet again to scour the Grünesauge. I had to keep myself busy, though I could not focus on anything the villagers told me of de Grey or the fauns, and when I returned home close to sunset to find Wendell still asleep, still shivering, I felt darkness settle over me. I murmured to Shadow, and he settled himself next to Wendell—his huge bulk would keep him warm. I wandered aimlessly into my bedroom, where the foot was poking its toes out from under the bed. It had disturbed the circle of salt, which I was forced to repair. I'd been right—I *had* heard the bloody thing shifting about in the night. Was it trying to get somewhere, or was it just restless?

I came down the stairs and found my notes and sketches still piled up on the table. I have not worked seriously on my mapbook in several days—indeed, there are times that I almost forget about it. Not once did this happen with my encyclopaedia; the project was at the back of my mind constantly. I cannot account for it.

I stood unmoving for a moment, one hand gripping the table. I needed to get away from the cottage—that ridiculously clean cottage, with the comfortable rugs and the silly knick-knacks scattered about.

"Emily," Rose said from his position by the fire, where he was writing in his journal. Just that.

"I need air," I said nonsensically—I had just come from outside. Neither he nor Ariadne tried to stop me as I pulled my cloak on, grabbed my pack, and darted out into the gloaming.

I went to the lake first, for no reason other than that it was familiar. Snowbell was nowhere in sight, nor did I spy the usual mist curling off the spring. Did the door to his realm close at night? Were the smaller Folk also afraid of whatever creatures lurked in the mountains after dusk?

I wasn't cold, but I couldn't stop shivering. I sat there until the sky darkened to ink and a horde of stars gazed through each break in the patchy clouds. From the direction of the village came the faint thrum of an accordion—one of the villagers, no doubt, practicing a song, yet the wind twisted and winnowed the notes, making them eerie. I became aware that an animal was howling somewhere in the distance, and my indifference abruptly shrivelled. Yes, I had Wendell's cloak—was that enough to preserve me from every danger?

The howling grew closer. It was not, in fact, an animal noise—it was a man. Garbled as it was by the wind, I knew what the voice was saying, and my breath froze in my throat.

"Professor?" I called, my voice catching. "Professor Eichorn?"

A brief pause, and then the shout came again, even closer this time. "Dani!"

I rose and made my way up the lakeshore, then over a little rise in the mountainside. "Dani!" the voice shrieked, and I winced, suppressing the urge to cover my ears. I had never heard anything so raw. It was a voice that had been shouting for hours without rest.

Something bright caught my eye, fluttering among the grasses. It was a ribbon, deep blue with a ragged edge. It was affixed to a root with a loose knot that the wind was already teasing free—someone had tied it there within the last few minutes.

"Dani!" the voice cried. I stowed the ribbon in my pocket.

I followed the voice down a slope, picking up ribbons along the way. It wasn't long before I stopped—I knew better than to chase spectres into the wilderness, and though I wanted very much to speak with Eichorn again, I had no idea if he was presently sane enough to recognize me. I could still see the cottage in the distance, the firelit windows beaming into the dark.

As was my habit, I clutched the coin in my pocket. I saw no evidence of faerie doors in the vicinity, but I was not fool enough to let my guard down. I knew now that part of the reason the villagers stayed in their homes after sunset was because it was too easy to stumble into Faerie then; after nightfall, doors opened that remained closed by light of day.

"Professor Eichorn?" I called. The wind sifted through the dry grasses, and I could still hear the soft plash of waves on the lakeshore.

"Dani!" the man howled again. He was farther away, moving much faster than I. Was it even Eichorn, or some echo of him imprinted on the wind?

Something moved to my left. A figure was outlined against the stars, descending a sort of natural staircase cut into the rock. A human figure, bundled up tightly in a hooded cloak and scarf that trailed in the wind. Despite the heavy clothing, it was clear that the figure was very slight. Not Eichorn.

"Good Lord," I murmured. It was a dilemma, but one I had faced before. I cast another glance back at the cottage—if I kept going, I would remain within sight of it for another fifty yards or so. I could still hear the distant strains of music from the village. I had my coin, my cloak, and the experience of having thought my way out of a dozen faerie realms before.

I followed.

The figure kept going, down and down. Eventually, their route rose again, terminating in a bluff. There the figure halted and seemed to survey the prospect. A few clouds scudded by below.

I stopped. I was near my self-imposed limit; any farther, and the terrain would block my view of the cottage.

"Professor?" I called. The figure didn't turn, though we were close enough to hear each other. "Professor de Grey?"

No response. It was possible that I was wrong, but I didn't think so.

"I've come from Cambridge," I said, hoping that the sound of a British voice might produce some effect upon her. "We're looking for the nexus. That was your discovery, wasn't it?"

At that, her hood twitched, as if she'd glanced in my direction—but it could have also been the wind. Without warning, she stepped off the bluff.

"No!" I cried. As she fell, her hood blew back. I caught a glimpse of a heavily lined face and waves of green hair.

I felt as if I had leapt at the same time, a dizzying weight-lessness. I ran desperately, stumbling over the uneven terrain. I fell once, scraping the heels of my hands, and was up and running again before the pain registered. The bluff was empty, the valley below lost in shadow. The chill wind howled and pawed at my hair and cloak. It could have been the edge of the world.

"Professor de Grey!" I shouted. I paced back and forth, shouting her name. Finally I forced myself to stop, pressing my hands into my eyes. I told myself that I couldn't be certain of what I'd seen—it may not have been de Grey, but some echo of her. A fae illusion.

"Dammit," I muttered when I turned around. As I had feared, fog had rolled over the landscape behind me. Still, I didn't panic. I'd been in similar situations before and knew that if I waited for the fog to clear, I'd have a better chance at finding my way than if I stumbled on through it. But the fog simply crept higher and higher until it enveloped the bluff.

Well, it was possible that it was a natural phenomenon—it had to be ruled out, at least. This was easily done when I walked back the way I had come and found that the natural steps de Grey and I had descended had vanished.

I returned to the bluff, simply to confirm what I already knew, but of course the bluff wasn't there anymore; it was now a ridge that descended steeply towards a forest of birch trees.

"Wonderful," I muttered. This was my own fault; but still I couldn't be upset with myself. I'd had to make some attempt to reach de Grey, futile as it may have been. All that mattered now was extricating myself from this mess.

I scanned the landscape. To my left, the grasses were faintly trodden, a path that curved gently around the mountainside. The terrain was roughest in the opposite direction, cluttered with boulders and precarious ledges, so I went that way. The stories are clear on this point—the Folk will always entice lost travellers farther into the wilderness with comforting deceptions: a distant glow, as from a cottage hearth; an easy path signifying the presence of other travellers. The correct path— that which might actually lead you back to civilization—is always treacherous or seemingly impassable.

I struggled along for some time and was rewarded when the fog began to dissipate. I began to feel that I recognized the landscape, that I was, in fact, on a bench in the mountain not far below St. Liesl. Naturally, that was the point at which my foot caught on a rock and I went tumbling end over end down a gully, landing fortuitously upon a dense carpet of moss. By the time my head stopped spinning, the fog had closed in again, and I was as lost as before. Only now my ankle was throbbing like mad.

I tested it, wincing. I didn't think it was broken—I could put weight on it, though it ached when I did, an ache that grew worse the longer I walked.

Grimly, I carried on, limping. Abruptly, I came to a cliff face—so abruptly I nearly walked into it.

I tilted my head back, squinting into the fog—was that a path between a cleft in the rock? It looked treacherous from where I stood, the crevice clogged with ice that likely never melted.

To my left, the path I'd been following continued at a gentle incline, and I even heard the thunder of a waterfall somewhere ahead. It was tempting to keep going that way, to see if the waterfall was one I recognized and could use as a landmark. Too tempting. I knew better.

As if it wished to lure me on, the fog parted on the easy path, revealing the mountainous landscape beyond. Most travellers would have surged ahead immediately in order to orient themselves, but I did not trust the behaviour of the fog. I surmised that the path ahead was a faerie door, and what sort of place did it lead to? The mountains I saw through the break in the fog were familiar, and yet something was off about them. They seemed too dark, somehow, and the nearest was riddled with hollows where tiny lights glimmered. The fog shifted again, and I was gazing at a luxuriant rose garden. The flowers were fat and healthy, but the garden itself was overgrown and had the air of abandonment, the rosebushes almost swallowing their trellises, some of which had collapsed. A little wind blew back the heads of the nearest roses, and I felt as if they were turning to gaze at me.

I shivered. This was no humble brownie door. And I would not be going that way.

Instead, I began the slow, painful process of hauling myself up the cliff path. It was painfully steep, though with enough jutting boulders to form a sort of rough staircase. I fell within the first few steps, my knee slamming into stone, wrenching my already wounded ankle. I had to rest a moment, my vision swimming.

However, the path grew easier the higher I went, as I had hoped; the impossibility of it had been mere illusion. Finally, I reached the top, and I was able to get the lay of the land.

My stomach clenched, and I felt the dizziness return. I recognized nothing. The fog swept over the landscape, and when it cleared, the cliff path I had taken was gone, as if some god had scrubbed it from existence with his thumb. Before me was a broad, easy track through a gentle valley. Or I could go right, along the ridge, towards a warm and distant glow that could have been a cluster of cottages.

I sat among the saxifrage, pressing my head against my knees. I would wait five minutes, I decided. Hopefully, the fog would sweep through again, and the landscape would rearrange itself once more. I simply had to keep going, and eventually I would find a way back to the mortal world. I had done so before.

I tried not to wonder how many times Eichorn and de Grey had told themselves the same thing.

"Emily!"

The call drifted to my ears from a distance, twisted by the wind. But the voice was unmistakable.

"Wendell!" I shouted, surging to my feet. "Here!"

"Emily?" He sounded even farther away this time. "Where on earth have you got to?"

I spun uselessly, trying to pinpoint the direction of his voice. Suddenly, in the midst of the drifting fog, a light flared. It was small and flickering—ghostly.

"Wendell?" My relief was subsumed by fear. Was this the doom of Eichorn and de Grey? Did they spend their waking hours wandering the fogs, chasing echoes and illusions? Was the light held aloft by some bogle, the voice fashioned from my own hopes, sure to vanish the moment I neared, leaving me more lost than before? When I had left Wendell, he had been unconscious, still shivering. What were the chances he had followed me?

"Emily!" Wendell's voice called again. "Goddamn this fog— now what is that there? *Another* door? This place is a regular bloody rabbit warren." This was followed by a series of curses.

"Where are you?" I shouted. I could make out no shapes in the fog. His voice seemed both close and far away.

The light bobbed. "Can you see that, my love?"

I was running before I made the conscious decision to move. *Stupid, stupid, stupid,* I thought. But the thought seemed completely detached from my feet, which were closing the gap with the light, leaping over stones and hillocks. If it *was* Wendell, I would not linger there a moment longer, shouting into the fog; if it was some faerie trickster, I would strangle the creature with my bare hands.

"Emily?" His voice was close now, I was sure of it. And then the fog broke, and I saw him—his familiar cloak, his familiar golden hair—standing a little ways up the slope, scanning the mountainside. Above his open palm hovered a tiny light, bobbing in the wind.

A smile broke across his face as he saw me barrelling towards him. He opened his arm, the one not holding the light, but he underestimated the ferocity of my embrace, and we toppled backwards into the grasses.

"Emily?" he said dazedly. "Surely not. I must have inadvertently summoned Danielle de Grey. My Emily would never be so flamboyant in her affections."

I gave a huff of laughter—it died quickly; the jest was ill-timed, given what I had witnessed. I closed my eyes as if that might shut out the afterimage of green hair splayed out as the woman fell, there and then gone.

"Should you be doing that?" I asked, drawing his hand towards me to examine the light.

"It's a small thing," he said, snuffing it in his fist absently as he propped himself up. "Do you know? I'm feeling much better. You put something in those cakes, didn't you? Where on earth did you learn to bake? I always thought you were allergic to kitchens—or at least the cleaning of them."

"I can take no credit for the cakes," I said, and briefly told him the story of Poe's door and my visit to Ljosland. To my surprise, he seemed pleased to learn that he had been named a member of Poe's family.

"You were right," he said. "He is a charming little creature, isn't he? Well, I don't have to ask what he would like as a thank-you gift. When I am well again, I will summon a grove of magnificent aspens for him and his descendants, and he may build himself a court and live as a lord among brownies."

"I believe the best gift would be your continued absence from Ljosland," I replied. "Poe seems to prefer to admire you from afar. Are we still in Faerie?"

"Hmm? Oh, no. You weren't actually in Faerie, merely the borderlands. There are so many realms in these mountains that many of them overlap, so that a mortal who stumbles in the wrong direction may end up several worlds away from home—what a mess!"

I examined the wild terrain. "I don't recognize this place."

"I'm afraid you drifted more than a mile from the village. We've a long hike before us, for it's all uphill."

I was certain I had not travelled so far. "Small wonder Eichorn went astray searching for Dani."

"And what a wretched place to wander for eternity!" Wendell lamented. "It's all up and down, up and down without ceasing. Bloody glaciers lurking everywhere. It's no mystery to me why he went mad."

He continued to exclaim over the ruggedness of the terrain; I didn't bother pointing out that the landscape was beautiful at least—I knew it would only provoke him to soliloquies on the wonders of green hills and gentle forests, and drizzle and mist every other day of the year.

I glanced at the steeply sloping landscape. We were in a sheltered nook in the mountainside, beyond which the wind fretted and groaned. I winced, rubbing my ankle.

"You're hurt," Wendell tutted, drawing my foot into his lap to examine it. "Why didn't you say so?"

"Because I don't wish you to sew my foot on backwards. It's not that bad."

"Perhaps we should stay here tonight," he said. "It will be easier going by light of day."

"Stay here?" I repeated, amused. "Perhaps *you* can burrow down into the turf and make from the moss a quilt, as the rhyme goes, but I cannot."*

He held out a hand. "Your cloak, Em."

I groaned, for I could guess what was coming. I unbuttoned the cloak and handed it over. He gave it a shake, then released it into the wind, which made it billow and twist until somehow it formed itself into a tent, neatly tucked into the landscape and as ordinary as a tent could be, save that it was the precise shade of midnight-black as my cloak.

"How many enchantments did you put upon my poor cloak?" I grumbled.

---

* *Pillows made of stones,*
  Bed of old kings' bones,
  Quilt of moss and earth,
  Deep beneath the turf,
  Sleeps the faerie child,
  Dreaming of the wild,
  Hidden and unknown.
  —From "Now the Faeries Sleep," a nursery rhyme originating in Kent, c. 1700.

"You will never reach the end of them," he said with satisfaction, running his hand over the fabric to straighten the creases. "That many."

I rolled my eyes. "Why didn't I guess?"

"We can keep going."

"No," I said quickly, for I had decided that it was time we came to terms with things. "This is perfect."

I ducked inside and found it pleasantly cosy, the uneven ground softened as if by a layer of cushions. He followed a moment later, summoning another tiny light, which he let loose to drift above our heads. I pulled the tent flaps together, shutting out the wind. They closed with the same row of silver buttons that fastened my cloak.

Wendell rummaged around a bit—I could not see exactly what he was doing—and pulled a handful of blankets from one of the folds.

I couldn't help laughing. "What else have you stored in here? A bottle of wine, perhaps?"

"I'm afraid not," he said cluelessly, preoccupied with folding the blankets into perfect rectangles. I supposed that I shouldn't have been surprised; I've never had a knack for flirtation. When he began sorting the blankets into separate pallets, I yanked the entire bundle away from him and strewed them upon the floor.

"What on earth are you doing? The creases, Em, the creases—"

"I've had enough of things being complicated between us," I replied. "I will never stop being terrified of the prospect of marrying you. How could I? It would make me queen of a land of nightmares. But I would like to settle *this* side of things, at least."

"This side of—?"

I kissed him matter-of-factly. He drew back, and at last he

seemed to understand the significance of my interest in spending the night in a tent, as well as my joke about the wine.

"You know," he said, beginning to smile, "the cottage would be rather more comfortable."

"The cottage is too crowded for my liking," I replied. "And I don't wish to give Rose another reason to scowl forebodingly at me. Would you prefer to wait?"

In answer, he kissed me—much more slowly than the kiss I had given him, and more skilfully too, I'm afraid. Afterwards he didn't lean back as I'd expected, but trailed his lips down my neck, sending a shiver skittering through me.

"You can begin by removing your clothes," I said. "If you would like to. To clarify, this is a suggestion, not a demand."

"Oh, Em," he said, laughing softly against my neck. I had my hands in his hair, which was now quite mussed, something that made me absurdly happy.

"I'm sorry," I said, self-conscious now. "Perhaps I shouldn't talk."

"Whyever not?" He drew back, examining me with a perplexed smile. "I like the way you talk. And everything else about you, in fact. Is that not clear by now?"

I felt laughter bubble up inside me, but I hid it behind a mock-serious expression. "I'm not sure."

His smile changed, and he trailed his hand down the side of my neck. "Let me show you."

6th October–late

I have never abandoned a field study before, and I do not wish to go, of course—we are too close to the nexus. And yet perhaps it would be for the best if we did leave—if we hid awhile, in Italy perhaps, or Switzerland, until Wendell has recovered from the poison, and then began our search for the nexus anew in Russia?

I am rambling. In truth, I have no idea what to do. But we certainly cannot sit here and wait for the villagers to come for us with torches.

But I am getting ahead of myself.

I woke before Wendell this morning. I have never known what to do in such a situation—I supposed that the romantic thing would be to watch him sleep, but I've never had much use for romance, and so I pushed open the flaps of the tent to admit the predawn light, pulled on the first item of clothing I came across amidst the scatter—Wendell's jumper—and settled in to write in my journal. He stirred shortly after and gave a murmur of laughter.

"Other women snore, or talk in their sleep. I don't recall ever being woken by the sound of vigorous pencil scratching."

"You could always ask one of those other women to marry

you," I said. "Though it may not be easy to find one who is quite so tolerant of faerie assassins and strange quests as I am."

He leaned his head against my shoulder playfully and watched me write, which I did not mind, much to my own surprise; normally I hate being observed when I am working. "Only you would put footnotes in your diary," was his only comment.

"Will you ever answer my question?"

He shifted slightly so that his hair tickled my neck. "Which one?"

"You know which one," I said. "The one you have been avoiding since that meeting in your office. Why is your step-mother after you now? I thought she couldn't kill you."

"She can't safeguard her claim to the throne forever. She must leave open a path to her defeat. There's a difference."

"Is there?" I closed my journal and looked at him. "If you won't overthrow her, who will? Are you not her only rival for the throne?"

He avoided my gaze, picking at a loose thread in the blanket. "She assumes that if I am killed, you will attempt to avenge me."

I choked. "I—will *what*?"

"I'm sorry, Em." He truly did look regretful. "Somehow she learned of my proposal to you last winter."

"How?"

"Spies, I imagine. We speak of it often enough."

I groaned, thinking of our jests.

"I should have known it," he said. "She has always been one to keep an eye on those she loves."

At this, I let out the ghost of a laugh. "She loves you, does she?"

He looked surprised, as if there were no contradiction at all. "Of course. She raised me from the age of seven. I have more memories of her than of my birth mother."

"So that's it," I said. "She is sending assassins after you because she thinks we are engaged, and thus her mad faerie logic tells her that I will devote my life to seeking revenge against her if she murders you."

"That's generally how these things go. You know the stories."

Of course I did. Deirdre and the River Lord; The Princess of Shell Halls.* "If she only needs to leave one of us alive, she could simply kill *me*," I pointed out. "That would leave you to your own devices. Woeful devices; you've proven yourself largely useless at tracking down your door."

"Yes, well, she is somewhat more worried about me than she is about you. She doesn't know how fearsome you are."

"Not fearsome enough to overthrow a faerie queen, I assure you."

He kissed me. "You needn't worry, Em. I have no intention of perishing, and if I do, I forbid you from seeking revenge on my behalf."

I felt oddly guilty at that—I knew it was ridiculous; he may not have intended to put us in this position, but nevertheless, here we were, all because of his ridiculous proposal. "You have no business forbidding me from anything," I said. "I certainly

---

* Deirdre was an Irish queen who sent her army into Faerie to avenge the death of her faerie husband at the hands of his brothers. The Princess of Shell Halls is likely of French origin, a variant of *La princesse et le trône de sel*. "Sel," meaning salt, was likely mistranslated as "shell," but the framework of the story is the same: a faerie princess of an undersea kingdom dedicates her life to avenging the death of her betrothed, the prince of an island realm. This despite the fact that leaving the sea condemns her to a slow death, to which she eventually succumbs only after murdering the last of the conspirators in her fiancé's murder.

would retaliate if she harmed you, if I had a shred of magic with which to go about it."

"What would be the point?" he said with a shrug. "I've never understood this addiction to vengeance many Folk have. I think it must be my grandmother's blood. The *oíche sidhe* may not have the most patient tempers, but they do not concern themselves with revenge quests, for what do they have to do with the practicalities of running a household? No, Em—if I am killed, I give you permission to write a paper about it. I know you will find that a more satisfying endeavour."

His fingers had begun to twine through my hair. I gave up arguing—for the moment—and set my journal aside.

Later, Wendell reached beneath my pillow and pulled free the ribbon that was trapped there. "You dropped this."

He handed it to me. It was green—one of Eichorn's, which I had placed in my pocket the previous night. There was a second one tangled in the bedding, blue with a frayed edge. I squeezed them together in my fist.

"Eichorn," I muttered, then bolted upright. "We can use these to find him. Can't we?"

He put his elbow over his eyes and gave a breath of laughter. The morning light pooled in the hollow between his collarbones and picked out the gold in his hair. "Well, I knew it was too much to hope for cuddling," he said, "but I expected to be allowed to sleep in at least."

"Don't you want to find your door?"

"No," he said, reaching for me. "At this precise moment, I can genuinely say that my only wish is to remain here with you. Those two have been stumbling around these mountains for fifty years; surely they'll survive another hour or two."

I glanced at him, and I could not stop my gaze from lingering on the spill of his hair and the sharp lines of his shoulders. Well, I would not have minded waiting either.

He seemed to sense this and took my hand with a smile. "Was I a disappointment?"

"No," I said—somewhat too emphatically, and felt my face redden. That was my mistake—his expression became dreadfully mischievous.

"Nothing compared to that Leopold fellow, though," he said.

"I don't know why you need to bring him into this."

"Well, you've mentioned him so many times."

"I have mentioned him all of three times in your presence," I exclaimed.

"Really?" He seemed genuinely surprised. "I could have sworn it was at least a dozen."

"Not to mention, I'd no idea you had any interest in me," I said.

"Yes, you did."

Fortunately, there was a ridiculous number of pillows scattered about. I seized one and flung it at his face.

He laughed and kissed me. I forgot everything for a moment, but when he pulled back, the opportunity before us reasserted itself.

"Could you track Eichorn using the ribbons?" I pressed.

"I doubt it. I'm not a bloodhound."

I made a frustrated sound. "He was so close last night. He and de Grey both. If only I could have spoken with them."

"How?" he said. "Eichorn has spoken with you before, it's true—but we don't know how he manages this, and each time it has been he who has taken the initiative. They are both trapped deep in Faerie. Her more than him."

I frowned. "How do you know that?"

But he only shook his head, examining the ribbons. "You know, it *might* be possible—I can sense that bumbling man when I hold these, as if they are a tether and he is flailing about at the other end."

"So you are a bloodhound after all."

"Perhaps . . . Do you remember those silly directions he gave you?"

"Is that relevant?" I asked, surprised. "I just assumed he was raving."

Nevertheless, I repeated the directions. We dressed, Wendell muttering complaints all the while. I followed him out of the tent, then eyed the thing, wondering how to go about transforming it back into my familiar old cloak. I grabbed a handful of the peaked roof, whereupon it folded itself back into its former iteration with a soft rustling of cloth. I could not help staring, and would have liked to examine it, as a child might examine a magician's sleeve for evidence of secret pockets and the like, but Wendell was already striding away. I threw the cloak back on and hastened to catch up.

"Surely Eichorn's directions are useless," I said. "How are we to know where his brother died? Or where he saw a ghost?"

"Oh, I don't think that has anything to do with Eichorn," Wendell replied. "It sounds to me like the sort of useless directions bogles enjoy giving lost mortals, the better to drive them to utter madness. It's a sport for them, but then they are miserable creatures with nothing better to do. I think if we find them, we may find Eichorn."

"Of course," I murmured. Eichorn's babbling hadn't been some sort of prophetic message delivered for my benefit—he had simply been repeating the bogles' directions to himself, under the mistaken assumption this would do him any good.

Wendell paused to glance down at the ribbons, then scanned the landscape with a wince. "I don't really know what

I'm doing," he admitted. "But I've found a bogle path. The little pests pass this way regularly."

He continued walking. I could see scant evidence that we were on any sort of path, beyond a few patches of dead grass here and there—even with my experienced eye, I would not have noted it. We reached a little meadow of wildflowers with a mist creeping through it in narrow strands. Wendell took my hand and led me around the edge.

"Bloody rabbit warren!" he muttered.

"Was that a door?" I enquired eagerly. Now that I wasn't in danger of being hopelessly lost, my enthusiasm for faerie doors had returned. "Where does it go?"

He merely shook his head darkly. "Just be glad you didn't stumble in this direction last night."

Over the next rise, he paused, squinting down at the ribbons, then at the supposed bogle path. "It's like trying to navigate with two broken compasses, each pointing in opposite directions," he complained.

I sighed. "Perhaps we should turn back."

"I didn't say it was impossible. It's just a rather irritating process. Come on."

He took my hand again and led me to the left for no reason I could discern, then through a boggy gully, despite the presence of an easier path only a few yards away, and then he insisted that we turn sideways and squeeze between two oak trees growing close together. I was just resigning myself to hours of this sort of tedious pussyfooting when he stopped and carelessly tossed the ribbons aside.

"Wendell!" I said. Then I turned in the direction he was looking, and there was Eichorn.

Professor Bran Eichorn stood upon a lonely boulder, one hand shielding his eyes as he scanned the landscape. He wore the same heavy cloak with ribbons spilling out of the pockets, and appeared to be somewhere in his forties. As we watched, he cupped his hands round his mouth and yelled, *"Dani!"*

"Well!" I said, more than a little dumbfounded. "I expected that to take longer."

Wendell gave me a look of disbelief. "We've been walking for *at least* half an hour. That's more than enough on an empty stomach."

Eichorn turned and spied us. We made our way over as he clambered down from the boulder. His expression was puzzled, almost afraid, and for a moment I wondered if he might flee. How mad, I wondered, was this particular version of Eichorn?

"You—" he began, gazing at me. "I remember you. Don't I?"

"I expect so," Wendell said. "You've been haunting her these past weeks, babbling nonsense at her."

"What are you going to do?" I said.

"He's trapped in Faerie. So I must pull him out, of course."

And that was what he did. It is not something I can adequately describe, for I did not see it. He reached out a hand to Eichorn—which the man took, frowning—and pulled him forwards. But I *felt* it—a sudden dislocation, akin to falling. A shiver went through the grasses, and for a brief moment, all was still.

And then the world righted itself, and the three of us stood upon a little hill that looked like the same hill we had stood upon a moment ago, but I knew now that we were in the mortal realm, and together had stepped out of Faerie. Eichorn was gazing at Wendell in wonder.

I expected him to ask the year, or perhaps where he was, to demonstrate some awareness that, at long last, he was free. Instead he looked at us both in turn and said, "I must find Dani. She is still out here, I know it."

"Professor," I said slowly, "we are going to find her together."

+ + +

We returned to the cottage to collect Ariadne and Rose—and Shadow, of course. The beast was beside himself with relief, and leapt all over me, tongue lolling. My ankle still ached, but it was a manageable throb now.

Eichorn's presence loomed large in the little cottage, and Ariadne and Rose were promptly rendered speechless when I made the introductions. Eichorn barely glanced at them; he was gazing around the cottage with a frown. I realized he had likely stayed here himself, half a century ago. Ariadne scurried out of her chair under the pretense of offering it to him, though I suspected she simply wanted to put distance between them. I didn't blame her. The otherworldly clung to Eichorn like dew; partly it was the fact that he showed little sign of fatigue, despite his decades of wandering the mountains.

"No breakfast?" were the first words out of Wendell's mouth. He was rubbing the space between his eyes.

"Julia hasn't come by yet," Ariadne said. "Are you all right?"

He waved her away. I said, "Professor Eichorn, you told Wendell and I that you had a hunch about where de Grey may have stumbled into Faerie. I suggest you take us there now so that Wendell can attempt to track her."

"Glorified bloodhound," Wendell muttered.

"Emily," Rose said in a scolding voice. "Aren't you getting rather ahead of yourself?"

"No," I snapped. "De Grey knows the location of the nexus, which we must find as soon as possible. At any moment, the huntsmen may return, or perhaps some new variety of assassin. One way or another, Wendell's stepmother must be stopped."

"Well, you're getting ahead of *me*," Rose said. "The danger is such that we must be *methodical* and *strategic*. De Grey was likely abducted by the fauns, so what is the plan if we encounter them? They are vicious creatures—no surprise, given the realm they inhabit." A vague gesture in Wendell's direction.

"I cannot argue with that, I'm afraid," Wendell said. "My realm is home to some unpleasant Folk. You are lucky I am one of the peaceable ones."

"Yes, you are a model of equanimity," I said drily as Rose gave Wendell an appalled look. Wendell took no notice of either the look or the sarcasm. I haven't yet worked out if he is not entirely conscious of his murderous fits when they come upon him or if he simply sees them as an unexceptional fact of life.

Rose turned to Eichorn. "How is it that you appeared to Emily at Cambridge? On the train? What is your connection to her?"

"He doesn't know," I cut in before Eichorn could speak. Wendell and I had already been over this with him. "He wasn't even aware he'd left the Alps, merely that he was talking to me."

"Hm!" Rose said. "Yet there *must* be a connection. Some sort of artefact, perhaps? Creating an anchor, a door?"

He seemed to be speaking to himself. "Dr. Rose, you may remain here if you wish, and work on your theories," I said. "The rest of us will find de Grey."

He stared at me. "*Emily.* We cannot simply go charging off with this man. I've said it before, and I will say it until it penetrates: your trust in the Folk is dangerously misplaced."

"Bran Eichorn is not Folk."

"He has been bumbling about in their realm for *fifty years,*" Rose thundered in indignation. "Who knows what enchantments they've placed upon him? He may lead us right into some bogle's trap."

"I am not enchanted," Eichorn said coldly. "And I am standing right here."

I briefly closed my eyes. *This is why I work alone*, I thought. I could have been out the door with Wendell already. "Farris, I have made my decision. This is my expedition, not yours—I thought we were clear on that."

He drew himself up to his full height—barely an inch more than mine. "You are headstrong and intemperate. These are not productive qualities in a scholar."

"And you have not had an innovative idea in a decade," I snapped. "You are so frightened of the Folk, of new methods of scholarship, of anything that interrupts your safe, comfortable routine at Cambridge, that you have rendered yourself irrelevant."

Eichorn slammed his hand down on the table. "What does this bickering have to do with Dani?"

Shadow began to howl. He lurched towards Wendell, only stopped by Ariadne, who grabbed hold of his collar. "What is the matter with him?" she cried.

"Shadow," I began, starting forward.

"I'm not going anywhere without a cup of coffee," Wendell announced. And then he collapsed.

Eichorn did not lead us into the wilds as I had expected, but the village. It was beginning to spit, though the turbulent grey clouds overhead seemed undecided on their intentions and parted every few moments to cast bright sunlight over the countryside. The wind, however, stayed fierce, whipping my hair from its tie and gathering up pine cones and bright leaves and hurling them across our path.

I had not wanted to leave Wendell behind, but what was to be done? Clearly, the effort of pulling Eichorn from Faerie quickened the poison within him; he had been nearly insensible as we led him up the stairs to his bed. His bedroom began to rain upon us, and a carpet of moss spread beneath our feet, speckled with daisies. Bird shadows flitted across the floor, though we saw no birds. I pushed open Wendell's shirt and found the shadows clustering there too. I had been terrified to leave him, but equally terrified to remain at his side. And so we had left him with Ariadne and set off in pursuit of the one person who knew the way to his realm.

And what then? I pushed the question aside. Wendell would recover. Somehow I would work out a solution.

It surprised me that Rose had insisted on accompanying us, given his protestations earlier, but the man was immovable.

"I will not let you go charging off on this fool quest alone," he said. It was a determination rooted in condescension, and thus deeply irritating, but I could not help being embarrassed by my criticism of him before. Rose was not a coward, and it had been petty of me to imply anything of the sort. He was, in fact, the reason we had been presented with this opportunity at all, for he had been the one to suggest retrieving Eichorn's ribbons. A part of me wished to make some attempt at healing the tension between us, but we had no time. The weather was turning, Wendell was deathly ill, and we needed to do *something*.

"We will be attempting to track de Grey without faerie aid," Rose pointed out as we stood in Wendell's damp, mossy room, watching him sleep. I let out a slow breath.

"Not quite," I said, and pulled out the collar I had borrowed from the dryadology museum. It seems a long time since Wendell and I fought the grey sheerie. And yet it was mere weeks ago.

Shadow initially seemed unaffected when I placed the thing around his neck. He has worn collars before, both the ordinary and faerie-made variety. But as we walked, his lumbering gait grew more graceful, and he paused frequently to sniff at things.

"What does it do?" Rose enquired.

"It's hobgoblin-made," I said. "They sometimes keep grims as guard dogs. The legend associated with it suggests that it will enhance Shadow's speed and senses."

Rose shook his head at this, but I could tell he'd run out of energy for lectures. Which was just as well, I thought, given his own penchant for faerie artefacts. In addition to the pocket watch, I had learned he also possessed a pair of boots that had been spiffed up by a household brownie and were impervious to the elements as well as to stray pebbles. Shadow's collar would protect us, but it would also protect *him*. Given his age, I have grown increasingly uncomfortable with the idea of taking my loyal beast into danger without offering him some form of armour.

"What are we doing here?" I asked Eichorn when we came to a stop upon the rise behind the church. A passing farmer whose name I had forgotten—one of the many Haases, I believe—gave us a nod as she cast a look of mild curiosity at Eichorn, seeming unaware that he was the same spectre who occupied such a prominent place in the local lore.

"I believe this is where she vanished," Eichorn stated. He is a man of few words, this Bran Eichorn, a characteristic I normally appreciate in others, but in his case, almost every utterance bears elaboration. I was also unable to get a handle on his level of sanity—not ideal, that. He does not rant or rave, and responds rationally when spoken to, yet he also appears utterly relentless in his quest for de Grey and displays little sign of appreciation—or, indeed, comprehension—of his own escape from a lonely imprisonment in Faerie. It is as if his time there reduced him to a walking myth, capable only of treading and retreading the familiar confines of his story.

I looked about, pausing to rub the stiffness out of my ankle. The hill had a line of scruffy trees growing up the backside of it, mostly dead or dying, which formed a partial screen from the church, and the human-made trail that ran below it was overgrown with prickly nettles. This created an unwelcoming atmosphere that cheered me instantly, for it set my instincts tingling. There was something here, I was sure of it.

"Our theory was that de Grey disappeared in the Grünesauge," I told Eichorn. "Her final ribbon lies upon the ridge that overlooks that valley."

"Yes," Eichorn said, "that is what the villagers thought. They thought she fell off the ridge. The Grünesauge is indeed the location of the nexus, but it is not where she vanished."

"Why not?" I prompted when he fell silent again.

"I believe she went to the Grünesauge the night of her disappearance. I believe she was forced to flee the valley that night, and so had no opportunity to leave additional ribbons. The creatures who chased her caught up with her here, and dragged her through a door on this very rise."

"How do you know?"

He led me over the purple clover to the crest of the hill. "There is the Grünesauge," he said, pointing.

"Ah," I murmured. It wasn't far, that dark clutch of trees, the little green-blue lake winking in the intermittent sunlight. My sense of geography is always disorientated by mountainous regions, and I realized that we were quite close to the valley there, at the northern end of the village; the lengthier route we ordinarily took was necessitated by the steepness of the terrain behind the church. We would have to scramble most of the way to reach it, at times lowering ourselves down faces of sheer rock.

"Dani could climb?" I said.

"Dani could climb," he confirmed with a quiet pride that

made him seem human again, at least for a moment, before the expression faded back into fierce preoccupation.

"Surely you found evidence she came this way," Rose said. "Otherwise this is all meaningless supposition."

"Yes, Professor," Eichorn replied. "The scholars of my generation may not have had your modern methods, but still we were not as hopeless as you seem to think."

He pulled a chain from his pocket. Dangling from it was a key.

I snatched it from him. "Where does this lead?"

The ghost of a smile appeared on his face. "Calm yourself, Professor Wilde. It is an ordinary, human-made key. It is Dani's, for the apartment we share at Cambridge." He paused. "Shared. One of the shepherds happened upon it shortly after Dani disappeared. I think she dropped it on purpose, so that I might know where she was taken."

"Where precisely was it found?" I said, already scanning the landscape.

He shook his head. "The shepherd couldn't recall. Only that it was by this hill."

"But you didn't find a door?" I pressed. Behind us, the church bells began to ring.

"No. I searched the hill and vicinity but found only the door to a simple brownie home. It was when I was returning to the cottage one night that the fog rolled over me, and I became lost."

"Understandable, given the number of faerie realms impinging on this landscape," Rose said. I think he was attempting to mollify Eichorn, who did not seem to like him much. Eichorn gave no sign of noticing.

"Shadow," I murmured, and the dog moved closer to me. Together we conducted a systematic search of the hillside. I found the brownie door easily—a hollow place in the hill with a lot of yellow buttercups outside it, jarring against the clover. It was perhaps an hour before I found the *other* door.

"There," I said. The rain was by this time falling in sheets, and we were all of us drenched and shivering, even Eichorn.

Rose, who had been huffing and muttering to himself the whole time, came to stand beside me with his arms crossed. "What? I see nothing."

"Those two stones," I said. "Do you see how they mark a sort of path?"

"Emily," Rose said, wiping the rain from his glasses, "there are a dozen such stones scattered about this hill. I suggest we take shelter in the church until the gale blows over."

"Sometimes the rain reveals them," I said. Cautiously, I reached between the stones and cupped a handful of dirt. Then I let it fall through my fingers in a shower of dust. Bone dry, as if the rain did not like to touch it.

Eichorn touched the dirt himself, as if he could not allow himself to believe it otherwise. Then he turned to gaze at me for so long I grew uncomfortable.

"I spent days here," he finally said. "Your instincts are a match for Dani's, Professor Wilde."

I shrugged this off. "The door may be closed to us. But I suggest I take Shadow and attempt to see what sort of realm lies beyond. I will not proceed far—we need Wendell."

I did not give voice to the plan I had been quietly forming— that I might meet with the Folk who had abducted de Grey and attempt to negotiate with them for her release. I have bartered with faeries before and have been more successful than most scholars. It struck me as quite likely more profitable to locate the jailers, particularly when the prisoner was capricious as a phantom.

"Absolutely out of the question," Rose announced. His flyaway mane of white hair was plastered to his head, which gave him an older, hangdog appearance. "We do not even know if we will find de Grey in whatever realm lies beyond the door."

"The realms are a labyrinth here," I replied. "They overlap and tangle. Not only that, but de Grey and Eichorn were lost in *time*. Just because I saw de Grey on that bluff as an old woman does not mean that a younger version of her is not beyond this door. Indeed, it seems perfectly probable."

"'Struth," Rose muttered, running a hand down the side of his face.

"Why is this difficult?" I said, frustrated. Rose had spent his career studying the Folk. He should be used to such paradoxes by now.

Rose gave no answer beyond a soft laugh. He knelt to examine the door. "It seems that I am forever a step behind you, Emily. Perhaps that is how we should proceed. I cannot very well allow you to go alone."

"You will only get in the way," I said, because we had no time for politeness.

"Hallo?" a voice called. "You need help?"

I turned. It was the elderly farmer we had passed before—I still couldn't recall her name. She stood a little ways up the path that led down from the back of the church, squinting at us.

"We're all right, Agnes," Rose called.

"What?"

"We're all right!" he hollered.

"Good grief," I muttered. A second villager appeared behind the first—Agnes's husband, I think, a grizzled little man with a prominent stoop. They conferred together in German, casting worried looks our way.

"Dark soon, you know," Agnes called to us. "Very idiot."

"Yes, we know," Rose replied. "We're conducting research."

"What?"

"Research!"

There was a blank silence. "I have not much English," Agnes said. "Go inside! Idiot!"

"We have to get rid of them," I said through my teeth.

Rose repeated himself in German. Agnes conferred with her husband again. Either Rose had convinced them, or they had resigned themselves to the suicidal instincts of the visiting foreigners, for they finally turned and made their way back to the church.

"Agnes makes a valid point," Rose said drily. "We are losing the light. I do not particularly wish to meet with the same creatures who have been clawing at our door."

"Then go back," I snapped. I'd had enough of listening to others' opinions. My instincts had never steered me wrong before—had I been alone, I would have been through the faerie door already with Shadow.

"What was that?" Eichorn muttered.

I turned. Through the fading light, I could just make out a shape—a creature thin and child-height, with something towering above its head.

Horns.

Rose fumbled for his lantern, and the light fell across a macabre countenance, visible only for a heartbeat. Luminous, distended eyes; a long snout that was like no creature I'd seen. The horns were twisted and bony—whatever scholar had likened them to tree rings had been a poetic soul, for they were scabrous things, like diseased growths.

"Good God!" I staggered back a step. It happened so quickly that I caught only a flash of movement: Shadow lunged forwards, the collar lending him a nimbleness his aged bones no longer possessed.

"Shadow, no!" I shrieked, but the dog paid me no heed. He was upon the faerie in an instant, and for a moment there was only a gnashing of teeth and a sort of wet gasp, and then silence. When Shadow emerged from the darkness, he had grown to twice his former size, his snout bloodied around his bared fangs.

Rose gave a cry and fell back. But several other fauns were behind him—I think. The creatures seemed to prefer keeping to the shadows, which would have been preferable given the looks of them, only that meant you never knew when the flickering lanternlight would snag upon their countenance, like a thread on a rusted nail. I felt enchantment wash over me, something cast by the fauns, but fortunately it was weak enough to shrug off—so weak that even without my cloak, I believe I could have withstood it.

Not wanting a repeat of the incident with the faeries of the Grünesauge, I wrenched Rose away from the fauns, but he fought me. It was as if something had possessed him; when he managed to shake me off, he marched back towards the fauns with the jerky gait of a marionette.

I swore. The enchantment I had so easily ignored had ensnared Rose completely. I had to trip him to stop him from throwing himself at the beasts; he landed with a drawn-out groan.

The fauns had packs of dogs with them on leads—small creatures with oversize mouths. I use "dogs" only for want of a better word—they were rather more like oversize rats in appearance, with the posture of small, hunchbacked men. There was nothing about them that made sense, and the part of me that recoiled from them kept forcing my eyes away. Shadow sighted the dogs and threw back his head, unleashing an ululating howl that filled me with visions of dark tunnels and writhing worms, until I clutched at the coin in my pocket and forced myself to count to five. As one, the faerie dogs fled their masters, snarling and snapping at those who tried to restrain them. One of the fauns had his leg near bitten off.

"Shadow!" I wrapped my arms around the beast's neck, trying to get a hold of the collar. His head whipped back and forth as he tried to shake me loose. He was even bigger now, his shoulders nearly reaching my own, but dreadfully skinny, bones poking through his skin. He was more a Black Hound than he ever was in his natural state, unglamoured. I cursed myself for putting the collar on him.

"Shadow—" I tried again, half sobbing, but he paid me no heed.

One of the fauns had hold of Rose and was dragging the man across the hill by his cloak. He lay eerily still, even as the cloak seemed to be choking him. Several had Eichorn encircled as he slashed at them with a broken branch. Others were chasing after their dogs silently—that was the worst thing about the creatures. Everything was done in silence. I finally forced Shadow back on his haunches and lunged after Rose, but suddenly there was light everywhere, flashing across the hillside.

"It's our good neighbours!" a voice cried in German.

"Shine the lights!" another voice returned. "Let them know these are our guests. Throw the offerings!"

Agnes and her husband had returned—I could just make them out, clambering unsteadily down the hillside with their lanterns raised. In an act of ill-advised and entirely undeserved kindness, they had gathered up a handful of villagers to ride to the rescue of the idiot scholars who had tangled with the most fearsome of the local Folk, despite their warnings. A strangled sound escaped me, something between a sob and a laugh.

"Get back!" Eichorn shouted at the villagers. Rose was

clambering to his feet, wheezing, for the fauns had released him to snatch at the "offerings" tossed their way by the villagers. I would have expected bloody hunks of meat, but instead, ludicrously, they seemed to be throwing vegetables—carrots and onions, predominantly.

How did it happen? The scene is a blur of noise and movement, to my memory. I believe I was laughing at the time—yes, laughing. The image of those nightmarish beasts appeased by a hail of carrots was too much for my frayed composure, and for a moment it seemed this would become another story I told at conferences or to rouse a laugh from my students. For the Folk are terrible indeed, monsters or tyrants or both, but are they not also ridiculous? Whether they be violent beasts distracted by vegetables, or creatures powerful enough to spin straw into gold, which they will happily exchange for a simple necklace, or a great king overthrown by his own cloak, there is a thread of the absurd weaving through all faerie stories, to which the Folk themselves are utterly oblivious. I believe I was thinking of this as everything fell apart.

Agnes's husband reached us first, with Roland Haas and Eberhard Fromm close behind. I have no idea what they thought they were doing; perhaps they intended to reason with the fauns or heroically interpose themselves between them and us. Shadow had just finished ripping apart another of the fauns which had strayed too close, in his bloodthirsty estimation, to me. He was so large now that he would intimidate a warhorse, his fur long and rippling like seaweed in dark undersea currents, and forming a mane about his head. Perhaps he didn't notice the villagers approaching and saw only a flicker of movement out of the corner of his eye, a potential faun lunging from the shadows. As Eberhard reached my side, Shadow struck, his huge jaws clamping round the man's chest, lifting him clean off the ground and shaking him violently, then tossing him aside.

I don't recall the sequence of events that followed; it was all mayhem. Eberhard Fromm, who had neither moved nor spoken since his initial, horrific scream, was spirited away somewhere by the villagers—they wouldn't tell us where. Most seemed unaware of what precisely had happened, in the chaos, or our part in it all. The others would inform them soon enough, I knew. There was nothing for us to do in that rain, which had turned torrential, with the threat of the fauns still hanging over us, but to beat a hasty retreat to the cottage.

And thus I sit here by the fire, scratching away in this journal as if making some sense of our plight might in any way relieve it. Every creak and groan of the cottage sends my heart racing for fear of unfriendly visitors, either of the faerie or mortal variety. For how long will we be permitted to shelter here, after what we have done? What I have done. I have done this.

7th October

Having read that last entry over, I fear the emotion of last night overwhelmed my rational faculties. Let me attempt to clarify the events. I feel that, now more than ever, it is important to leave an accurate record of what may prove to be my last days alive.

What melodrama! Yet I cannot see how it is inaccurate.

Naturally the cottage was a nightmare when we returned. Vines spilled from Wendell's window and clambered all over the roof. The grasses were now filled with bluebells, a flower that had no business being in this part of the world, and from the cliff behind the cottage came the mysterious sound of waves. Most bizarre was the rain, which lessened from a gusty mountain downpour to a gentle drizzle, but only when one stood within a few yards of the cottage, as if someone were holding a slightly leaky brolly overtop of it.

We found Wendell awake, stumbling about the cottage in search of his boots, clearly determined to go after us. Ariadne, who trailed after him in a great fluster, hurriedly explained that she had forced one of Poe's cakes down his throat as he slept, after which he had roused himself, demanding to know where I had gone. She had prevented him from lurching out into the night only by hiding his cloak and boots—and a good thing she had, for he was pale and shivering and clearly in no state to be venturing even as far as the garden. He enveloped me in a fierce hug when I entered, scolding me for leaving him behind, and I was able to guide him into one of the chairs by the fire. Ariadne hurriedly tucked a blanket around him, as if that might prevent him from charging off again.

"Where the bloody hell did you hide my things, you imp?" he demanded.

Ariadne gave him a weary but victorious grin. "Your cloak is in the closet inside Dr. Rose's spare one, which I turned inside out. You looked right past it. As for the boots, one is in the flower box outside and the other is in plain view in my bedroom, which you hate to look at because of the mess."

"Good Lord," Wendell muttered. "You have your aunt's devious mind."

Rose took the armchair opposite Wendell, leaving me with the footstool between them. Ariadne and Eichorn sat at the table. Eichorn had stated that he would return to the faerie door at first light to attempt to trace de Grey, whether the fauns gave him trouble or no, and since then had settled into a pensive silence, evidently deciding that nothing beyond this was worth commenting on. Shadow crept to his usual position at my feet, his tail lowered. I had not berated him for what he had done, but he knew—he knew. I had removed the collar, of course; it fell somewhere on the hill, proving the vexatious Dr. Hensley correct in denying me the loan. As soon as the collar was off, Shadow was his old self again, only a little tired—he had fallen behind us a few times during the return journey, hobbling along determinedly until I noticed and ran back to him. I hugged him each time, my guilt brimming over, but still he knew that something was amiss between us, and tensed whenever I did this, as if he did not know what to expect, an embrace or a blow.

"I hate fauns," Wendell said when I finally stuttered to the end of our tale of misadventure, and Rose had added his pessimistic assessment of Eberhard's injuries. "Tedious creatures! I shall banish them to the depths of the Weeping Mines when I am king again."

He reached down to pat Shadow's head. Wendell's reaction to my account of Shadow's terrifying rampage had consisted primarily of puzzlement at the fuss we were making over it, coupled with lavish praise of the beast for defending us from the fauns.

"It was dark, Em," he said, noticing my expression. "Those dreadful creatures were attacking—the villagers meant well, but they should not have got in the way. You cannot blame Shadow, surely."

"No," I said, leaving unmentioned the fact that, while I did not fault Shadow, he had frightened me. I was frightened of my own dear beast, and it felt like a sore I could not stop touching. "What happened was my fault alone. I brought him here. I put that collar on him, when I did not know the effects it would have beyond a few stories I had read." God, what an idiot I had been.

Wendell smiled and gripped Shadow's muzzle between his hands, giving him an indulgent neck rub that made the dog's eyelids droop. "Personally, I've never thought Shadow to be in need of enhancement. Are you, dear one?"

"I do wish *they* would stop," Ariadne said, shifting in her chair. She was paying little attention to the conversation, too distracted by the ominous scrapes and bumps coming from the other side of our door. We had never heard our nightly visitors so clearly before. I wondered if the lashing rain had summoned them somehow, the worst storm since our arrival. While it did not touch the cottage, we could hear the howl of the wind through the valley. Ariadne had risen three times to check that the lock was properly engaged.

Rose had been nearly silent since we returned to the cottage. Now he bestirred himself from the armchair opposite, where he'd been sat in a contemplative slump with his hands folded over his rounded belly. I braced myself for the invective I deserved, but Rose simply said, "I believe we should pack up our things. I will venture down to the café at first light to enquire after Eberhard's health—and to get a sense of the mood. But I think it likely the villagers will evict us. We riled up their Folk, and were the cause of an attack upon a local notable. Dryadologists have been chased out of villages for less."

"Yes," Wendell agreed. He was holding my hand—I had not noticed him take it—and was gently running his thumb over my knuckles. "Don't take it too hard, Em—it's not as if we've had much luck here. We will try one of the Russian sites."

"You're in no condition to be travelling to Russia!"

"Oh—another of Poe's cakes will set me right," he said blithely, but I did not believe him. He was trying to assuage my conscience. A cold fog settled over me as I realized the extent of my mistake, which may have not only taken the life of one of the villagers, a man who had shown us nothing but welcome and kindness, but destroyed our hopes of finding the nexus, perhaps for good. Darkness blotted my sight.

"Perhaps the villagers will not be so set against us," Ariadne was saying as I stood and made my way towards the stairs. Wendell gave me a sharp look but did not try to stop me. "I'm friends with several of the Haas girls. They may be able to talk the others round."

Rose murmured something in reply, but I did not hear. I stumbled up the stairs to my bedroom—Shadow did not follow, which only increased my feeling of wretchedness. I found the bloody faerie foot halfway across the floor, and it began a slow drift towards the door as soon as I opened it. I snatched the thing up—was it my imagination, or did it feel warmer than before?—and shoved it back under the bed. I must have left a gap in the circle of salt, and I carefully poured another thick ring around it.

My door opened as I stood with the salt in one hand, the other resting upon the windowsill as I gazed unseeing into the storm. I turned, expecting Wendell; but to my surprise, it was Rose.

"Ah," I said. "So you've decided to respect my dignity a little, and upbraid me away from the others."

He frowned and merely continued to stand there. "Well?" I prompted. "You might as well begin. My arrogance has made me too unafraid of the Folk, too dismissive of the danger they represent. No, never mind—you could skip over that, since the thought has run through my head a dozen times in the past minute alone."

"Emily," he said, "I find the fuss you are making over this rather ridiculous."

I was so astonished I nearly dropped the salt. "You *what*?"

He sat at the foot of my bed. "We could use you downstairs to strategize our next move, and yet you seem occupied with beating yourself up over what happened on that hill."

I let out a sharp breath. "You sound like Wendell."

"The one time we'll agree then," Rose said. "I don't say any of this out of callousness. But it's rather self-indulgent, isn't it? Because of your mistake, everything's gone to pot. Now you must help us find a way out of it, not shut yourself away to sulk."

I sat heavily beside him. "I thought for a moment you were going to offer me some inspirational story. Something very wise to motivate me to find some solution to what I've wrought here."

"I wouldn't patronize you. There is no solution to what happened to Eberhard. You will carry it with you for the remainder of your days." He paused. "Why—would you like a story?"

I gave a breath of laughter and rested my face in my hands. "Yes, I suppose I would."

"Very well. Though I make no promises on the wisdom front. Here is a tale from one of my first forays into the Alps.

"I have been studying the folklore of this region since I was a young man—no, I will not specify how long ago this was. Suffice it to say that the era was archaic enough that some of the older scholars were still speculating about the existence of other supernatural entities—ghosts; witches—and arguing over whether certain of the Folk should be categorized as separate creatures entirely. Of course, we are now reasonably certain the reverse is true—many of the old tales attributed to demons and haunts and the like were, in fact, about the Folk, or those mortals who had formed a close relationship with them and were thus believed to have their own sorcery. In any case, I had just arrived from a sojourn in Scotland, investigating a particularly tetchy boggart who liked to impersonate various individuals in the village he had claimed as his home— unusual, that,* which naturally the locals found unsettling.

"I was happy to have a more straightforward subject of study in the Swiss Alps—disproving the existence of a ghost, which the locals thought haunted an abandoned cottage high in the alpine. The hypothesis I formed—which I eventually

---

* Boggarts, bodiless faeries who can take on any shape they choose, generally attach themselves to a single household. Often they remain even after their mortal family is deceased, which is why so many Scottish ruins have boggarts living in them.

proved correct, though it took two seasons of fieldwork—was that the supposed ghost was in fact a type of Swiss banshee known as the 'shrieking kobold' elsewhere in the country. At the beginning, though, I was greatly baffled. I slept in the cottage for a week, whilst the creature wandered about in the attic, moaning and rattling chains. I should have known then that someone was having a spot of fun with me, but I took myself very seriously at that age, and the possibility failed to cross my mind. I was further baffled when, during various interviews with the local populace, villagers would suddenly start spouting utter nonsense. I would ask them to describe their sightings of the ghost, and they would begin telling me about the intricacies of hummingbird husbandry, or the proper way to launder a rosebush. Each villager I spoke to had no memory of the encounter when I saw them the next day.

"Perhaps you've guessed the cause of all this already—yes, I can tell you have. That bloody boggart had hitched a ride in one of the artefacts I'd brought with me all the way from Caithness, a portrait of his last human companion. He had been impersonating the Swiss villagers as he'd done in Scotland. He also impersonated the supposed ghost. He stole the villagers' clothes—women's dresses, bathrobes, the priest's cassock, you name it—and paraded through town in them in his invisible form. Naturally the villagers knew this wasn't *their* ghost, which had never done such a thing, and so they simply found him a nuisance. They began threatening to turn me out, and while I pleaded with the boggart to stop his nonsense, he insisted on parading about the village in the mayor's Sunday best, making that silly chain-rattling sound. The whole thing ended rather anticlimactically—eventually the boggart grew tired, as boggarts always do, and curled up inside the portrait frame and went to sleep. I was able to mail him back to Caithness, not that the locals had missed him."

We were quiet for a moment.

"That was a very silly story," I said. "Was it supposed to cheer me up?"

"It was," Rose admitted. "A sorry attempt, now that I think about it. I'm not—very good at this sort of thing."

"Nor am I," I said. "One of my students broke down in tears in my office last month. Her cat had died, and I had further ruined her week with a bad grade. I think I threw some extra credit assignment at her and invented an excuse to hurry off. I've no idea how to comfort a person."

"Yes, I do hate it when they cry," Rose said.

"Well," I said, "I appreciate the effort either way." And, to my surprise, I found that I truly did.

There was a little silence. Rose scratched at his ear absently, and the silver flickered in the lamplight. Wendell had done that, I reminded myself, and I made myself sit with this for a moment. I did not know the limits of Wendell's magic, and perhaps I never would.

Then Rose said, "I think *I* should write the foreword to your next book."

"You—" I felt like shaking myself, it was so unexpected. "You want to write the foreword."

"Emily," he said with some of his former condescension, "while I don't doubt that feckless creature can tell you a great deal about the Folk, he has nothing whatsoever to teach you about being a scholar. Research. Methodologies. I have mentored many bright young minds in my day, you know. I do not wish to breathe down your neck, but, well—my door will always be open."

He said it a little awkwardly, which is how I knew he meant it. "Thank you," I said, because what else could I say? I was still reeling.

"I am well aware you think me pompous and unimaginative," he said. "I doubt I will become less so with time—we settle into patterns with age, I'm afraid, that grow difficult to shake off. But I am adept at recognizing young talent, and offering guidance. You may think you have nothing to learn from me, but—"

"In fact, Professor, I am more aware of my shortsightedness now than I have ever been before."

"Excellent," he said, and we both laughed a little. My guilt had not lessened, but there was hope mixed up with it now. An awkward silence followed, as neither of us knew how to end that sort of heartwarming moment.

Fortunately, we both became aware of an odd noise emanating from downstairs. I had been conscious of it for a while, distantly—a sort of thudding sound—but had taken it for the noise the kettle makes sometimes when it is allowed to boil over, which causes it to swing back and forth on its hook, knocking against the fireplace.

"What on earth is that?" I said.

"I don't know," Rose said. Like me, he appeared relieved by the interruption—both of us, it seemed, would rather confront a supernatural intruder than fumble our way out of an emotional exchange. We proceeded downstairs, whereupon we were confronted with a chaotic scene.

Ariadne dashed back and forth in a panic, hauling chairs to brace against the door, then stacking firewood upon the chairs. Eichorn was pressing his own weight against the door, which was rattling alarmingly as someone—some*thing*—that must have been the size of an ox at least, judging by the brute force of it, pounded on the other side. I had never heard a more dreadful din, as the pounding was accompanied by a violent scraping sound, as if the boards were being simultaneously hacked at with a saw. It was clear that our nocturnal visitors had abandoned their attempts at scratching their way through our door and were now determined to smash it to bits. Another particularly vicious *boom* summoned a hail of dust from the ceiling.

Wendell, meanwhile, remained sat in his chair with the blanket over his legs, looking interested but not particularly alarmed by the proceedings. He was having tea.

"Why is this happening now?" I demanded of no one in particular.

"It's the offerings," Ariadne said in a moan. "What with everything, we forgot to leave them out! Oh, God—they are going to eat *us* now!"

"The offerings," I repeated. I turned to Wendell. "Is that it?"

He gave me a faint smile and shrugged, then went back to watching the door, one long finger tapping thoughtfully against the teacup.

"Aunt!" Ariadne cried. She was pressing herself against the door now too, as a long crack appeared in one of the boards. "Perhaps it's the faerie foot—what do you think? Could it be the faun who lost it, come to demand that we give it back? Perhaps if we handed it over, they would leave us alone."

"Hmm," I said, considering this. It caused a number of memories to surface—Wendell's dismissive attitude towards our nightly terrorists; their disdain for our offerings. Eichorn's appearance, how he'd haunted me like a ghost—the foot was connected to *that* too. I'd smuggled it out of that dusty basement archive in Scotland only two days before he first appeared to me.

"Professor," I said to him, "you don't have something belonging to the fauns on your person, do you?"

He tore his gaze away from the door. Rather than responding, he considered my question in silence, then calmly drew another chain out from around his neck. From it dangled a single tooth, disturbingly long and sharp, like something one might expect to see in a museum display on carnivorous dinosaurs.

"Dani set a trap for the fauns," he said. "Perhaps a month or two before she disappeared. She thought she might convince one to lead her to the nexus in exchange for its freedom. But the trap accidentally killed the creature. She kept one of the horns for her own research, then had the body sent back to the dryadology department at Edinburgh for display at their museum. They decided to keep only a few parts and sold the rest to some American university."

"A foot," I murmured. "They kept a foot."

He nodded slowly. "And this tooth. I thought it might come in handy when I went in search of her—a bargaining chip, perhaps—so I brought it with me to Austria."

I absorbed this. "Yes. It all makes sense to me now." I turned to Ariadne. "Yours is a clever theory. I'm embarrassed to admit I had not considered the foot before as a possible reason for our nightly pestering."

She blushed and looked relieved. "Then—then we will return it? Perhaps if we tossed it out the window, they would not—"

"No," I said. "The foot remains with us. Stand back, both of you."

They stood back, though Eichorn remained at the ready to brace himself. Eerily, the pounding and scraping ceased as I removed one of the chairs, then the firewood, then went back for the final chair.

"What—what are you doing?" Ariadne said.

"What does it look like?" I started back with a strangled cry as the pounding resumed, a battering ram only inches from my face. Ariadne and Rose screamed. The crack in the plank grew longer—I could see a flicker of movement through it now, though it may have been only the drenching rain and blown leaves.

"It looks like you've gone mad," Rose shouted over the din.

"Aunt," Ariadne said faintly as I removed the final chair from beneath the door handle, which was shaking as if in an earthquake. "If you would only tell us—"

She gave another scream, for one of the hinges had given way beneath the onslaught—stalwart things, they had at last been pushed beyond endurance—and the pin went flying across the room, shattering the glass on one of the photographs Wendell had hung up. Ariadne dove behind a chair, whilst Eichorn took up an iron poker and brandished it before him.

"Emily," Rose blustered, "you must *not*, under any circumstances—Eichorn, should we restrain her?"

The wind funneled through the crack in the door—it was high-pitched, like a woman screaming. I took hold of the doorknob, and the pounding ceased once more, as if whatever was without could sense my intention.

"Emily—" Rose began, moving towards me.

I opened the door.

As soon as I pulled it back, the wind pushed it from my hand and slammed it into the wall with a tremendous bang. I braced myself for attack—for, even though I was reasonably certain my hunch was correct, "reasonably certain" is not an ideal scenario where potential faerie monsters are concerned. But I needn't have worried.

Standing in the rain, her hood framing her pale face, was a woman of about my stature. She wore a heavy, fur-lined cloak in a Victorian cut, which had several ribbons spilling from the pockets, and she held a large, twisted horn in her left hand, with which she had evidently been assaulting our door. Her face was half in darkness, but I had the impression of wide-set, mischievous eyes overshadowed by a brooding brow; a generous, upturned mouth framed by frown lines—an unusual face, full of contrasts. Her hair, which the wind whipped round her face in thin strands, was a vivid green.

Eichorn gave a cry—a raw sound, as if torn from the depths of his being. Then, without warning, the woman was gone—that version of her, anyhow, as if blown away by the wind. We now gazed at an old woman, her shoulders slightly stooped, her frown lines deepened, though her hair was as green as before. There was another ripple of wind—or perhaps it was a ripple in the worlds themselves—and the young woman was back, only she seemed, to my eye, even younger than before. Fog drifted over the doorstep, and for a moment the woman was gone. When she reappeared, she was like a ghost, the fog half erasing her from existence.

Eichorn cried out again and lurched forward, half running and half falling. He was restrained, however, by Wendell, who had appeared behind us soundlessly.

"There, there, my friend," he said sympathetically. "You will only be caught yourself. She is trapped deep in Faerie—much deeper than you were. It hangs about her like layers of chains."

"You might have mentioned this," I said in a sharper pitch than usual. "Just a bit."

"I'm sorry, Em," he said, gesturing at de Grey. "This is not my story. It belongs to the mortal world, and it was only right for you to work through it yourself."

"Oh, damn your faerie logic to hell."

De Grey reappeared, middle-aged once more. The fog spilling over her was like disembodied hands, little filaments tugging at her cloak. Her expression, I could see now, was one of puzzlement, as if she were viewing us from a great distance—or, more likely, as if she had lost the ability to separate reality from faerie illusion.

"Will you help her?" Eichorn demanded. He wasn't looking

at me. He only had eyes for Wendell. "You will not allow her to fade back into Faerie?"

"Of course not," Wendell replied warmly, rubbing his hands together. "I'm so glad you asked! Ah, what a charming re-union this will be! No, no, my friend, it will be my pleasure to give you back your beloved Dani."

A sudden horror gripped me. "Wendell, what if you—"

He reached through the fog and the ripples of the world, or perhaps it was many worlds rippling together, and took de Grey's small hand in his. Then, with the air of a gentleman drawing a lady from a carriage, he pulled her into the cottage.

As you might imagine, what followed was rather a blur. I will try to sort through it as best as I can; at the time, I was solely aware of Wendell.

No sooner had Danielle de Grey staggered out of myth and into our little cottage than Wendell sagged against the wall. Rose caught him before he fell, and together we lowered him to the ground—he was shaking as violently as if he had spent hours in a Ljosland winter. I could hear those fell birds, beating their wings inside him—they *are* inside him, I'm certain of it now; it isn't some illusion. I wasn't paying attention to Eichorn and de Grey at the moment of their reunion, but when I became aware of them again, Eichorn had her enveloped in his arms, and they both sat in a heap against the door. Ariadne fluttered about thrusting blankets and tea at people. Rose spent the time pestering me with questions, most of which I barely heard. It was only after we had laid Wendell down on a makeshift pallet by the fire and draped him in blankets, which caused the worst of the shivering to subside, that I was able to attend to Rose, or anyone else.

"It was the foot," I said finally. "That is how I knew." I knelt at Wendell's side, the fire hot at my back, trying to force a little tea down his throat—I'd had no success getting him to eat another of Poe's cakes.

"The foot!" Rose cried, looking about the cottage as if expecting someone to share his indignation. "She thinks that's an explanation! Emily, you owe us more than that. How did you know it was de Grey out there, and not some faerie beast?"

"I should have worked it out before," I answered honestly. "Look." And I pointed at the stairs.

Ariadne screamed. Rose swore and stumbled back, tripping over a chair. Eichorn and de Grey ignored us all completely.

The faerie foot stood (the word seems inaccurate, when unattached to a person, but I don't know how else to describe it) on the fourth stair from the bottom, toes pointed towards the door.

"How on earth did it get there?" Rose cried, gesticulating at the thing wildly. "How on *earth*—"

"As with much of folklore, the *how* is less important than the *why*," I explained. "They were taken from the same faun. The foot. The horn carried by Danielle de Grey—the villagers' stories mentioned it, but I did not realize the significance until just now. And finally, the tooth Eichorn wears round his neck. They have been drawn to each other all along—out of some primal desire to reunite themselves, I suppose."[*]

"Yes, of course," de Grey murmured. I had not realized the

---

[*] There is ample evidence to support such a thesis. To name just two examples: the Black Hound of Dingle, an Irish tale in which a hunter recovers an animal leg from one of his traps, eats it, and is then stalked from one end of the country to the other by a huge black dog with a missing leg; and a strange story from Ljosland I recorded last year, wherein a farmer shoots a raven without realizing it is one of the snow king's pets and gives one of its feathers to each of his children. The family endures generations of ill luck until one plucky maiden seeks the advice of a local brownie, who suggests that the feathers be reunited again, after which the family's difficulties are miraculously resolved.

woman had been listening to me. She looked at the horn she still held in her hand. "That is why it kept leading me here. I had no concept of time, in the Otherlands, and my memories blur. It has brought me here several times, has it not?"

"Fourteen, in fact," I said. "At least, that is how many times we have discovered fresh holes in our door in the morning."

She did not apologize for her nocturnal reign of terror, but merely nodded. "Yes—I wished to get inside. I was never quite certain why. I suppose the horn must have bent my will to its own—not difficult, given the muddle I was in half the time. It was like moving through the shadows of a nightmare."

I wondered if she had truly left the nightmare. Her focus seemed to sharpen with each passing moment, and yet she had the same quality I'd observed in Eichorn when he wasn't speaking, a sort of charged stillness, like an ancient statue posed at the precipice of some act of heroism. Her manner of speaking was quieter than I had expected of someone of her colourful reputation, almost shy, but there was something intimidating about the critical way that she examined the four of us in turn, seeming to come to some private conclusion in each case that I knew, somehow, would be unsparing.

"Then—" Ariadne's brow was furrowed. Like Rose, she seemed to be struggling to keep up—though Rose, who was now slumped in a chair with an untouched cup of tea before him, rubbing his eyes, seemed to have abandoned the attempt. "Then the *foot* is also why Eichorn was drawn to you?"

"Yes," I said. "He appeared to me shortly after I recovered it from the University of Edinburgh. Somehow the foot created a connection between us, a sort of fleeting and temporary door.

"I suspect," I continued, thinking out loud now, "that the faun's remains are also what kept the two of you locked in the same orbit. The faerie realms here are a labyrinth, and yet neither of you wandered so far away from this region that the villagers did not still catch a glimpse of you from time to time. You were drawn to each other even as the realms—and, I suppose, the mischief of the Folk—kept you apart."

Eichorn and de Grey were no longer listening to me—they were once again speaking quietly together. I had the unpleasant sensation of being extraneous—an overlong denouement who did not realize it was time to fall silent. It was irritating—I had many questions for de Grey, after all. One loomed larger than the others.

Eichorn stood and helped de Grey to her feet. "We will leave you now," he said in an almost offhand manner.

"*What?*" Ariadne and I cried together.

"Dawn will come soon," Eichorn said. To my astonishment, I realized he was right—a greyish light was spilling through the windows. "When it does, we will borrow one of the villagers' horses and make our way to the train. I have no intention of lingering here a moment longer than necessary. Numerous Folk made sport with us while we were trapped, and they will not be pleased to find their playthings have escaped their realms."

"Hasty departure is understandable," I said, and it was an effort to keep my voice steady. "Yet you agreed to show us the way to the nexus."

"It has become abundantly clear to me that some mysteries are not meant to be solved," de Grey said. She fixed me with her piercing gaze. "Bran tells me that you wish to find the nexus not for science, but so you may put your faerie lover back on his throne. It is the height of stupidity to involve yourself in their politics. You will thank me one day."

I stared at her in dumbfounded agitation. This was not how it was supposed to go. I had imagined Eichorn and de Grey full of gratitude for our assistance and eager to help in our search for the nexus. Not condescending, dismissive, and—well, bloody rude.

To my surprise, it was Rose who came to my defence. "Our reasons for seeking the nexus are beside the point. A promise was made, and we have the means to see it is kept."

"Do you?" De Grey cast a cool look in Wendell's direction where he lay by the fire, little more than a lumpy collection of blankets and a tuft of gold hair. "This faerie king, as Bran has termed him, does not seem to be made of strong stuff."

"He pulled you both out of Faerie, you ingrate," I snapped. "Not to mention out of *time*. If you do not help us, I will see to it that he throws you into a realm far more unpleasant than the one you have left behind, with a populace decidedly less well mannered than the fauns."

A little silence followed this.

De Grey gave a sharp laugh. "Oh, you will regret this, child," she said. "As have many lovesick fools before you. You want the nexus, hmm? Very well: I will show you the way."

"Dani," Eichorn protested. "She is hardly a child. She should know better—and we must not delay."

This was such an outrage that I could not stop myself from exclaiming, "You're the one who promised to help us, you two-faced tosser."

Again, they both ignored me. "Apparently I'm near a century old," de Grey told Eichorn, giving his chest a playful poke. "I may call even that silver-eared eccentric over there a child if I like. What odd company you have kept in my absence, dear."

Her gaze softened when she looked at Eichorn—I wondered if he was the only person to have ever received such a look from her. They moved off to the kitchen, murmuring together, where Eichorn began preparing de Grey's tea. Neither seemed inclined to move more than a few inches away from the other. Small bursts of laughter drifted towards us.

"God," I muttered.

Rose grimaced. "No one has ever described Danielle de Grey as amenable. Charming, yes. Sympathetic, no."

"I know." Yet I had not expected her ruthlessness to be turned upon *me*. Again I had the sense that I was intruding on someone else's story—good Lord. This was *my* expedition. I, as much as Wendell, had rescued the two of them, succeeding where dozens of scholars had failed. And who was Danielle de Grey? A woman best known for twitting fusty curators and getting herself lost in Faerie.

My ego thus dubiously bandaged, I went to Wendell's side. His eyes drifted open when I placed my hand on his face. But his gaze was distant, and I could not be certain he knew me. I noticed Rose eyeing the two of us in an unhappy sort of way, and I realized that I was still stroking Wendell's cheek. But he turned away without lecturing me, and Ariadne too removed herself tactfully to the kitchen.

I tried again to feed Wendell one of Poe's cakes, breaking off small pieces to press against his mouth. But his eyes drifted closed.

My hand closed around the cake, crushing it. I realized that part of me had been waiting for Wendell to make a miraculous recovery. To rescue us all, as well as himself, just when we needed him most. It would fit the pattern of innumerable stories.

But perhaps Wendell wasn't part of his kingdom's story anymore. Or he was, but merely as a footnote, a trial for his stepmother to overcome as she rose from powerful to unstoppable—to irrevocably weave herself into the fabric of her world, as the king of Ljosland had.

And if he was a footnote, what did that make me?

I leaned close, breathing in the smell of his hair—the salt of sweat; smoke from the fire; and the distant smell of green leaves that never left him.

"My answer is yes," I whispered in his ear.

I sat there a moment longer, idly combing through the tangles in his hair. He would not eat the cakes, I was thinking, so perhaps I could visit Poe again and ask for a tea. The wan light brightened, and I saw that the beech trees had lost half their leaves in the storm last night, the sharp angles of winter poking through the magnificent yellows and oranges.

Shadow came to sit at Wendell's side. His tail was lowered, and he settled gingerly on his haunches, blinking away from my gaze.

It was too much. I flung my arms around him and dragged him into my embrace, which sent his back legs windmilling.

"You must not be afraid of me," I said fiercely, kissing his head. "I will not allow it. In any case, what happened was all my fault."

Shadow seemed alarmed, his black eyes bulging—small wonder, for I am not normally partial to such displays of affection—but his tail had begun to thump against the floor. I could hear Rose sigh behind me, but I didn't care. If the lesson I was meant to learn was that I was too close to the Folk, that I trusted in them too much, then I would refuse to learn it where Shadow was concerned. I kissed him again, and he licked my nose, unleashing the usual deathly smell of his breath.

"Emily," Wendell murmured without opening his eyes.

"I'm here," I said. I felt embarrassingly pleased that he was dreaming of me—not what I should have had top of mind, I know, but there it is. Shadow gave a grunt and pressed his snout into Wendell's hair.

He murmured something else, and his eyelids fluttered. His

dark green gaze caught on me, and I was certain he knew me this time.

I reached for the cakes, intending to cram the lot down his throat, but he gripped my hand. To my horror, I saw the flicker of wings behind his eyes, wheeling in and out of the green.

With an oddly deliberate manner, he reached up and brushed the hair from my face with one fingertip, tucking it behind my ear.

At that, the world split in two.

I was still crouched upon the stone floor by Wendell's pallet. But I was also thrown back in time, days, weeks, to a moment shortly after we came to St. Liesl. Wendell and I were tucked into a little alcove in the mountainside, sheltered from the wind, peaks all around us. Shadow lay at Wendell's side, tail twitching gently.

"Is there a moment you would relive more than once?" Wendell was asking me.

"No," I said, because this conversation had already happened, and I was caught in it, powerless to alter or prevent its unfolding. "I'm quite fond of my sanity, thank you."

He smiled and tucked a strand of hair behind my ear, the gesture identical, his fingertip tracing precisely the same path over my skin. The sensation rippled through me, and I felt the two moments overlap, and as they overlapped, they melded.

Somehow, with a simple gesture, Wendell had stitched these two moments together. I'd seen him play with time before, but I'd had no idea he could do *this*. Something so uncanny, so momentous, that it terrified me. And yet that was less important than the *why* of it.

Well, that was easily answered. He wanted to send me a message. But what?

We had been talking about his cat, the formidable Orga. I was still thinking about her—my past self was, anyhow, worrying more than I would ever admit to Wendell that the beast would hate me upon sight. And another part of my mind was turning over his description of her: *She has many talents. Several I'm not allowed to reveal . . . Suffice it to say that I would trust her with my life.*

"That would be mine," he said as his finger followed the curve of my ear. "It's always in your eyes."

"You're in a strange mood," I told him, and somehow it was a coda, bringing the moment to a close.

I started backwards, bumping into the armchair behind me. I was back in the cottage—or rather, *all* of me was back; I was no longer existing simultaneously in two moments in time. Wendell was asleep again, face turned slightly away from the fire so that it was half hidden in shadow. He looked so peaceful that it was hard to believe he had woken at all, let alone unleashed a new and terrifying magic upon me.

I pressed my hands to my face and willed myself not to be sick. It was worse than when he turned back time, I decided. *That* at least was something I could halfway comprehend.

"Aunt Emily," Ariadne said, coming to my side. "Are you all right?"

"I know how to cure him," I murmured. My vision swam with afterimages: Wendell's smile flashing in the sunlight; the blue mountains surrounding us. "My God!"

"How?" Ariadne whispered, clearly anticipating something dreadful. Well, isn't that the truth? I still felt the brush of his fingers against my ear, and I knew that, as before, his touch would linger for some time.

"How?" she prompted again when I made no reply.

"I believe," I said, "that I have to fetch his bloody cat."

8th October

It seems the jar offers enough light to see by, so that is *some* use for it, I suppose. The act of writing is one I find soothing, so write I shall, for as long as I am able.

I've read that last entry over, and I'm certain Wendell will be disappointed in me. He would not like his proposal to be accepted whilst he lay sprawled unromantically on the floor with his hair tangled, and me in my torn and rumpled dress. And, of course, there was the anticlimactic nature of the response, due to his being unconscious.

Well, if he wanted romance and high drama, he should have asked Danielle de Grey to marry him.

After the unwelcome revelation regarding the cat (God), I informed de Grey that we would leave within the hour. I bathed, ate, and attempted to snatch a nap before giving it up as a lost cause and dedicating much of the time to scribbling down the previous journal entry. Ariadne kept hurrying in and out of my room rather irritatingly. I had instructed her to pack my bag with enough provisions to last several days, yet she kept coming to me with questions: would I be needing snacks, and what weather would I be dressing for, as if I knew what the bloody temperature would be in Wendell's realm.

"How do you know the cat can heal him?" she finally asked,

which of course was what she'd been wanting to ask all along, but hadn't been able to work up the courage.

"It would take too long to explain everything," I said without looking up from my journal. "Suffice it to say that Wendell gave me a hint about his cat's special abilities before, which I have now understood. He was prevented by some enchantment from telling me directly, so he used a roundabout method to get the message across." By which I meant, of course, an insane method. "I think it likely that he hoped I would never need it, that he planned to fetch Orga himself once we found the nexus, but clearly he is unable to save his own skin at this point, so he needs me to do it."

I said this with a great deal of satisfaction. I had, after all, intended to be the one rescuing him this time. I could almost convince myself that the terror coiled in my stomach was excitement. Almost.

The Silva Lupi. Dryadologists have found their way into that realm before, it's true; none have found their way out again.

"And—you will do this—how?" Ariadne said.

"We have succeeded in our aim here. We have the location of a door to Wendell's realm, but Wendell cannot overthrow his stepmother in his current state. So I will go there myself, obtain the cat, and return. Simple."

"Simple," Ariadne echoed in a blank sort of way. She continued to stand there, motionless. I ignored her.

After a few more minutes had passed, she said, "You cannot go alone."

"My going alone is the only option," I said. "Cats despise Shadow. *You* are certainly not coming—what sort of monster would I be to drag my nineteen-year-old niece into Faerie? And as for Rose, he would be worse than dead weight. Back on that hill, he was overcome by the simplest enchantment.

Clearly that healing spell has made him more susceptible to faerie trickery, as Wendell suggested it might."

She continued to stand there like a mule. "I am coming with you. I've already packed my bag."

"No," I said—just that word. That was the moment she should have backed down, as she always did. I had placed her and her objections from my mind almost before the word left my mouth, returning my focus to my journal.

But instead of turning meekly away and leaving me in peace, she said, "If you do not allow me to come, I shall write to my father."

I gave a sharp breath of laughter. "You think he will sympathize with your desire to go charging into Faerie? I will rise in his esteem for refusing you—though admittedly this is because his expectations of me are at ground level."

"You don't understand," she said. "I shall write to him to say that you have given me little in the way of supervision, and allow me to wander the mountains at all hours, despite the danger. And *then,* after I have sent the letter off, I shall follow you into the nexus. And what will happen, do you think, if I do not catch up to you?"

We gazed at each other in silence for a long moment. Ariadne looked pale, and several times she had the appearance of biting back an apology, but she did not apologize. Nor did she drop my gaze.

"You wretched brat," I finally said. "I will tie you to your bed."

In answer she beckoned at the door and called, "*To me.*" I thought at first that she was calling for Shadow, but then a scarf—the periwinkle scarf Wendell had given her—came slithering into the room in a most unpleasant manner. Ariadne calmly picked it up and settled it over her shoulders.

"I worked out what it does," she said. "It obeys basic commands. It can open doors and fetch things. It seems to like it particularly when I ask it to wrap around my neck in the latest style. When I ask for anything complicated, though, like making my tea, it simply lies there, twitching. But I'm certain it would be capable of fetching a knife to cut a bit of rope. Likely it could even seize the rope and tie it round *you* before you got near me."

Bloody Wendell! Naturally he could have me tearing my hair out even when he was unconscious. I closed my journal slowly and said, "Your life is worth more than a silly scarf. Don't think I won't make ribbons of the thing simply because it's important to you."

"You could try, but I tore it on a thornbush the other day and within twenty minutes it had mended itself."

I swore under my breath.

"I'll finish packing your things," she said, and left the room.

"That was not agreement!" I called after her.

But really, a little voice whispered, *would it be so dreadful if she came along?* Ariadne could be irritating, but she was also clever, resourceful. She was a cat person; not ordinarily a prerequisite for a scientific expedition, but in this case?

And did I have time to figure out a way to stop her?

In the end, it was this last point that decided things. Just as I was discussing the situation with Rose, there came an alarming knock upon our door. It had nowhere near the violence of de Grey's, but served as enough of a reminder to fray our collective nerves.

Rose opened the door, and in charged one of Julia Haas's many daughters—Elsa, I thought. She was red-faced and panting.

"What has happened?" I demanded. "Have the fauns—"

"No, no," the girl said, and then she had to bend over, clutching her side.

"Astrid!" Ariadne cried, and I recalled then that this was the girl Ariadne had formed a particular friendship with. "Is it Eberhard? Has he passed? Here, sit down."

She pulled out a chair, but the girl shook her head. "No time," she said in a gasp. "Eberhard lives—barely. I've come to warn you. The villagers—they are gathering to throw you out."

"To throw us out!" Rose cried—not indignantly, but with a kind of wearied exasperation. "Well, of course they are: it's no more than we deserve."

"Indeed," I said grimly. "Still, the timing is inconvenient. When are they coming?"

The girl looked at me wide-eyed. "Now! I had ten minutes for a head start—perhaps twenty. They will come with Peter and the cart, and if you do not go willingly, they will gather up your belongings and escort you to the train themselves. They do not intend any harm, but as you have angered our Folk, they do not think—"

"They do not think it safe for us to remain among them," I finished. "Yes. I see."

The girl collapsed in a chair, and Ariadne sat beside her, patting her arm reassuringly as they murmured together.

"No pitchforks, at least," Rose said drily. "I had that once—a group of Northumberland farmers thought I was riling up their barrow-brownies."

"Wendell should not be moved in his condition," I said. "Farris, perhaps you can attempt to reason with the villagers. Inform them that Wendell is sick—perhaps they will allow you to remain another day or two. Long enough, I hope, for me to conclude my business in Faerie."

Rose nodded slowly. "And if they do not listen?"

"Then you must retreat to Leoburg, and await me there." I hated the idea of Wendell being bumped and jostled down that winding mountain path, but there was nothing to be done. I turned to de Grey, who was hovering in the kitchen door with Eichorn at her shoulder, watching the scene unfold with only distant interest. "We will proceed to the Grünesauge immediately."

Astrid looked frightened. "If you attempt to hide, the villagers will be angry."

"I am not hiding," I informed her. "I will leave. I shall simply go by a different path."

Fog clung to the mountains like layers of silk, pooling in gullies and softening the jagged edges of ridges and bluffs. We had to wade through it, despite the dangers it posed, and only when we reached a parting of the grey folds, a few yards of early sunlight before the fog closed up again, was I able to breathe easily. I was so familiar by now with this path to the valley that it was I who led the way, not Eichorn or de Grey, whose memories of the topography of the mortal realm had been hopelessly muddled by their years spent in Faerie.

As we left the cottage behind, de Grey's scrutinizing gaze had come to rest on Shadow. "Does the beast offer some form of protection from the Folk? It is my understanding that dogs can sense them at a distance, though I've never used them in the field myself."

"Shadow is not here for my protection," I replied. "But yours. He will return to the cottage with you and Eichorn. He is a faerie beast, a grim, and he can guard you from Folk who may wish to lure you back to the Otherlands."

De Grey blinked. Eichorn said, "Thank you," which sounded as hollow as one might expect, given that I had threatened them into helping after he attempted to stab us in the back. I did not bother to reply.

De Grey, though, was watching me with newfound interest.

Her gaze is unnerving, as there is no sense of reciprocity about it—she simply stares at you until she has drawn her conclusions, regardless of any discomfort this produces. "You tamed a grim?"

"In a manner of speaking," I said, for I saw no reason to tell her that Shadow had chosen me, more than I him, after I had saved his life—I doubt that any of the Black Hounds can be tamed in the conventional sense. Nor did I see the need to pursue further conversation with either of them. I strode ahead, trailed by Ariadne.

I had not spoken to my niece since we left the cottage. I was not in an ideal humour, which was compounded by the girl's inability to perceive my mood. I had never granted her leave to accompany me; I had simply run out of time to stop her. Yet she insisted on prattling on about her preparedness for the journey; how extensive were her readings on the faerie realms of Ireland; the benefits of her daily exercises, which lent her great stamina, clearly under the assumption that I was preoccupied with worries for her safety, instead of fantasies of shoving her through the nearest bogle door.

"If you fall behind," I said, when she at long last paused for breath, "if you cause me the slightest delay or prove an impediment to this expedition, I will leave you for the *fuchszwerge* to devour."

She did not speak another word.

We hurried through the fog, passing a few errant sheep browsing the grasses, but no human residents. I paused a few times to orient myself. On one of these occasions, I thought I felt something tugging at the hem of my cloak, which I ignored, assuming it had snagged on a rock. Then I felt something prick my lower back—a twig, perhaps, thrown by the wind?—but when I brushed my hand across it, there was nothing there.

A moment later, de Grey said, "Emily," in a sharp voice. She was staring at a place behind my right shoulder, and her expression was very strange. I glanced down—and there was Poe, clinging to me like an insect, his long needle-fingers digging into my epaulet.

I was so startled that I shrieked, which I immediately regretted—poor Poe leapt down and scurried behind a tree in fright.

"I'm so sorry," I called over my thundering heart. "I wasn't expecting you, little one. How on earth are you here?"

Poe edged out from behind the tree. "It was *my* door I gave you," he said, as if this explained everything. Perhaps, to him, it did.

I crouched among the toadstools. It was clear that Poe was frightened by his own boldness in venturing so far from his tree-home—he was trembling lightly, which made his furry hood slip down over his eyes, and his gaze darted from side to side.

"Come here," I said soothingly, and then Poe, quicker than a blink, was crouched in the shadow of my knee. He looked much calmer there.

"What is this creature?" de Grey enquired. "Some manner of sprite?"

"Scholars don't use that word these days," I said. I suppose it was petty to correct her, but that did not lessen the satisfaction of it. "Faerie nomenclature has been greatly streamlined since your era, though some of the old words remain, used loosely. He is one of the Ljosland tree brownies. Wendell and I made his acquaintance last winter, when he proved himself very helpful indeed. We are now fortunate enough to be counted among his family."

Poe stood up a little straighter at this. "I am the fortunate one. I had no mortal family before—I always hid when their noisy boots came crashing through the forest. And now I have a mortal *and* a prince of the high ones as my *fjolskylda*! It is a wondrous thing." He looked rather terrified at the reminder. "He is not here?"

"Wendell is back at the cottage," I assured him. "Please tell us why you came."

"You wished to hear news of his lordship's realm," he said. "I have news!"

"That's wonderful," I said, feeling genuinely emotional. There was something about Poe sitting there vibrating with fear and proud excitement that made me wish to hug him.

"Yes—I have spoken with a great many Folk, who come from near and far to marvel at my tree," Poe explained unnecessarily—he seemed to enjoy repeating this point.

"As is only natural," I said.

He nodded. "I have asked everyone I met for news from the summerlands," he said, and then he added a word in Faie I have never heard before, which sent a little chill down my back. It translates loosely as "the place where the trees have eyes."

"Where the Trees Have Eyes," I said. "You mean Wendell's kingdom?"

Poe nodded. Wendell has never told me the Faie name for his kingdom—well, I cannot imagine why. It is such a prepossessing moniker.

"I spoke to a travelling tinker," Poe went on, "and she told me that the queen there has made a great mess. She has conquered all her neighbours, and now the high ones fight among themselves. All the tree-Folk and river-Folk and barrow-Folk do their best to hide, but it is frightening, with the high ones fighting everywhere, stamping and charging about with their wolves and horses."

I felt faint. "Then Wendell's stepmother controls—how many of the Irish kingdoms? Three?"

"Four," Poe said.

"Good Lord," I said. Over half of the Irish realms! That would make her the most powerful faerie monarch in the whole of the British Isles. No wonder she wanted her only rival to the throne properly out of the way, with a fractious kingdom seething beneath her. Surely it was not just because of me, as Wendell had supposed. Perhaps she was not even aware of my existence.

"Mother would not wish me to be going to and fro like this," Poe said, weaving his fingers through my cloak—I winced as one grazed my skin. "But I do not care! It's very exciting." He went pale and gripped my cloak harder. "Though I do miss my tree!"

"You shall return to it presently," I said. "And know that you have my eternal gratitude, and Wendell's, who will no doubt wish to gift you with a very fancy new addition to your tree home."

"There is also this," Poe said. "From the Fair One—I watched as she read your letter, and then she hurried away very fast. When she returned, she brought this, which she left beside the spring."

My breath caught. With shaking hands, I accepted the small bundle of paper. It turned out to be a letter, hastily written and blotchy, folded into eighths. Tucked into one of the folds was a compass, which I barely glanced at, instead fixing all my attention on the letter.

Dear Em,
This is because I know that you are going to his realm—
aren't you? Perhaps you are already on the way. Margret says

you are not that mad. I do not think you are mad, but I know—how well I know!—how determined you are, my friend.

Margret inherited this on her wedding day. Apparently it was a gift from the Tall Ones to one of her ancestors. We've never been able to get it to work—but something tells me you might.

Please be careful! Write to us as soon as you are back.

Much love,
Lilja

Poe was wringing his hands. "Was it right to bring it to you?"

"It was right," I said quietly, brushing the moisture from my eyes. "Very right indeed."

"What does it do?" Ariadne asked, examining the compass over my shoulder. It was a simple, graceful little thing, carved from willow wood, with only a tiny pearl affixed to the rim to indicate north. The needle appeared to be a delicate flake of obsidian, glistening and knife-sharp. It reminded me of the Hidden Ones, somehow—all sharp lines and stark beauty.

"I suppose we shall find out." I tucked the compass into my pocket and turned to Poe. "I have only one more question for you, little one."

I reached into my pack and drew out the glass jar where I had stored the strange substance that appeared after our battle with the grey sheerie. Tiny embers of light drifted to and fro like moths. I had sealed the jar with a metal stopper, which seems to contain the substance adequately.

Spilled magic, Wendell had called it. And also, even more curiously, *lint.*

"Do you know what this is?" I asked Poe.

He tapped his finger against the glass. "Yes, yes—*sweepings,* we call it. Left-behind magic. The air is full of it after the high ones have their battles." He shuddered.

I felt deflated. "Then—then there is no use for it?"

"I do not know," Poe said. "All small Folk keep away from it. We mind our trees."

I tucked the jar back in my pack. Well! Perhaps it was a mere curio that I had lugged across Europe. Yet it is not for nothing that I am so frequently cited for my work on the patterns found in faerie stories. So I will lug the jar into Wendell's kingdom, much as I might feel silly about it, because I know full well that, in the stories, it is such incidental little things that often prove themselves unexpectedly useful.

"Have I helped?" Poe said, weaving his fingers together.

"Very much," I assured him. "But how will you get home? Where is the door?"

"*You* have the door," he said with some exasperation, as if I were being deliberately obtuse. "Mortals have terrible memories."

And he vanished—somewhere behind me, I thought, as if he'd stepped through my shadow.

"How," de Grey began, then stopped. "How does that work? Your connection to the little one?"

"He gave me one of the doors to his home," I told her. "It seems that has allowed me to act almost as a portal myself—for Poe, that is."

"I see." I could not read her expression. "Yes, I formed a similar connection with a pixie in the Lakes."

I doubted that. Perhaps she was simply attempting to make conversation, but either way, I made no reply, and we continued our march. Moments later, I felt another tug at my cloak, and found that Poe had returned, one of his loaves tucked beneath his arm.

"Thank you," I said as I took it carefully. I tucked it into my pack—it was already quite full, but there was no question of leaving Poe's gift behind.

"It will keep warm," he informed me offhandedly, then disappeared once more.

Not long after that, we came in sight of the Grünesauge. I half expected de Grey to balk, for according to Eichorn it was here that the fauns had attacked her, chasing her back to the village and apparently inducing her to scale a mountain along the way, but the woman simply said drily, "Not much changed since our day, is it, dear?" to which Eichorn gave a chuckle.

"It's in the forest, isn't it?" I demanded. For despite the horrors awaiting me, the mystery that was the nexus still gnawed at me, a riddle whose answer seemed to hover on the tip of my tongue. I tried to convince myself that I had *not* failed to find it; I had simply succeeded in a more roundabout way, but it remains a bruise upon my ego, I'm afraid.

De Grey merely shook her head and led us into the valley, through the forest and up the slope of the mountainside.

We had searched here, of course. We had searched everywhere in the valley, apart from a few precarious slopes I'd been eyeing with increasing desperation in recent days. Was it possible that the nexus had moved? Yet I kept my doubts to myself as de Grey led us up the scree. Ariadne slipped and slid a yard or two, sending a rain of stones down into the valley. Just what we needed—to draw the attention of the *fuchszwerge*.

I thought de Grey was following a different path until she took a turn by a cluster of red, cup-shaped flowers, heavy with dew. She led us along a spare little ridge, then abruptly halted, indicating a door tucked into the landscape.

"Oh, for God's sake," I said.

The faerie door blended so completely into the mountainside that it was nearly invisible, apart from the odd, crystalline doorknob, which winked in the sunlight. It looked only a little different from the last time—the painting had brightened to match the sunlit contours of the mountain slope, and a red flower had been added, to further blend it into the meadow.

"But," Ariadne protested, her brow wrinkled in confusion, "that can't be it. Dr. Bambleby looked there."

"Then he did not look very thoroughly," de Grey said. "There is another door within."

"Wendell was a little distracted by the occupant of the place," I said, remembering the hail of pottery. "One of the winter Folk, apparently. He did not like us waking him, and made his displeasure known."

"When I came here, the house was empty," de Grey said. "There were a few old dishes upon the table—no other signs of habitation. I could only catch glimpses through the door from a distance; there were too many fauns about."

"We saw no fauns when we came here," I murmured. I thought it over. De Grey had visited St. Liesl in winter. Perhaps the faerie we had met had been roaming the countryside then. Probably off breathing frost against the villagers' windows or sharpening the icicles, or whatever it was the winter Folk did for amusement when the world rolled round to their season. And perhaps this was also when the fauns preferred to travel between realms, when they did not need to fear disturbing the door's temperamental guardian.

"How does this work?" I asked, indicating the painted door, which stood only a little taller than my boot.

"Simply walk through," de Grey said.

I nodded thoughtfully. *Walk through*. A cloud drifted over the sun, and the painting darkened as the landscape did. My absent finger gave a ghostly twitch.

I knelt, and Shadow's nose was instantly pressing into my

face. I wrapped my arms around his comforting bulk and drew him close.

"You must look after him," I murmured into his fur. "Do you understand? Stay by his side. If I do not— If he—then at least he will have someone."

I think the beast understood me—certainly his tail began to wag again. "Remember to stay out of sight," I instructed him. Rose had already promised to conceal Shadow should any of the villagers show a desire for vengeance, but nevertheless, I knew the worry would weigh upon me throughout my journey. I gave his forehead one last kiss and stood.

I felt little need to bid farewell to Eichorn and de Grey— Eichorn had already turned away, his hand reaching instinctively for de Grey's to begin the trek back to the cottage. De Grey, though, had fixed me with another one of her assessing stares. She seemed to come to some decision.

"We will speak for him," she told me. "Before we leave. We will invent a story—say that the fauns bewitched your pet, driving him to violence, as they bewitch their own dogs. I am a very convincing liar." She flashed me a startlingly genuine smile.

Words failed me, and I could only stare at her. Finally, I said quietly, not fully trusting my voice, "Thank you."

She nodded. "Take this."

I blinked at the horn in her hand. "What on earth would I do with that? I haven't any scholars to terrorize in the night."

She gave an irritated sigh. "There's poison in the tip, you headstrong child. It works on faeries and mortals alike. A useful deterrent for all but the fauns themselves. Did you think I carried it round with me for dramatic effect?"

"More so than anything else." But I paused, my attention snagging on the coincidence of her words. "What manner of poison?"

"Most Folk were put off by the mere sight of it," she said. "Those who weren't—I did not remain long enough to witness its effects."

I took it. In fact, I may have snatched it from her hand, such was my eagerness. "I—thank you. Again."

She gave a little nod. And with that, she and Eichorn left us. Shadow did not go so easily, but I spoke to him quietly, reminding him of his duty to Wendell, and he eventually slipped away, tail lowered. He stopped every few paces and looked over his shoulder, clearly hoping that I would change my mind and call him back. It was such a depressing sight that I had to turn away.

I tucked the horn into my pack—what an eclectic hoard of faerie treasures I was bringing with me on my journey! A jar of embers, a compass from a foreign realm, and a horn. Would any of them be enough to save me, if it came to that? Certainly Rose would not approve one bit.

"I will go first," I informed Ariadne. And then, because I am not one to stand on ceremony, I simply opened the door and walked through.

I believe I was only able to do it because I had watched Wendell—otherwise I would have flinched or shrunk back at the impossibility, and the door would not have let me pass. Ariadne had more trouble—she could not get in on the first attempt, and merely stood blinking at the door, her eyes crossing.

"You must not hesitate," I informed her. "You must walk through like one of the Folk, who simply ignore the impossible until it ceases to be so."

I turned to examine my surroundings. It was a cosy little hovel, the walls wattle-and-daub, the stone floor clean of all but a few cobwebs. The mantel was crowded with figurines made of some sort of black, lumpen clay. There were birds;

fish; rabbits; all clumsily made—*well*, I thought, *I suppose even the Folk need hobbies.* My head cleared the ceiling, but only just. There was a low wooden table, also clean, and a washbasin with a few dishes stacked within, waiting to be scrubbed. The room was lit by a lantern left upon the table and the crackling fire.

I was relieved not to immediately stumble upon the faerie who had taken such offence to Wendell. Evidently, though, he was still in residence, for I heard several muffled thumps and creaks, as of someone moving about in another room.

"Quiet," I whispered at Ariadne, who had finally staggered across the threshold.

I gazed about the place, but the only door I could see was not really a door, but an opening for a hallway that led, I assumed, deeper into the faerie's house. I did not like the idea of proceeding in this direction, as it was also the direction whence came the creaks, as well as the odd rheumatic cough.

"Examine the cupboards," I whispered to Ariadne, who was clutching at her scarf as she gazed about in mingled terror and delight. "I'll look for hidden doors."

I trailed my finger along the mantel. This brought me close to the faerie's art, the little figurines. These were rather woeful, but perhaps the faerie had not been at it long. There was something unpleasant about the clay, I noticed now. It took me another moment to realize that, in fact, the figurines were not made of clay at all. They were fingers, mixed with a few toes, all stuck together with some sort of glue. Human appendages, blackened with frostbite, a process I have been unlucky enough to observe on one occasion, when one of my students became lost overnight during a nasty cold snap in the Brecon Beacons. The little faerie's collection numbered in the hundreds, from what I could see of it.

I stumbled back so quickly that Ariadne looked up, startled. I gave her a tight smile, which naturally only served to alarm her further, but at least she kept her eyes on me and not the mantel.

I turned towards the front door, which had swung shut behind us. It now appeared tall enough for me to walk through if I ducked my head just a little. I gave a breath of laughter and motioned to Ariadne.

The door had six knobs on its inner side: the uppermost, which matched the outer one, a square of frost-furred crystal, and five beneath it, placed in an uneven row. The first two were of some sort of dark stone, one icy and the other matte and slippery-smooth. The fourth had the look of a tiny aquarium, a cylinder of turquoise sea shafted with sunlight. The bottom two were made of wood. The first was pale, carved with an intricate floral pattern. I could not tell if the second was similarly decorated, for it was largely covered in a wet moss woven with constellations of tiny white flowers.

Ariadne's hand slipped on the cupboard door, and it thumped back into place. We both froze. But there was no change in the sounds emanating from the hall, apart from—perhaps I was imagining things—a slight pause.

Though I could guess which doorknob was for Wendell's kingdom, I could not resist trying the loveliest first: the tiny turquoise sea. Hardly daring to breathe, I turned the doorknob, and the door swung open with a gentle sigh.

Salt wind spilled into the faerie's house. Before me stretched a dry, rocky coastline punctuated by groves of yellowish trees. The turquoise sea was endless and far too bright, broken only by an ellipsis of rugged islands. Just beyond the door was a spindly olive tree and a cairn of white pebbles. Largely to see if I could, I reached through and took one—the sun beat down upon my arm, a most curious sensation, while the rest of me felt only the cosier warmth of the faerie's alpine home.

I closed the door. "Greece," I murmured. "I think. It looks to be situated either in the mortal world or a place of overlap, like Poe's door. I had no idea the nexus led there—they have no stories of tree fauns in Greece. Perhaps they do not use it much?" I touched the second-highest doorknob, the one covered in ice. "This must be Russia. The edge of the steppe. This one—" I touched the stone doorknob beneath it. "This, I don't know—the other Russian site, perhaps? Or is that the carved doorknob?"

"Which is the one to return to St. Liesl?" Ariadne said in a worried voice.

"Here." I turned the crystalline doorknob and swung the door back, and we were once again gazing down at the mountainside and the green-blue lake of the Grünesauge. I could even make out three small dots in the distance, moving along the ridge—de Grey and Eichorn, with Shadow trailing behind. It was a relief to note that the passage of time had not already warped, but then we were only at the edge of Faerie.

"My," Ariadne breathed, and then fell silent, staring at the door.

I touched her arm, for I understood the look on her face. "Breathe slowly," I advised her. "You might also try counting to ten—it helps, I find, to have something to root you to the mundane."

"Is someone there?" called a high, tremulous voice from somewhere down the hallway. "Is that you, sister?"

Ariadne squeaked. I closed the door, but in my haste, I allowed it to slam. At that, a blast of icy wind rattled through the room—the fire went out with a *whoosh,* and the lantern toppled on the floor and shattered, and we were thrown into darkness.

"Burglars!" the voice wailed. "Trespassers in my home!"

"Aunt Emily!" Ariadne cried. "The door!"

"Yes, I know!" I scrabbled through the blackness for it, cursing my curiosity. My hand hit the Greek doorknob again—it was warm and dusted with sand grains. Wendell's was the lowest one, covered in moss.

Or was it? Could it be the doorknob patterned with flowers? Or the one made of smooth stone? My stomach lurched. I thought of the frostbitten fingers, neatly arranged—was it my imagination, or was there a rustle of movement from the mantel?

A horrible shriek filled the air, and there came the pitter-patter of small, bare feet against stone, growing steadily closer.

"Aunt Emily!" Ariadne kept crying. She too was pawing at the door now. "Aunt Emily!"

There—my hand met moss, wet with dew. Praying desperately that my supposition was correct, I threw the door open. Dim blueish light—dawn, I thought—spilled into the room, along with the scent of oak, pine, moist vegetation. I shoved Ariadne through first, then leapt after her, swinging the door shut behind me with an echoing *thud* as another shriek rattled through the faerie house.

I paid no heed to my surroundings in that moment; I grabbed Ariadne's arm and dragged her with me behind the nearest cover I saw, a weathered standing stone.

The outside of the nexus here, in what I hoped was Wendell's kingdom, was the same shape and size as it appeared in St. Liesl, but the painting now matched the green hillside in which it was embedded. The doorknob was not crystalline, but mossy, a match for the sixth doorknob on the other side.

We waited, hearts thundering, peeking out from around the edge of the stone. But the faerie did not follow—perhaps, fooled by the scent of the sea lingering in his entryway, he had gone charging into the Greek countryside. After a moment passed, Ariadne wanted to leave our hiding place, but I dragged her back.

"He didn't seem too terrible," she protested. The surge of adrenaline seemed to have left her giddy, and far too keen to view the close call as part of a merry adventure.

"One of the guiding principles of dryadology," I said, "is this: do not cross the sort of Folk who make collections of human body parts."

We waited a few moments more before I deemed it safe. Then I stood and turned my back on the door.

If before I had doubted I had chosen the correct door, I no longer did. We were in Wendell's kingdom—every way I looked, every shade and colour and detail, convinced me.

How? I cannot say. True, the landscape accorded with the longing speeches Wendell was always making about his home. But there was also something strangely familiar about the place that I could not put my finger on—did my closeness with Wendell somehow also imbue in me a closeness with his realm? I cannot imagine how this would be so, and yet there is a kinship between the Folk and the natural worlds they inhabit that eludes the understanding of us mortals.

We stood upon a hill, green and studded with pale stones. Below us was forest, bluebells undulating among the trees, a tide of purple dissolving into shadow. There was a lake—no, two lakes, the second a mere line of glitter in the distance. At our back, behind the nexus and extending to the northern horizon, were mountains of indigo and layered shadow, some darkened to black by the moody sky overhead, some greyed and smudged by shafts of sunlight.

Must I even say it? It was beautiful—of course it was. The forest in particular, which glinted here and there with silver as the wind rode the branches, as if someone had clambered into the canopy to hang baubles. And yet I had the sense that I was not seeing the entirety of it, that the shadows were thicker here, more obscuring, than those in the mortal realm, and many of the details were clouded by a dreamlike haze. Even now, as I write these words—I am still in Wendell's kingdom!— I find the memory of that view trying to slip from my mind like a bird darting through the boughs, so that I catch only the flickering edge of it. Perhaps there is some enchantment embedded in the place, or perhaps it is simply too much for my mortal eyes to take in.

Where the Trees Have Eyes. I allowed myself a small moment —a very small one—to lose control, and a sob escaped me, quickly stifled. I let the panic wash over me, the weight of my task settle on my shoulders. And then I locked it all away.

"It seems I will not have the guided tour this time," I murmured. "If your precious hills and forests unleash their monsters upon me, I shall become the most gruesome of ghosts and haunt you for eternity."

"Aunt Emily?" Ariadne came to stand beside me.

I shook my head. "There," I said, pointing to a narrow path leading into the trees. Ariadne started forward, clearly as eager as I to leave this exposed place and hide among the shadows, but I stopped her.

"Let us conceal ourselves first," I said. As she stared at me, I removed my cloak.

"Would you—" I began, then stopped, feeling ridiculous. I was talking to a *cloak*. "Would you help us? If you can, please help me to avoid notice—to blend in."

The cloak made no reply, thank God. I'd no idea what magics Wendell had woven into its folds; if he had ever considered that I might have a need like this. *Inconspicuous* is not a criterion I have ever seen him apply to his own wardrobe.

I slipped the cloak on. It seemed eager to be back in place—

it slid over my shoulders without any aid from me, which was new. I drew the hood up.

"Anything?" I asked Ariadne.

She squinted. "No—but perhaps it only works on the Folk."

"Perhaps," I said. "Make the same request of your scarf, then pull it over your hair."

Next I taught Ariadne the Word of Power—not the one for lost buttons, of course, but the Word I had used to good effect several times, most recently against the grey sheerie.

"Do not trust it to grant you full invisibility," I warned her. "Certainly not against the courtly fae. But it will make us less interesting, and hopefully that will be enough."

And so we proceeded into the green shadow of Faerie, heads covered, chanting the Word as we went like a small, strange procession of monks.

9th October

Again, the date is conjecture. We have been in Faerie a full day, if one trusts the passage of time in Faerie, which I do not. Perhaps a month has passed in the mortal realm. Perhaps an hour. I can only hope for the latter. For the sake of convenience rather than accuracy, I will continue to count the days as I experience them.

The obvious flaw in my plot to abduct Wendell's cat— besides, well, the entirety of it, I suppose—was that I did not know the way to his court, the castle in which he had been born and raised, then exiled from at the age of nineteen, and where his stepmother now sat upon her stolen throne. He has spoken of it occasionally, but never in reference to its situation.

They live in the mountains to the east of my court, he had said of the fauns. This was my sole clue. We had emerged through the fauns' door into said mountains, and thus if we travelled west, we would be moving in the correct direction. I assumed— *hoped*—that once we drew nearer, we would encounter sign- posts, or perhaps a convenient viewpoint.

And so I set about navigating by the sun and stars. Sadly, the compass Lilja had lent me was no help at all. It seemed hopelessly confused by Wendell's realm, the needle at times pointing west, others south, and so on. At one point I began to think there was a pattern to its perplexity, and spent a relatively contented hour or two mulling over titles for an academic paper. *"Constant as the Northern Star: The Effect of Faerie upon the Magnetic Field"*? It was a useful distraction from my creeping terror of the place, but also, there is a scientific part of my mind that never truly shuts off, even in such situations.

It was immediately and horrifically apparent, once we stepped into the cool shadow of the forest, how Wendell's realm came by its name. Yet I—

I have had to set the pen down for a moment. I do not think I can write the words; the thought of attempting to describe such a thing, of allowing my mind to dwell on it for longer than a second, is too much. Perhaps when I have returned to the mortal world, and have distance, the words will come easier. For now, to keep myself sane, let me focus instead on the bluebells carpeting the forest floor; the misty sunlight that broke through the clouds, blurring the edges of things and turning the world to watercolours. The occasional glint of silver from the treetops. These are indeed baubles—I climbed up into one of the oaks to check—but larger than the ones mortals place on Yuletide trees, globes of delicate silver, hollow and light as eggshells. Something about them put me in mind of faerie stones, and I hastily released the bauble to drift back into the trees, among which it hovered like a puff of mist, disdaining the notion of gravity.

The path that led us into the forest eventually brought us to a wider, clearly more well-trodden route. As this was heading in roughly the right direction, we followed it for a time before arriving at a crossroads, where we again took the westward path. We crossed pleasant streams and exposed hills crowned with butterflies and cheery yellow flowers. We also passed through groves so thickly treed that no light could get through, as if the night had turned rebel and set up permanent residence. The air in these groves was cloyingly damp, and the bark of the oaks seemed in places to move—until I realized that this was merely the slow progress of dozens of slugs. They were curious creatures, their skins speckled with yellow that glowed in the darkness. Before we entered these places, I drew Ariadne close to me and wrapped part of my cloak around her, which obligingly expanded itself for this purpose. I've no idea if this was effective, but nothing menaced us—though we often heard a rustling in the boughs, disturbingly close, which seemed to shadow our progress. And, of course, there were the eyes—

But I will not speak of that now.

During our daylong march, we encountered Folk only occasionally. Mostly their movements were heard, not seen: laughter in the distance, often alongside the clomp of horses or other large domestic beasts, or music playing, though never a tune I could remember for more than a moment after it faded. I think there were dwellings located just off the road, for occasionally I could make out signs of trampling in the grass at the margins of the path, or two white stones placed in parallel, with enough room for a horse to pass between. Sometimes, a curious brownie could be seen peeping at us from a branch or knothole in one of the trees, but I caught only glimpses of these—an impression of wet black eyes and long fingers; the odd moss-coloured hat.

Later, we heard someone humming up ahead and came round a bend to find another traveller plodding along at a little distance. It was a tatterdemalion faerie only a little smaller than me, a stained and oversize hood drawn over their head, dragging a cart that made a rattling sound as it bumped along, as if stuffed with tin pots.

I pulled Ariadne behind a tree immediately, but the traveller took no notice of us, though I found it difficult to believe they had not heard our clumsy mortal footsteps. We followed them for a time, but the traveller was moving much more slowly than we wished to go, and so we were forced to pass, skirting around the cart as we muttered the Word. All I could see of the faerie's face was a long curtain of dark hair spilling out of their hood, woven with pine cones. The creature did not so much as glance in our direction, and we soon left them behind, and yet the humming persisted for hours, echoing softly through the trees and driving us both to distraction.

10th October

Ariadne and I sleep in shifts, of course, one waking the other halfway through the night; only an amateur falls asleep in Faerie without some form of alarm clock. We slept on the shore of one of the lakes the first night, unrolling the sleeping mat over the sand, which proved quite comfortable, the murmur of the waves ensuring a restful slumber, provided one could ignore the curious little lights dancing on the water, as well as the occasional reptilian groan emanating from somewhere out in the depths.

Neither of us was hungry, but we managed to force down a little of Poe's bread, which was, as ever, delicious, buttery with a hint of chocolate, and very refreshing. Having finished the water we had brought with us, we were now forced to drink from creeks and streams. I was not happy about this, but there was no alternative.*

"What are you doing?" Ariadne asked, turning over on the sleeping mat to watch me. Something—my guilty conscience, no doubt—could not help noting that I would not be sleeping

---

* In some stories, drinking from faerie streams has the same effect upon mortals as faerie wine.

at all if not for Ariadne's company, or at least not without significant risk.

"Hypothesizing." I had my knife out and was sawing carefully at the faun's horn. It felt oddly warm in my hands, though I told myself I was imagining it. After a few moments, I had removed a sliver from the tip, leaving the horn still sharp.

I took up a flat stone and set the fragment upon it. Another rounded stone served as an adequate pestle, and I was able to grind the sliver to a fine powder—reddish-brown, easy enough to disguise in a glass of wine, surely. Could it pass one's lips undetected? I thought it likely—the powder had no smell whatsoever.

Could this be what had poisoned Wendell? In the stories, Folk could be healed by consuming certain plants native to their realm, but the reverse was also true. Here was a poison drawn from a creature of Wendell's own realm, and easy enough for his stepmother to obtain.

I told Ariadne this, and she said, "Could this help Dr. Bambleby? If we know what poisoned him, perhaps we can work out an antidote."

"Perhaps," I said. It was an interesting idea, but I'd no idea how it might work in practice. Could we examine the powdered horn under a microscope? Take it to a scientist of medicine?

I gazed at the horn, the long, corkscrew curve of it, the tip so sharp it was not actually visible to my mortal eyes, except as the narrowest of shadows. It filled me with the strangest desire to touch it, as if it were a spindle and I the hapless witch-touched maiden.

11th October

Last night was cool and rainy, and neither Ariadne nor I had much desire to sleep in an exposed location. Particularly as we had spent the day dodging mounted Folk who would come abruptly thundering along the path every hour or two. As soon as we heard the hoofbeats, we had only seconds to dive off the path and hide ourselves behind some tree or shrub. I could never get a look at them, as they went by too fast, a blur of shadow and sometimes a colourful pennant. They were courtly fae, that was clear, riding beasts that had the rough shape of horses, though there was something off about them—I could never quite determine what it was.

Just off the path, screened from view by tall ferns, was an enormous yew. Its bole was too large for several men to link arms around, splitting itself into a dozen knotted limbs with foliage so lush it looked black. Its old, hoary branches were curved protectively over a patch of flat ground cushioned with moss.

"How convenient!" Ariadne said. "It blocks the rain entirely!"

I did not like the look of the tree one bit, nor trust faerie "convenience," but I was too exhausted to protest. Clear evidence that the place had been used as a campsite before could be found in a blackened ring of stones placed beside a smooth stump, which served as a comfortable chair. I chose—unwisely, as it turned out—to see this as a favourable sign.

As has become my habit, I took out the glass jar of "lint"—or "sweepings," as Poe had called it—and set it between us to serve as a lantern. The little embers offer enough light to write by, which is an enormous comfort. I do not know what I would do with myself if I did not have this journal to distract me from the night noises of Faerie.

I took the first watch, which passed uneventfully enough. A rider thundered past once or twice, its mount snorting wolfishly all the while. I spent most of those hours thinking of Wendell. During the day, what with the fatiguing nature of our journey and the constant threat of the Folk, I am able to avoid worrying about him, but I experience no such respite at night. Has he awakened? Is he safe, or has yet another round of assassins tracked him to the Alps? It is some comfort to know that Shadow is with him; often it is that thought alone, the image of the great shaggy beast curled up at his side, that eases me into sleep.

After waking Ariadne, I decided that I would likewise keep watch for the remainder of the night—my instincts were not entirely overwhelmed by fatigue, and I had only grown more suspicious of the tree with each passing hour. The bloody thing was too quiet.

"Stay close to me," I instructed Ariadne as she yawned and stirred at the embers of our fire. And then my instincts betrayed me, and I fell asleep.

I was on my feet the instant Ariadne started to scream—I'm not sure I was even fully awake. The foolish girl had not left the shelter of the tree, but she had strayed a yard or two from my side to gather branches for the fire, which were now scattered in all directions. Her scarf was still draped over the stump, where she had left it to dry. Ariadne was on her back, kicking and flailing, her hands clutched around her hair, by which she was being dragged into the shadows by an astonishingly hideous faerie.

It was perhaps the size of a small man, with the slippery dark skin and rounded head of a frog, and it moved like one, too, its limbs splayed and ending in enormous toes that gripped tight to the huge roots of the forest floor. In the darkness, I could not get a good look at it, but what I could see was enough to identify the thing as a *deara*, a faerie beast found at the margins of wetlands and lakes across the south of Ireland. Deara do not eat mortals—they are thought to be vegetarians— but they take great offence at our presence in their habitats, particularly if we light campfires; if given the opportunity they will drag us into the dark and hold us underwater until we drown.

I did not hesitate, for I had planned for this eventuality, and was thus able to react on instinct. I seized the hem of my cloak and flung it over Ariadne's writhing body. The garment unfurled itself, as it had during the fox faerie attack, the folds wrapping her like a shroud.

The faerie howled, an unending cry that made my hands fly to my ears in a futile attempt to muffle the sound. I could not tell if it was anger or fear, but the creature released Ariadne and pressed its sinuous body to the ground in obsequious obeisance, crawling backwards as it moaned. When I took a step closer, it flinched away from me, then slid back into the darkness of the forest, howling all the while.

11th October—evening

We decided to make an early start to the day after that—the sky was just beginning to lighten, and anyway it was impossible for either of us to contemplate going back to sleep. I was lost in thought, and nearly burned the oatmeal.

"What is it?" Ariadne said, and I realized she had been watching me worriedly. Apart from a few bruises, she was largely unharmed, and now that the shock had worn off she seemed to view the attack as a thrilling tale ripe for scholarly documentation, and was already making notes on the subject. An entirely unhealthy response to attempted murder, of course; I have never been more convinced that she has the makings of a dryadologist.

"The cloak," I said. "The faerie knew Wendell had tailored it. His magic left a trace, one the common fae recognize and fear—perhaps it's also why we've been left unmolested thus far."

"And so?"

"And so," I said, "if the common fae know us to be friends of their lost king, then so will the nobility."

"That's good," Ariadne said. "The queen has enemies, the little one said. If Dr. Bambleby has friends among the courtly fae, perhaps they will help us."

I shook my head. "Do not assume that any friends of Wendell's will be friends of *ours*. It is more likely that they will see us as valuable pawns, and shut us away in some gilded prison for safekeeping. The courtly fae have a tendency to underestimate mortals, and they are completely unpredictable—perhaps they would believe in the importance of our mission, and perhaps they would not. And anyway, it is just as likely that we will stumble across one of Wendell's enemies."

Ariadne chewed her lip. "What can we do? We need the cloak."

I had no answer to this—our need for the cloak was as undeniable as the danger it placed us in.

And so we continued on our westward course, though I found myself increasingly filled with self-doubt. Not only regarding the cloak, but our path: we did not seem to be getting anywhere. The mountains were perhaps marginally farther away, but I could see nothing to guide us, certainly no castle helpfully poking up out of the trees.

Ariadne, despite my admonishments, was wont to exclaim over something every few minutes, whether it was two fat red toadstools forming the rough outline of a door, or the silver mirrors that flashed from knotholes in shady groves, or a spiderweb with tiny clothespins dangling from it, as if for laundry. At first I ignored her, hoping this would induce her to be silent, but after a time I realized that her tireless and ill-advised enthusiasm for our quest had the same effect upon me as my journalling—namely, that it prevented me from dwelling on darker things.

Sometime that morning I became aware of an odd pattern in the natural soundscape of the forest. It had stopped raining, but the boughs kept up their steady *drip-drip-drip*, and yet I thought I heard, buried behind that sound, the light patter of footsteps, as if someone small were attempting to match their pace to the raindrops. It is not something most mortals would have noticed, but I have had a great deal of practice.

Eventually I stopped and murmured to Ariadne, "We are being followed."

The girl's mouth trembled. "By what?"

"I don't know. But it has been behind us for several hours."

Someone giggled in the distance. Ariadne froze. I scanned the path, but naturally there was no movement but the drifting leaves, and the sunlight playing through the evaporating rain curling off the forest floor.

I thought quickly. "But perhaps I am wrong," I said. "Perhaps it is only the leaves."

"Leaves!" a small voice echoed. "No, no, it's me! I have been following you all this time, not only for a few *hours*."

Snowbell crept out of a foxhole that I had not noticed before. Ariadne made a strangled sound and fell back a step— I knew exactly which memories she was reliving. I hid my trepidation and said politely, "Good day to you."

"I wish to help with your quest," the creature said in his small voice. "It *is* a quest you're on, isn't it?"

I blinked at that. "You have already assisted me," I said, hoping that I was correct in identifying the faerie as Snowbell. The *fuchszwerge* are identical to my eyes. "Your debt to us is paid."

The faerie flicked his tail. "You can't make me go," he said in the voice of a mutinous child, and the path seemed to darken.

"I would not think of it," I said quickly in a soothing tone, for I thought I could guess what this was about now. Many of the common fae—most brownies, and some of the trooping faeries—are intrigued by mortals and our affairs, much as they might affect lack of interest, and enjoy involving themselves in our lives. That this involvement is often of a detrimental nature to the mortals in question is beside the point.

After showing me the way to Poe's door, was it possible that this violent little beast had developed a taste for being useful?

"Naturally we would be honoured to have the assistance of Folk as handsome and clever as yourself," I said, trying to keep the grimace out of my voice. But I am too pragmatic to be above flattering the common fae, even if they have recently dined on my friends.

Snowbell shrugged this off, but he stood a little taller, his ruff bristling. "I found you a path to the winterlands," he said in a bragging voice. "It was easy! I simply looked about and found the way. But then *I* am not a bumbling mortal oaf."

Good grief. "Indeed," I said. "I was terribly impressed."

"Ha!" he crowed. "It was easy!"

"Do you know this realm well?" I asked.

"Of course!" he said. "We often sneak through the door when no one is watching. It's great fun."

"We are trying to reach the queen's castle," I said.

"The castle?" Snowbell frowned. "Hum! Then why do you travel this way?"

"What do you mean?" I said, after a confused pause. "Is this not the direction of the queen's court?"

"You are taking the long roads," he said. "Few travel this way. Only outcasts and thieves. Bad Folk. You should take the short roads. Safer, quicker. It will take you days, weeks, going *this* way."

"The *short* roads?" I repeated. Already my head was beginning to ache.

"Through the barrows." He smirked. "Do you not know this? What stupid mortals you are!"

"Dreadfully stupid," I said. "We are fortunate indeed that you followed us."

"I like quests," the faerie said. "But I have never been part of any."

"Well then!" I gave the faerie a bow. "We would be honoured if you would join ours. Would we not, niece?"

Ariadne had been regarding the fox faerie with a glazed, nauseated look. She swallowed and said, "Very—honoured."

"Would you show us the way to the royal court of Where the Trees Have Eyes?" I enquired. "Shall I speak my request three times?"

The faerie was twitching with excitement. He seemed to make an effort to control himself, but could not quite manage it. "Very well, then," he said in a haughty voice, while his eyes glistened.

I repeated it. No sooner had the last word left my lips than the faerie was racing ahead, calling gleefully over his shoulder, "Come on, come *on*. It's this way! I know the very best way to go."

Ariadne and I had to sprint down the path to keep up—several brownies ducked behind trees as we came thundering unexpectedly round a corner, which confirmed my suspicion that we had more faerie observers than we had noticed. Snowbell darted left along a side trail, little more than a line of trampled grass and ferns. To my astonishment, there was a wooden signpost with the word "castle" written on it in Faie, and then, below it, the same word in Irish, English, and Latin.

"What the bloody hell," I exclaimed, too incensed to be more articulate.

"You didn't see them?" Snowbell paused, eyeing me over his shoulder. "The signposts are everywhere."

In response, I could only let out a string of curses.

"Why bother with the mortal tongues?" Ariadne said. "They—do the Folk *want* us to find our way to their court?"

"The high ones in this realm like mortals," Snowbell said. "Some they lock away and make pets of. The boring ones they feed to their wolves or use as prey in their hunting games. Still others work in their court as advisors. The high ones are often fickle and silly that way," he added in a disdainful voice. "Everyone knows that mortals are only good for eating."

"They *like* us," Ariadne repeated. She was looking nauseated again, and I could understand why. This erratic attitude towards mortals Snowbell described, in which some were granted political power while others were used as animal fodder, was somehow more disquieting than hearing that these Folk threw us all to the wolves as a matter of course.

"The queen sends her guardians into the woods to hunt her enemies," he said. "Sometimes they also capture stray mortals." He shuddered. "I do not like the queen's guardians."

I didn't either—though I knew nothing about them, I hazarded that any Folk capable of frightening Snowbell would be monstrous indeed.

"They did not capture us," I said. "We didn't even see them."

"They saw you," Snowbell said.

I went still. "What do you mean?"

"I followed you all along," he said. "I saw them watching you from the treetops as you went into the forest. I do not know why they did not attack. They watched and watched, and then they soared into the sky, and seemed to talk together."

I forced my panic down. That I hadn't had the faintest inkling of any of this was unsettling, to say the least. Yet the creatures had not immediately flown off to alert Wendell's stepmother—that was something. "Tell me," I said. "Were these guardians loyal to the former king?"

"They are loyal to the ruler of the realm," Snowbell said scornfully, as if it were the most obvious thing in the world.

I nodded distractedly. Clearly these creatures, whatever they were, had recognized my cloak. And yet they had not attacked us. Could it be that they were torn between loyalty to their present queen and loyalty to Wendell, their absent but rightful king?

My cloak, I realized, was behaving strangely. When I turned and tried to carry on along the castle path, it felt as if some small child was grabbing at the hem and tugging me back. It wasn't enough to stop me, but it was impossible to ignore.

Ariadne gazed at it worriedly. "It doesn't want us to go this way."

"I believe you're right," I said. "Well, I *did* ask it to help us avoid notice—marching up to the queen's castle will hardly accomplish that. And then Wendell has placed upon it various protection spells which may also be triggered by such suicidal intentions as ours. Perhaps the cloak is to blame for us missing the signposts." For the bloody hood had been wont to fly up over my head several times a day for no reason I could discern.

"We must go this way," I told the cloak. I no longer felt strange talking to it—hardly a hallmark of sanity, but I did my best not to dwell on this. "Would you trust me?"

I tried to imagine I was speaking to Wendell—which in a sense I think I *was,* or at least a ghostly afterimage of him. His magic was woven into the cloak, and faerie enchantments are not like inanimate human workings; they often seem to have a personality and can retain a distant connection to their maker. The cloak ceased its irritating tugging and allowed me to proceed, though at the same time the collar developed a distinct itchiness, as if to remind me of its disapproval.

Snowbell led us along the narrow path to a grassy barrow.

It had no door, merely a frame of three large stones surrounding a square of darkness.

I paused, trepidation overtaking my sense of haste. Was the cloak correct? Was it madness to be guided by this feral little creature? For some reason—a fragment of a half-remembered story?—I pulled out the compass and held it before me.

To my astonishment, the needle slowed, then ceased its maddened spinning. It drifted a bit, back and forth, and then it pointed—not at the yawning door but at Snowbell.

"Interesting," I murmured.

"What?" Ariadne had stopped too—she likewise looked none too pleased with our present course.

"I'm not sure," I said slowly. "But I think we should trust him."

I turned to Snowbell. "If this is a shortcut," I said, "then we will be bypassing a great deal of Where the Trees Have Eyes."

"Hum!" Snowbell said. "I suppose so. The Weeping Mines, for one—terrible waterfalls where the high ones harvest their silver. The Gap of Wick, which a nasty boggart has claimed for his own. Also the darkest part of the forest, the lands of the hag-headed deer, which they call the Poetry. And many other perils besides."

He said it in his usual bragging tones, assuming that I would be nothing but grateful. And I was, I suppose; but another part of me wept at the thought of finding my way to the Silva Lupi, a place of scholarly legend, so magnificently fascinating and terrible, and then hurrying through like a busy shopper at a market.

"You will show me," I murmured to the cloak. "You will show me all, when you are well again."

It was both a promise and a prayer. I followed Snowbell into the barrow.

13th October?

I find the passage of time increasingly difficult to track, as I did when I was trapped in the snow king's court. My memory grows patchy and threadbare. I wonder: is this truly the product of enchantments woven into Faerie designed to muddle human minds, as we scholars have always speculated? Or is the explanation more innocent, and yet more terrible: that in Faerie are things that lie beyond the limits of human understanding, and thus the primitive system of record-keeping that is our mortal memory?

But away with all this theorizing—I am not writing a paper for peer review. In maintaining this journal, I am trying, more than anything else, to keep myself sane.

I believe the barrow we passed through contained a faerie village. I have retained an impression of lantern-lit doors built into trees; silver ladders leading up into a silver-strung canopy beneath a glittering night sky—were we still in the barrow then? Was it truly sky, or enchantment? And certainly there were many Folk, Folk of all descriptions, some human-seeming and some decidedly *not*, though my memory fails me particularly at this point, apart from a few fragments of terror lodged there like splinters. There is an image of an enormous fox with the long legs and mane of a horse, tied to a hitching post outside a—tavern, perhaps? Music and laughter spilling out into the road. I do not recall us attracting attention, perhaps because we were not the only mortals there. I remember a pack of feral-looking human children running through the lanes with a white wolf, and a lone woman, her clothes filthy, her hair tangled and growing past her knees, curled up on a doorstep, sobbing.

There was another barrow after that, also containing a starlit village, but of this I can say even less. Were there fireworks? For I remember a crackling sound and an explosion of lights in the sky; Folk *ooh*ing and *aah*ing. But it is also possible that it was some display of magic, perhaps a duel. We spent a night there—possibly two.

And then, abruptly—I have no memory of the steps that led me there, nor when we left the second barrow—I was gazing at the castle of Wendell's stepmother.

For a confused moment, it seemed as if there were two castles, one of which was upside-down, before I realized that the castle was perched on the bank of a lake so still and glasslike it mirrored every detail of the world above. Behind it reared a forested hillside, which the clouds covered in a shifting tapestry of shadow. The forest glittered here and there; through the wind-tossed leaves I caught glimpses of bridges made of silver suspended between the treetops. The castle itself was as magnificent as I could have hoped, a stretch of pale stone walls and battlements far longer than it was wide, for there was only a narrow bank of flat land between the lake and the steep hillside, into which the castle folded itself in a neat, catlike way.

We were gazing at the castle from across the lake, which was compassed by a path dotted with comfortable benches for Folk to lounge upon and take in the view. Fortunately, there were none in the vicinity, for it was barely dawn, the western horizon behind the hillside maintaining a dark, violet hue, even while the sun splashed the stones with warm golden light.

It was Ariadne who saw them first. "Aunt," she said in a whimper, clutching at my sleeve.

The castle parapets, at first glance, had an uneven look about them. Closer inspection suggested they had been adorned with some sort of gargoyle, perhaps to keep the forest birds away. Upon still closer inspection—

"I suppose those will be the queen's guardians," I said, and then felt the need to sit down on one of the benches. Ariadne was shuddering in spasms, as I'd seen her do less dramatically whenever Shadow ate a spider, which he is disturbingly fond of. I was very grateful for the cloak of shadows cast by the trees around us.

The guardians were owls, more or less—less, I suppose. Twice as large at least as any owl I'd seen, they had an ancient, cronelike appearance, all sinew and mange with sparse, mottled grey feathers, hunched upon their perches. This was not the worst of it. It was that their lower halves ended in six limbs—long, spiderish things that extended far beyond the central framework of their bodies and gripped the stones like pincers.

"Why spiders?" Ariadne moaned. "I hate spiders. It could have been anything else."

"If we trust our friend," I said, motioning to Snowbell, "at least a few of these creatures followed us for some time without attacking."

Snowbell was nodding. "I never saw them do that before. Except when they are very full. Then they track their prey until they have worked up an appetite again."

Ariadne made an inarticulate sound.

"How many guardians does the queen have?" I said.

"Ten or more," Snowbell said. "Ten's the most I've seen at once."

I counted the ghastly owl-things on the parapets. Eight. So several were missing. Were they lurking in the treetops above even now? Would they drop upon us like spiders, or swoop like birds? I could not suppress my own shudder.

I gripped the coin in my pocket, more for comfort than anything else. Snowbell, meanwhile, was yawning, not a pleasant thing to witness—his great fanged jaw swings open like a hinge, and his teeth have a disturbing, pinkish stain around the gums.

I turned away and scanned the forest. "Let us rest here a few hours. I will proceed to the castle—alone—at full daylight."

"The creatures are on every parapet!" Ariadne cried. "How on earth will you sneak in?"

"I will not *sneak*. I will simply walk."

The collar of my cloak had begun to itch against my neck like sandpaper. I ignored it.

Ariadne looked as if she thought she'd misheard me. "What?"

"I've done it before," I said. "Once at a goblin court in Shetland. Last year I walked into a winter fair in Ljosland and made off with two captives. You cannot hope to evade the notice of the courtly fae in their realm; the only option is deception. Pretense."

"And—who will you pretend to be?" Ariadne said slowly.

"Someone who will not surprise the Folk," I replied. "Myself."

?–October

I have never felt so spent. Yet I must write what happened—for how else will it be known? Already the details drift from my mind like dandelion seeds scattered by the wind. The price of too much time spent in Faerie—yet at least I have kept my sanity.

I think.

Before I left the camp I'd made with Ariadne and Snowbell—a sheltered nook in a gully, over which a fallen tree formed a natural shelter—I wrapped her in my cloak. It could be of no further use to me.

"At least take my scarf," she begged.

"It is too great a risk," I said. "Wendell tailored that too, and no doubt his enemies among the courtly fae will know it."

"Aunt Emily," Ariadne protested. She was pale, and crying softly. I do not think she slept at all.

"It will be up to you to help Wendell if I do not return," I told her. "Gather as many of the edible faerie mushrooms as you can—you know what they are, for you took the course—as well as a selection of berries. Consuming the food of his own realm may cure him."

I did not, of course, believe this, and said it mainly to keep the brat from following me. I would not trust her nor anyone else to walk into the royal court of the Silva Lupi and come out in one piece. I was the only scholar I knew capable of such a feat, and even so, the odds struck me as rather unfavourable.

Fortunately, my words had the desired effect. Ariadne brightened, and Snowbell exclaimed, "Oh, good! The quest will not end, then, when you are eaten."

"I will see that Professor Bambleby recovers his magic," Ariadne promised. "I have several ideas for teas that might be brewed from the flora of this realm. If you do not return, he and I will rescue you."

I thought of the state Wendell had been in when I left, the dark wings beating beneath his skin. But I only nodded.

She put a hand on my arm as I turned to go. "I put the remainder of Poe's bread in your pack."

It was such a small thing, and yet it was this that almost shattered my composure. Before the tears could escape me, I touched the side of her face in thanks, ignoring her startled expression—I do not believe I have ever touched her before, at least not in affection—and hurried away.

As I walked, I removed a spare notebook and pencil from my pack. I made no effort to conceal myself, even as I reached the edge of the castle grounds, where flowering gardens, complete with elegant gazebos, began to replace the woodland. Every few moments I paused to scratch something in my notebook. I plastered a dazed smile on my face and craned my neck to gaze in every direction like a tourist. I knew I had to keep my terror in check, that my very life depended on it, but it was difficult, nigh impossible, with those creatures staring down at me. And the castle itself was much larger than I had guessed from across the lake—not a serene, orderly thing, but a labyrinth of balconies and parapets. Worst of all: I could see no way in.

Several of the courtly fae thundered past me on their horses—these were at least horse-shaped, not monstrous else-things, but far too large, their propulsion akin to massive boulders rolling downhill. They shook the ground as they passed, so much so that I kept being thrown off my feet. Once I nearly rolled beneath their massive hooves and had to scurry away on hands and knees, which was objectively horrifying— not only because I was nearly killed, but because I inadvertently crushed several snails beneath my fingers, which emitted tiny, high-pitched screams of agony.

Once I was off the path, I hid myself inside a weeping willow and bowed my head against my knees, shaking. My heart would not stop thundering, and the all-encompassing fear made it even more difficult to clear the blur from my mind. The castle was affecting me more than I'd predicted, either its interwoven layers of enchantment or my inability to make sense of it.

I counted to ten several times over, squeezing my coin. I thought of my office at Cambridge, assembling it in my mind piece by piece. The grandeur of the oak desk, smooth-topped and velvet-drawered; each meticulously organized bookshelf; Shadow's bed in the corner; the window with its pastoral view of green lawn and pond. I felt marginally more myself after this exercise, and knowing that was as much as I could hope for in Faerie, I set off again, grimly minding my step for snails.

I drew closer to the castle, entering the long shadow it cast over the hillside and gardens, yet still I could make out no door. I lost the road I was on somehow and stumbled around the garden paths for a while, occasionally tangling myself in overgrown wisteria. There were Folk lounging in the gardens, but they paid me little notice—either because my disguise was effective, or because, as I thought more likely, I was simply not that interesting a person to look at. There are advantages to being a smallish, dusty-looking scholar.

Their lack of interest was not reciprocated, I promise you. It was impossible not to stare at each of them, not only because my encounters with the courtly fae are so rare I could count them on one hand, but because they were more lovely and more disturbing than any faerie I had set eyes on before. The Ljosland Folk had seemed shaped from the harsh landscape of their home, a pattern that seemed to extend to the courtly fae of this realm.

The memory blurs, much as I try to pin it like a butterfly in a display case. The best I can do is record the impressions I've retained: a woman with her hair a cascade of wild roses; a man with tiny leaves dotting his face, like freckles. Several faeries with their skin faintly patterned with whorls, like tree rings, or in the variegated shades of bark. Another woman who flashed silver-blue in the sun, as if she were not made of flesh and blood but a collection of ripples. Some were less human in appearance than others, so much so that I had to wonder: is the division between courtly and common fae less rigid in this realm than others? Or have we scholars overestimated its importance in our haste to find neat categories for things?

I glimpsed several castle guards—I assume they were guards, as they wore gleaming silver breastplates and swords that nearly came up to their shoulders, and seemed to be patrolling the grounds in an established pattern. I kept away from these, but they paid me as little heed as the others did.

It's possible I would still be there, adrift in helpless fascination, if a mortal had not taken me by the elbow and steered me to the edge of the garden, which is also where my memory grows decidedly less hazy.

"You cannot be here," he said, holding my gaze with a quiet

intensity. He spoke English with an Irish accent that I could not place; there was something old-fashioned about it—how long had he been in Faerie? His hair was a glossy auburn and his skin like fresh cream, his well-proportioned frame sumptuously attired in silver-embroidered silks, and generally he gave off the impression of a man in the sort of ideal health only wealth and ease can afford. "Whoever you are, you must go back. Do you understand?"

I smiled at him. "I am here for research. I am a scholar. Isn't Faerie wonderful? It is my first time here. I will write a book about it, I think."

He released me and stepped back, frowning. I wasn't convinced that he thought I was beyond saving, so I began to ramble about paths and crossroads—borrowing heavily from Eichorn's nonsense—until he left me. I would have liked to question him—he was obviously under some faerie's protection, to appear so comfortable here, not to mention unaffected by enchantment—but naturally I could not do so without giving myself away.

I found my way to the castle eventually, for my next memory is of standing beside a balcony, gripping the stone railing, which had another one of the fat, spotted slugs crawling along it. At some point, having failed to locate the gates, or whatever form of entrance this castle had, I must have decided to enter via unconventional means. I could see nothing past the balcony—the room was shielded by black curtains patterned with roses.

Abruptly, I staggered back, because the balcony had darkened, and a figure loomed before me.

It was one of the guards, as tall and slender and beautiful as the rest, with black hair that cascaded past his waist, tied back from his face with silver thread. His dark skin had a similar whorled pattern as some of the others', and his eyelashes were green and shaped like ferns.

"Who are you?" he said, frowning at me. "Are you one of the little ones' pets? I have not seen you at court."

I could tell instantly that I could not have met with worse luck. The man was out of humour about something—perhaps he had recently quarrelled with another guard—and from the sleekness in his voice and the way he looked me up and down, he was of a mind to skewer me on the spot and resolve the problem of my identity later. Pleas would have no effect on one of the courtly fae in such a mood, but perhaps I could appeal to his mercurial humours.

"I am a professor, sir," I informed the man, giving him a dreamy smile, as if he had not already leapt lightly over the balcony and moved towards me with his sword unsheathed. "Professor Eustacia Walters—a scholar of dryadology."

I meant no malice towards Professor Walters, only hers was the first name that popped into my head, likely because she is such a nuisance to me back at Cambridge, with her incessant throat-clearing and her habit of entering my office when I am absent to borrow my books, which she rarely returns. I continued, "I was researching fauns in the south of Ireland when somehow I stumbled into your realm—what a fascinating place it is! Beyond my wildest dreams. I plan to write at least a dozen papers on the subject. Please forgive my intrusion; only I wished to see inside the castle."

"A scholar!" the faerie exclaimed. His face lit up, the irritation vanishing like a shadow in the sunlight, and I almost wept with relief. "How lovely! Scholars are such charming little things, with your notebooks and your questions." He leaned casually against the balcony, resting his sword tip upon the grass with the air of a man indulging a welcome distraction from a tedious day. "Yes, we have had scholars here from time to time—the last one was gobbled up by the queen's owls, I'm afraid. He grew rather tedious in the end, as you all do—ranting away and tearing at his hair, often forgetting to bathe! Mortals who do not bathe are most unpleasant company."

"Oh, dear," I said worriedly, because while I wished him to think me addled by enchantment, I did not want to seem quite so addled as the poor, unhygienic scholar in question. God—had I known him? Off the top of my head, I can think of at least two dryadologists who disappeared during fieldwork in Ireland in the past decade.

The faerie added quickly, "I would not want you to worry, dear—it is not a fate that one so fair as you will ever have to think about."

It was a lie, of course, but I pretended to be soothed by it, giving him a relieved smile, which he returned with equal relief. I am not much of an actor, but then the courtly fae are not difficult to fool; their pride and self-satisfaction rarely admit the possibility that a mortal might even attempt to outsmart them. "Sir—" I began hesitatingly. "I wonder—I am working on a paper about the courtly fae of Ireland. It would be such a kindness if you would tell me a story about yourself."

"Of course, of course," he said, waving his hand and giving me an indulgent smile. I could see that my request pleased his vanity, that he had even been looking forward to it, and I could not help being reminded of little Snowbell, the smug pleasure he took in my reliance on him, and even Poe, always eager to present me with a fresh loaf.

The faerie told me a very long story revolving around a hunting expedition he had undertaken recently, while I took notes. It did not seem to have a point, being merely a long list of all the poor creatures he had murdered and how, and for the first time I am glad for the haziness of my memory. Once he had finished, he moved closer to see what I had written, which was pure gibberish—an assemblage of nursery rhymes and inane doodles, sometimes just the word "LOST" over and over, which I thought a nice touch. I smiled at him as if I saw nothing amiss, and he smiled back in a patronizing way, then shook my hand.

"Lovely to meet you," he said. "Good luck with your paper."

"Thank you, sir," I said, giving him a curtsy. He left me, and I turned to watch him go, feeling more than a little self-satisfied.

The feeling faded, however, when I turned back to the balcony and found that it had vanished. In its place was a dark casement, its frame glittering with silver, and it was locked.

"Oh, sod off," I muttered. I ran my hands along the frame, but I could not locate the latch. I gave the castle a kick.

"Professor Walters?"

I turned and found the red-haired mortal man I had met in the garden eyeing me curiously.

"Oh—hello," I said, irritated by the interruption, which I tried to cover with my former affectation of dazed goodwill. "Have we met, sir? In the forest, perhaps? It is a wondrous place, the forest, with so many paths, paths of shadow and sunlight; paths that seem to lead one into eternity—"

"You're a dreadful actor," the man said. "You can stop babbling. I can tell you aren't enchanted."

I stilled briefly before recovering my composure. "Nor are you," I pointed out.

He gave a dismissive shrug. He was strikingly handsome, I could not help noticing—well, so are most mortals who attract the attention of the Folk; Wendell is rather an aberration in that respect—with the long, fine-boned hands of a musician. "I am wed to one of the queen's brothers," he said, "and under his protection. There are a few of us in similar positions, deemed valuable for one reason or another. We are able to live here without going insane. Yet this cannot explain *you*—can it? Unless you are some new paramour of one of the nobility."

"I am perhaps not so sane as I appear," I said slowly. "Only I have more experience with the Folk than the average mortal, and am better equipped to resist falling prey to the madness that often grips those who stumble unknowing into Faerie."

He looked a little doubtful at this, but also intrigued. "My name is Callum Thomas. A maker of harps, once upon a time—a time that no longer exists, I think. What is your business here, Professor?"

I searched his face. I could detect no malice there, but did that mean anything? What were the whims of his husband? Of his friends among the Folk? If, through Callum, they learned of my intentions, it could go very badly for me.

And yet there was something in his gaze that made me answer honestly, "I am on a quest, the specifics of which I cannot divulge. But I need to enter the castle and locate the chambers of the former king."

"The former king," Callum repeated in a musing voice. I had the odd impression that he was trying not to smile—was he laughing at me? "I wonder who you mean. For there is more than one person who fits that description. Indeed, this realm has a plethora of deposed kings, and queens to boot, whose legacies are largely forgotten and collecting dust."

I studied him. "Something tells me you know exactly whom I mean."

He was not smiling now. "Come with me," he said.

I was uncertain of the wisdom of obeying, and yet it was clear that my focus improved in the presence of a fellow mortal—perhaps that alone would allow me to find a way forwards. He led me through the garden to a quiet little nook where there was a bench nearly concealed by a drapery of ash boughs, upon which a faerie lounged with a glass of wine and a book.

He was, at first glance, more human than many of the others, but that was only when I looked directly at him—then he was a man somewhere in his twenties, perhaps, black-haired and pale-skinned, almost alarmingly so, with enormous dark eyes and red, bow-shaped lips. But when I saw him from the corner of my eye, he was a figure made of branches and moss, or rather, the shadow of one, for his dark eyes were the only part I could clearly make out.

I felt a thrill of panic race through me. The faerie reminded me of the snow king of Ljosland—not quite so ancient, perhaps, nor so inhuman, but there was a similar pattern to his movements and the drift of his gaze. If this was the queen's brother, did that make him an enemy of Wendell's? It seemed probable, yet the loyalties of the Folk rarely follow such straight lines. Likely, though, he would have been at the queen's side when Wendell was exiled and his family slaughtered. When he glanced at me, even in the bored way he did now, I felt as if my will had been washed away, leaving a pleasant blankness; I think I would have done anything he asked, told him anything he wished to know.

"Don't enchant her, dear," Callum said. "She says she is on a quest. I think we should help her."

"A quest?" the faerie drawled, closing his book. "How quaint."

"She wishes to explore the castle," Callum added. "In particular, the chambers of our erstwhile king."

The two of them exchanged a look that I could not read at all. The queen's brother gave me his full attention now, which I did not find preferable.

"I see," he said, amusement flickering in his dark gaze. He was as beautiful as any of them, but not in a way that I found appealing—quite the opposite; I wanted to run in the other direction. "Well, why not?"

I have sat for several moments, trying to work out what happened next, but it is a blank space in my memory, so thoroughly scrubbed of even the hazy impressions I have from the garden that I can only assume the faerie placed an enchantment upon me.

And yet it seems clear that he helped me—or so I assumed at the time. Given that I could not even locate the door to the castle, it seems unlikely that my next memory should be of my standing in a magnificent bedchamber, gazing out the paned window at what was unmistakably the garden far below, with the lake unfurling beyond it.

It frightened me to think that I could be in the debt of a creature like that. I almost wished they had left me stumbling around in the gardens.

I turned and found myself alone. *Very* alone—the room was empty but for the huge oak four-poster, which had been stripped. Beyond an archway I could make out another room, similarly vacant. The ceilings were high and airy, and mysterious shadows shifted over the floor, as if from light filtered through a forest canopy. Even empty, the place reminded me of Wendell's apartments back at Cambridge in all but the cleanliness. There was a thick layer of dust upon every surface and clear evidence of leaks, with mushrooms sprouting in the corner and the smell of damp. The window by the bed had been shattered, and some sort of alarming tree with blackish leaves and deathly looking black berries had shoved its way through, as if wishing to lay claim to the place. The bed had dark stains from where the berries had fallen and rotted away.

I wrapped my arms about myself, feeling suddenly cold. I tried to imagine Wendell here, luxuriating in princely comforts. But all I could think about was that this was where he had slept the night his family had been murdered and he had been forced to flee Faerie. He had given me only the barest of summaries of the event, but I knew he had escaped out the window.

The strangest part of the tableau, however, was the dining table in the centre of the room. It was long, draped in silken cloths, with a cushioned, thronelike chair at either end. The table was the only part of the room that was clean and free of dust, as if someone were in the habit of coming here to sit and revel in the room's decay. What's more, the table was set: there was a decanter of some dark wine with two glasses; a platter of meats and cheeses; two loaves of a sweet-smelling bread with seeds pressed into the crust; a bowl of fruit.

I touched one of the grapes and found it still chilled, as if it had only moments ago been taken off ice. I withdrew my hand, shaken. I had no explanation for all of this, though several possibilities occurred, none of them pleasant.

I lingered by the wine for a moment. Then I lifted the decanter to the light and swirled it around—faerie wine always looks dark and has an almost oily thickness. I did not drink, of course, though I was thirsty. With a feeling of trepidation, I set the wine back down.

That will have to do, I thought. I had no time to ponder all the possibilities, after all. My thoughts were still blurred—some aftereffect of whatever the queen's brother had done to me? Or simply the product of too much time spent in Faerie?

Was Wendell's cat still lurking in this part of the castle? I realized that I had no way of knowing—I was operating on a guess. Perhaps the creature had abandoned hope that Wendell might return and slipped away into the forest, or taken up with another member of the queen's household. I could never imagine Shadow abandoning hope for me thus, but cats are fickle, self-involved creatures.

I wandered through the rooms for some time—let us say an hour, why not; the moments bleed together—investigating barren closets and peering beneath the few scraps of furniture that remained. No cat could be found, though I did see evidence that one had resided there at one point: upon a dusty divan shoved into a corner was a thin layer of black fur. However, I was also looking for definitive proof that these were, in fact, Wendell's rooms, and this I found at last.

Beside the divan was a low table of a simple but symmetrical design, like the rest of the furnishings, with a silver sewing needle stuck into the underside, as if someone had stored it there temporarily whilst in the middle of a project, then forgotten about it.

"Orga!" I called in a hushed voice, heartened by this discovery. "Here, puss!"

I don't know if I have ever felt more out of my depth than I did hunting for that bloody cat. Finally, an idea clicked into place, and I pulled the jar of lint from my pack. This was precisely what I'd been hoping for—the moment I might find a use for the strange faerie artefact I'd lugged here from Cambridge. Unfortunately, in the same moment, I discovered that the horn was missing.

I swore, hunting through my pack. But it was gone. It must have fallen out at some point, perhaps when I'd nearly been trampled by the faerie horses.

This seemed an ominous development, to be without any means to defend myself at what was surely the most dangerous part of my journey, but what could I do? Nothing at all. I kept searching. As I did, I released the faintly glimmering lint, hoping that it might entice the cat into appearing. It was Wendell's magic, after all. Unfortunately, my thoughts kept blurring, and I think I searched the same rooms and furnishings over and over, for I would often forget that I had looked somewhere. I clutched at my coin, but it could do little to protect me in the very heart of Faerie.

When I finally found her, I do not think it was through any skill of mine, but rather because the creature decided that she would not mind being found. During what was at least my third search of a sunny chamber I had begun to think of as the dressing room, due to the presence of several large, empty wardrobes that looked like the hollowed trunks of old trees, my gaze happened to snag on the wardrobe closest to the window. Again, I had searched this wardrobe several times. Yet now, perched atop it with one black paw dangling lazily over the side, there was a cat.

Or, at least, there was something that was approximately a cat. The posture was feline, as were the insouciant golden eyes, but the creature had no definite form; it seemed but a collection of gently rippling shadows, or perhaps the absent brushstrokes of an impressionist who had seen a cat once, at a distance. The creature seemed to stretch, at which point I became aware that it had claws somewhere in its tenebrous bulk—of course it did.

Nevertheless, I could have wept with relief. "Orga?" I called, very awkwardly. I do not think I have ever spoken to a cat before.

The beast gave me a long look. Her ears—again, I use this word only in a rough sense; they were more like little tufts of shadow—twitched. She leapt easily from the great height of the wardrobe to the floor, then stalked through a door that had not been there before.

Cursing under my breath, I wrenched the cage from my pack and followed her. This "cage" was, in fact, a burlap sack through which I had woven several coils of metal wire. It was not an elegant thing, but I'd had little time to create something more elaborate before leaving for Faerie. If I could get close enough, I could drop it over her head.

The door led to a narrow hall, then to what looked like a storage closet lined with shelves. To my surprise, there were garments here, lying in several piles upon the floor. They looked like the sort of thing Wendell would have worn in Faerie—silk tunics and frilled cloaks and the like—and bore evidence of his immaculate tailoring. They also bore evidence of tooth marks, as if the cat had dragged them here, as well as cat-shaped indentations lined with fur.

The cat was standing by a door at the other end of the closet, looking over her shoulder at me as if I were supposed to follow. Beyond the door came the sound of distant voices— was the beast leading me into a trap? Or was she simply hoping for a meal? How on earth did one tell with cats?

"Come, Orga," I said again, holding out the makeshift cage without much optimism. I wanted to find my way back to the bedchamber—both because I did not wish to become lost again and because I was of a mind to attempt escape out the broken window. The tree had seemed climbable, and leaving that way meant I would not have to navigate the castle, where I might bump into any number of the queen's courtiers.

The cat let out a low growl and pawed at the door.

Bloody hell. "Orga," I said in a reasonable voice, "we cannot go that way. You must come with me. I will take you to your master. Do you understand? Do you remember your master?"

The cat gave me what I can only describe as a withering

look. The voices beyond the door grew louder—there came a piercing laugh—then faded again.

Partly out of curiosity, and partly because my muddled mind had only just remembered it was there, I pulled the compass from my pocket. The needle spun slowly once, twice, three times—and landed squarely on Orga.

"God," I muttered. I could still hear the sound of distant conversation beyond the door. The compass must be mistaken—I could not trust the wayward inclinations of a cat, not with so much at stake.

The cat gave a long yowl. She turned and began scratching at the door. Her claws were long and fiendishly sharp, and the sound seemed to echo through the room.

Bloody cat! Cursing, I snatched the creature up by the scruff—she *felt* like a cat, at least, though rather more slippery than any mortal beast—and threw her into the sack, which I was certain would result in my painful demise as soon as I released her again. Indeed, the beast hissed and spat, thrusting her shapeshifting paw through the narrow opening at the top, which I bound shut with another coil of wire, trying to claw at any inch of me she could reach. I ended up with a nasty gash on my arm and another on the back of my hand. Yet the metal wire held, and for all the faerie cat yowled and carried on, it was clear that she could not escape.

I stuffed the cage into my pack and took off at a run, the unfortunate and now determinedly murderous feline bumping and jostling against my ribs. Back through the maze of rooms, which kindly refrained from reordering themselves, towards the bedchamber. Orga's protests only grew louder as I ran, as she seemed determined to tear her way through both cage and pack. She managed, somehow, to get a paw through the flap and rake her claws over the nape of my neck. I shrieked in pain as a trickle of blood slid down my back. The fiend began to claw at my hair, and I had to remove the pack and sling it under my arm. It was a little like trying to maintain a grip on a bag of wasps.

I didn't immediately notice anything amiss when I came crashing through the door to the bedchamber. The cat went still, however, her paw sliding back into the pack.

One of the chairs at the banquet table was now occupied. A tall woman sat there, absently peeling an apple with a knife. She did not seem surprised by my appearance, but merely gave me a cool look, as if we two had made an appointment and I had arrived five minutes late. Behind her, on either side of the door, stood two faerie guards. This identified the woman as much as her sumptuous robes, which pooled at her feet and trailed behind her across the floor, layers of stiff silk and embroidered velvet studded with thousands of silver beads. She was Wendell's stepmother, the queen.

She was also of mortal blood.

I could see it in the dusting of grey at her temples and the lines on her forehead. She had large, dark eyes in a long, pale face, her hair the same wispy red-gold as her eyebrows—striking, perhaps, though not beautiful as the courtly fae generally are.

The queen popped a piece of apple into her mouth and chewed without any particular haste, watching me as I stood frozen in speechless panic.

"You are my son's betrothed," she said eventually. "What is your name?"

Her voice was clipped and precise, slightly nasal, also unlike the Folk with their melodious tones. It was, in other words, an imperfect voice—a mortal voice. But there was enchantment in the words nonetheless, and before I could stop myself, I said, "Emily."

"Emily," she repeated. She ate another piece of apple.

"Please tell me how you slipped past my guardians in the forest."

I fought against the enchantment in her voice, my heart hammering in my throat, but again I found my usual defences stormed by this part-mortal woman. I said, "They knew me—knew me by the cloak I wore, which Wendell—I mean, your stepson—tailored."

"I know the name he goes by in the mortal realm," she said, waving her hand. She stood, graceful despite the yards of fabric trailing behind her, and walked over to the wine. She poured two glasses and handed one to me, then motioned to the platter of food. "Eat," she said. "Drink. I can see you are undernourished—mortals often forget their meals when they are in Faerie. I had the table set for two. I'm sorry I was delayed, but I trust you've been busy in my absence." She eyed my pack with a hint of amusement.

As I hesitated, she gave me a smile that seemed to have an edge of bitterness in it. "Don't worry—it is not faerie wine. I cannot drink that any more than you can."

I wasn't certain I believed this, for it looked like all the faerie wines I'd seen. But again, there was some form of compulsion in her words, and I took a nervous sip, grimacing at the aroma. It was floral in an unpleasant, bittersweet way, as if it had actually been comprised of the juices of crushed flowers.

"So," the queen continued in her businesslike manner, settling herself back in her chair with a rustle of fabric, "my loyal guardians are not so loyal after all."

"I don't know about that," I said. Why was I still talking? "I suspect they are simply uncertain of which loyalty comes first—their loyalty to the one who currently holds the throne or the one who *should* hold it."

She did not seem offended by this, but merely sipped her wine, gazing at me over the rim. I could not tell if there was doubt there, or resentment. I could not read her at all. She was one of those people who keep their thoughts behind a fortress, either by preference or necessity.

"How did you know who I am?" I said as I fought against the terror. This was the woman who had murdered Wendell's entire family.

She shrugged. "I have had Folk watching him—so carefully that he was perfectly unaware. Mind, he has never been a particularly observant creature. I was also able to ask the elder huntsmen—those who survived my son's sword—to give me an account of you. They saw three mortals with him that day, and only one seemed unafraid of him. A little mousy girl with her hair in tangles." She smiled. "I think of these things as they do not."

They. It was unmistakable to whom she was referring.

"You do not—see yourself as Folk?" I don't know why I asked it. I knew exactly what I needed to be doing: placating her; flattering her vanity—halfbloods are said to be every bit as vain as the Folk, and even more sensitive to slights.

"Clearly I am not Folk," she said. "Though I had a faerie mother, that does not prevent me from aging, or from being gripped by an inescapable urge to dance when I consume their food and wine. Neither am I human, like my father. I am myself. I am singular."

I was speechless. I had never heard of a halfblood rising to the throne of a faerie court—well, that is not precisely true; it is a motif in some versions of the tale of the Earl of Wenden,[*] but that is the only instance, to my knowledge. I recalled what Wendell had said about his stepmother's ability to manipulate those in her orbit—a very human trait. The Folk may

---

[*] See, for instance, John Trelgar's *Fairie and Folke Tales of the Westcountry* (1608).

scheme, but few bother with manipulation; it isn't something that suits them, capricious as they are, particularly when they can simply enchant others into giving them what they want. Creature of habit that I am, even in the most ridiculous of circumstances, my fingers itched for pen and paper—I doubted I would ever encounter a research subject more interesting than the woman before me.

"Come closer," the queen said, and I obeyed thoughtlessly. Yes, there was enchantment in her commands, but there was also a human version of authority there that I recognized. Were the king of England to order me to speak—or, for that matter, the chancellor of Cambridge, a small but forbidding man—I would have found it similarly difficult to disobey. For there are certain mortals who are quite capable of intimidation and dominance without the aid of magic, particularly when they are used to it, when they possess a certain stature, inherited or earned. And the force of this woman's personality was immense; she seemed to possess her own gravity, to which I was helplessly drawn.

"Yes, you're common enough," she said, after examining me for a moment. Up close, I could smell her perfume— something spiced and also very human. "I admit I'm surprised—my son was always a superficial creature. But perhaps he's changed."

"What do you want from me?" I said. For surely she wanted *something;* a woman with such high regard for her own cleverness would not go to the effort of arranging this meeting merely to gloat.

She finished her apple and a piece of cheese, then poured herself another glass of wine, taking her time with it all. I took the opportunity to surreptitiously calculate the distance to the window. The guards would not reach me in time, and I did not think she could, either, in her heavy fabrics. But could I evade her enchantments? My hand clenched round the penny in my pocket.

"They need us," she said at last. "You know this by now, I'm sure. They're hopeless creatures. Incapable of consistency, which a kingdom needs to prosper. Before I ascended to the throne, this realm was in chaos, as were all its neighbours."

"From what I heard," I said, "in expanding your borders, you have only increased that chaos."

"A temporary thing," she said. "As was the chaos that followed my husband's death. I see beyond the present as the Folk do not—another failing of theirs. Why do you think I have decided to murder my son? I've known he was at that university for some time."

The sudden shift in subject made me pause before I replied. "Because you are having trouble maintaining power given your recent conquests, and want him properly out of the way."

She laughed. "Trouble maintaining power! I have had no real trouble. Not from my court, and certainly not from my son, airheaded young creature that he is. I expected a century or more to pass in the mortal realm before he presented any real threat to me, if he ever did. No, Emily—it was *you* I worried about. From the first rumours I heard of you, of your cleverness, your high regard for my silly son, I knew you were the real threat. Mortals always are, aren't they? If you read the stories. The arrogant faerie prince who can make gold from straw is always undone by the humble miller's daughter, not some powerful rival of his own stature."

My stomach grew queasy. I had never felt so out of my depth when conversing with one of the Folk, not even the snow king of Ljosland. Wendell had been right, but it was no comfort to know that his stepmother had been afraid of me. I am used to being underestimated by the Folk—nothing could be more dangerous than the opposite.

"You're a talented woman," she went on. "I like the talented ones—in fact, I have my own little collection of mortals, from perfumers to painters to chefs. You would be the crown jewel, a mortal clever enough to find a long-lost door to my kingdom—that is how you came here, yes?"

I held my features still, but there must have been some re-action, for she nodded and went on. "My son couldn't have managed it, and this is *his* kingdom." She let out a surpris-ingly genuine laugh. "So, here is my proposition: remain here with me, and help me bring about my son's death. There is nothing special about him, Emily, I promise—oh, he's more beautiful than most, even among the Folk, but beyond that, you will not miss him. Once you have spent time with other faerie nobility, you will see what I mean. If you still desire a husband, you may have your pick of the nobles of my court."

My pulse thrummed as I watched her set the wineglass aside. She looked weary—or perhaps it was my imagination. I realized that I had been absently tearing at a piece of bread and forced myself to stop. Had I eaten anything at her table? I couldn't remember. I was losing my ability to focus, which frightened me even more than the woman before me. "I as-sume the alternative is my death," I said.

"I will allow you plenty of time to consider before it comes to that," she said.

"How generous."

She smiled. "You wish to remain here. Don't you?"

Some part of me recoiled from answering this particular question, and so I fought against the compulsion, but once again, she drew the truth from me. Because I fought it, my answer was torn free, overloud. "*Yes.*"

Her smile widened. "I knew it."

I stared at her, my breath coming in shallow gasps. Yes, I wanted to remain here in Faerie, with Wendell. Yes, I knew it went against reason and common sense—ordinarily two of my strengths. My arguments with Rose had been nonsense all along, because the truth was that I agreed with him. Of course it wasn't a sane decision to befriend a monarch of the Folk, let alone marry one, particularly if he reigned over the Silva Lupi. Nor did I think Wendell was different from other Folk, particularly—kinder, less enigmatic, or somehow more human. I simply didn't care. I loved him, and I suspected that I would grow to love this beautiful, horrifying place if given the chance. I *wanted* the chance. I wanted Faerie, its every secret and its every door.

If there was danger in my decision—and I knew there was—then so be it. I would accept danger, if it meant I could have this.

The queen was still studying me, but there was something absent about it now, as if I were a riddle that had been solved to her satisfaction. "I know you will refuse my offer presently," she said. "You think you still have a way out. I can see it in your face—what is it? Something you have in that pack of yours? A weapon, perhaps?"

I went still, even as my heart kept up its gallop. I clutched at my scattered thoughts—it was like trying to catch fireflies without a net. "No," I said. "I had a weapon with me, but—I lost it."

For the briefest of moments, she looked confused. I cannot say for certain—my memory of these moments is poor, and also, I have never been skilled at reading others. But I am, of course, an expert in the ways of the Folk. And whatever else she might be, the woman before me was inarguably Folk.

"What was it?" she said.

"A horn," I replied. "The horn of a faun."

She did not move, though something in her face relaxed.

"That would have been a fearsome weapon indeed, for one brave enough to wield it. Pity."

I nodded. "Fortunately, I had made a little powder from the tip, which I had in my pocket before you came in."

It was not my imagination—the queen was visibly tired, exhausted even. It had come on quickly. She seemed to make an effort to focus on me.

And then I saw the moment she understood.

Her hand clenched around the fine tablecloth. "You—"

"Yes," I said. "I put it in the wine. At least, I'm fairly certain I did—you'll have to excuse me, but Faerie does not agree with my memory. Of course, I did not know you would come here to taunt me—but I thought it a possibility. I suppose you were right: the capacity for forethought is an advantage we mortals have over the Folk."

She sagged back against her chair, her mouth falling open as she inhaled in shallow gasps. She had begun to tremble lightly—I remembered Wendell doing that. He had ingested the same poison, after all, that I had fed to his stepmother.

"I wonder what the effects will be?" I said, and it was not fear making my pulse race anymore, but a sudden wave of fury. The thought of the suffering Wendell had endured, all for this woman's poisonous ambition, had awakened it in me. I didn't see her as a research subject anymore, but merely as a foe, and the simplicity of it was satisfying.

"I imagine they will be more intense than for someone of Wendell's power," I went on. "The poison made it difficult for him to use his magic. In the end, it was difficult for him even to speak." I stepped forward so that my body blocked the guards' view of the queen. "I may not be a miller's daughter, but you are not so different from the Folk as you think, Your Highness." I lifted her wineglass and dashed the remainder against her face, spilling it across her mouth and into her eyes.

I meant it to be dramatic. I have always wished to dash wine in someone's face. But I've never had the knack for drama; my aim was poor, and much of the wine sloshed upon the queen's dress. And yet this produced a gruesome effect: the red stained the queen's bodice to the neck, like blood from a cut throat.

The queen gave a choked cry and clutched at the neck of her dress. The guards had not been paying us much attention before, but they were now, perplexity writ large across their faces. I had the sense that they had never observed their queen betray weakness in any form. The larger of the two stepped forward. Panicking, I turned and leapt out the window.

Perhaps I should not say *leapt*—the word implies a grace I do not possess. Say instead that I half stumbled, half fell, catching at the branches awkwardly, the bloody cat banging against my spine. She had been quiet before, but now she yowled as the pack jarred and jostled. I barely noticed; all my attention was on scrabbling down the tree, which writhed as if determined to shake me off. I reached the ground all the faster for its efforts, though with a great deal of bruises and a wrenched shoulder.

I should not have been able to escape, but if there is one fault universal to faerie monarchs, it is overconfidence. Yet I did not count on this protecting me for long—it was a head start, that was all.

As I charged through the gardens, dodging bemused Folk, I realized I would need some form of disguise—several of the guards were eyeing me with narrowed eyes, and one faerie woman came forward, as if to offer help. No doubt I presented a pathetic figure with my torn dress and hair tangled with leaves and berries. So I began to sing as I ran, a hodgepodge of childish lullabies, and the Folk fell back, their sympathy and suspicion giving way to irritation at the noise this maddened mortal was making—a thoroughly unsympathetic Ophelia I was, with my dreadful singing voice. All seemed pleased to see the back of me.

I released Orga shortly thereafter—it was either that or have my back clawed to shreds, as she had managed to excavate her way through both the pack and my dress, and seemed eager to further vent her spleen upon my flesh. A little voice whispered that setting the beast free was madness, but I had made my decision—I would place my trust in Lilja and her gift.

The compass had pointed at the cat. I had ignored it before; I would not do so again.

As soon as her paws touched the ground, Orga darted towards the dark forest that overhung the garden. She paused beneath a stone bench, glancing over her shoulder as if expecting me to follow.

"No," I said, despair making my voice crack. "We must reach the other side of the lake. My friends are waiting for us."

I felt on the verge of shattering—to have come so far, through so much, and to have this creature abandon me was beyond my ability to endure. I began to babble something about Wendell and how much he needed her—it should have felt ridiculous to plead with a cat, but it did not. Orga did not seem moved. After regarding me for a moment, she turned and folded herself through a narrow gap between two rosebushes.

"No!" I lunged after her, the bushes tearing at my skin and depositing more foliage in my hair. To my astonishment, I was no longer in the gardens, but standing at the edge of the lakeside path just before it entered the castle grounds. Orga sat a few feet away, tail curled round her paws, regarding me with tolerant condescension. She set off along the path at a trot.

I let out a whimper of pure relief. It was at that moment that the screaming started.

It echoed through the gardens and over the lake, and, I suspect, through every corner of the forest and hills. It was a cry of rage and sorrow.

After the first echoes died, there came a distant rustling, a gathering sound that, in its inexplicability, was worse than the screams had been. Orga took off at a loping run, and I followed blindly, crashing through shrubs and branches.

I risked a glance over my shoulder—which naturally caused me to stumble over a root—and found that a dark line had appeared in the sky, broken by the branches that draped over the lakeside path.

The guardians.

They were approaching the place where I stood with uncanny speed. They had been agnostic about me before, and allowed me to pass through their realm unchallenged, but now I had attacked their queen—perhaps fatally—and this, clearly, had made up their minds.

Orga yowled at me, and though my stomach was now lurching with nausea, I kept running, following the flicker of her black tail through the green shadow. Something stirred the air at my back—that was all I noticed, a gentle breeze—and suddenly Orga had turned and lunged at something behind me, so swiftly she seemed to melt into pure shadow. When I turned, I found her rolling across the forest floor in a tangle of feathers and long, horrific black legs, her jaw locked around the guardian's neck. The creature went still a heartbeat later, letting out a final, wet wheeze as its legs twitched.

Orga was off running again before I had comprehended it. I tried not to look at the creature, which was somehow more sinister in death, but my memory supplies the image anyway. Up close, I could see that the beast's legs were covered in feathery down.

My memory suggests that we came upon Ariadne and Snowbell immediately thereafter, perhaps because Orga led us through another one of her shortcuts, but it is possible that we had been running for some time, dodging the guardians as we went.

"Aunt Emily!" Ariadne cried. The girl was weeping. "We heard the screaming, and I thought—oh, I don't know *what* I thought, but I am so relieved—"

"No time," I said as the rustling intensified again. This time it was accompanied by the bugle of horns, which I took to imply that we would soon contend with pursuers on foot as well. Ariadne handed me my cloak, and I threw it on—just in time too. One of the guardians had plummeted out of the trees, wings and all six legs fanned wide, but it broke off abruptly with a raspy hoot. The cloak, and the memory of Wendell it summoned, had given it pause again, but I doubted this would sway the creature for long. I had, after all, poisoned their queen.

Snowbell let out a shriek of terror as another guardian swooped past, only diving sideways when Orga lunged at it, hissing. "The queen's guardians are attacking!" the little faerie cried excitedly. "Oh, what a quest this is!"

We plunged along the path, Snowbell taking the lead once more, as Orga did not know the way to the nexus. At this point, my memory of the journey folds in on itself again—perhaps I could smooth out the creases with time and effort, but I am so weary as I write these words, my vision blurs. Orga, following at our backs like a hissing, spitting shadow, repelled the creatures again and again, and then I believe we lost them for a time when Snowbell led us through one of the barrows—a "short road" that perhaps the guardians did not see us take. I recall one of the guardians briefly sinking its talons into

Snowbell, raking him from neck to tail, which the little beast proceeded to crow over with a bloodthirsty delight that I preferred not to dwell on.

We came through another barrow—was it a barrow, or merely a bend in the path?—and one of the guardians was waiting for us. This one was larger than the others, an ancient, hulking creature with rheumy eyes. Orga did not seem so eager to pounce on it, but she interposed herself between us when it spread its wings, and it hesitated in the face of her yowling fury long enough for Snowbell to lead us down a side path, merely a deer trail, and—and what? What happened to the guardian? I remember Orga running behind us again— was this before, or after? Ah, my eyes are aching. But eventually we broke free of the forest—yes, that memory is clear. We broke free, and there was the nexus. The nexus—

9/10/10

Well, I have tucked you back into bed, but I shall keep watch this time to ensure you stay there and do not leap up again to resume your frenzied scribbling. Really, Em— I found you at your desk with your face buried in this journal, snoring soundly, yet even so I nearly had to wrestle the bloody thing away from you. Did I not advise that you were better off catching up on your sleep than immediately recording every detail of your sojourn in my realm? When you awaken, we must have a discussion about this obsessive journalling habit of yours. It is not healthy, and while none of your acquaintance would be surprised were you to expire from overwork— specifically, with a pen in hand, hunched over a book—I ask that you have a little mercy on your poor fiancé.

Yes. I heard you.

I hope you will not mind that I took the liberty of reading your previous entry, nor—since I am rather bored, as I generally am when I do not have you to talk to—that I will be completing it for you. And so you will have at least a few pages in here that are legible—your handwriting, Em! It is so blotched and mangled you might give this book to Shadow in place of his bone and scarcely notice any difference in readability.

Anyway, I have made a pot of tea and helped myself to several of Julia's tarts, so I suppose I am adequately prepared for the labour ahead of me. You may thank me when you awaken. Shadow is at the foot of your bed, watching you sleep as the wind howls beyond the curtained window—a storm that, I am happy to say, is entirely natural, and should not, this time, be carrying another round of assassins to our door. My dear Orga is here on my lap, sleeping blissfully after I spoilt her with the best cuts of meat from the café and a great deal of cream. Rose made several withering remarks about the devilish nature of faerie cats, as well as my indulgence of her, which he seemed to think a bit maudlin, and yet I saw that old hypocrite sneak her several morsels from his dinner plate when he thought I wasn't looking. Like Shadow, she has adopted a glamour here, and presently looks every bit the part of an ordinary mortal cat, apart from her eyes, which flash like gold coins.

First off, I have to say that the greatest mystery to me in all this is Lord Taran's motive in helping you. That is the name of my stepmother's brother—part of it, anyhow; I don't know the rest. Because it is obvious to me that they helped you, Em, even though it is also true that they informed my stepmother of your presence. For did they not also leave you an opportunity to escape, which likely you would have done, had you listened to Orga and followed her through that door? It is a door I enchanted myself in order to sneak out at night during my teenage years—it leads directly to a hidden stairway that takes you down to the forest at the back of the castle. Taran's husband always struck me as a thoughtful sort of person; could he have influenced Taran to intervene on your behalf? Was it sympathy for a fellow mortal? Ambition? I admit that I know neither of them very well; I spent most of my youth flitting from party to party, after all, and they are both older than I, and not much for the social scene.

I can picture you shaking your head at me. I'm sorry to break it to you, Em, but not all of us spent our adolescence worshiping at the metaphorical feet of Posidonius. Some of us had fun. Though admittedly too much, in my case.

Ariadne has just stopped by. I encouraged her to sleep, but she keeps coming in here to check on you. Were you aware that she has come to love you very dearly? I was beginning to think it would never happen; while the girl has always idolized you, there has been far too much terror in her regard for love. At some point, my dear dragon, she has ceased to worry about you burning her to a crisp—perhaps this will come as a disappointment to you, but there it is.

Anyway, where did you leave off? Ah, yes. You were fleeing the guardians.

I did not learn about this until I awoke, of course, but apparently Rose had been keeping a watch for you in the Grünesauge, together with that friend of Ariadne's, Astrid Haas. You were gone one day, Em, in the mortal world. One day and one night. Eichorn and de Grey intervened on our behalf with the villagers and convinced them to allow us to stay a few more days, so we are not in any immediate danger of being tossed out of the cottage. It was thoughtful of them, I suppose, though I understand from Ariadne that they were not inclined to be helpful before, and so perhaps there was some guilt on their part. Fortunately, Eberhard seems to be on the mend. I've already taken the liberty of making some form of reparation—do you recall that insipid mushroom stew they serve at luncheon in the café? Well, nothing was easier than conjuring a garden of wolf's paw, a fungus that grows in abundance in the deeper forests of my realm. Very tasty, perfectly safe for mortal consumption, and the caps have the added benefit of offering a pleasant luminescence at night. Their growth can be unpredictable, it's true—some will never be larger than a shilling, others, for some reason, sprout up as large as cows—but better to have more than less of a commodity, is that not so?

So, you and Ariadne came racing out of the nexus this morning as if you were being chased by monstrous fiends, and naturally Rose was greatly alarmed, but no fiends followed you out the door—not immediately, that is. And so he led you back to the cottage, bruised and battered as you were, Orga forcing him to carry her.

According to Ariadne, Orga ran ahead as soon as you rounded the bend and came within sight of the cottage—no doubt she could smell me at that point. I was stirring a bit, though still very weak—I don't know how much time I had left by then. It's possible that one more spell would have finished me off. But then the two of you came charging through the door, and I barely had time to open my mouth before she pounced.

Not on me, exactly, although I suppose that's what it looked like. Instead, she pounced on the poison lurking beneath my skin, which had been inside me for so long that it was beginning to take on the shape of faerie blackbirds— dreadful things, always lurking at deathbeds as they do. They were terrified, naturally, for Orga is a fearsome predator, the nightmare of all birds and mice and other small animals unlucky enough to cross her path.

The creatures fled my body, and suddenly the cottage was full of wingbeats—dozens of them, together with the panicked croaking of birds as they searched for an open window. But alas for them, it was already too late, and Orga killed them methodically, one by one. I believe one or two may have escaped, though I cannot be bothered to care—they are no longer inside *me,* and that is all that matters.

Does this help, Em? For you seemed rather lost afterwards,

and kept staring from me to the feathers scattering the floor. Fortunately, when I stood and swept you into my arms, you seemed to lose interest in the mechanics of faerie poisons and simply buried your head in my neck, which I appreciated. I can help you write a paper on the subject of blackbirds later, if you like.

You managed to give me a brief, garbled account of the events while I stroked your hair—you had poisoned my step-mother, who was now dead or dying—oh, Em! You miraculous creature; I did not wish for you to have anything to do with her. I merely hoped you would bring me Orga, a simple enough errand, given that she would have known you as my friend by the cloak you wore. But you cannot do anything halfway, can you?

Em, I must confess—I am in awe of you. I believe I am also a little frightened.

I would have liked to have held you for much longer, particularly given that you seemed to be crying—an uncharacteristic display of emotion that I believe I have only ever observed once before—but Ariadne and Rose were standing about awkwardly, and Orga was creating a dreadful ruckus.

"Come here, my dear," I said, bending to scoop her up. I assumed she was merely jealous, but she slithered out of my arms and onto my shoulder, still yowling her head off. Shadow, who had been eyeing her with trepidation from beneath the table, suddenly added his voice to hers, as if something had been communicated between them.

"We were followed," you blurted. "But surely they didn't—they did not follow us through the nexus, I'm certain of it—"

"Followed by whom?" I said, but your grip on reality seemed tenuous at that moment, and you only kept rambling about the nexus and your narrow escape from that stupid brownie in the bathrobe—something about fingers?—which was of no use to me. And so, sunk into a melancholy sort of mood, I opened the door and went outside, wondering what form of assassin my dear stepmother had sent after us this time.

I doubt I need say it, but I was in no mood for a fight just then; while the poison might have left my body, I still felt its aftereffects, a bone-deep weariness, and desired only a cup of coffee and a good hearty breakfast, not another swordfight with some bloody bogles. And why is it that my enemies always come at me when I am tired and hungry? Why cannot I deal with my stepmother's hirelings on a full stomach, having had a good night's rest in some comfortable bed? (Present lodgings excepted—the lumps in these mattresses, my God!) Assassins are a monstrous breed. Either they attack when you are at your worst, or they are having a go at you on your birthday. I have never known a more dishonourable profession.

Where was I? Yes. Ariadne, who had followed me out the door, began to scream. I shook my head, trying to clear the dizziness brought on by fatigue, and saw them a second later.

Or, rather, I saw *him*. Razkarden, the ancient leader of my stepmother's guardians—who were once *my* guardians, at least for the day I held the throne, and my father's before that. Does this seem traitorous, that the creatures would offer their services to my father's killer? It is not—for they were not loyal to my father, nor are they loyal to my stepmother. They are loyal to the throne. Who occupies it is largely immaterial to them.

Razkarden's shrieks echoed over the valley and across the mountains—likely they could hear him in the neighbouring villages, so there is another thing for the locals to hold against us. I was initially quite pleased to see him. He is of my kingdom, and I have missed him to the degree that you *can* miss a kind of sentient gargoyle like him.

But it was immediately apparent that he was in one of his rages, and clearly intent on rending you and anyone who stood in his way to pieces. Behind him, flying in a long, dark line like an arrow, were at least twenty more guardians. So there is our reason they were delayed: they had not been thwarted by a simple faerie door, but had been gathering the numbers for a full-on assault.

I tried to shove Ariadne back towards the cottage, but it became clear that there wasn't enough time. You ran to join us, despite my shouted warnings, to try to drag Ariadne back yourself. But Razkarden was almost upon us, his enormous wings carrying him over the landscape faster than a winter wind. And so I drew you both towards me, and summoned the Veil.

I had seen my father do it before, but never tried myself. I've never had the slightest inclination, nor did I wish to in that moment—but needs must.

All faerie monarchs can summon the Veil. Or, at least, a small edge of it—a trailing hem, if you will. It is thought to be an ancient faerie realm, long lost and very unpleasant. Some of the more learned members of my court believe all Folk lived there once, before splitting off and building much more pleasant realms in which to dwell, but the Veil is still there, in the cracks between our worlds. When my father summoned it, I recall he seemed to disappear within a column of darkness. It is properly horrifying to one's enemies, for all Folk fear the Veil.

It was as if night had fallen, swift and sudden, a night studded with glittering stars. Wind whipped around us—how cold it was! The Veil is said to be frigid, and filled with creeping monsters who would have died long ago, and perhaps wish to, but they are immortal and so cannot leave the Veil even by that path. Unearthly howls filled the air, and I smelled nothing but sand and dust—dry; frozen; foul. The smell of ancient civilizations corrupted by something within.

Razkarden was trapped in that wretched place with us, and he screamed—in terror now, all bravado gone. I could leave him there, and he knew it—for I had summoned the Veil, and I alone could banish it; Razkarden had no power over it whatsoever.

But I am not vengeful, and so I stepped forward through the darkness as he screamed and begged and flapped around us in desperation, and held out my arm. The creature accepted my offer immediately, diving towards my arm and landing so hard I nearly toppled over. He wrapped two of his legs around my left shoulder, and the rest around my outstretched arm, shuddering and emitting a raspy *too-woo* sort of sound— almost like a mortal owl.

I banished the Veil. Doing so created a fierce gust of wind, and Ariadne fell forward onto the grass of the mountainside. You remained upright, because you had kept hold of me, but you released me with a strangled sound once you realized Razkarden was clinging to my shoulders. The old guardian needed a moment to calm himself, and I gave it to him, stroking his forehead feathers as his shudders subsided.

My wrist aches dreadfully. What a tedious business journalling is. You see, this is why I generally dictate most of my formal writings to one of my students. Anyway, Razkarden and his flock departed, and Rose and I managed to drag you and Ariadne up to your respective beds, for neither of you appeared to have slept much in days and were nearly fainting from exhaustion.

I returned to the nexus, not because I had any notion of marching off immediately to claim my throne—God, what a tedious business that will be, given the chaos that will have followed my stepmother's poisoning; not one to be undertaken in my current state, and particularly not on an empty stomach—but merely to have a glimpse of my realm at last, after all these years. One breath of the forest.

By the way. I do not know what is so troubling about the trees of my realm. They are perfectly harmless, Em, provided you leave them be.

But when I reached the Grünesauge, I found the guardians circling the valley in alarm, and it did not take me long to discern the cause. That bloody brownie had somehow sealed the door against us; I could find no sign of it in the mountainside. Well, I suppose I cannot blame him too much; it cannot be enjoyable to have mortals stumbling through your foyer all the time, and also I suspect the guardians made a dreadful mess when they followed you through.

And yet it was—disappointing. I may have made a small hole in the mountainside in my anger.

When I returned to the cottage, I found you as I described: out of bed, your hair in utter disarray, asleep over your journal. I put you back into bed and washed the ink stains from your cheek. I confess that, as I have been writing this, I have had to stop myself several times from waking you, to hear the story from your own lips again.

How I missed you.

"It was only a day!" I can hear you reply. Well, a day is far too long.

Do you know? Rose asked me why I was not more surprised by your feat. He does not understand you as I do, Em, but as you seem to consider him a friend now, I told him the truth: in order to be surprised, I could not have known already that you are capable of anything.

12th October

I was certain we would miss our train this afternoon. Given my few personal effects, it took me less than an hour to pack, but naturally it was an eternity before Wendell had himself organized. He and Ariadne went to the shop twice, on the hunt for additional suitcases, as well as clothing boxes and silk wrappings. Then there was an extended conversation about Thermos bottles for the journey to the train, at which point I absented myself to sit outside in the autumn sun with Shadow.

In any event, I cannot be too annoyed with him, for the westbound train out of Leoburg was delayed some hours, and we arrived with time to spare. I am sat upon a bench beside the tracks, which offers a pretty view of the mountains we just descended.

Bloody wind! It keeps snatching at the pages, taunting me with glimpses of Wendell's handwriting. If he *insists* on writing in my journals—all right, fine, it can be useful when he does—could he not refrain from showing off? I refuse to accept that anyone's handwriting, faerie or no, could be as neat as his without a great deal of effort. I could almost believe he placed an enchantment upon my journal, but he swears he would not dare. He knows where the line is, at least.

I slept later than I intended this morning—it was sunrise before I stirred. It seems I have adapted to St. Liesl too well, and now keep the villagers' hours, dawn to dusk. Wendell's side of the bed was empty, which was astonishing. It is exceedingly rare for him to rise earlier than I do.

As soon as I opened my eyes, my vision was obscured by a large quantity of black fur, a cold, wet nose, and an enormous tongue. I was not offended at all—quite the contrary—and let Shadow lick my cheeks before burying my face in his neck.

"Poor dear," I murmured. "There, there—you needn't worry about me leaving you again!"

He has been like this each morning since my return, but I can scarcely object. I missed him as much as he missed me, and have vowed never again to venture anywhere he cannot follow.

Somehow I became aware of Wendell's presence. Sure enough, when I looked up, he was leaning against the doorframe, watching me with one of his unreadable smiles.

"Since when are you a morning person?" I demanded.

"I'm not," he said emphatically. He entered the room and dropped onto the bed in a sprawl, leaning against the wall with his legs across mine. "Only those two were fighting again, and I felt I should break things up."

"Not again."

To put it mildly, Shadow and Orga have not taken to each other. I am not at all surprised; cats are terrified of Shadow—undeservedly so, I've always thought, given that he barely notices their presence. Orga appears to be the first cat who has ever frightened Shadow, and she seems to take a malicious pleasure in this, hiding in dark places to pounce on him, claws extended.

"Mostly her fault, I'm afraid," Wendell said. "She taunts him."

"She's a bully," I said, irritated on Shadow's behalf. "A vicious, bloodthirsty monster."

"And that is barely scratching the surface," Wendell agreed fondly.

He leaned over and kissed me. I twined my fingers through his hair and lost myself for a moment, before the sounds of clattering cupboards and laughter from the kitchen below brought me back to my senses.

"I must say," he murmured, running his thumb over my lower lip, "I am rather looking forward to returning to Cambridge. To my apartments, that is."

"Temporarily," I said.

He smiled. "Temporarily."

When we emerged downstairs, we found Julia Haas, her husband, Albert, and all four of her daughters bustling about, clearly in the process of preparing a lavish send-off feast— apart from Astrid, who was standing by the fire with Ariadne, in the middle of an excited conversation about something. Rose was making the coffee.

"Shall I leave my order with you, then?" I enquired as we passed.

He gave me a scowl. "I merely volunteered to help. A gesture of good will."

"How thoughtful," I said, maintaining a straight face. "Extra cream in mine, please."

"Careful, you."

The door swung open, and in strode Roland Haas and his two sons, one of whom had a baby tucked under his arm. To my alarm, they were followed almost immediately by a couple I recognized from the café, and then three youths who called out greetings to Ariadne.

"I invited them," Ariadne explained, in response to my expression. "Well, I doubt all of the villagers will wish to send us off—some will be happy to see the backs of us—but look, here's more!"

The cottage was now too full to accommodate everyone, and so Julia ushered everyone out into the yard, where she assembled a bonfire, whilst her husband and daughters went back and forth, bringing everyone coffee. I found myself in a conversation with Julia and Roland about a crystal cave in a neighbouring valley we did not have time to explore, where reside three singing faeries who will complete whatever small labour you leave at their doorstep, be it an unfinished bit of knitting or linen in need of bleaching.

"Well, you had so much else to worry about, didn't you?" Julia said kindly. "Next time you're here, Papa will show you the place."

"Spring is a lovely time in St. Liesl," Roland assured me, and before I knew what was happening, I was promising that I would return then, in "May or June, when the meadows are all in their finery," as Roland put it.

The villagers know about Wendell now, of course—it was unavoidable, given the state of the cottage, which is presently surrounded by a meadow of bluebells and has a fine crop of Irish moss sprouting on the roof. Not to mention that Julia and one of her daughters witnessed Wendell's encounter with Razkarden when they were on the way to ours with breakfast.

"Was all well last night?" Wendell enquired.

"Oh, yes," Julia said, giving him a warm smile. "Everyone got home safe and sound. Certainly some had a wee bit too much to drink, but never mind. We've never had a midnight bonfire in St. Liesl! I've been to one in my sister's village up north, but for plenty of folk, including some of the old timers, it was their first."

Wendell has banished the fauns back to his kingdom. How they shall make their way there with the door sealed in the

Grünesauge, I do not know, but Wendell does not seem worried. They shall no longer trouble the inhabitants of St. Liesl, and while there remain plenty of nasty Folk in the vicinity to keep the villagers on their guard—Snowbell and his ilk among them—it seems that the *krampushunde* were the primary culprits behind most of the deaths and disappearances that have plagued St. Liesl over the generations. Thus the villagers may sleep a little easier now—even if they must still exercise caution after dark.

Julia gave Wendell's arm a squeeze. The villagers' easy attitude towards him is a bit unsettling—they do not seem at all in awe of him, or nervous in his presence, as the villagers in Hrafnsvik do. I suppose it is owing to their faerie heritage. They are certainly grateful to him, but in an absent sort of way, as one might be grateful to the sun for quickening one's crops.

"Ariadne," I called, and she broke off her conversation with another one of the Haas girls. "May I have a word?"

"Of course, Aunt," she replied, and followed me over to the bench at the edge of the garden. The beech grove was almost bare of leaves now; only scraps of foliage clung to the boughs, shivering in the wind.

"Did I do wrong in inviting the villagers?" she said nervously. "I thought it would be best to maintain good relations—we may need to return here after all, for further research."

"Yes—I mean, no, it was not wrong to invite them," I said. "You did well. I only meant—" I stopped, gathering the words. "Ariadne—I've been too harsh with you at times, I think. You have proven yourself an immensely capable assistant, and were a great help to me in Faerie. I hope you have learned something from me, and I hope you will come to me whenever you need guidance. I may not always remember to be tactful, but I will always answer your questions because—because you have grown to be important to me."

I felt I should add some sort of conclusion, but I had not thought to come up with one when I practiced the speech in my head the previous day, and so lapsed awkwardly into silence. Ariadne looked stunned. Well, I don't think I've ever said that many words in a row to her before, outside of instructing her in fieldwork techniques and what not. Then she said, in a hopeful sort of voice, "Thank you, Aunt Emily. I mean, I always thought—I wouldn't say I doubted, but—well. Thank you."

"You see, I'm not used to having an assistant." I stumbled over the word a little, because I didn't just mean assistant, of course. I have never been close to my family—not my brother, who finds his purpose in life in the enlargement of his bank balance, nor my parents, good-natured, hardworking folk with all the scientific curiosity of a pair of field mice. But Ariadne seemed to understand, and her face broke into a warm smile.

"I'm not used to any of this!" she said. "I thought I'd be stuck making dresses for the rest of my life. Oh, I like dresses, but not *that* much. This is what I love, and it's only because of you that I felt brave enough to tell my father. And now, here I am—I just saw Faerie! Thank you, Aunt."

She leaned forward and wrapped me in a tight hug, then kissed my cheek before going to rejoin her friends.

That was a to-do, I thought, grateful that the moment was over. Yet I found myself returning to the memory throughout the day, as a person might absently touch a favoured piece of jewelry.

I helped myself to a mug of chocolate and settled myself on the grass to watch the impromptu band. Rose wandered over after a while, and we returned to the debate we had been having about Bertocchi's latest theory, which had been generating much polarization within the dryadological community. I think both of us were a little weary of company at that point, and happy to rest a while within the metaphorical library of the intellect. We ended the conversation still at loggerheads, but amiably so, and Rose retreated inside for a nap.

Wendell, meanwhile, was occupying himself at the outdoor table where Eberhard was seated with his family, with whom he was engaged in a conversation involving a great deal of elegant and elaborate hand gestures, no doubt promising them all manner of nonsensical gifts as recompense for Eberhard's injuries, which Eberhard, by his gestures and expression, seemed to be attempting to refuse, though not very forcefully.

I felt a pang of unease, or perhaps it was just another layer of guilt. Shadow lumbered over from the pleasant patch of sun where he had been napping and flopped down at my side. I rubbed his stomach until he drifted back into a doze.

Wendell joined me a little while later, leaning back into the grass in a lazy slouch. "Now, Em, what does that particular scowl signify?"

I shook my head. "He's forgiven me too easily. They all have."

"Good!" Wendell said. "Much more convenient that way. Grudges are a tiresome business."

"I almost killed him," I said. "It should take more than a magic fruit tree, or whatever you've promised, to win back their affections. It feels—like trickery, somehow."

"You would like for them to chase you from the village, or pelt Shadow with stones?"

"No." I didn't know what I wanted. I only knew that the villagers' warmth unsettled me, and made me feel as if I were already coming unmoored from the world I knew. And what awaited me beyond the horizon?

Wendell cocked his head, considering me. I didn't have the sense that he understood my discomfort, though I certainly appreciated the efforts he was making with the villagers on my behalf. Perhaps he simply had a greater affinity with them than I did.

"Don't bother," I said drily. "I don't expect you to comprehend a guilty conscience. You're going to strain something."

He laughed at that. "I almost forgot," he said. "You missed this. He must have come by this morning while we slept—it was on the table downstairs."

He handed me a small basket covered with a cloth. When I pulled it back, I found one of Poe's loaves—unmistakably his; it was as immaculate as ever, studded with dried blueberries and topped with a sprinkle of sea salt. I inhaled the sweet, yeasty scent gratefully.

"I must admit, it's impressive, what the little one did," he said. "Giving you his door—I'm not sure I would know how to do that. He's surprised me."

"That is because you underestimate them," I said. "All of them. The common fae are cleverer and more resourceful than you give them credit for."

"Mm," he said, tearing off a piece of bread.

"It's true," I protested. "You cannot overlook them just because they are small. If it wasn't for the fauns, you wouldn't have found a way home."

He was quiet for a moment, playing absently with the bread. "You're right."

This brought me up short—I had been prepared for an argument, or another breezy dismissal. "I am."

"Yes, Poe has been helpful; the *fuchszwerge* too. And what business do I have, looking down on the creatures, when I am as good as one of them? My grandmother would be disappointed in me."

I believe my shock must have shown on my face, for he laughed. "I'm not likely to forget about my failings with you at my side, Em."

"That's good. You won't notice them otherwise, and will get yourself into all sorts of trouble because of it."

I expected him to laugh, but instead his green eyes grew serious, and he took my hand. "Never be afraid to tell me."

"Tell you what?"

He frowned. "My father was once a humble man whose main concerns were the care of his children and keeping a clean house. There is a reason he was drawn to my mother, whose own mother was of the *oíche sidhe*. I have no memory of this, but my eldest sister told me stories . . . I knew him as a man who would cheer as Razkarden tore his enemies apart, and who started silly fights with neighbouring realms simply to have a war to occupy himself with. And as for my stepmother, well, she doted on us all. In her case, it was *desire* for the throne that infected her. Sharing it with my father wasn't enough—she wanted it for herself alone. And then there is your previous suitor—what a piece of work he is! It seems a fate that befalls all monarchs of Faerie, to grow as sharp and cold as a winter's night."

I examined his face. It was strange to hear him talk like this—well, like all the Folk, he is not made for self-reflection. But then a smile tugged at my mouth.

"What?"

"I'm sorry," I said. "But I do not believe I could ever be frightened of someone who cannot stir out of doors if his cloak has a wrinkle."

He gave a breath of laughter and turned away. But I reached out and took his hand, pressing it between mine, and when he looked at me, his face relaxed into a smile.

"I will be with you," I said quietly. "I'm not going anywhere."

I leaned my head against his shoulder, and we watched Roland pluck at his harp.

"What we were discussing before," I said, "about the common fae—"

"Ah, yes. You had a point to make, didn't you? I could feel it. Something I won't like. Well, let's hear your arguments."

"Not a *point,*" I said. "Only an idea. And you may like it more than you think."

29th December

We arrived late last night and slept late this morning. The house—it is most certainly a house, bordering on a mansion, for Wendell has announced that he is finished with "dusty cottages" once and for all—is situated on a hill above the shoreline, where the turquoise waves beat against the seashell-coloured limestone. There is no beach, per se, for this is a rugged, rarely visited corner of the country, though there is a path down to the water, where one may dive from the rocks. Wendell moped a bit over this, but I have no use for sand, which only gets into my books and makes Shadow's fur a nightmare to comb. In any event, we would not be staying long.

It feels strange to be writing again. I don't know why I found myself unable to return to journalling before now. Perhaps Wendell was right, and I overtaxed myself somehow in my frenzy to record every detail of my journey into his realm before it slipped from my memory like an elaborate dream, filled with scenes of both loveliness and horror, which Faerie seems to possess in equal measure.

I rose this morning before Wendell awoke and went to sit on the shore. I removed my shoes and dangled my feet in the water, which was ridiculously warm for winter. I have visited Greece only once before, chasing stories of nymphs, and do not know the country well. That was no impediment in locating the nexus, for I had memorized the shape of the coastline and the islands that I glimpsed through the winter faerie's door, and Wendell and I were able to locate the spot easily enough after a few days of scouring maps back at Cambridge. While it was possible that the creature had sealed the entrance as he sealed the one in Austria, Wendell said it was unlikely, as apparently doing so is a difficult and tiring business.

The house we rented is likely no more than a twenty-minute walk from the door, which I know will have a doorknob of glass filled with sunlit seawater.

It feels fitting that we are making this journey now, at the close of the year. It will be my second winter in a row spent in Faerie, but I will be aware of the old year's passing this time, for I will be under the protection of Wendell's magic, and so will not have to deal with the dreadful fog that settled over me during my previous two visits. He has additionally promised to alter the course of time in his realm, so that it is roughly synchronous with the mortal world. Of course he informed me of this in his most offhand manner.

We do not know what we will encounter in Wendell's kingdom, of course. Not exactly. Wendell believes his stepmother is dead, based on the quantity of poison I put into her wine. At the very least, she will have been rendered unable to use her magic, as he himself was.

But what does that mean? Will we be met with a world thrown into chaos? One in which some other faerie has stepped into the vacuum of power and seized the throne? We shall see. Either way, I believe that Wendell will succeed in claiming the throne, not only because he is Wendell, and apparently capable of manipulating space and time itself (that bloody "Veil" he summoned gave me nightmares for a week), but also because he has *them*.

A shape passed overhead. I knew without looking, for there is a sharp chill in their shadows that I do not believe I am imagining, that it was Razkarden. He regularly patrols Wendell's residence, wherever it may be, shifting his glamour to suit his surroundings. This morning he resembles a spotted owl whose tawny colouring blends into the scrubby countryside. The other guardians are scattered among the nearby hills, waiting.

And that is not all.

I could not see them at that moment, thankfully. But I caught glimpses of them last night, lurking in the darkness of the hillside. The glitter of overlarge eyes; the even deeper darkness of shadow cast by their knifepoint horns when the starlight touched them.

Wendell does not know how they found their way here. Nor does he seem to care; he commanded them to come, and they came. It is clear that the fauns' knowledge of the hidden paths connecting faerie realm to faerie realm, and to the human lands they border, is even deeper than we imagined. They brought their dogs, whose haunting, whining howls broke through our slumber last night.

And still that is not all—there is a family of trolls, at least a dozen in number, sent to us by Poe. I had never seen a troll before; they are found mostly in the remote, cold regions of Northern Europe and Russia—they are a hardy lot, the scholars who make such creatures the focus of their research. These trolls are perhaps three feet in height and would put one in mind of well-dressed medieval peasants if not for their bulbous features and greyish complexions. Each carries an implement of some sort—further evidence of a cultural emphasis on tradesmanship?*—varying from hammers, shovels, and saws to baskets and nut gatherers. They speak very little, mostly muttering among themselves and then backing away into the underbrush when I try to engage them in conversation, but according to Poe, trolls like nothing better than to explore, roaming hither and thither and establishing temporary villages where they offer their services to the locals, then packing it all up and moving on again. They were happy to ally with Wendell in exchange for the right to travel his realm at will.

And then, last but not least of our allies among the common fae, there are the *fuchszwerge*. When Snowbell told his kinfolk of his journey into Wendell's realm, they were beside themselves with jealousy and demanded to be invited along on his next quest. They await us in the Grünesauge. When Wendell and I enter the winter faerie's house—which will be abandoned now, in the depths of the cold—we will first open the sealed door to St. Liesl and admit them. And then we will proceed into Wendell's realm all together, an army of miscellaneous nightmares.

I collected my shoes and walked barefoot back to the house. It was an edifice of gleaming white stone with six bedrooms and three balconies, absolutely ridiculous accommodation for two people staying only one night. In the kitchen, I found Wendell awake, cracking jokes with our on-site cook, who came with the rental. At least, I assume he was cracking jokes—I speak less than a dozen words of Greek.

The cook, a reassuringly plump individual with a very red face he was often swiping with a tea towel, had already pre-

---

* Evelyn Dadd documents her observations of blacksmithing in a troll village in the Kainuu region of Finland in the most recent (1909) edition of her undergraduate textbook, *Introduction to Dryadology: Theory, Methods, and Practice.*

pared our breakfast. This consisted of an omelet made with tomatoes, sliced fruits mixed with yogurt and honey, some manner of spiced flatbread piled with vegetables, and, of course, plenty of coffee.

Wendell kissed me when I came in, which I do not ordinarily like to do in front of others, but he is in such a good mood these days that I find myself similarly cheered around him, and so did not mind. Our cook gave a short bow and retired to the servants' quarters.

"There," Wendell said at length, once we'd eaten our way through a large percentage of the dishes, leaning his chair back as he sipped yet another cup of coffee. "Now *that* is the civilized way to begin retaking a kingdom."

"You would say it is the civilized way to begin any endeavour," I said, amused. "Or a day of lazing about."

"One needs a great deal of time to laze about after one has been poisoned," he said in a complaining tone. "Not all of us wish to go charging off to the library to terrorize the librarians and scribble out three papers or more immediately after a traumatic experience."

I merely shook my head and took another piece of toast. He appears entirely well again, though he sometimes complains of headaches when he uses his magic. It took him weeks to recover from his stepmother's poison, which gave us another reason to return to Cambridge for the remainder of the fall, in addition to the need to tie up loose ends.

I went upstairs and woke Shadow. He had been asleep on the foot of the bed, and sat up with a snort, tail wagging. Then I packed a bag—very light, only a few items, including my journal and my draft of the mapbook. I have returned, slowly, to working on it, and it is now nearly complete.

My hands shook slightly. Naturally, I am beside myself with excitement to be returning to Wendell's realm. No, I have not forgotten the horrors that I endured there, which nearly included a descent into madness. Truly, there is something wrong with me.

We will be taking a long sabbatical from Cambridge, both of us. Wendell does not believe he will return, and why would he? The scholarly life was for him merely the means to an end, the end being finding a way back to his home. But I know that I will, if only from time to time. Perhaps a semester here, a semester there. A tenured scholar has a great deal of freedom, after all, and once the article I have written on my journey into the Silva Lupi (much redacted and condensed, of course) appears in next month's issue of *Modern Dryadology,* Cambridge will be all the more eager to retain me. Rose, who acted as co-author, and actually deigned to allow my name to appear first in the publication, is certain it will send the scholarly community into a tizzy.

And also—I will have my mapbook to publish.

Wendell was leaning gracefully against the window, gazing at the sea, as I came downstairs with Shadow at my heels. He wore his lightest cloak, a deep brown with silver buttons that brings out the green of his dark eyes. He would take nothing with him—apart from Orga, of course, who sat patiently by his feet, tail twitching.

"Well," he said, holding out his hand with a smile. "Shall we?"

I took it, and we left the house, not bothering to close the door behind us.

The story of Emily Wilde
and Wendell Bambleby
will continue in Book 3.

About the Author

HEATHER FAWCETT is the author of a number of middle grade novels, including *Ember and the Ice Dragons* and *The Grace of Wild Things,* as well as the young adult series Even the Darkest Stars. She has a master's degree in English literature and a bachelor's in archaeology. She lives on Vancouver Island.

heatherfawcettbooks.com
Facebook.com/HeatherFawcettAuthor
Instagram: @heather_fawcett

About the Type

This book was set in Legacy, a typeface family designed by Ronald Arnholm (b. 1939) and issued in digital form by ITC in 1992. Both its serifed and unserifed versions are based on an original type created by the French punchcutter Nicholas Jenson in the late fifteenth century. While Legacy tends to differ from Jenson's original in its proportions, it maintains much of the latter's characteristic modulations in stroke.